"You have touched me in a way I've never been touched before," Nate murmured softly.

Tenderly, she looked up into his face. "And you have touched a place in me."

Nate's gaze drifted from her ebony eyes to her promising lips. A sheen of moisture caused their fullness to shine, beckoning him once again to touch them with his.

A chilling weakness encased Raquel as his mouth covered hers. Nate's deepest desire was to feel her give in to his touch, and from the moment their lips met, he knew she was all there for him.

"BEGUILED is a sensual, exotic thriller."

—Maggie Davis, author of
THE AMYMTHIST CROWN

"Eboni Snoe has crafted a fast-paced story full of
suspense, intrigue, and sensuality.
I devoured it in two sittings."

—Alexandra Thorne, author of LAWLESS

EBONI SNOE
BEGUILED

PINNACLE BOOKS
WINDSOR PUBLISHING CORP.

PINNACLE BOOKS are published by

Windsor Publishing Corp.
850 Third Ave.
New York, NY 10022

First Pinnacle Printing: August, 1994

Printed in the United States of America

With love, I'd like to dedicate this book to my husband Larry and all of my children, Na'imah, Ali, Dawn, and Larry, Jr.

Chapter One

"I just can't handle it, Raquel. It's over, that's all. I don't have anything else to say."

The finality of Clinton Bradshaw's words echoing in her head made her insides churn. After four years, all she'd gotten was a phone call to tell her they were through! Clinton hadn't even had the decency to tell her to her face. That phone call had been six weeks ago, and she hadn't seen or heard from him since.

Raquel Mason's trembling fingers twisted the top button of her neat, high-necked blouse. It was one of the many nervous habits she'd developed recently, although no one at the clinic where she was a social worker seemed to notice.

Raquel was an uncommonly beautiful woman whose velvety brown skin had a hint of red. Her thick, curling black hair, which she wore pulled severely back, framed a face with huge, sable eyes, a delicate nose, and full, sensual lips. Always conservatively dressed and perfectly groomed, Raquel appeared completely in control and coolly serene, no matter how heavy her caseload. But over the past few weeks, only Raquel herself knew how dangerously close that flawless facade had come to cracking.

She hadn't been paid in weeks, she was two months behind in her rent, and her other bills were mounting up. Everything in her life was going wrong, and Clinton's abrupt rejection had made matters even worse.

I have to cope, she told herself. *I can't let myself fall apart. I'll manage somehow . . .*

"Hey, ma'am, you gonna pay for that?" The cashier's voice broke into her thoughts, and Raquel realized she was holding up the line.

"Yes—of course. Sorry." Embarrassed, she placed the mango and the banana on the counter. The pearl button she'd been twisting popped off and fell beside them.

"Eh, pretty lady, what's wrong?" a young, deeply accented male voice asked from behind her. "Why you stand there breaking the buttons off your little blouse? You uptight 'cause you ain't got no man?"

Another young man began to laugh. Raquel ignored them both as she carefully counted out the money and put the fruit into her briefcase. With her back stiff and her head held high, she walked swiftly to the exit, her full, colorful skirt swirling around her slender legs. The *whoosh* of the automatic door wasn't loud enough to drown out the first kid's words.

"Next time you need somethin' to hold onto, baby, you just give Roberto a call, okay? I got plenty." More raucous laughter followed Raquel into the street, and she realized that she was trembling again.

I ought to be used to comments like that by now, she thought wearily, as the warm, humid evening air surrounded her like a damp blanket. She knew the young guys in the neighborhood didn't mean any harm. Raquel might even have seen Roberto's mother or sister at the clinic for counseling, and his mother would be the first to say she had tried to teach him better than that. Ordinarily, Raquel would have paid no attention to the boy's words, but tonight she was so tense that his sexual innuendos made her heart pound with irrational fear.

It was at moments like this, all too frequent lately, that Raquel realized what power her own mother's unreasonably strict religious upbringing still exerted on her. Even after all these years, she could hear Lucy Mason's shrill voice warning her against the dangers of the "sinful world," threatening her with the wrath of God if she ever strayed from the paths of righteousness and the fires of Hell if she sampled the forbidden pleasures of sex unsanctified by marriage.

Well, Mama, maybe you were right about that one, Raquel thought, as Clinton's image flashed before her mind's eye. Handsome in a conservative, buttoned-down sort of way, he was a rising CPA in a small but successful Miami firm. *I'm suffering, all right, but I'm twenty-six years old, and Clinton's the only man I've ever been with. I honestly thought we were going to be married. That's what he told me. He said we'd be married in a church . . .*

Much of Raquel's youth had been spent in church or participating in church activities, always with her mother. Lucy was grimly determined to balance the amount of time Raquel spent among the unrighteous with a steady diet of her own joyless, repressive brand of religion. The only fun Raquel had gotten out of it was once a year at a church-sponsored summer camp she was permitted to attend by herself. She had looked forward eagerly to that one precious week when she could mingle with girls her own age, free from her mother's eagle-eyed supervision. Always the overachiever, even at camp, Raquel had excelled at weaving beautiful, elaborate baskets which were then sold to raise much-needed money for the church. She had once brought one home as a gift for her mother, who had grudgingly allowed that it was almost—but not quite—perfect.

As far as Lucy Mason was concerned, nothing less than perfection would do in every aspect of life— perfection and careful planning. Day after day, year after year, even now, when she was bedridden in the nursing home, she said the same thing: "Take control of your own life, Raquel. Never leave anything to chance. Trust in the Lord. And most important of all, don't depend on no man. They'll let you down every time. Believe me, I should know!"

Raquel would then be forced to listen to the story of how her immigrant father, frustrated at being unable to learn English or find a job here in Miami, had finally returned to his home in the Dominican Republic, abandoning his wife and baby daughter. Lucy always finished by saying, "That man left us dirt poor, you and me, but we didn't stay dirt poor for long, no sir. I worked my fingers to the bone for you, Raquel, and don't you ever forget it. The Lord will punish an ungrateful child. You pay me back by making something of yourself, you hear?"

"Yes, Mama, I hear," Raquel always replied, and she had. She worked hard, she planned carefully, and she strove for perfection. Was her mother proud of her for putting herself through school and becoming a social worker? Did she love her for it? Did she love her at all? To this day, Raquel didn't know. "Love" was not a word that had ever been spoken between them.

As she walked along the cracked, uneven sidewalk in her practical, low-heeled pumps, avoiding the crevices that might cause her to trip, Raquel felt her racing heart gradually regain its normal rhythm. She absently returned the friendly greetings called out to her by the people sitting on the steps of their rundown houses, knowing that even though it was getting dark, she had nothing to fear in this low-income, mixed-race neighborhood. She was a familiar figure here—the clinic was only a few blocks away, and that was where she was headed now.

Conscientious to a fault, Raquel had recently made coming to work in the deserted building after hours a part of her daily routine even though her salary was so far in arrears. Without the distractions provided by her co-workers, she found its peace and quiet conducive to studying and evaluating the cases she'd dealt with during the day. By focusing all her attention on her clients' problems, she was able to forget her own for a while longer.

As Raquel approached the clinic, a streetlight flickered on in front of it, revealing a man who stood outside. He seemed to be doing something to the double doors. Was he trying to break in? Raquel slowed her pace, prepared to turn and run if that proved to be the case, but as she came nearer, she saw that he was putting a padlock through the door handles. The man wasn't breaking in—he was shutting *her* out!

"What's going on?" she called, striding up to the man and glaring at him.

"Por favor, señorita, no hablo ingles," he muttered, sounding apologetic.

Just like my father, Raquel thought bitterly. Although

she knew he couldn't understand, she cried, "You're locking up the building where I've worked for two whole years, and you can't even tell me why?"

The man shrugged and repeated, *"No hablo ingles."*

Controlling herself with effort, Raquel took a deep breath. She knew she hadn't been fair. She'd needed to lash out at someone, and this man, who was probably just following his boss's instructions, had borne the brunt of her ill temper.

"Sorry," she murmured.

He shrugged again, then turned away and crossed the street. Raquel watched him climb into a battered pickup truck and rev the engine. As the truck pulled away from the curb, her dark eyes widened in disbelief. The back of it was filled to overflowing with furniture—the office furniture from the clinic.

Raquel turned to stare at the padlocked doors. This couldn't be happening on top of everything else. It just wasn't possible! She'd known for some time that her job was in jeopardy, but she had never dreamed that the administrators would simply close the clinic without a word to any of the staff.

What am I going to do? Raquel wondered, panic-stricken. *I'm unemployed, I can't pay my bills, or Mama's at the nursing home. I'll be evicted from my apartment. Before I find another job, I could be homeless!*

A Latin song blaring at top volume from a passing car jolted her out of her daze. Shaking her head to clear it, Raquel started to walk slowly, stiffly, toward the lot where she had parked her car earlier that day. She was still so overwhelmed that she didn't even hear the whistles and lewd suggestions from a group of young men hanging out in front of the coffee shop across the street.

When she reached her Toyota, Raquel popped the trunk open and tossed her briefcase inside. Closing the trunk again, she leaned against the car, her knees suddenly too weak to support her.

"Damn it! They could at least have warned me!" she moaned aloud, as the tears she had been fighting began running down her cheeks.

But in a way, Raquel knew she had been warned. She had just been too blind, too trusting—or perhaps too naive—to read the handwriting on the wall. Week after week, the administrators had promised to make good on the back pay they owed her and the other employees, but no checks had been forthcoming. Twice Raquel had approached the director of the clinic, inquiring about its financial stability, and each time he had smilingly fobbed her off with a lot of double-talk. Why had she let him get away with it? She should have insisted on a reasonable explanation and demanded a straight answer. Now it was too late.

The only faintly bright spot in this whole disastrous mess was Raquel's knowledge that her mother would continue to be taken care of, at least for the time being. Four months ago, when Lucy's multiple sclerosis had advanced to the point that she needed professional care, Raquel had had no choice but to put her in a nursing facility. She had located one with an excellent reputation not far from the apartment she and her mother had shared, and since Raquel was still receiving a salary at the time, she had paid Lucy's board six months in advance.

Although Raquel felt no great love for her mother, the decision to entrust her to the care of strangers seared her with guilt. Clinton, however, had been wonderfully supportive. He'd seemed delighted that he and Raquel would at last be able to spend night after night making love, now that she didn't have to race straight home to tend to Lucy's needs. At first Clinton's ardor was all Raquel could desire. Thinking about it now, she realized that it was only when she revealed how much Lucy's nursing home was costing that he began to cool toward her. Was he afraid he would be responsible for Lucy's bills if he and Raquel married? Was that why he had broken off their relationship?

But at the moment, none of that really mattered. What did matter was that Clinton was gone, her job was gone, and Raquel was virtually penniless. She was also terrified.

The stumbling footsteps of a man who'd had more than enough to drink aroused a different kind of fear, making her realize how dangerous it was to be standing alone in the dimly lit parking lot. Raquel quickly got inside her car, locking the door behind her. Tears still clouded her vision, and she fumbled with the key before she was able to put it into the ignition. Her hands were shaking so much that she could hardly fasten her seatbelt.

I can't drive like this, she realized. *I might kill somebody— maybe me.*

Taking a tissue from her purse, Raquel carefully dried her eyes. Then, folding her arms on the steering wheel, she rested her head on them and took long, steadying breaths until she was sure she could function normally. Only then did she trust herself to drive out of the lot.

As she stopped for a red light at the corner, Raquel watched the usual Friday-night crowds pouring into The Sunbreeze, a popular Caribbean nightclub. Snatches of laughter and a sensuous tune could be heard each time the green door opened. Raquel felt a sharp stab of envy at the sight of the carefree couples lured inside by the festive sounds and flashing lights. She sighed heavily. If only her life were as simple as theirs appeared to be . . .

The music was seductive, hypnotic. Raquel leaned back against the headrest, soaking up the sound as she waited for the light to change. Ever so slightly, her body swayed in rhythm to the beat. It would be sheer heaven to dance, to laugh, to have just a moment's release from the worries that burdened her so heavily.

A car behind hers honked when the light changed. Sitting up, Raquel inched the Toyota forward, but instead of crossing the intersection, she impulsively flipped on her turn signal and swerved into the parking lot of The Sunbreeze.

"If I'm going to be homeless in a few days, I might as well spend one night trying to drown my sorrows like everybody else," she declared with a defiant toss of her head.

She got out of the car and quickly made her way to the club before she could change her mind.

Once inside the green door, Raquel found a line of people who she assumed were waiting to pay the cover charge. As she opened her purse and searched for her wallet, a pang of guilt hit her. How could she spend part of what little money she had left on a frivolous night of drinking and dance? She'd never done anything like this in her life.

I must be out of my mind, she thought. *I'd better go home right now!*

Turning to leave, Raquel bumped into the man behind her. He was tall and dark-skinned, and he had a beautiful smile as he openly assessed her. When he spoke, his rich, deep voice revealed his Jamaican origins.

"Eh, lady, you lookin' good tonight. Would you like to spend some time wit' me? I got moanee, plentee of moanee."

With one glance, Raquel could tell this man was not accustomed to being turned down by women. The sparkle of many conquests lit up his dark gaze, so she was sure her refusal would not put a damper on his night.

"I don't think so," she said, tentatively returning his smile. "But there must be plenty of other ladies who would be glad to take you up on your offer."

He shrugged his broad shoulders. "You may be right, but plentee women are plucked. It is the few, like you, who are chosen."

Raquel blushed but made no reply, not wanting to encourage him. Seeing that her exit was blocked by the noisy crowds surging in, she was forced to move forward. When she reached the front of the line, to her surprise, there was no cashier. Instead, a husky woman approached and began patting her down, searching for "hardware." The shock of it immobilized Raquel. Did the woman actually think she might be carrying a gun?

"Could you step on through the door, please?" the woman asked politely. "There are quite a few people waiting to get inside."

Disconcerted, Raquel did as she was told, emerging from the partially lit search area into a dim world of throbbing music, drinking, and dancing she'd previously witnessed only on television.

Despite the restraints her mother had placed on her, as Raquel had grown older, she'd occasionally been allowed to date, and the boys had sometimes taken her to clubs. But those were nothing like The Sunbreeze. There was a flagrant sensuality exhibited by the dancers here that created a familiar tingle deep inside her. It reminded Raquel of hot summer evenings long ago when she would sneak next door to Paulette's and watch her perform her native dances. Paulette was Jamaican, and her daughters, Dottie and Pauline, were young teenagers like Raquel.

Naturally, Lucy Mason thought all dancing was sinful, particularly the kind of dancing Paulette enjoyed. That's why those stolen Friday evenings at Paulette's were so exciting. Their neighbor would treat herself by listening to all her favorite island tunes, accompanied by a bottle of rum and frequent closed-door visits to a little room in the basement. A pungent scent mixed with incense would always accompany Paulette when she returned. Then she would laugh and dance as if all her cares were gone.

One evening when Raquel's mother was attending church, Raquel had feigned illness in order to stay home, then run to Paulette's.

"This time, *you* dance," the woman said. "There be no young men aroun'. C'mon girl, it not be wrong to dance here in my basement. Your mama, she so afraid of anythin' resemblin' sex. How she think you got here, girl?"

Surprisingly, Raquel's first efforts weren't too bad. But it took several more secret Friday excursions, listening to Paulette's instructions to "bump, grind, and roll," before Raquel became really good. Once she had mastered the technique, she discovered that dancing at Paulette's released something wild, sensual, and free within her, something that had been rigidly suppressed all her young life. Raquel had not danced that way for many years.

Now she caught herself staring at a particularly handsome couple whose simulated sexual gyrations were hotter than any of the others. Embarrassed, she began twisting at one of the remaining buttons of her blouse and turned away, looking for a place to sit. All the tables were taken, but when a tall, slim man rose from his place at the bar, she rushed over and slid onto the stool.

"Do you have any piña coladas?" she asked the bartender nervously.

He grinned. "Sure do."

"Are they made with real pineapple juice and real coconut?"

"Nope. All we got is mixes."

Raquel frowned. "I see. Well, in that case, I'll take a lime daiquiri."

"Frozen?" the bartender asked.

She nodded, and turned back to survey the crowd. Even though the evening was young, most of the dancers had already worked up a streaming sweat. Some of the men had opened their shirts to get what little air they could and to show off their muscular, glistening chests. One woman held melting ice cubes in both hands, rubbing them over her sweltering neck and then depositing them between her ample breasts.

"Here you go—one frozen daiquiri," the bartender said.

"How much?" Raquel yelled over the music.

"No problem. The gentleman down there has taken care of it." He indicated a man sitting at the end of the bar. "Pretty lady like you'll get plenty of free drinks."

Raquel glanced at her benefactor, smiling in grati-

tude, but made sure their gazes didn't meet for very
long. Lowering her lashes, she sipped thirstily at her
drink through a plastic straw. It was cold, sweet, and delicious. She hardly ever drank anything stronger than
the herb teas she concocted to ease the pain of a tension
headache, so the alcohol gave her an immediate, pleasurable buzz. The daiquiri was gone far too soon, and
Raquel ordered another, paying for that one herself.
She tried to drink the second one more slowly, reminding herself that she had a twenty-mile drive back to her
apartment.

The stifling heat of the club combined with the rum
she had just consumed was making her perspire, and
Raquel opened the top two buttons of her blouse, fanning herself with a cocktail napkin. The tapes and CDs
had now been replaced by a live band kicking up a fan-
tastic beat. Colored lights flashed on and off, further
contributing to the crowd's mood of abandonment. The
dancers seemed to have let go of all their inhibitions, if
they'd ever had any to begin with. As she had in the car,
Raquel swayed slightly to the music's pulsing rhythm,
her eyes half closed. Was it her imagination, or was that
one of the tunes she'd danced to long ago in Paulette's
basement?

"Eh, beautiful. Come and dance wit' a man like me,"
purred a voice close to her ear.

Opening her eyes, Raquel saw a slim, sinewy, dark-
skinned man stretching out his hand.

Why not?

Almost without her own volition, she put her hand in
his and let him lead her to the dance floor. They found
a space barely big enough for the two of them, but there
was plenty of room for the languid, undulating moves of

Caribbean dance. Shedding her inhibitions as the others had, Raquel surrendered to the music as the singer crooned, *"All we have to do is live in love and harmony."*

A tendril or two escaped from the tight knot on the crown of her head, clinging to her damp face. Then the knot itself loosened as she moved, and a stream of thick black curls cascaded over her shoulders and back. Feeling the beat deep within her, Raquel raised her full skirt high on her thighs as she descended slowly, her legs spread apart, swiveling and pumping her hips in a provocative rhythm. Completely unaware of her partner, or of anything else except the music, she deliberately made her mind a blank. As long as she was dancing and more than a little drunk, it was easy to blot out the things she didn't want to remember.

Her partner, however, was not content to be ignored. Aroused by Raquel's seductive movements, his hands roamed eagerly over her body, clutching at her buttocks and caressing her full breasts. Under any other circumstances, Raquel would have been outraged, but tonight it didn't seem to matter. Nothing mattered anymore. Laughing almost hysterically, she responded to his amorous pawing.

Three men in business suits sat at a table nearby, watching Raquel's gyrations intently.

"I t'ink we've come to the right place," the one in the brown suit said to his companions.

"I think you're right," said the man in gray pinstripes. "She's not her twin, but pretty close to it."

"Yeah," the first man said, licking his lips. "Everyt'ing about her looks perfect, right down to her little round—"

"All right, Benjamin, that's enough. Watch your

mouth," the third and most elegantly dressed man snapped.

"I'm sorry, mon. No need to get excited, since it's not your sistah anyway. Can I help it if this one does what she's doin' so well?"

"This looks like it's going to be easier than we expected. One club, and we find the right girl." The third man rose, a faint smile on his thin lips. "Fifty thousand should do it, but that's the limit. I'll be leaving now. Make sure you two don't let her get away."

Brown-suit grinned. "Don't worry about a t'ing, mon. We got it covered."

As the third man made his way to the exit, the throbbing island music eased into a slower song. Raquel lifted her dark curls from her perspiring neck and slipped out of her nameless partner's grasp. She waved goodbye to him and quickly lost herself in the crowd, searching for the ladies' room. Glancing briefly over her shoulder, she saw him gazing after her with a wistful expression on his lean, dark face.

Less than an hour later, Raquel pushed open the double doors and stepped outside. Humid though the night air was, a cool breeze pressed her sweat-soaked blouse against her breasts and back, making her shiver. Wearily she headed for her car, feeling completely drained. The frenzied euphoria of the past few hours was gone. Though many strangers had bought Raquel drinks, the liquor's effect had been dissipated by her strenuous dancing. Now that she was cold sober, the memory of all her troubles returned in force, and with it a deep depression. She had no lover, no money, no job, and soon she would have no home. Raquel had always prided herself on her ability to take charge of her life and to overcome a number of obstacles that would have daunted many others. Yet all her hard work, resourcefulness, and careful planning had led only to this dead end. Try as she might, Raquel could think of no way out.

Head bowed, she did not notice the black limousine parked around the corner near The Sunbreeze. But at the sound of brisk, determined footsteps following her, Raquel was instantly on the alert. It sounded as if there were two of them. This was a bad neighborhood after dark. Were they muggers? She quickened her pace. The footsteps quickened, too. What if they had knives, or even guns?

With a bravado born of desperation, Raquel stopped under a streetlight and spun around to face her pursuers. After all, she had nothing to lose but her life, and bleak as her future seemed at the moment, that wasn't worth much.

Eyes flashing, she shouted, "Go away! Leave me alone!"

"Calm down, lady," said the taller, slimmer of the two. He wore a brown business suit and an ingratiating smile. "We not going to attack you or do you any harm. We jus' want to make you a business proposition."

Raquel was so amazed by this unexpected statement that all she could do was stare at him.

The shorter man in gray pinstripes pulled a large brown envelope from inside his jacket and thrust it into her hand. "We want to solicit your services this evening. These papers will explain everything. You might be interested to know that there is also one thousand dollars cash in the envelope, the down payment on the deal, should you accept. You'll receive nine thousand more if you come with us to the appointed spot, and a final payment of forty thousand dollars will be forthcoming when you complete the assignment."

I must be dreaming, Raquel thought, stunned. *Either that, or I'm so upset by everything that's happened to me lately that I'm having some kind of wild hallucination! This can't be happening!* Still speechless, she stared from one man to the other.

"If you will be so good as to supply us with the name of your bank and your account number, the forty thousand will be deposited there," the man in the gray suit went on. "I hope that's satisfactory?"

Raquel finally found her voice. "Satisfactory? *Satisfactory?*" she echoed. "What is this, some kind of a practical joke?" Then her eyes narrowed. "Oh, now I get it. You're undercover cops, right? If I accept your 'business proposition' and your money, you'll arrest me for prostitution. Well, thank you for your kind offer, gentlemen, but no thanks! I may be on the streets in a few days, but I'm not there yet. Now please let me pass!"

But the man in the brown suit, still smiling, grabbed hold of her arm before she could turn away. His grip, like his voice, was surprisingly gentle. "Pretty lady, you got it all wrong. We talkin' real business—no sex, no drugs, nothin' illicit. This a job, and you the only one can do it."

"I'm sorry if you feel the amount is insufficient," the other man said. "Unfortunately, we are not authorized to offer more. On the other hand, perhaps you don't need the money . . ." His voice trailed off as he watched Raquel closely.

"Not need the money!" She gave a short, strangled

laugh that was more like a sob. "Oh, my God, if you only knew!"

In Raquel's present circumstances, fifty thousand dollars seemed like a vast fortune. With that much money, she could make a new start. She could pay all her bills and Lucy's with plenty left over. She wouldn't be evicted. She could take as much time as she needed to look for another job, a much better one than the one she'd just lost.

"What—" Raquel swallowed hard. "What would I have to do?" she whispered.

Gray-suit said, "As I told you before, the papers will explain everything. Please open the envelope."

Raquel's hands were trembling so much that she could hardly do so. When she did, the first thing she saw was a neatly banded sheaf of ten hundred-dollar bills.

"Why don' you put the moanee in your purse?" Brown-suit suggested, releasing her arm. "It be a shame to drop it on the ground, the way you shakin'."

Numbly, Raquel placed the packet of bills in her handbag. Then she took out the letter and began to read it by the light of the street lamp.

Chapter Two

"Would you care to hear some music?"

The chauffeur's disembodied voice drifted to Raquel's ears over the intercom in the sleek black limousine as it purred almost soundlessly along dark, tree-lined streets. She thought they were somewhat in the vicinity of Fort Lauderdale, but for all she knew, they might have been in the Kingdom of Oz. So many bizarre things had happened during the past few hours that at this point, nothing seemed impossible. Looking down at the scarlet, stiletto-heeled pumps on her feet, Raquel was reminded of Dorothy's ruby slippers. Would they protect her from evil influences?

"Music, madam?" the chauffeur repeated more loudly, breaking into her thoughts.

"Yes, please," she replied.

"What kind? Rock, rhythm and blues, reggae, pop, or classical?"

"Do you have any jazz?"

"Yes, I do. If you care for anything to drink, the wet bar is in the compartment directly in front of you."

Moments later Raquel heard the plaintive wail of a

jazz saxophone ˏcoming from the speakers. *Branford Marsalis?* she wondered vaguely, leaning back against the plush seat.

Raquel had no interest in the contents of the liquor cabinet. Instead, she turned her attention to the scene passing swiftly by the limousine's tinted windows. This was obviously an affluent neighborhood, where mansions set back on lush, floodlit green lawns were barely visible behind high walls and wrought-iron gates. Presumably she would soon be delivered to a similar mansion where she would embark on the assignment she had agreed to accept. Would she be equal to the task? What if she blew it? The two men who had hired her insisted there would be no danger, but could she believe them?

Thinking of the ten thousand dollars safely tucked away in her purse, Raquel decided she could. The second lieutenant had been delivered exactly as promised, and it was hers to keep. Even if the additional forty thousand dollars was never deposited in her bank account, which she realized was a distinct possibility, she would still be better off than she had been before Brown-suit and Gray-suit had approached her.

Raquel closed her eyes, picturing in her mind the beautiful, smiling face in the photo that had been enclosed with the letter and the first thousand. The young woman's caramel skin tone, bountiful black hair, dark eyes, and generous lips bore an uncanny resemblance to her own, but there was one major difference: Jackie Dawson had disappeared, and for some reason as yet unknown to Raquel, she had been hired to make one public appearance at a Caribbean soirée tonight, pretending to be the missing girl.

Opening her eyes, Raquel picked up her handbag, took out her compact, and studied her reflection in the small mirror with something approaching awe. A turban in a wild floral print of red, green, and mustard yellow crowned her head, concealing her unruly black curls, and huge gold hoop earrings dangled from her ears. Her face was heavily made up with vibrant purple eyeshadow and brilliant red lipstick. Raquel hardly recognized herself beneath the elaborate mask. The only other time she had worn so much makeup was on the rare occasions when her mother had allowed her to attend a masquerade party in the church basement. But Lucy would have tanned Raquel's hide and locked her in her room if she had ever attempted to leave the house dressed as she was tonight.

Glancing down at the costume she was wearing, Raquel felt her cheeks burning, glad that her mother couldn't see her now. Little was left to the imagination. A skimpy bralike top in the same print as the turban revealed far more of her full breasts than it concealed. The flounced skirt, above the knee in front and dipping to ankle-length behind, flared from Raquel's hips well below her navel. Brown-suit, who was called Benjamin, and Gray-suit, known only as Mr. Smith, had presented her with the outfit in their hotel suite less than two hours ago, telling her that it reflected Jackie Dawson's flamboyant tastes.

Raquel was appalled. Even at the beach, she never wore anything so bare, preferring a simple one-piece in a dark, sober shade. How could she possibly appear in public half-naked? She had been tempted to refuse, but the thought of all that money and what it could mean to her and her mother was a powerful incentive. Casting

modesty to the winds, Raquel had donned the borrowed
finery, telling herself that it was merely a costume to be
worn, part of the role she had been hired to play. Now,
although she was still somewhat uncomfortable, she also
felt a tiny thrill of excitement at the prospect of submerging her own personality in that of a woman who
was obviously the complete opposite of herself. It was
nothing but a masquerade, and after all, it was only for
this one night.

Raquel dropped the compact into her purse, then
picked up the brown envelope lying on the seat beside
her and took out the papers. Back at the hotel suite, she
had gone over them several times. Benjamin and Mr.
Smith had coached Raquel endlessly about the woman
she was to impersonate, but now, in the soft glow of the
limousine's courtesy light, she carefully read yet again
the information concerning Jackie Dawson to commit it
to memory.

Actually, there wasn't all that much to remember.
Jackie was twenty-six, Raquel's own age. Like Raquel,
she was an only child. Unlike Raquel, however, Jackie
was the ultimate party girl. She lived with her father,
who was something of a tyrant and strongly disapproved
of his daughter's frivolous ways. Her mother was dead.
Jackie's personal preferences and political views were
briefly mentioned, and the names of some of her friends
were listed, along with the restaurants and clubs where
her crowd hung out. Mr. Smith had assured Raquel that
she had nothing to worry about. The information contained in the letter, meager though it was, would be sufficient to see her through the festive evening. But when
she asked why it was so important that the other guests

at the party think she was Jackie Dawson, his expression became suddenly grim.

"As we have already told you, Ms. Dawson is missing. You are impersonating her tonight in order to buy us more time to find her," he said. "That is all you need to know. You are being paid—and paid very well, I might add—for what is really a very simple job."

Benjamin's perpetual smile had held more than a hint of lust as he'd looked Raquel up and down. "I know 'bout pretty women. Pretty women like pretty t'ings. You jus' enjoy the party, and t'en tomorrow you take some of the moanee and buy yourself somet'ing nice, okay?"

Raquel had asked no further questions.

Now, as she put the papers back in the envelope, she glanced out the window again. They were driving along a road bordered by tall palm trees and a massive stone wall which blocked her view of whatever might lie behind it. Suddenly the car slowed its pace. Looking up ahead, Raquel saw the red taillights of many other vehicles that were waiting to make the turn into a gateway in the wall. Two huge wrought-iron gates stood open, and the gateposts were topped with crouching jaguars carved in stone. A uniformed attendant checked what appeared to be an invitation handed to him by the driver of each car before allowing it to enter. Feeling a surge of panic, Raquel realized she had reached her destination.

As the black limousine inched forward, following a gleaming silver Porsche that had just been permitted to pass through the gates into a floodlit courtyard, the chauffeur rolled down the window and presented a white card to the attendant. While the attendant scanned the invitation, Raquel read the words *Glimpse of Glory* inscribed on a bronze plaque behind him. Apparently that was the name of the estate where "Jackie Dawson" was to do her thing.

Raquel's nerves seemed to be vibrating throughout her entire body, and there was a weird ringing around in her ears. She knew these symptoms heralded the onset of one of her tension headaches, and desperately wished for a cup of soothing herb tea. Since that was not a possibility, she steeled herself to resist them. The thought of the money in her purse calmed her somewhat, but she had been instructed by Mr. Smith to leave the purse in care of the chauffeur when she entered the mansion. Unsure whether this man whose face she had never seen could be trusted, Raquel furtively took out the banded stack of ten hundred-dollar bills. Breaking the band, she quickly tucked them into her top, placing five under each breast. Even if the chauffeur absconded with the rest, she would still be a thousand dollars richer.

When she looked out the window again, the limousine was making its way around a circular driveway to the entrance of the mansion which was built of stone the softest shade of pink, in the style of a Mediterranean villa. Through its tall, arched windows, Raquel could see brightly attired revelers, laughing, talking, and drinking.

It's like a fairy tale—or a movie, she thought, *one* of those made-for-TV movies about the rich and famous that aren't anything like real life. I never knew people actually lived this way!

The sliding glass panel that separated Raquel from the chauffeur opened soundlessly, and a dark hand presented her with an ivory envelope as the limousine glided to a stop in front of the broad staircase that led to the mansion's main entrance. Another uniformed attendant stepped forward, bowing and opening the car door. Clutching the envelope in her hand, Raquel got out. With a pounding heart, she ascended the stairs behind a couple whose scanty costumes were adorned with multicolored feathers. Compared to what they were wearing, her outfit was positively demure, and Raquel began to feel less embarrassed about the amount of skin she was showing.

When she reached the top of the stairs, she followed the feathered couple's lead, placing her envelope on an embossed silver tray proffered by yet another attendant. Then she passed through a vast, marble-paved entrance hall lit with crystal chandeliers into an even larger and more impressive chamber. It was crowded with guests, some of whom were fantastically costumed, while others were formally dressed. Drinks and hors d'oeuvres were immediately offered to Raquel by an obsequious waiter. Sipping a crystal flute of champagne, she assumed the persona of Jackie Dawson and casually looked around her.

It was obvious that her arrival had caused something of a stir. Various couples and groups of people whispered and threw surreptitious glances in her direction, but no one approached her. Was that because they knew Raquel was an impostor? Had the attendant to whom she had given her invitation realized that she was not who she claimed to be and alerted the others? Was someone even now preparing to throw her out bodily?

"Ms. Dawson?" The tentative voice addressed her

from behind. Turning, Raquel saw a tall, slim young man in an immaculately tailored white linen suit.

"I presume you're Jackie Dawson—that's what everyone is saying." He smiled shyly. "You see, we've never met before, but I spoke to you on the phone about three weeks ago. You *do* remember, don't you? My name is Johnson—Derek Johnson. Jim, a mutual friend, encouraged me to call."

Raquel did the only thing she could under the circumstances. She furrowed her brow as if she were trying to remember. "Derek? I'm not sure . . ."

"The conversation was very short. Your father was furious because I called you, and he cut us off before I could tell you why I was phoning."

Thinking fast, Raquel said, "Oh, yes! Now I remember. I'm terribly sorry things didn't work out for us, Derek."

"Me, too." He seemed satisfied by her apology and hurriedly walked away.

Raquel thought that her conversation with Derek might have encouraged other of Jackie Dawson's acquaintances to approach her, but none of them did. Puzzled yet relieved, she finished her champagne, placed her empty glass on a passing waiter's tray, and took another.

As the evening progressed, champagne and colorful drinks that Raquel didn't dare sample flowed endlessly. Soon the lights dimmed, replaced by flashing red bulbs. Couples began to dance as the music changed from laid-back, standard pop tunes to reggae and rhythm and blues. Wandering through a pair of French doors onto an enormous flagstone terrace, Raquel saw that servants were placing flaming torches all around it and along the wide steps that led down into a beautiful tropical garden. Obviously preparations were being made for some kind of special event, but she had no idea what it could be.

"Eh, babee. Where you been?" asked a deep, insinuating voice behind her.

Startled, Raquel spun around and found herself face-to-face with a well-built man in a tuxedo. He was standing much too close, and the smirk on his face conveyed that he knew a lot more about Jackie Dawson than the other man who had approached her. Who was he and what did he want? she wondered apprehensively. Unsure of how to respond to his question, Raquel remained silent, regarding him with a cool, supercilious expression that belied the frantic pounding of her heart.

"I didn't hear from you for so long that for a while there, I thought you'd left the city. Why you leave me hanging like that, huh?" The man moved even closer, so close that she could feel his hot breath on her cheek as he whispered, "I thought we had a real good time the last time we were together. That glass dick was fire."

Fortunately, at that moment people began surging through the French doors onto the terrace, separating Raquel from her unsavory companion. Quickly losing him in the crowd, she could hardly believe what she'd just heard. *Glass dick?* Many times at the clinic she had heard her clients use that term for a crack pipe, but it was difficult to imagine how a woman whose life was so rigidly controlled by her father could be involved with crack cocaine. Her curiosity about Jackie Dawson increased, as did her apprehension. If the woman was deeply into the drug scene, Jackie might very well be dead by now. *Oh, God, just let me get out of this without any-*

thing going wrong, Raquel prayed silently, and checked her watch, relieved to find that in only thirty more minutes the limousine was scheduled to pick her up and take her home.

By now the guests had ranged themselves around the terrace. Suddenly there was an explosion of color and sound as twelve male dancers burst onto the scene with a loud shout. Their faces were concealed by elaborate masks made of red and black feathers, and the torchlight flickered on gleaming bodies that were bare except for the briefest of feathered trunks. Accompanied by the throbbing music of wooden instruments played by a group of musicians in the garden below, the dancers leaped and whirled, letting out barbarous yells that sent chills down Raquel's spine. Still, she couldn't help being fascinated by the frenzied performance. Caught up in the display before her, Raquel didn't notice the man who had taken his place at the top of the stairs until a passionate drum combination attracted her attention.

The drummer was a magnificent specimen of manhood whose very posture exuded power. A tall drum sat between creamy brown thighs that tensed and bulged each time he rose to the balls of his feet in response to the drumbeat. Taut muscles rippled in his arms, and his hands moved so rapidly that they were nothing but a blur. Raquel couldn't tear her eyes away from him. She felt something stir deep within her that blotted out all conscious thought, a primitive, sensual response to the hypnotic rhythm.

The dancers had begun to entice some of the female guests to join them, and when one of them took Raquel's hand, she was powerless to resist. Dancing with even more abandon than she had at The Sunbreeze, she lost all track of time. When the dance finally ended, she was horrified to discover that more than half an hour had gone by. What if the chauffeur had gotten tired of waiting for her? If the limousine had come and gone, not only would Raquel have no way of getting home, but the precious nine thousand dollars would be lost as well.

She pushed her way through the crowd blocking the terrace doors and raced back into the mansion, retracing her steps to the entrance. As she ran outside, to her great relief, Raquel saw the black limousine sitting in the driveway. An attendant opened the door for her and she slipped inside, sinking down into the plush seat with a grateful sigh. One quick glance assured her that her purse was where she had left it; another glance inside proved that the money was all there.

As the limousine circled the driveway and passed between the jaguar-crowned gateposts, soft jazz began to play—the chauffeur had remembered her preference. Leaning back, Raquel closed her eyes and smiled, completely relaxed for the first time in weeks. It was over, all over, and so were her worries. Soon she would be home safe and sound and solvent. She might even use some of the money she had earned to take a long-delayed vacation. Only one problem remained: Raquel had promised her employers she would tell no one about tonight's adventure. That in itself didn't concern her, but sooner or later she would have to come up with a plausible explanation for her sudden wealth. The lottery, perhaps? Or a legacy from a rich relative? Raquel laughed out loud. It was all so incredible! Only a few hours ago she had been frantic because she had no money, and now she had to figure out what to do because she had too much!

Lost in her pleasant reverie, Raquel didn't notice that the limousine was slowing down, but when it came to a halt, she sat up and opened her eyes, a puzzled frown wrinkling her brow. They couldn't have reached her apartment already. Perhaps there was a problem with the car. She peered out the window, but saw nothing but pitch blackness since the moon had disappeared behind a bank of clouds. Not knowing how the intercom system worked, Raquel decided to attract the chauffeur's attention by tapping on the glass partition. She had just leaned forward to do so when there was a terrible crashing sound as the window through which she had just been looking was savagely smashed.

Raquel screamed and covered her face to shield it from flying glass. In a flash, someone reached through the broken window and unlocked the door. Almost before she knew what was happening, she was being dragged out of the car by strong hands. She couldn't see the man's face. Limp with terror, she didn't resist. If her attacker wanted money, he could have all of it as long as he let her go. Then, as the moon emerged from the clouds, Raquel saw the figure of another man standing beside the open door of a nondescript car in front of the limousine. It was one of the masked dancers from the party. Panic-stricken, she began to struggle with all her might, kicking and scratching at anything within reach as she tried to break free of her captor's grasp. Her nails raked away skin, blood, and a feathery mask, causing the man to curse and momentarily loosen his grip. Raquel lunged forward, and the other man yelled, "God damn it, hold her! Hold her, I said!"

"I'm tryin', but this one fierce bitch!" her assailant grunted, throwing both sinewy arms around her. "She clawin' me to death!"

She aimed a vicious kick at his shins with one sharp-heeled shoe. He let out a yelp of pain, and as his confederate ran to his aid, two other men jumped out of the car. Outnumbered and overpowered though she was, Raquel continued to struggle, kick, and scream while one of them yanked off her turban and slipped a pillowcase over her head.

"Lady," a silky, threatening voice warned from a few paces away, "we don't want to hurt you, but we may have no choice if you don't shut up."

"Hush, mon!" said one of the others. He sounded nervous. "You must not offend her, or you will be offending the *gubida* as well."

"Ah, but so far we have no proof that she is linked with the ancestors," came the casual reply.

The two men holding Raquel dragged her forward, and one of them shoved her into the waiting car's back seat so vehemently that she fell on her hands and knees. As she scrambled upright, she heard the same voice that had just spoken address the man who was getting into the seat beside her. This time his voice was not sensual or silky at all.

"That's enough, Jay! There's no need to be so rough."

"I should've done more t'an t'at," the man called Jay muttered. "My face is bleedin'! Besides, I don't remembah anybody puttin' you in charge, Meester Nate Bowman. We were told not'ing about t'ese changes you talkin' about."

"I put myself in charge. Would you care to challenge my authority?"

The question was asked very softly, but there was such menace in it that Raquel shivered. The man called Jay made no reply.

"As for your face, don't worry—you'll live," Nate Bowman went on. "If the lady is too tough for you, I suggest you consider backing out while there's still time."

"She not too tough! *I'm* tough, or I would not be a membah of Shango!" Jay blustered.

One of the other men got into the back seat on the other side of Raquel, effectively blocking any possibility of escape. The third man and Nate Bowman got in the front seat, and the car lurched forward as the driver stepped on the gas.

Crushed between two of her abductors, unable to see, barely able to breathe inside the bag that covered her head, Raquel had never been more terrified. Her thoughts spun wildly out of control. *Shango? Gubida?* What were they talking about? Where were these men taking her? What did they want with her? Suddenly she gasped. As far as the kidnappers knew, she was Jackie Dawson. If she told them she was not, they might let her go!

Before she could speak, the man called Jay gave an unpleasant chortle. "You right, Meester Nate. Another woman I would kill for what she done to me, but I will not hurt Mees Dawson. She is too valuable to all of us." He gave one of Raquel's breasts a painful squeeze. "But I cannot promise anyt'ing else. It's goin' to be a long trip to Dangriga."

Realizing how close she had come to signing her own death warrant, Raquel slumped over in a dead faint.

* * *

Raquel remained unconscious for several hours, coming to only when powerful, unseen hands shook her awake and led her out of the car. Stumbling over rough terrain, Raquel would have fallen many times if it had not been for the two men who gripped her arms on either side, their fingers digging into her soft flesh. As her captors led her down a treacherously steep slope, the foul stench of rotting fish and stale urine accosted her nostrils and she fainted again. One of the men must have carried her from that point on. When Raquel awakened the second time, she was dimly aware of being set on her feet and pushed through an open doorway. A moment later, she heard the door close behind her, and the sharp *click* as someone turned a key on the outside, locking her in. Still groggy, Raquel ripped the pillowcase from her aching head and took a deep breath of salt-tinged air as she looked around.

The tiny room in which she found herself had no window and was so dimly lit by the single flickering candle that even without the bag, she could hardly see. Taking a tentative step forward, Raquel promptly banged her knee against a sharp object. It turned out to be the corner of a bed that jutted out from one wall and took up most of the floor space. There was only one other piece of furniture, the small bureau on which the candle sat, and practically no room to walk except for about two feet at the bed's end and along either side. Leaning down to rub her throbbing knee, Raquel suddenly felt the floor heave beneath her, knocking her off balance. As she sprawled on the bed, she realized that she must be aboard a boat. And from the way the rocking motion continued, that boat was most likely heading out to sea.

Raquel plunged into total despair. On dry land, there was always the chance, however small, that she might attract the attention of some passerby or even make a desperate run for it. But on the ocean, there was no way to contact a potential rescuer and no possibility of escape. Burying her face in the bed's small, hard pillow, Raquel surrendered to a storm of hopeless tears until, exhausted, she fell into a troubled sleep.

Chapter Three

For the first few seconds after Raquel opened her swollen eyes, she didn't know where she was, but too soon the memory of all that had happened to her came flooding back. Sitting up on the bed, she squinted at her watch, trying to determine how long she had slept, but the crystal was cracked and the watch had stopped. The candle had almost burned itself out. Afraid that once it was gone she might not receive another one, Raquel quickly pinched out the flame.

The tiny room, however, was not completely dark. She realized that what little light there was came from a plastic hatch in the ceiling of the stuffy cabin. Desperate for fresh air, she stood on the bed and pushed against the hatch, but it wouldn't budge. Frustrated and more furious now than frightened, she shoved it with all her strength. Suddenly the hatch sprang open an inch or two, and a cool, salty breeze carrying the scent of the sea embraced her. Peering through the crack, she could catch a glimpse of moonlit sky. Over the sound of waves she heard two male voices. Standing directly below the hatch, Raquel listened intently to their words.

"He jus' don't understan'," one voice declared. "No one orders Jay, *Dada*, aroun'."

"No one, my brother?" asked the second. He sounded skeptical.

"No one! I simply obey the *buyei* because of my respect for him."

The second speaker said something else, but apparently the two had moved away, because Raquel couldn't hear what it was.

Sinking back down on the bed, she tried to gather her wits about her in an attempt to make some sense of her situation. These men who had kidnapped her were very strange. They spoke English combined with a language foreign to her, and they seemed to think that she—or rather, Jackie Dawson—was connected in some weird way with their ancestors. Raquel remembered one of the men warning the one called Nate Bowman not to anger the ancestors. He seemed to be afraid of them, and fortunately for her, that meant he probably feared Jackie, too.

It was also clear that the group's loyalties were divided. The man named Jay did not like the one he called Mr. Nate. From the snatches of conversation Raquel had heard, she gathered that the four men had never worked together before. So why had they conspired to kidnap Jackie Dawson? And why were they taking her to Dangriga, a place she had never heard of? Who owned this boat on which she was a prisoner?

Wondering if she would ever know the answers to her questions, Raquel lay down, but even exhausted as she was, it was a long time before she fell asleep. In that cloudy world between sleeping and waking, one of the words she had heard that night suddenly struck a familiar chord.

Shango or *Chango,* the god of power and passion. Paulette had once spoken of him—or was it one of the other gods of the Santeriá religion? They all sounded so much alike. Paulette had warned her never to speak of them to her mother and she never had . . .

Finally, Raquel drowsed off again.

Jay's hands were sweating as he slowly turned the key that had conveniently been left in the lock of the woman's door. Nervously, he glanced over his shoulder, but the narrow passageway was empty. He had never thought it would come to his confronting Jackie Dawson face-to-face, but as things stood, he had no other choice. He had to get rid of her, somehow making it look like a suicide. Then Nate Bowman would never be the wiser.

His bulbous eyes gleamed in the darkness as he cautiously pushed the door open. Pausing for a moment, he took in the woman's voluptuous figure lying on the bed and licked his lips. Perhaps he would make one small detour from his intended plan . . .

The slight scraping sound of the door closing roused Raquel from her slumber. She could barely make out the shadowy figure before he was on top of her, pawing at her flounced skirt and parting her thighs with strong, eager hands. Although she was still half asleep, Raquel fought like a tigress, biting and clawing at him with talonlike nails.

"So you want to hurt me again, do you?" His hot, fetid breath scorched her cheek. "First I pay you back for what you did to my face. If you try to scream, believe me, I will make it very painful for you."

Raquel did not scream, but neither did she stop struggling. Before she gave in to this animal, she would gladly die. She raised one leg and kneed him accurately in the groin.

With a yelp of pain and outrage, Jay grabbed both her hands with one of his and pinned them above her head while with the other hand he ripped off her lacy underpants.

"Get off of me, you big ape!" Raquel screamed, writhing beneath him.

"I strongly suggest you do what Ms. Dawson says, Jay."

The silky voice from the broad-shouldered figure silhouetted in the doorway caught her assailant unawares and he momentarily froze.

"Screw you, Meester Nate!" he growled. "I do what I want to do, and what I want to do is t'is!"

Raquel heard a faint metallic click.

"Really. And now—do you still want to do it?" Nate Bowman spoke almost in a whisper and his face was shadowed so that she could not see his expression, but the menace in his voice was unmistakable.

He moved with the swift, lithe grace of a predatory animal. As Jay's heavy body rose abruptly from Raquel's, she saw moonlight reflecting from the switchblade Nate pressed to Jay's jugular vein.

"I'm warnin' you, Meester Nate. You will find yourself in big trouble if you mess wit' me," her attacker muttered.

"I'm willing to take that risk. At the moment, however, *you* are the one in big trouble." Nate Bowman grabbed Jay's beefy arm and hauled him to his feet. "Now, listen carefully, because I'm only going to say this once. While we are on this voyage, *no one* is to touch Ms. Dawson in any way, understand? I would appreciate it if you would relay this message to your brother, Al, as well."

"What you care if we have a little fun wit' her?" Jay asked truculently.

"If she is linked with the *gubida*, you will be grateful to me for stopping you. If she's not, I don't care what you do with her. But until we find out, Ms. Dawson is not to be touched, understand?"

Nate stepped aside and Jay edged out of the room, cursing under his breath.

When he had gone, Raquel wrapped the longest portion of her skirt around her and huddled near the head of the bed, trying to control the frantic racing of her heart. Had this man saved her from Jay only to use her for his own lustful purposes?

Although Nate Bowman was still shrouded in shadow, a ray of moonlight from the partially opened hatch touched Raquel's tumbled curls and smooth bronze skin. Looking at this beautiful, desirable woman, Nate knew that she had every reason to be wary of his motives. He could hardly blame her. In spite of what he had said to Jay, why should she trust him right after one of his henchman had attempted to rape her?

"Ms. Dawson . . ." he began, but Raquel cut him off.

"I suppose I should thank you for rescuing me, but gratitude isn't uppermost in my mind right now," she said acidly. "If you expect me to repay you with sexual favors, you are very much mistaken! Please leave me alone."

Responding to the challenge she offered him, Nate moved forward. He flashed the switchblade once more, then he murmured, "I don't take orders from anyone, lady. Just because I'm protecting you from the Shango doesn't mean you can do or say anything you like. I'm in charge here, and don't you forget it."

Raquel caught her breath. The lips of this man whose face she could not see were only inches away. Terrified though she was, she refused to grovel.

"Get out," she grated.

"That was my intention, and this time I'll take the key with me. But first . . ."

His mouth descended on hers. With a gentle sucking motion, Nate captured her lower lip, exploring it with the tip of his tongue. Before she could react, he strode out of the little room, closing the door behind him, and she heard the key turn in the lock.

Trembling violently, Raquel wiped her mouth with the back of her hand in a gesture of disgust directed as much at herself as at Nate Bowman. Try as she might, she could not deny the tiny spark of desire his kiss had ignited. What was wrong with her that she would respond to him this way? Knife or no knife, she should have lashed out at him as she had at Jay, but there was something masterful about him that had melted her resistance. He had proved his point. Nate Bowman was definitely in charge.

In an attempt to erase the memory of her disgraceful reaction to his kiss, Raquel decided to focus on the issue at hand. Nate Bowman had said he was taking the key of her cabin with him, and she was fairly certain that she had nothing to fear from him. But that might not be the only key. If Jay had another one and planned to attack again despite Nate's warning, she was determined to be ready for him. The first thing she had to do was provide some light.

Turning to the bureau next to the bed, Raquel opened drawer after drawer, fumbling in each one until she found what she sought—a book of matches. When she had lit the stubby candle, she rose to her knees and began looking around the cabin. She discovered the long strip of cloth that had formed her turban lying on the floor along with her ripped panties, but that was all. Raquel's abduction had happened so fast that she had left her purse in the limousine, which she now realized was providential. Though she regretted the loss of the nine thousand dollars, the purse also contained her driver's license, credit cards, and other information clearly establishing her true identity. If she had taken it with her, there was no doubt in her mind that the kidnappers would have opened it, and when they'd discovered she was not Jackie Dawson, Raquel was sure they would not have hesitated to kill her on the spot.

Thank God for small favors, she thought. At least she still had the thousand dollars she had tucked into her top. It might very well come in handy at some point. But at the moment, she had to do something about her half-naked state.

Since her underwear was beyond repair, she pulled the tail of her skirt between her legs and began tucking it into the waistband in order to transform it into a pair of ruffled, knee-length pants. Intent on what she was doing, she didn't hear the key turn in the lock. Suddenly the door swung open. Primed for Jay's second assault, Raquel opened her mouth to scream, but the scream died in her throat as Nate Bowman reentered the room.

"Did I startle you? Sorry—I didn't know you were dressing. I suppose I should have knocked," he said.

For the first time, Raquel was able to see the man's face, and she couldn't help staring as the flickering candlelight cast strange shadows on his ruggedly handsome features. Nate Bowman's skin was the color of cappuccino, his nose broad and well formed. Black hair, cut close, hugged his shapely head, and dark brown eyes fringed with long, thick lashes regarded her with cynical amusement. Full, smooth lips beneath a pencil-thin mustache quirked in a slight smile. It was the kind of mouth Paulette used to say could "turn a woman inside out."

Lowering her gaze, Raquel took in the man's slim yet muscular physique. A white shirt, open to the waist, revealed his glossy brown chest, and skin-tight jeans outlined powerful thighs and calves. As he lounged in the doorway, every inch of him exuded a confident masculinity that made her heart pound erratically.

Embarrassed and ashamed by her reaction, Raquel tore her eyes away. Yes, Nate Bowman was attractive, more attractive than any man she had ever seen, but he was also a criminal, and she was at his mercy. While they were on this voyage, he would protect her, thinking she was Jackie Dawson. But once they reached their mysterious destination, there was no telling what would happen. She shuddered as she remembered his words to Jay: *"If she is linked to the gubida, you will be grateful to me for stopping you. If she's not, I don't care what you do with her."*

Raquel had no idea what the *gubida* was, or how the woman she was impersonating might be "linked" to it. But since she was not Jackie Dawson, no such link was possible, and when Nate Bowman found that out, he would turn her over to Jay without a qualm—unless she could somehow manage to escape after the boat docked. That hope, faint though it was, bolstered Raquel's flagging courage and steeled her against her captor's insidious appeal.

"What do you want?" she snapped, scowling at him.

His reply surprised her. "I brought you something." Raquel had not noticed the small bag he held in one hand until he tossed it on the bed. "I planned to give you these when we reached Belize, but perhaps you might like something less—shall we say, *revealing*—than your present outfit to wear in the meantime."

Peering into the bag, she saw that it contained what looked like a shift of some sort, undergarments, and a pair of flat shoes. "Thank you," she said grudgingly. Then it hit her. "Did you say Belize? In Central America?"

Nate raised one dark brow. "Is there another Belize? Come now, Ms. Dawson. Has it been so long since you visited Dangriga, the home of your ancestors?"

She paused. "Yes. Yes, it has."

"It's a shame you must be taken to Belize by force." His apology actually sounded sincere. "But you should have more respect for your ancestors and their beliefs."

As Raquel gazed into his dark eyes, she thought she saw a flicker of compassion there. Seizing his hands in hers, she cried, "You talk about shame, but it's *you* who are forcing me, *you* who should be ashamed! Mr. Bowman, I beg of you, let me go! I promise I won't tell a soul about any of this!"

She must have imagined the hint of compassion, because his eyes now glittered as hard and black as obsidian. Looking down at her hands, he sneered as though they were dirty, unworthy of touching him.

A hot wave of humiliation washed over Raquel, and she quickly released him. "I should have known I couldn't expect the likes of you to do what's right!" she snarled.

Nate Bowman regarded her with undisguised contempt. "Right, Ms. Dawson? I doubt if you know the meaning of the word!"

With that, he turned on his heel and left the room. In a fit of impotent rage, Raquel took one of the shoes out of the bag and hurled it after him, but it bounced harmlessly off the closing door.

"You bastard!" she hissed through clenched teeth. "You no-good, arrogant bastard!"

Chapter Four

When she had calmed down a little, Raquel noticed that the light coming through the hatch was much brighter now. Standing up on the bed again, she looked out and caught a glimpse of azure sky. Obviously it was early morning, and Raquel suddenly realized that she was ravenous. She had had nothing to eat since noon of the previous day except for the hors d'oeuvres at the party. Surely her captors didn't intend to starve her!

She got off the bed and marched over to the door, intending to yell at the top of her lungs, demanding that somebody bring her food. Raquel had just raised her fists to pound on the door when to her surprise it inched open and a young man stuck his head in. He was slighter in build than either Nate or Jay, his skin was chocolate brown, and he was holding a tray of fresh fruit, bread, and cheese.

"Good morning, *pataki*," he said softly. "My name Art. Meester Bowman say to bring you breakfas'. May I come in?"

His demeanor was so different from that of the other men Raquel had encountered that she felt no fear of him. Stepping aside, she allowed him to enter. As he placed the tray on the little bureau, he kept casting furtive glances at her over his shoulder. When he turned around, he actually bowed.

"Is there anyt'ing else I can do for you, *pataki?*" he asked, regarding her almost with reverence.

Raquel couldn't figure out why he seemed so much in awe of her, but it was such a welcome change that she smiled at him. "Well, now that you mention it, there is. I assume this boat must have a bathroom somewhere. Would it be possible for you to escort me to it?"

Art hesitated. "Meester Nate didn' say nothin' about bathroom."

"I hardly think he will object. After all, I can't very well escape while we're at sea, now, can I?"

"I guess it will be okay," the young man finally replied. "Come with me, *pataki.*"

Wondering what the strange word meant, Raquel followed him into a narrow passageway to a small door. Art positioned himself outside while she used the facilities, then washed her hands and face thoroughly using a sliver of soap and some paper towels she found next to the tiny sink. There was no mirror, which was probably just as well, Raquel thought. She must look a mess. Running her fingers through her tangled hair, she stepped outside and followed Art back to her cabin.

Before he left, she said, "There's one more thing you could do for me, Art. Do you know if there's a needle and thread on board?"

"I do not know, but I will see."

Art bowed himself out and Raquel perched on the edge of the bed, devouring every scrap of her breakfast. When he returned, he handed her one needle and a spool of thread, then picked up the tray and left the cabin.

Raquel had once made many of her own clothes, and now she wasted no time converting her turban fabric into a sleeveless shirt. Although she was determined not to give Nate Bowman the satisfaction of seeing her in the clothing he had provided and had shoved the shift and shoes into a bureau drawer, she was unaccustomed to going without underwear. She took off the skimpy top she was wearing, careful to remove the thousand dollars she'd stashed there, and put on the bra and panties, which fortunately appeared to be new and spotlessly clean. Next she slipped out of the skirt. Examining the waistband carefully, Raquel distributed the ten hundred-dollar bills along the inside facing and sewed it securely to the body of the skirt before she put it back on. Then, after recreating her ruffled pants, she slipped into the makeshift shirt, securing it around the waist with the costume's original top. On impulse, she concealed the needle in a fold of the shirt's fabric. It wasn't much of a weapon, but it was the only one she had.

All dressed up and no place to go, she thought, surprised that under the present circumstances she still retained her sense of humor.

Just then Raquel heard a soft rapping on her door, and her tension returned. "Who's there?" she called out.

"It's Art, *pataki,*" came the young man's soft voice. "Meester Nate say you can come topside now if you want. The door not locked anymore."

Heart pounding at the prospect of release from her prison cell, Raquel leaped to her feet and quickly opened the door. Art smiled shyly at her. "T'is way, please." He led the way along the narrow hall and up the companionway at its end.

When Raquel stepped out onto the deck, her eyes were so dazzled by the brilliance of the sun that for a moment she could see nothing at all. Then her vision cleared, and as she looked eagerly around her. she discovered she was on a sailboat. The motor she had heard the night before must have been used to propel the boat out of the harbor, but now pure white sails bellied out against an incredibly blue sky as the boat skimmed over the water. The craft was good-sized, maybe forty feet or so, with ample sleeping space for the four men aboard and their prisoner. Glancing into the main cabin, Raquel could see that its couch had obviously been used as a bed—Nate Bowman's, she assumed, since he was the boss.

Filling her lungs with clean salt air, she knew the sensation of freedom she felt was only an illusion, but still she reveled in it. Raquel had always loved boats, and knew quite a bit about them. One of her high-school teachers, a sailing enthusiast with his own boat, had formed a sailing club. Amazingly enough, Raquel's mother had not objected to her joining, so she and several of her classmates had spent many happy hours learning all Mr. Rutherford could teach them about the art of handling a sailboat. Raquel, always an apt pupil, had often earned his praise for her skill at the sport.

Deliberately ignoring Nate, who was manning the wheel, she sat in the corner of the long padded seat, lifting her face to the wind and gazing out across the bluish-green water. Raquel was a strong swimmer. If there had been any land in sight, however distant, she would have considered jumping overboard and taking her chances. But there was nothing but water as far as the eye could see, and Raquel knew that was why she was no longer locked in her cabin. The only possible escape would be death by drowning, and she refused to surrender to despair. She was a survivor, and survive she would.

Nate Bowman studied her as the wind whipped a tangle of black curls away from her beautiful features and pressed that ridiculous outfit she had concocted against her body, molding the fabric to the curves of her ripe breasts. He knew perfectly well why she had refused to wear the clothing he had given her. She was stubborn, proud, and strong, qualities he couldn't help admiring. Her fiery temper and rebellious spirit both infuriated and impressed him, and he had an inkling of how much it had cost her to beg him for her freedom the night before. Looking into her dark, pleading eyes, there was a moment when he had almost weakened. Instead of the shameless woman he knew she was, he saw one of the young women of Dangigra who had pleaded for mercy on that terrible day so long ago. It was a day Nate would never forget.

Ironically, it had begun as a day of celebration. A truce had been called between the two warring religious groups, the Garifuna and the Shango. The festivities commenced at noon and continued all day. He and his cousin Cecilia, both in their early teens, were having a wonderful time. Nate's mother had raised Cecilia from infancy, feeling it was her responsibility to give the baby a loving home when her sister died in childbirth. Cecilia's father had totally abandoned her shortly thereafter when he'd taken another wife.

The Shango had traveled the long distance from

Punta Gorda to the outskirts of Dangriga with slabs of *gibnut* in tow. Armadillo and brocket deer were stewing in pots over huge open fires, along with a medley of seafood, cow-foot soup, beans and rice, and various vegetables and tropical fruits. Wine made from cashew fruit was offered to everyone, even youngsters Nate's age. His people believed that it strengthened the blood, and young men needed to be strong so they would sire many healthy children when they came to manhood.

Everyone was in a happy mood, and there was much dancing in addition to eating and drinking. Nate smiled, remembering how for the first time Cecilia had joined the dance of the young virgins. She was so lovely, so slender and lithe. Occasionally she would giggle when she caught the eye of an interested Garifunian male, but she was still too young to do anything but flirt. Nate himself had been very proud because he was allowed to join the band, playing a large drum his father had fashioned for him. Everyone had praised him, saying how much his drumming added to the ensemble of instruments.

Slowly Nate's smile faded. As the day wore on, people from both villages mingled freely, enjoying each other's hospitality. Like many of the Garifuna, some Shango men found Cecilia beautiful and desirable. Unlike the Garifuna, however, the Shango were unaware of Cecilia's extreme youth. That night, as the wine flowed freely and the dancing and celebrating reached fever pitch, several Shango men who desired Cecilia refused to be dissuaded by her objections. Some young women from Dangigra willingly went into the brush with the Shango, but there were others who were forced. Cecilia was among them.

When this outrage was discovered by the Garifuna, fierce fighting broke out between the two factions. Eventually the Garifuna were able to drive the Shango away, but not before some people were killed and many others injured.

The days that followed were sad ones for the entire village, and especially so for Nate's family. Cecilia's young, tender body had been so badly abused that his mother had sought out the priestess to help heal her. Despite the woman's assurances that Cecilia would survive, her condition worsened every day. After two weeks, the priestess declared that there was nothing further she could do. The girl had lost her will to live. Something inside her fragile spirit had been broken and she no longer wanted to remain on this side of life. Nate and his family sat helplessly by, watching Cecilia die.

Even though he was little more than a boy, Nate vowed that when he became a man, he would never force himself on a woman no matter how much he desired her, nor would he permit any other man to do so if he could possibly prevent it.

That was the last time the Garifuna and the Shango had come together in peace. Now a truce was being called because of a prophecy—and Jackie Dawson.

Nate's eyes flickered over the young woman sitting on the bench. Like Jay, he was sexually aroused by her, but he would keep his distance and make sure that Jay kept his. She was Nate's responsibility and he would not allow her to be harmed in any way.

Following Raquel's gaze, he saw that she was watching Art, who was looking at the fluttering mainsail, a concerned expression on his face.

"We're losing speed," Nate called to him. "I'm going to sail her straight into the wind, so prepare to jibe."

Art nodded, and Raquel watched him trim the jibsheet, then slacken the lines to allow the boom to swing.

"Pakati," he said, bowing to her, "you must move now. The boom soon be swingin' in your direction and I would not want you hurt. It would be best I t'ink if you go below."

Touched by his concern for her safety, she smiled. "Very well."

Raquel rose and headed for the companionway. Art was the only man aboard whom she did not hate or fear, and she wondered how he had become involved in this criminal undertaking. Suddenly she stopped in her tracks. If she made friends with Art, he might help her escape when they reached Belize! She would gladly pay him the entire thousand dollars if he would.

Lost in thought, Raquel didn't notice the short, stock, light-skinned man who sidled up to her.

"My brother Jay tells me the big man says we cannot force you, eh? Maybe I won't need force. Al got somethin' here the ladies like." He grabbed his manhood through his pants and grinned suggestively. "How 'bout you and me havin' some real fun?"

She was about to brush past him when Nate's shout of "Jibe-ho!" rang out. Raquel ducked just in time, but Al wasn't so lucky. The heavy boom struck him a cruel blow before continuing on its way, and the man crumpled like a rag doll at her feet, blood flowing from a deep gash on the side of his head.

Jay had come up from below deck in time to see the whole thing. Dropping to his knees, he called his brother's name, but Al did not answer. He looked up at Raquel, and the malevolence and fear on the ugly face she had scarred with her nails made her cringe.

"It's your fault, woman!" he accused. "You are *echu!*"

Nate suddenly appeared behind Jay. "This isn't the time to talk about whose fault it is. Let's pick him up and carry him into my cabin."

"Stay away!" Jay shouted. "You say this woman be a link to the *gubida,* but I say she *echu,* an evil spirit! Look what she done to my face, and now to my brother. I take care of him myself!"

Nate shrugged. "Do as you please. It's no concern of mine."

Bulky muscles straining, Jay began dragging Al's limp body to the stern of the boat, and Nate turned his cool gaze on Raquel.

"Al was our cook," he said. "From now on, you have kitchen duty. You *can* cook, can't you?"

Raquel stared at him in disbelief. "Cook? You're asking me if I can *cook* when one of your men has been badly hurt? You should turn this boat around right away and take him back to Miami where he can get proper medical care!"

"Lunch is to be served at noon, and supper no later than six," Nate continued, as if she hadn't spoken. "You'll find everything you need in the galley. If you don't know how to operate the stove, ask Art."

He returned to relieve Art at the wheel, leaving Raquel sputtering with rage. Even she, who detested both Al and Jay, felt compassion for Al's plight, but Nate Bowman felt nothing at all. The man must have ice water in his veins! Unfortunately, however, she was his prisoner. She had no choice but to follow his commands.

With Art's assistance, Raquel soon familiarized herself with the galley and prepared lunch. When it was time to eat, Jay eyed both the meal and her with suspicion and emphasized his distrust by spitting at her feet. He grabbed a can of baked beans from a shelf and returned to his brother without a word.

Jay's lust had frightened Raquel, but it was nothing compared to the enmity he expressed from that day on. For the rest of the voyage, she avoided him as much as possible, spending most of her time in her cabin. But whenever she came topside, Jay's vengeful eyes never seemed to leave her.

One day Raquel heard Nate tell Art they would arrive in Belize tomorrow. That night her heart pounded in wild anticipation. By now she was sure that she would be able to persuade Art to aid in her escape, and as she went to bed, she planned to offer him the money first thing in the morning.

She was awakened in the middle of the night by the boat's wild bobbing. Angry waves were crashing and pounding the hatch above her. Mingled with it was another noise, a high, constant screech like the cry of an animal in pain.

From the hallway outside her room, Raquel heard loud voices.

"Meester Nate need you to help bring the sails down or we will lose them," Art was shouting.

"Do it yourself," was Jay's angry reply. "I got to look after Al. Don' you see how he's actin'? He's out of his

mind! What if he gets out of here and jumps overboard?"

"Al just one man. If we don' take care of the boat, we
will all drown in t'is storm!"

"Go to hell! I'm not leavin' my brother. I don' know
nothin' about sailin' a boat, no way. You and Meester
Nate were supposed to take care of t'at!"

Of all the odds that confronted her, Raquel had never
contemplated the possibility of going down with her abductors in the Caribbean Sea. Now, because of Jay, their
chances of survival were almost none!

She leaped out of bed and pounded on the cabin
door, which was still locked every night for her own protection. "Art! Can you hear me?" she shouted. "Let me
out of here! *I know how to sail!*"

It was several agonizing minutes before she heard the
key turn in the lock and Art opened the door. "Meester
Nate say you will only be in the way," he told her apol-
ogetically. "But he know an extra pair of hands better
than none, so he say come on."

Since Raquel slept in her clothes, there was no need
to change. She raced after him down the hall and up
the stairs. As soon as they reached the deck, the howling
wind nearly knocked her off her feet, but she quickly
caught hold of some rigging. Torrential rain mixed with
seawater immediately drenched her as she turned to
Nate for instruction.

"What do you want me to do?" she yelled.

"Can you steer?" he yelled back.

"Yes!"

Nate turned the wheel over to her. "Hold her as
steady as you can." To Art, he said, "We have to bring
those sails down fast!"

Raquel planted her feet wide apart to steady herself, holding onto the wheel with all her might. The cool metal burned the palms of her hands as she squeezed it tightly. Already the forty-foot craft was heeling dangerously as it battled the waters.

Nate and Art scurried to bring down the jibsheet, the wind whipping the material in their faces, fighting them every step of the way. Finally, they managed to tame it, tying it off just enough to secure it against the storm's vengeance.

Nate exuded sheer power as he fought the elements. Every muscle in his upper body was tense. His eyes burned with determination.

"Now the mainsail," he shouted above the storm, then turned to Raquel. "You're doing fine. Just keep holding her steady."

The wheel resisted her effort to control it, and she bent her knees, giving her more leverage against its opposition. Her eyes and face stung from the savage lashes of the seawater, yet she never slackened her grip.

Nate and Art tried to haul down the large sail, but something was caught. Several other attempts to free it resulted in one of the main lines disengaging.

"I've got to go up there!" Nate determined. "It's the only way we're going to get it down."

Art stepped between Nate and the mast.

"No—I better go," he shouted. "You bigger and heavier than me. I'll be able to cling closer to the mast. The wind will have a smaller target."

There was only a moment's indecision before Nate nodded his approval. As Art turned toward the mast, Nate suddenly grabbed his forearm, concern burning deep within his gaze. "Be careful."

Clutching the mast, Art shinnied his way to the top. Raquel could see his brown hands grabbing for the evasive hook as it swung wildly in the storm. He leaned out further, finally catching the rope in his hand, but at that moment a mountainous wave crashed against the craft, forcing Nate to grab a block attached to loose rigging, and casting Art into the raging waters.

Raquel screamed as she witnessed Art's slim body disappear overboard and with it her hope of escape. She nearly let go of the wheel to reach out for him, but she stopped herself just in time. It would have meant instant death for them all.

Nate hung onto the rigging for dear life. The white cresting waves went washing over him time and time again, while his black head resembled a bob on the end of a fishing line. Raquel watched in sheer horror, knowing there was no way she could help without causing all their deaths.

She had no idea how long she steered, but suddenly it was all over and the storm dissipated as quickly as it had appeared.

Once the waves became smoother, Nate collapsed onto the deck, weak from exhaustion. Upon seeing him, Raquel released the wheel, her arms and legs shaking uncontrollably from the ordeal, and knelt down beside him.

"Are you all right?" Her voice came raspily.

He nodded his head once; he could do no more. It was hard for him to believe the woman he had placed in such danger had actually saved their lives.

Consciousness was beginning to evade him, but he could hear her breathing deeply beside him and felt the wet mass of her tangled hair lying limply over his arm.

He wanted to thank her, to touch her. Then all went dark.

Raquel lay upon the deck, exhausted, allowing the boat to drift in whatever direction the wind took them. She was too tired to care or even cry.

Looking at Nate's inanimate body, she realized that now he was the only one she could depend on. Art was dead. There was no way she could trust Jay, and she knew his brother Al was an invalid. Suddenly she found herself clutching at Nate's bare chest and she began to sob against it. He mustn't die. He mustn't!

Almost as if from a distance she heard her own hysterical laughter, and she tasted the saltiness of her tears mixed with seawater upon his muscular chest. As Nate lay unconscious beneath her, Raquel knew with every fiber of her being he was her only chance for survival.

Chapter Five

The shady porch of the inn was only several feet away, but Raquel was unsure if she would be able to make it. The storm had caused them to beach much farther south than Nate had planned, and considering the condition of the boat, they were lucky to reach Belize at all.

Nate turned to see how far she lagged behind. After reassuring himself of her closeness, he switched his heavy duffel bag to the other shoulder. Heavy lines appeared in his handsome brow. Now his initial plans would have to be altered. It could take another day or so before they reached their intended destination. He entered the inn deep in thought with Jay and Al following closely on his heels. Nate was uneasy about what this unexpected change would mean for the woman.

On top of all that had occurred, Raquel was badly shaken by Art's death. The fact that he was an accomplice to her kidnapping was of little importance. She had never before seen another human being die.

Nate, however, showed no outward signs of being affected by the drowning. He appeared totally preoccupied with his own thoughts. So despite the closeness they experienced while battling the storm, their relationship was barely cordial.

Raquel's thoughts drifted back to before they had reached Belize. They had exchanged a few unkind words after he'd criticized her sailing. His thickly lashed eyes had appeared worried, and his handsome features had displayed lines of strain around the mouth. He was impatient with their lack of progress and accused her of not concentrating. She couldn't believe his audacity. She was literally a prisoner helping to sail a boat to God knew where . . . and he had the nerve to be rude and ungrateful!

Angrily Raquel lashed out at him. "You don't care about anything but what you want. You don't care about anybody else, do you?" Her dark eyes were cutting and cold as she spoke. "I have feelings of sympathy for someone like Art. But I believe you choose to be the way you are just so you can justify anything wrong and ugly that you do."

For a second, the anger in his eyes made her think that he would slap her. Then his face became the image of controlled rage and he simply walked away.

After Art's death, Jay had been forced to perform more of the duties on board. Al was of little help. The blow to his head had deeply affected his ability to reason. His sentences were disconnected and his ability to concentrate was minimal. In other ways he exhibited the behavior of a man who'd gone completely mad. He ate ravenously, as if he didn't know how to stop, and his sexual penchants had become disgusting. Foul language poured out of his mouth at the most peculiar times, mixed with a tongue Raquel did not understand.

After a particularly vulgar outburst, Nate suggested Al

should be locked in the cabin until they beached the craft, but Jay would have none of it.

"It is your fault, as well as the *echu*, that he is like t'is. Now you want to lock him away so you don't have to see what you have done. No way, Meester Nate."

Raquel felt that in some perverse manner Jay took pleasure in Al's demented behavior, especially when it was directed at her. She could not pass within arm's reach of Al without being mauled openly. A glazed look would enter his eye and a string of the foulest terms she'd ever heard would tumble from his slack lips. Jay laughed hysterically during these uncomfortable moments—daring Nate to stop his brother's actions, knowing a man whose mind was as disturbed as Al's appeared to be was not responsible for the things he did.

The tension between Nate and the two brothers seemed to worsen as the journey progressed. Raquel was concerned over how things would go now that they had reached land. Jay needed Nate in order to reach Belize. But now that they had arrived, she feared Jay would not hold back his negative feelings toward either one of them.

They had little trouble during the long trek up the coastline of white, sandy beaches but the sinking sand made the journey difficult. As Raquel passed by the last clapboard house in a row of six, the heat of the sun was nearly unbearable—even her tongue felt dry as she tried to swallow. Still her tired, anxious eyes scanned the place for a building that might house the local authorities. But from the look of the tiny, underdeveloped settlement, the inn was the only place of business other than a poorly stocked, smelly fruit stand. There wasn't even one telephone pole in sight. The settlement seemed to sit in the middle of nowhere, with a thick, imposing forest on its inland side.

Suddenly, Raquel found it hard to breathe. Here she was on foreign soil, totally ignorant about the country or their present location. Could a somewhat modern city be beyond the wall of trees and brush? Or was her nearest possible avenue of escape miles away?

Raquel had been holding onto the belief that once they reached land she would make a way to contact the authorities and get help. But seeing what awaited her drained all hope. It felt as if the last ounce of physical strength she possessed was replaced by anxiety and fear. It was hard for her to think straight, and she had to force herself to mount the stairs to the inn. She felt as if heavy weights had been tied to her feet, making the simple motion a strenuous task. As she looked around, it was evident the inn was not a popular spot for tourists. From the look of the settlement, she doubted they received any tourists at all.

Inside, the furnishings revealed that one would get nothing but the bare necessities at this inn. There would be no modern conveniences. Yet compared to the straggly clapboard houses with little shade from the hot, tropical sun, it was a virtual Shangri-la.

Raquel sank into a large chair that had obviously seen better times. Dog tired and mentally worn, she watched Nate negotiate with a short man behind the counter. The language was totally foreign to her.

Out of desperation she considered throwing herself on the innkeeper's mercy until his dark eyes focused upon her. With one sweeping gaze he took in the dirty, flamboyant costume she wore, and his conclusions were plain. Scorn filled his eyes before he looked away. Humiliated and helpless, Raquel knew he had no room for understanding and any attempt to garner his help would be futile. And she knew she had to be careful—she did not know how her kidnappers would react to an attempt to escape on her part.

"There is only one room left, and that one is mine," Nate informed her. "I've arranged for you to have part of the back porch area that's sometimes used for guests. You can bathe in my room if you like."

Since the storm, Nate had begun to treat Raquel with a little more respect; still, he did not speak to her unless it was necessary. She knew she should not have expected him to give her the one room that was available, but somehow she had hoped. Her sable eyes mirrored her disgust as she listened to his decision.

Behind them, the Creole innkeeper eyed Al as he walked over to a bowl of fruit and began to take bites out of each one. The innkeeper, waving his arms emphatically, called to Al to stop. Finally, he snatched the bowl away, then placed his flat palm under Al's nose, demanding payment for his deed.

A verbal spat ensued between Jay and the Creole. When Jay pressed the man about a place to sleep, he turned over the small registration tablet and gave it a final slap. With an extensive stream of words Raquel did not understand, he pointed toward the door, then determinedly showed Jay and Al his back. Raquel felt a tinge of relief knowing at least that night Jay and Al would be sleeping under another roof.

Slipping into the sudsy water of the old-fashioned tub, Raquel felt her feelings of fear and anxiety float away like the bubbles of her bath. She lay in the steaming, soapy waters at her leisure, wondering how she would be able to gain her freedom. The warm water soothed her aching muscles and eased her mind.

Her thoughts unwittingly drifted to Nate as she wondered where he was and what he was doing now. He puzzled her more than she cared to admit—he had kidnapped her, yet he had protected her from Al and Jay. But he wouldn't set her free and he wouldn't say why he'd kidnapped her. Raquel was sure he needed her for some mysterious purpose.

Nate had taken his time in the bath before he'd allowed Raquel in the room. When he'd opened the bedroom door, she'd noticed his dark hair glistened from being freshly washed and he smelled of soap and a mild spicy scent. His carmel colored skin was freshly shaven, leaving only his trimmed mustache.

"How much time do you need?" he asked, buttoning his shirt over his bare chest.

She averted her eyes, yet a hazy vision of his powerful brown chest remained with her. "I don't know. Do I have a time limit?" she asked sarcastically.

"No," he replied, then extracted several Belizean dollars from his billfold and placed them on the bed. "Take your time. You can buy a meal downstairs once you're through." He disappeared down the hall without a backward glance.

She didn't bother to thank him. If it wasn't for him she wouldn't be in the situation she was in. Raquel thought of the thousand dollars sewn inside the belt of her costume. She hoped at some point it would come in handy, perhaps as an adequate bribe to get someone to help her. Ironically, it was a need for money that had gotten her into this situation. Hopefully, money, and lots of luck, would get her out.

As she allowed her fingers to float upon the water, she realized her kidnappers apparently had no intention of killing her, at least not yet. Her presence—or rather, Jackie Dawson's presence—was needed for something special, and that something was keeping her alive.

Raquel did not really believe Nate would harm her. But she wasn't sure. There was something beneath his cool exterior, an ability for cruelty if the need arose. Whereas Jay was a different story altogether. She believed the two men's desire for Jackie Dawson's presence was connected, but the motive for it was not the same. There was little doubt in her mind that Jay would kill her with pleasure, if the proper moment arrived, but only after degrading her further.

An involuntary shudder ran through her at the thought, and she reinforced her decision to be wary of him.

Raquel put on the shift Nate had given her. Afterward she washed the costume she'd worn for the past two days. The truth was, the frilly material had been extremely hot and uncomfortable, and already she could tell the airy shift would be much more practical. After all, she shouldn't cause herself more discomfort just to annoy her taciturn abductor.

Instead of going to the small dining room as Nate suggested, Raquel settled herself in the functional space provided for her. It contained a cot, and a battered nightstand that served as a dresser. The mattress was soft enough, and the linen was clean. Raquel needed food, but right now her need for rest was greater, and she tumbled into a deep sleep moments after her head lay on the flat feather pillow.

A feeling of disorientation swept over Raquel when she opened her eyes and it remained dark. Finally, she realized she must have slept through the entire afternoon and it was night. The distant sound of a guitar came from the direction of the dining room, along with several unusual but delicious smells. Raquel's stomach grumbled in response to the aroma.

The outside wall of the meager dining room was constructed of netted wire, enabling a constant flow of cool air to come off the sea. There were few decorations other than plants which grew lushly in the tropical climate.

Raquel felt self-conscious as she walked into the room filled with men and one female whose purpose was plain. Her tattered shift hung unattractively on her slender frame, and the only thing that appeared remotely appealing was a lock of shiny black hair that hung from beneath a dirty scarf she wore.

Because of the young Indian woman's unkempt appearance, Raquel could not imagine anyone wanting to take her up on what she was offering. Yet only moments later, when several pairs of lustful eyes focused on her, she was glad for the woman's presence.

An older female, whom Raquel assumed to be the innkeeper's wife, ambled over to the table where she sat. There was no menu and the woman spoke no English—from this Raquel knew her choices for a meal would be nonexistent.

The woman stood over her smiling and gesturing expressively with her hands. At the end of her presentation, she pointed to the plate of a man sitting nearby.

Still smiling and in a heavily accented voice she nodded affirmatively toward Raquel. Raquel had no choice but to agree. She would eat whatever the woman was offering.

Nate sat silently by himself in a corner. Two bottles of wine were the only things on his table. One was totally empty and the other was half full. With barely focused eyes, he stared at this woman called Jackie Dawson. Out of the colorful frock and heavy makeup, she was still lovely. *More lovely than any woman has the right to be,* he thought bitterly. But he knew about women like her, and despite her beautiful face and desirable body, he wanted nothing to do with her. He would do his job and leave her alone.

Raquel looked uneasily around the room and felt a sense of relief when she saw Nate. She had the urge to get up and join him until she saw the bottles of wine on the table and the blank look in his eyes. Raquel returned his look with disgust. Not only was he a criminal; he was an alcoholic as well.

Jay and Al had come to the inn for dinner, and were conversing with two other men as they shared two bottles of wine and food. Raquel was amazed to hear the language they spoke was different from the one used while communicating with the innkeeper, and she wondered how many languages were spoken in Belize.

Deep-pitched, raunchy laughter erupted in the room as one of the men grabbed a slim cheek of the prostitute's bottom. The woman gave no sign of rejection or acceptance in response to his actions. Moments later, as the innkeeper's wife served Raquel her food, the two of them disappeared down the hall, noisily shutting a door behind them.

The dish Raquel saw before her resembled a gumbo, containing pieces of fish, shrimp, rice, and beans. Raquel ate gratefully. She finished her meal quickly, rinsing it down with a glass of cool limeade. To her dismay, as she emptied the glass, Al took a seat beside her. His breath stank of liquor and onions as he breathed heavily through mouth, which was slightly open.

Al's bleary eyes focused on her breasts. A shaft of light angling off of a small lantern nearby made them clearly visible through the flimsy material of her shift.

"Juicy hooters," he slurred, making obscene motions with his mouth and tongue, then looking expectantly into Raquel's face.

Jay laughed boisterously, followed by a low remark to the men at the table. Their deep guffaws joined his.

It wasn't enough that she had been kidnapped and shanghaied clear across the sea. She also had to stand being ridiculed and degraded by this group of degenerates!

"Get the hell away from my table!" she hissed, dark eyes flashing with rage.

Al's idiotic features suddenly sharpened into a mask of livid sadism. Quick as a flash he had his large hand about her neck and his eyes were bulging with madness.

Raquel sputtered and gagged as she tried to remove Al's hand, but his grip was like steel. The weight of his large body caused the chair to tip over and they fell to the floor. Somewhere in the room she heard glass shatter as she kicked and squirmed to break loose from Al's deathly hold.

"Call him off, Jay, or I'll split his throat wide open," Nate's voice cut through a haze. "Now! Or he's a dead man!"

Raquel could see blood trickling down the side of Al's heavily veined throat. The tip of the jagged wine bottle, which Nate held, was already cutting deep into his skin.

"Stop, Al. Stop!" Jay called to his brother. "It is *Dada* who speaks to you."

Like a mad dog with a cherished bone, Al was reluctant to let go. Jay's insistent tug on his wide shoulders finally persuaded him, and Raquel rolled on her side, coughing and clutching her throat, while Jay led Al out of the building.

Raquel still held her throat as she tried to catch her breath. She could barely focus on Nate as he knelt down beside her, allowing the dazed young woman to lean on him as she stood.

"Are you all right?"

Raquel nodded blankly, even though she wasn't very sure. Stunned, she let him accompany her back to her place. Tears brimmed in her eyes, but she refused to cry. She'd cried more in the past two days than she had in her entire life. She would not cry again.

For a moment their eyes met, and Raquel thought there was something Nate wanted to say. Instead, he silently left her alone in the semidarkness.

The thought of sleeping unprotected on the porch without a door with a lock petrified her. She could still see Al's insane eyes and feel his iron grip about her throat. There was no way she could stay there without protection. Desperate, Raquel ran after Nate.

"You cannot leave me out there alone!" Her voice was nearly hysterical as she stopped him outside his door. "What do you think they will do to me while you sleep?" Her frantic gaze searched his, and she noticed his eyes were slightly bloodshot.

"So what do you want? I'm not sleeping out there."

Stung by his apathy, Raquel retorted, "Then I'll just have to sleep in here with you."

A veiled look descended over his dark eyes. He did not answer her, and his steely gaze pinned her against the door.

Raquel was afraid his silence meant he would not accept her suggestion. She had noticed Nate kept to himself, never shared moments with anyone for the simple sake of company. It was obvious he treasured his privacy. Even his strange reaction to Art's death was a sign this man danced to a different drummer. She guessed that somewhere inside he carried a deep scar, but he had gone beyond the need to heal it. Perhaps that scar was his motivation. Somehow, she felt Jackie Dawson's presence in Belize was a key to his personal dilemma.

Desperate that he would reject her, Raquel resorted to the only weapon she possessed.

"I'm not that bad to look at, am I?" She spoke the suggestive words softly, looking deep into his eyes.

Never in her life had she propositioned a man, and the meaning behind the words she had just spoken caused her heart to pound. Through the years more than once her mother had accused her of being hot-blooded, and had made her pray for hours for what she called her sinful actions. And now here she was, offering herself to this man like a common prostitute. Was there a chance that her mother had been right?

Fortifying herself against her own traitorous thoughts, Raquel drew in a deep breath and her almond eyes narrowed. *I am nobody's prostitute, and I intend to survive all of this. Right now, this man is the only thing I can count on. Once we leave this hole-in-a-wall settlement it will be a whole new ballgame.*

Her sense of survival was strong, and her own brazenness amazed her. A slightly trembling finger lifted to his neatly trimmed moustache. Systematically she began to run it through the coarse hair, then placed it upon his smooth lips.

Like lightning his hand caught her wrist, giving it a slightly painful squeeze.

"This is not a good time to tease me, lady." Nate's dark, thickly lashed gaze penetrated hers.

"Who's teasing?" was her raspy response. She was breathless from fear.

Something like a low growl emanated from his throat as he caught a handful of Raquel's curls in his fist. She winced with discomfort as he slowly drew her head toward his, then buried his face in her ebony tresses. Seconds later he lifted her off the floor and carried her inside, kicking the door shut with one foot.

"So you have decided to *give* it to me?" His hot breath heavy with alcohol grazed her as she lay pinned beneath him on the tiny bed.

"Yes." Her whisper was almost inaudible.

"Then you must show me how much you want to." A knowing glint entered his eyes while he straddled her.

Raquel's sable gaze widened. He must know she did not want to go to bed with him. But his need to control everything was surfacing in his words. She would ultimately seduce Nate, but he would remain dominant by telling her how.

The young woman wrestled with her outrage and her need to survive. It was only a matter of moments before survival triumphed. Without Nate's protection, she would be lost.

"All right."

With her consent, he rolled off her, and she climbed to her feet, standing a small distance away from the bed. Slowly she removed the shift.

Her body trembled ever so slightly, and the brown tips of her breasts hardened from an inner chill. She stood naked before him, allowing him to soak up the even, copper-brown softness of her skin. The tender valley between her breasts, their dark peaks, and the lush, curly triangle below were the only visible variations in color.

Raquel forced herself to look into his face and felt humiliated when she saw how impassive his expression was as he sat on the side of the bed. His hooded eyes made it impossible for her to read their message.

"Come here," Nate huskily commanded.

The young woman stepped forward, closing her eyes to brace herself against his rough exploration.

He watched her come toward the bed with her eyes clenched tightly closed, her face an anxious mask surrounded by masses of shiny black curls. She was breathtaking in her nudity, her womanly curves at full blossom. He observed the tip of her tongue darting nervously about, licking her full bottom lip in tense anticipation of his actions. Like this, she exhibited none of the fire he knew burned deep inside her.

An audible intake of breath escaped Raquel as he gently slid his hands around her hips and drew her body closer, placing his face against the swell of her lower abdomen.

The sting of tears burned behind her eyes, tears that she would not release.

"If I take you like this," his voice was silky and low, "it would still be taking you by force, and that I don't plan to do."

Raquel's eyes flew open, relief flooding their depths, and she looked down at the top of his head as it rested against her.

"But I intend to have you, now that you have offered yourself to me." He stared up into her face intently. "I've wanted you ever since that first night on the boat, but taking a woman by force is not what I'm about."

Her shapely eyebrows rose in astonishment. Here she stood, his captive, and he spoke to her of his principles!

"I did not say I am without faults. I am simply saying I am no rapist," he concluded. Then he released her.

"You are welcome to sleep here," he indicated the bed where he sat.

Raquel bent down to retrieve her clothing from the floor, but Nate's strong grasp stopped her.

"No. You must sleep just as you are."

At first, humiliation filled her richly lashed gaze, but it quickly turned into a stubborn glint.

"I will not," she hissed between clenched teeth. She had stooped as low as she intended to go by offering herself to him. She would not sleep beside him in the nude like a willing lover.

Once again she kneeled down to get her shift. This time he did not interfere.

Raquel walked around him, climbed into the bed, and slipped beneath the plain white sheet. She turned her back toward him, and her eyes rested on the fiberboard wall in front of her.

She was totally confused by this man. He was her abductor! He had forcefully brought her to an unknown land, and now that she had offered herself to him, albeit unwillingly, he refused her, saying he would only do it when she was willing. How could he expect that would ever be?

Nate climbed in the tiny bed beside Raquel. Gently he drew her body against his, and she could feel his heart beat, as well as his hardness against her. Raquel stiffened from the contact, but forced herself to remain deathly still, feeling small and helpless against his strong, masculine body. Protectively a muscular arm lay draped about her waist, and the top of her head fit perfectly in the space beneath his raised chin.

Minutes later she found her guarded state unnecessary as she heard his even breathing. Relieved to know he had fallen asleep, eventually she slept as well.

Chapter Six

"Punta Gorda is much closah," Jay snapped, his chin lifting to a challenging angle. "We should go there first, before travelin' to Dangriga."

Nate's voice remained icily calm despite the opposition Jay presented. "Our plans never included going to Punta Gorda. The main *dabuyaba*—temple—" he explained for Raquel's benefit, "is in Dangriga. That's where we planned to go in the beginning, and that's where I intend to end up."

"Have it your way, Meester Nate, but Mez Dawson is goin' to Punta Gorda wit' Al an' me." Jay tried to look beyond Nate into the bedroom.

Nate shook his head, a snarl of a smile crossing his lips. "That's not going to happen. Anyway, I doubt if she'd even arrive in Dangriga if I left her alone with the two of you."

"Ah, that's the key to this situation, Meester Nate," Jay said with a malicious smile. "There is only one of you, and two of us. How are you going to stop us?"

For the first time Al stepped from behind Jay, like a trained animal responding to its master's command.

Nate's cool, steely gaze took in the two of them, and his half-nude body moved slowly from its relaxed position where it blocked the half-open bedroom door.

"Don't worry about me, Jay. I can be quite resourceful."

He purposely allowed the two men a better view of the dresser behind him, where the sun's early rays reflected off the Glock compact pistol that lay menacingly out in the open.

"Now, you may want to take a chance and try to overpower me, but I assure you, I'm a man who never addresses an unknown situation empty-handed."

Jay's glance darted to Nate's right arm that lay relaxed against his side. Then, for the first time, he became aware that his left arm remained hidden behind him.

Throughout the exchange Raquel lay very still, listening. But the sight of the deadly weapon lying several feet away from the bed caused her to start. She had anticipated a confrontation, but she'd had no idea it would happen so soon. Like Jay, Raquel wondered if Nate held another weapon in the hand that was also hidden from her sight, and she gasped.

Jay heard her quick intake of breath, and saw the slight movement of the sheet on the bed.

"That would not be Mez Dawson in your bed, would it, Meester Nate?" He tried to conceal his anger. "Not aftah you have warned us to stay away from the precious piece. You haven't broken your own rule?" His voice turned derisive.

"Whatever I do is none of your business. But rest assured, there was no force involved." Nate gave a meaningful smile. "You see, unlike you, I am man enough to arouse a woman."

It took all the control Jay could muster not to strike out. The side of his face twitched with unleashed anger, while his eyes burned into those of the man in front of him.

"T"is must be your lucky cycle, Meester Nate, because once again you have won. But we are in Belize now, and t'ings will be different. Al an' I have rented the only four-wheel drive vehicle available here, so travelin' won't be too easy for the two of you," he smirked, then continued. "We are goin' to Punta Gorda. A healin' must be performed on my brother by the *buyei*. But after t'at, at anytime, Meester Nate, be assured, you will look up one day and I will be right t'ere. And I promise you t'en the situation will go the way I want it to go."

Nate waited for them to walk away before he closed the door. Veiled eyes cast a glance in Raquel's direction before he strode over to the dresser and placed the Glock in his pocket. Raquel saw his right hand had been empty.

Nate turned a knowing, steady gaze in her direction.

"Well, I guess you heard all of that. We've got a long journey in front of us, Miss Dawson. I hope you realize it's not going to be easy, and I believe if Jay has anything to do with it, it's going to be rougher than anything you have ever experienced. Just don't make any waves and you'll do fine."

Raquel held the sheet up against her as she sat bolt upright in the crumpled bed.

"You're forgetting one thing, Mr. Bowman. If it wasn't for you and those two goons, I wouldn't be here in the first place!" she snapped. So don't give me a pep talk like I'm a partner in crime, or something. I'm the victim here, and if you just happen to wear a similar hat at this moment . . . that's your problem."

"You know what? For someone who's in the position you're in, you sure talk a lot of stuff." He gathered the rest of his belongings together and began to pack them in the duffel bag. "But if I were you, I would be getting dressed. You see, it's still the rainy season, and the tourist trade will continue to be slow for a few more weeks. And let me inform you, there's not much law around here. Nobody cares about this little area. It's not a big money-maker as far as crops are concerned, and it sure as hell ain't no great tourist attraction. So if you want to remain here and become like the woman you saw in the dining room last night, I'm sure those men would be more than happy that you decided to give her some help."

He turned his bare back to her as he sat on the side of the bed and began to put on his shoes. Defined muscles rippled and spread out powerfully as he bent over to tie the laces.

Frowning, Raquel looked out the window at the elegant palms and profuse ferns basking in the dazzling sunshine. It hadn't rained during their long walk to the inn, nor did it look like it would rain anytime soon. What if he were lying just to scare her? With Jay and Al gone, she could refuse to go with him, and she definitely had enough money to buy her way back home.

The young woman brushed the thick black curls that hung in her face back in a defiant gesture. "I don't believe a word you're saying," she stated. "I'm not going with you. So what are you going to do, shoot me? If so, you better do it now."

She stood up in the path of the sun's revealing rays, challenging him with her eyes, her breasts rising and falling rapidly beneath the flimsy shift as she backed against the flatboard wall. She could hear him cuss beneath his breath.

"Pataki . . . don't push me." His response was threatening. "We crossed a sea to get here. And now that we are here, and things have developed as they have . . . I intend to do whatever I have to. And there's one thing you need to understand. I need you with me in order to accomplish that. So . . . no, I won't shoot you, but I can make your backside so sore that you may wish that I had."

"You'd *spank* me?" Raquel gasped incredulously.

"Right where the sun don't shine, baby." His features remained impassive, but his eyes gleamed wickedly. "As a matter of fact, I might find it quite enjoyable . . . so might you."

Raquel stood rooted to the spot.

"So, are you going to get dressed? Or am I going to have to give you a sample of what I'm talking about, while you're so conveniently attired?"

The thin shift did little to conceal Raquel's voluptuous body. Almost by instinct she could feel Nate's mind turning from business to pleasure. His dark gaze became smoky with desire as he stood staring at her for the first time during their entire exchange.

Nate's searing look made her pointedly aware of her nudity beneath the material and the very vulnerable position she was in. His long legs were spread apart as he watched her in a stance of readiness. Raquel knew, feeling fear mixed with excitement, whatever task he took on he would do it well, be it fighting, lovemaking—or tanning her hide. Just the thought of his ability to master her in whatever way sent an odd tingle through her body. Yet it appalled her to realize how much he fascinated her.

She weighed her chances of escaping Nate Bowman. He was far more powerful physically than she and knew Belize far better, too. She was fairly confident that he wouldn't rape or kill her, but Raquel had no such guarantee with the men downstairs. She reluctantly admitted to herself that Nate was her best and only hope.

Stoically the young woman dropped her gaze and crossed to the bathroom in silence, where she noisily slammed the door behind her.

Nate let her go, but he was quite aware of the variety of thoughts which plagued her. They were plainly written in her dark, sable eyes. He knew that she feared him, but she had come to him, seeking refuge from an even greater threat. Just thinking about making love to her aroused him. It had been torture lying next to her last night. And he was irritated that his body had betrayed him. She was so beautiful, and there was something about her that touched an instinctive part of him. It felt almost like a kind of integrity, something he had come to believe no longer existed.

"Integrity?" he chided himself. "How did I come up with that? Women like Jackie Dawson are a dime a dozen!" Whenever he took her, she would willingly give herself to him, just as he believed she had given herself to countless other men.

Raquel let out a started shriek as several frantic turkeys and an armadillo were chased out of the abandoned clapboard building, heading right in her direction.

The meaty arms of the innkeeper's wife waved menacingly behind them before she turned and gave a broad smile to Nate, then gestured toward the rusty minibus inside the dilapidated structure.

It had been only moments earlier that the woman's now beaming features had been a mask of anger. It was when the young Indian prostitute attempted to interrupt her conversation with Nate. The disheveled female kept repeating the words "Nim Li Punti," after Nate had mentioned the unfamiliar phrase. Raquel thought she acted like a woman possessed, until the hefty female threatened her with the back of a raised hand. Finally, she shied away like a frightened animal. Until that moment Raquel had not realized how young the prostitute was, and she couldn't help wondering how she had ended up in such an awful predicament.

Nate circled the vehicle kicking its tires, and checking under the hood before he began to haggle with the innkeeper's wife. In the end their negotiations didn't take very long. Nate needed the minibus, and that was all there was to it. It was the only transportation in the settlement, and therefore could be had at whatever price she demanded.

Despite its run-down condition the van didn't need much coercing before it raucously cranked up and headed for a well-hidden road. Raquel didn't know what was worse—the road, if you could call it that, or the nonexistent shock-absorbers of the squat vehicle. Large plants brushed and pressed against the filthy windows as they drove down the narrow route, its uneven surface causing them to bounce about on the torn seats.

Raquel had refused to sit beside Nate as he drove, so she chose the longer seat behind him. She sat where she could have a clear view of the path, even though that was of little consequence; there was nothing to see outside of the thick foliage. Suddenly she realized the road was so narrow it would cause a major problem if another vehicle approached them traveling in the opposite direction. One of them would have to completely drive into the brush in order to allow the other to pass. In all her life the young woman had never seen anything like it. This was truly a wilderness, and her apprehension began to mount as she anticipated what could be in store.

Raquel would have chosen to sit on the back seat, if it had not been covered with old blankets and clothes that looked as if they had been there forever. Their musty smell floated toward them from the rear, causing her to cover her nose in disgust.

Raquel hated to admit to herself the other reason why she wanted to keep a safe distance from Nate. She found his nearness much too disturbing.

Looking at the back of his head and broad shoulders led her thoughts to earlier that morning, when the two of them still lay in bed. She had been strongly aware of the feel and smell of the man beside her. It had been warm and vibrant, almost comforting, unlike the cold nights and mornings when she'd gone to bed and awakened alone during her months of celibacy.

Raquel had offered herself to him the night before as a matter of survival. But it was hard to accept even the slightest possibility that she might actually want him, in light of all that had passed.

It took both hands to unlock the rusty device that controlled the sliding window. Sweat glistened on her limbs and face after she managed to open it. Abruptly a large branch forced its way inside the vehicle, leaving some of its leaves as the minibus continued on.

Nate glanced back over his shoulder. "I don't know if that's such a good idea."

"Why not?" she asked, plucking at the front of her shift to stimulate a flow of air.

"First of all, you never know what insects may want to hitch a ride. But mainly it's because some of those plants are poisonous. If they just touch your skin, you could be in a world of trouble."

"I'm already in a world of trouble," Rachel shot back. "But right now, I'm extremely hot as well."

"It won't be long before this road widens a bit. Until then you might want to remove some of those clothes you have on beneath that shift."

"No way! I'm fine just like I am."

In the bathroom that morning, Raquel had donned the bralike top of her calypso costume, and had turned the turban into a slip of sorts underneath the creamy fabric of the see-through shift.

"Suit yourself, then," he replied with a shrug.

Taking his own advice, Nate took off the shirt he was wearing, and unsnapped the waist of his jeans.

It was unmercifully hot inside the van even with the window open, and the clothes stuck to Rachel's back and under her thighs where her body made contact with the vinyl seats. Yet she preferred enduring the discomfort to following his advice.

Soon the road broadened as Nate promised, but this was accompanied by the inconvenience of enormous potholes. Raquel could see where the Belizean government had attempted to modernize the road. A thin strip of asphalt ran down its center, but after years of neglect, huge sinkholes dotted the sides, making it that much more dangerous. It was impossible to travel at a speed that would create a welcome breeze since the roads were so treacherous.

The clunk of tires moving in and out of potholes was soon accompanied by an occasional spatter of raindrops. In a matter of moments the rain became heavier until it developed into a torrential downpour. A deluge of water found its way through the window and into the vehicle. *So this is what the rainy season is like,* Raquel thought. Grudgingly her thoughts drifted back to Nate's warning, and just for a moment, she was glad Nate had persuaded her to come with him.

It didn't take long for the shabby roadway to run into a muddy trench. The potholes filled with water, causing the minibus to spin its wheels in an effort to drive through the mud. The rickety windshield wipers did little to clear the sheets of water streaming down the front window, and Nate peered uncertainly out at the road in front of him.

Suddenly, an unexpected drop into a massive pothole halted the vehicle with a jerk. The continuing whir of the minibus's tires buried the vehicle even further in the mire.

Raquel watched as Nate got out to evaluate the situation, fastening his skintight jeans before stepping out into the downpour. Repeatedly he wiped his thickly fringed eyes as he looked down at the embedded wheel, torrents of rain spilling over his muscular chest and back. He cursed savagely as he looked about him, deciding what would be the next move to make.

A gust of water blew inside the van as he climbed

back into the driver's seat, and began to don his shirt over his drenched flesh. Impatiently Raquel waited for his assessment of the situation, but he didn't speak.

"What are we going to do now?" she prodded, after her nerves could take no more. Her question was met with silence as Nate slipped back out into the downpour and disappeared into the forest.

The thundering rain that assaulted the minibus increased in intensity as the minutes ticked away. Raquel could feel panic rising inside her with the steady tilting of the vehicle into the massive hole. Where was he? Had he left her here in the middle of a Belizean forest just so he could save his own tail after finding their predicament impossible? A man like Nate Bowman, a criminal, was capable of that and more.

Scraping sounds from the back of the bus caused Raquel's heart to lurch and the hairs on the back of her neck rose up. The thought of a savage animal awakening from slumber flashed in her mind, but it was quickly cast away by the sight of the prostitute from the inn rising out of the pile of foul-smelling blankets on the back seat.

Two pairs of frightened eyes stared at one another.

Suddenly the girl lunged for the door nearest the driver's seat, and the stench that surrounded her nearly caused Raquel to gag. She watched as she bounded out of the minibus into the rain, then stopped. The driving rain pushed the filthy scarf she wore onto the back of her neck.

Raquel was surprised to see straight, jet black hair hacked to shoulder length, and a hint of deep reddish-brown skin beneath the film of dirt on her face which washed downward in the rain.

The young woman stood as still as a doe listening for danger, then her head swiveled to survey the landscape. Suddenly she stopped and stared far into the distance. Raquel darted to the opposite side of the bus to try and see what had captured the girl's attention. Through the wall of water it was hard to make out the large object far to the east of them, but it resembled an enormous hill or mountain, and a large portion of it was covered with trees.

Eyes filled with excitement and trepidation focused on Raquel once more, before she too disappeared into the thick foliage.

"Wait!" Raquel yelled. She rushed out into the rain after the only human connection she thought she had.

"What's the matter?" Nate's voice projected from behind her.

She whirled about to see him stepping out of the thicket.

"That girl was in the bus all the time," she explained excitedly, her face lighting up from the thought of it.

Nate's countenance reflected his confusion as he approached her.

"The young prostitute. She managed to hitch a ride with us and we didn't even know it. Don't you see? She escaped under their very noses," she yelled madly above the downpour. The young girl's victory was a cause for jubilation—there was hope in this ugly jungle.

Nate watched her with the rain plastering her inky curls against her face and shoulders, causing her clothes to cling enticingly to her breasts, hips, and thighs. The sparkle of life glistening in her eyes at that moment struck a cord of longing deep inside him, a long-forgotten yearning for that kind of belief in the good things of life. For here she stood, a captive in a strange land, not knowing what fate would befall her, but having the faith and courage to rejoice in the happiness of someone else.

Raquel's wet feathery lashes shielded dark, shining eyes as she looked at him. He knew she saw him as her enemy. What else would a kidnapper be? Yet he longed to possess her, to consume the light of faith that burned so brightly about her. Maybe it would help resurrect his own.

Yet, to Nate Bowman, possessing this woman did not simply mean possessing her body. She had already offered that to him out of a pure need to survive. No, he wanted more than that. He wanted the fire that he knew would consume her when she gave herself fully to a man, not the ember of fear.

"We're going to have to leave the bus here," he stated, climbing back inside to retrieve his duffel bag. Once outside again, he looked around him. "Which way did she go?"

"She entered the forest there," Raquel pointed. "It was like she recognized something. I think it was that mountain in the distance."

"Well, let's head that way. It's better than nothing."

"What do you mean, it's better than nothing?" Exasperation was apparent in her voice. "You mean to tell me you don't know where we are?"

"That's right *pataki*, at the moment your guess is as good as mine." A half-smile crossed his rakish features. "I couldn't very well take the main roads, could I, even though there aren't that many here in Belize. This is a small country, everybody knows everybody, and we would be easy to find."

"In other words, to cover up your criminal activity, you brought us out here in the jungle and now we're lost!" she accused.

"Partially."

"What do you mean, partially?"

He entered the slumping vehicle again, leaving her standing in the rain while he rummaged through the articles in the back. Momentarily, he emerged with a couple of blankets and a rusted ax, then he picked up their conversation where he left off.

"If you want to make it easy for Jay to find us, that's your business. I just think it would be better if he and his brotherhood had a somewhat difficult time doing it. Maybe we can make it to Dangriga before they do."

Raquel reared back and looked at him skeptically. "I don't understand this. All of you were together when you kidnapped me. Now all of a sudden you expect me to believe it's you and me against the world and all that jazz? Do I have this right?"

"You can believe what you want to believe." He entered the forest at the spot where Raquel had indicated.

"Well, I want you to know, you're no better than they are," she responded, annoyed by his offhanded remark.

"Maybe so, maybe not. Here, carry these blankets while I try to cut down some of these bushes." He tossed the smelly objects into her arms.

"I don't want to carry these!" she sputtered, imagining some of the filth had involuntarily flown into her mouth.

"That's up to you. I've got something inside here to use in case I need it tonight. You're the one who's going to need it, not me."

Reluctantly Raquel tried to fold the sodden covers so

they would be easier to carry. The wet moss, leaves, and dirt beneath her feet had begun to soak the cheap shoes Nate had provided for her, making the trek that much more unbearable.

They walked for what felt like hours before the torrential rains stopped, giving way to a glistening green world sprinkled with vivid color. It was almost magical, the moment-to-moment transformation that occurred. Like a conductor motioning for an orchestra to commence, the sun's rays struck the flowering plants and trees causing them to come vibrantly to life, the cries and calls of numerous birds and animals only adding to its complexity.

Raquel was out of breath when they reached a partial clearing. As she began inhaling deeply, the rich smell of damp earth and plants was powerful. She plopped down on a rotted trunk covered with lichen and other symbiotic plants.

Nate stood not far away. He dug into his duffel bag, producing several soggy fry jacks, breakfast leftovers from the inn. Reluctantly Raquel accepted the limp corncake he offered her but threw it down in frustration after it crumbled when she attempted to bite it. She watched Nate impassively chew the crumbly mess.

"How can you eat that?" Her stomach growled in frustration as she observed him consume it.

"Simple." His dark gaze raked her insultingly. "There's nothing else to eat, and won't be until we come across something edible, or run into a McDonald's. Whichever comes first."

Nate's sense of humor was quickly becoming irritating to Raquel. She looked down and observed the yellowish hunks she'd thrown on the ground being quickly devoured by a swarm of ants. Hunger caused her to raise her eyes longingly toward the last morsel Nate was popping into his mouth. It surprised her to see the young prostitute quietly watching them several yards away.

"Hey," Raquel whispered. "That young woman is standing behind you."

He turned just as she called to them in a strange language, then motioned for them to follow her.

"She's a Mayan," he said, fastening the duffel bag and rising to his feet. "That could be lucky for us."

"A Mayan! I had no idea there would be Mayans so near the shoreline."

"We have traveled much further inland, *pataki*. It's quite widely known that the Kekchi Indians live near this area."

She paused, then asked softly "Why do you call me *pataki?*" The foreign word was difficult on her tongue. "Art referred to me with the same word." Her rich gaze clouded over with the memory of his being thrown into the sea.

"I remember, and that is one of the reasons I use it."

Raquel looked at him in surprise.

"It means 'legend,' " he informed her. "But I am sure my reasons for using it are quite different from Art's, because he has never seen you naked, as I have." His dark, smoldering eyes appraised her reaction to his words, then he continued. "But you are also believed to have a connection with the *gubida*, the spiritual ancestors of our people. That is why Art called you *pataki.*"

Raquel swallowed hard, then looked again for the girl. She was gone.

"Hey! Where in the heck did she go?"

The Mayan's quick disappearance was like magic.

Raquel knew they needed the girl, since Nate wasn't sure where they were.

"I don't know, but it would be to our benefit to find her."

They gathered up their belongings and hurried further into the rainforest. They were so intent on finding the girl, they almost stumbled over her as she knelt down caressing the purplish petals of a flower growing in the midst of several other plants. As they watched, she began to dig with nimble fingers until she unearthed a large tuberous root.

"It's a sweet potato!" Raquel excitedly announced, bending down to dig up the root of a similar flower.

The girl's blackened teeth dominated her smile as she showed her pleasure in presenting the food to Raquel and Nate. Nate swaggered over and took the vegetable from her hand. "Well, well. I think we've made a rare but valuable friend."

The Mayan's grin broadened and she returned to the task at hand. After digging up several of the orangish-yellow roots, the girl took them to a rock overhang.

Looking at the curious pair, she struck one hand repeatedly against the other.

Nate shrugged his broad shoulders, "What is it? What are you trying to say?"

Sensing his confusion, the girl turned her imploring eyes to Raquel.

"She's hitting her hands together," she said almost to herself. "Hitting . . . *striking* her hands together. She's striking her hands together! I bet she's asking for a match," Raquel adeptly guessed, then pulled a book of matches out of her purse.

The girl shook her head affirmatively, pleased that

Raquel had understood. Next she began to gather a small group of dry twigs and leaves which she found nestled against the wall beneath a large, jutting stone. Once she felt she had enough, she made a fire, then dug a hole for baking the roots. It wasn't long before the sweet potatoes, encased in packed mud, were cooking in a smartly built natural oven.

Raquel was amazed as she watched the girl. Some of the history and stories she had heard about Mayans and their culture buzzed through her mind. Her thoughts of grandeur and power were such a contradiction to the young woman who stooped before her.

The filthy, tattered shift she wore barely covered her small breasts—the armholes of the garment were cut so large. She would have been a pitiful sight if it had not been for her eyes, which were extremely alert and knowing. She watched Raquel and Nate with the same intensity as Raquel watched her.

Nate, on the other hand, proved to be more restless than they. Constantly he rose and entered the forest, each time in different directions. He always returned to the overhang within moments, his face a taut mask. On his third return the Mayan girl went into a string of words ending with "Nim Li Punti," patting her breasts, then pointing into the forest.

"So that's it. She hitchhiked a ride with us because we were headed in the direction of the Mayan ruin, Nim Li Punti."

After hearing Nate say it, the girl repeated the phrase.

"Did she come from there? And if so, how did she end up at the inn?" Raquel wondered aloud.

"I doubt it. Some archaeologists began digging out there about ten years ago. There were several reports, but I never heard about people actually living there. There is a Mayan village not far from it, but I would think someone as young as she would have learned either English or Spanish as a second language if she lived there. No," he eyed the young girl speculatively, "I think she's from one of the more isolated Kekchi settlements. Of all the Mayans, they are the ones who have attempted to remain less dependent on other cultures, keeping to themselves."

The young girl's almond-shaped eyes lit up as Nate mentioned "Kekchi," then quickly dimmed with some unknown understanding.

It didn't take long for the sweet potatoes to bake. Raquel felt as if she were cracking an egg as she burst open the hot-baked mud surrounding her meal. Piping-hot steam rose off the tender root. She had to remind herself to be careful as she plunged into the soft orange insides, burning her fingers in her hunger.

Once their meal was completed, the girl covered the still-smoldering fire with lumps of mud before the group continued on. Refreshed, Raquel followed the young girl and Nate, and the impact of how her life had changed over the last few days pressed upon her.

This was a far cry from working in the Miami clinic and her quiet nights alone reading, listening to music, or taking in an occasional television program. She wondered how her mother was faring. She knew she would be worried—hardly a day would go by without them talking, at least by phone. She hoped Lucy had concluded she'd taken that long-awaited vacation she'd mentioned for the hundredth time during their last visit.

Raquel knew her mother still felt guilty because of her breakup with Clinton. Sometimes, when she wasn't quite herself, she would babble about it. Many times Rachel had wished she hadn't broken down and told her why she thought they parted. Now, over six weeks later, walking through a Belizean jungle, with a Mayan prostitute and a handsome kidnapper, she knew the truth. Clinton simply hadn't loved her enough to chance it. That was all.

Rachel's bundle of blankets began to unravel, causing her to lag behind. Muttering to himself, Nate approached her, offering to take the awkward package, only to be stopped by the Mayan girl.

Astutely she began to look around. After measuring several vines, she chose one she felt was right for the task and motioned for Nate to cut it. In no time at all she had rolled the blankets into a neat bundle and strapped them to her back. She turned and smiled her not-so-attractive smile in Raquel's direction before continuing to lead them through the woods.

The sun was beginning to lower in the sky when they reached a roughly constructed highway that crossed a smaller road. As they were stepping out of the thicket the Mayan girl's frame abruptly stiffened, and she held her lean arm out to prevent them from passing in front of her. Instinctively Nate and Raquel followed her actions as she knelt behind a lush plant.

"What's going on?" Raquel queried, her heart pounding.

"I don't know, but I guess we'll find out in a few minutes," was Nate's composed response.

It was less than that when three Mayan men, shirtless and dressed in calf-length pants and sandals, passed on the opposite side of the highway, then entered the forest. The girl stooped lower as their voices floated toward them. Raquel caught a hint of humiliation and remorse in her eyes as she glanced in their direction.

"This must be the Southern Highway," Nate whispered. "And if so, Nim Li Punti is not far away. Those men are from one of the Mayan villages, and from her reaction I would say it's the one she comes from. I can't imagine why she would hide after doing all the things she's done to get here."

The girl's sad eyes roamed over the stained, torn shift she wore, and Raquel understood exactly why the girl had reacted the way she did.

"Did you say there may be a couple of Mayan villages in the area?"

"Yes," Nate answered, curious at the intense sound in Raquel's voice.

"Are there any stores in them or nearby that would sell clothes or material?"

"Why?" He eyed her suspiciously.

"Can't you see the girl's embarrassed to return to her people looking like this? God, sometimes you men don't know anything, and are blind as bats on top of that!"

"You trying to tell me that this—*woman* is ashamed?" A hint of mockery lay beneath his words.

"And what if she is? Are you trying to say she shouldn't be? We don't know how this girl fell into that situation back there. And neither one of us is in a position to judge her. She just wants to go home."

"Are you speaking for yourself or the Mayan, *pataki?*" His voice was soft, knowing.

For a moment dark, fanlike lashes concealed her feelings, but when she looked into his face again, determination edged her soft features.

"What difference does it make? Would you be willing

to forget about what you're doing and see me back safely to the States?"

Nate never answered but his steady gaze remained on her face.

Taking his silence as a negative, Raquel continued, "Well, then, why did you ask? Without this girl we might not have made it this far. At least we can go and find her something decent to wear."

The Mayan girl's discerning gaze locked on the two people who knelt beside her.

"Decency is not my forte." His voice was low and silky. "And how do I know this is not a ploy to help you escape?" he asked warily, his lips close to her ear.

Raquel forced a chuckle. It was a defense against the electricity his close contact roused in her. Suddenly she stood and switched her round hips back and forth in front of his face sassily.

"And just where would I go, Mr. Bowman, I guess I'll just take a stroll down that big old highway into the city, and catch me a plane back to Miami."

His strong fingers caught hold of the soft flesh of her upper thighs, eliciting a quick intake of breath from her.

"Don't taunt me, *pataki*. I am immoral enough to take what you offered me, right here in front of the girl." His unyielding gaze assured her this was no idle threat.

Raquel caught his large wrist within her hands, challenging him with narrowed eyes. "And what you would get would be about as fulfilling as that hole she dug in the ground a few hours ago!"

"Do you think so? There are many ways to light a fire. Some are easier to start than others if the wood or charcoal is primed just right." He let his fingers drag enticingly along her inner thigh before withdrawing his hands.

She shivered involuntarily. Their battle of wills was over, at least for the moment.

Slowly he stood beside her, taking out his map.

"Well, now, at least I know where we are," he looked around them. "Right over there is Big Falls, the only warm springs known here in Belize. You two can stay there and maybe bathe while I go to the village." He looked at Raquel pointedly. "Now, I'm telling you this for your own good. You need to find a place where you're out of sight, because you'll be trespassing on somebody else's property. Of course, you might come up with the bright idea that they might help you, which indeed they might. But keep in mind, the fellow you seek help from could be as bad or worse than Jay," he warned, leaving her to make her own decision.

At first the Mayan girl tried to follow him, but Raquel held her back, speaking slowly and signing that he would be back with clothes or material. The Mayan girl's eyes shone brightly, not quite understanding what Raquel was trying to say, but obeying her command anyway.

Moments later the two women headed in the direction Nate had indicated. It didn't take long before they arrived at the bubbling mineral waters. Just the thought of submerging her exhausted body in the vibrating liquid began to relax her, but the warning Nate had given surfaced in her mind. Part of her wanted to take the chance and see if the people who owned Big Falls would help her. But what if they *were* like Jay and his brother Al? Or what if Jay was actually there?

A streak of terror ran through her, an aftershock from

her encounter with the two gruesome Belizeans. No. She was safe with Nate, as safe as she could be, under the circumstances.

She looked around cautiously, then pulled the Mayan girl into the safety of several bushes beside her. As Nate suggested, the women waited until the sun had been completely replaced by the bright half moon before they entered the soothing waters.

Activity in the Mayan village of San Pedro was grinding to a halt when Nate entered its midst. It was nothing like the dusty clapboard settlement in which they'd slept the previous night. No, compared to that, it seemed like a unique metropolis.

The houses, though a few were constructed from clapboard, were much more creative in design. Well-built thatched-roof structures constituted the most popular design. Most had strong stilts, with wooden stairways leading up to a platform which allowed one to gain entrance. Some had wooden verandas surrounding the one-story edifices; others were less endowed.

Not many people were on the narrow roads as evening began to turn to night, and Nate knew if he were to have any luck at all in locating a merchant who would be willing to sell to him at this late hour, he would need to hurry.

Nate saw a construction of thatched-roofed stalls as he entered what appeared to be a main road. A Mayan man busied himself inside one of the areas, putting away items he obviously had not been able to sell. Two Mayan women dressed in long wraparound colorful skirts and Latin-style blouses were leaving his store carrying baskets filled with goods. Shyly, they looked at Nate as he passed by.

The salesman stopped his removal of several items and eyed him with interest.

"Yoo need help?" The merchant's English was oddly accented.

"Yes, I do," Nate answered. "Do you have any women's clothing?"

"Yees." A spark of interest shone in the man's deeply creased eyes. "Ovar theere." He pointed out several folded squares of colorful material stacked neatly on a handmade bench, then crossed to the objects to display them for his unusual customer.

"They arr the skeerts our women wear. Eer arr the blooses." He held up several tops adorned with embroidered yokes. "The woman yoo arr buying theez for, she deed not want to come?"

"No." Nate turned hard eyes upon the little merchant.

"I oonderstand. Eet eez late. Maybe she deed not want to come out at sooch a late hour," he tried to appease the sullen man. "Arr yoo stay here at the lodge?"

"No."

"Oh." Curiosity continued to burn in his deep-set eyes. "Then where . . . ?"

"We're not staying in the village."

"No? But there eez not many place nearby to stay. Punta Gorda eez near, but eet eez too far to travel een one night by foot, and yoo do not have a carr." He looked around a second time to make sure.

A wary tone crept into the nosey merchant's voice. "There eez two other village. The Forbidden Village eez one of them. But they would not welcome your keend

there. Sometime toureests do not understand thees." He
tried to see if his words had sparked a response in the
standoffish man, but seeing none, he continued, "No
doubt, they arr my brothers and sisters, but they arr the
Kekchi, who have held to the ancient ways more than
eeny of us. Theirs is a strong hate of change. Ponti
knows how mooch," he pointed to a young Mayan
crossing the road in their direction.

"Tell him, tell him, Ponti, he would not be welcomed
een the Forbidden Village, would he?"

A strange mix of emotions crossed the young man's
face as he looked at Nate.

"You're planning to go to *Balam?*"

The man's impeccable English caught Nate off guard.
He eyed him suspiciously before answering.

"No, not necessarily."

The merchant seemed to perk up as he waited for
Ponti to speak again, and Nate noticed how the younger
man watched the merchant warily. Finally, the man
Ponti decided to continue on his way.

Nate was on the verge of telling the curious merchant
to mind his own business, for he quickly realized it
might be to his benefit to listen to what the young Kekchi had to say. With purposeful strides he caught up
with Ponti.

The young man stopped, still eyeing the disappointed
merchant several yards away.

"Forgive me. Usually I'm not this rude, but the
merchant loves to spread everybody's business across the
village. Right now I have enough troubles already."

"So, is what he says true?" Nate questioned. "Is staying away from Balam a wise thing to do?"

"I can assure you it would be. I was born there," he paused.

There were lines of frustration marring his young features. Nate waited patiently for him to continue, and when he did it was as if he were finally relieving himself of a burden.

"I did not want to spend my entire life living the way my people have chosen to live. So I ran away, then worked and went to school in Belize City for a long time. Finally I acquired the papers I needed to go to the United States for college," he kicked at a stone near his foot. "But my school aid was soon cut, and I had to return to Belize. I had missed my family over the years, so I decided to come back to Balam. They would not even let me in,' he commented with exasperation. "I was told to wait here for word when I would be allowed to reenter the village. That was over a week ago. No word has come, yet. So as you can tell, if they are hesitant to let me come to the village. Strangers would not be welcome at all."

"Interesting." Hooded lids descended over Nate's dark gaze, "Thanks for the information." Nate and Ponti parted ways.

Bent on completing his task with as little conversation on his part as possible, Nate placed several Belizean dollars in the merchant's hands before he picked up two skirts and two blouses. "I think that should do it."

Then without another word he nodded his goodbye, and headed down the moonlit road.

Through trial and error the two women found a smaller offshoot of the heated springs, nestled in the middle of a clump of trees and bushes. Stealthily they removed their clothes and entered the luxurious waters.

Raquel lowered her eyelids as the heated currents surrounded her. The sensations were so satisfying she succumbed to their bewitching powers, completely becoming oblivious to her surroundings. Like the swaying watch of a hypnotist, the moon hobbed back and forth in the heavens to the rhythm of the currents that propelled her body. With time, the sounds of the Mayan girl splashing along beside her became one with her state of relaxation.

Raquel had no idea how much time had passed when two hands gently embraced her waist. Startled, she opened her eyes to find Nate inches away from her. A groggy look of surprise crossed her beautiful features as he easily moved her into a pocket of intensely bubbling water, in a private nook along the densely forested shore.

"What—what are you doing," she stammered, blinking away the drops of water that had attached themselves to her long, curly lashes. Strangely she realized there was no fear as he touched her, only a sense of unsolicited excitement.

"Hush *pataki* and continue to relax. I just thought you would find this portion of the water . . . what should I say . . . more stimulating."

The pocket of currents in which he had maneuvered her ran and bubbled more rapidly than the others. The vibrations of the silky, warm water massaging her body felt like knowing, insistent hands. She tried to fight the relaxing sensations the flow encouraged, but her tired body betrayed her as it gave in to the wet caresses, enticing her mind to relax and enjoy the pleasurable feelings.

Nate's muscular thigh rubbed against a smooth boulder submerged under the vibrating waters. It was just what he had been searching for as he forced Raquel's nude frame gently against it. He could tell she was giving in to the gripping motion of the water as she let herself relax upon the stone. Her elbows easily supported her on its moss-covered surface, and her legs hung limply down the rock's smooth edges.

A thick feathering of dark lashes lay upon her high cheekbones as she totally gave into the wonderful sensations. Nate watched as her well-formed chin tilted upward toward the splendid star filled sky, and her inky hair formed countless curly locks, the lower strands floating and bobbing within the animated currents.

Each forward movement of the water threatened to encase the top of her slender shoulders, yet a backwards motion, just as natural, temporarily revealed a wider glimpse of her rich velvety brown frame.

Raquel was aware of her nudeness, as well as his. She told herself there was nothing she could do under the circumstances. But a voice deep inside insisted she lied. She could leave Nate here in the water and seek the safety of the shore, reconfirming her stance of wanting to have nothing to do with him. Then whenever she did give in to him, if she did, it would be him forcing her hand.

Yet, she felt helpless as the mesmerizing sway of the bubbling waters held her captive. She was tired. Tired of fighting the inevitable. If he was to take her, let him do it now in her state of lethargy. Her eyes remained closed as she anticipated his move.

Silently she waited with masses of soft, stimulating bubbles forming around her. A forceful current had formed between her legs, massaging her inner thighs.

Almost unconsciously she allowed the silkly flow access to the most sensitive part of her. A natural expression of mild surprise and pleasure crossed her beautiful features.

Part of her wanted to move, to extract itself from the vulnerable, yet needy feelings that rose within her. But the sexual desires that were awakening inside her were so strong, she could not pull herself away.

The soft, but lapping current worked its way deeper within her, and she found herself welcoming it with a further spreading of her slender thighs. The pleasurable sensations began to build in intensity and Raquel wantonly gave in to her feelings, forgetting about the man who stood within the waters not far away, watching every change of expression that crossed her sensuous features.

They were expressions he wanted to arouse in her, and he longed to be where the pulsating water churned, evoking the looks of delight nearly bordering pain, that arose consistently as her body thrilled to nature's caress.

Raquel could not believe the height of excitement the gushing waters were propelling her toward. She lay there a prisoner of her own desires, her body soaking up each silky stroke.

Suddenly the current stopped. Raquel's shocked, lust filled gaze opened to find Nate standing between her legs. His eyes were full of the knowledge of her readiness, and the desire that encased his features told her, he too, was near the point of no return. She rose up further upon her elbows to see if his shaft would substantiate her belief, and she saw the shadow of it beneath the somewhat calm waters was immense.

Abruptly, an involuntary moan escaped her lips as she thought of it entering her.

Their smoldering gazes met then held, and Raquel wanted to scream out her impatience, but her pride wouldn't allow it.

Nate was very much aware of the flicker of emotions passing over her moonlit features. His body trembled as he restrained the most natural thing in the world to do, while he watched Raquel's body arch in readiness. Yet, he knew it was her eyes that told the true story. She wanted him, yes. But her desire for him, even now, could not mask an even stronger resentment.

Somehow she knew the moment when he had changed his mind, and she reluctantly opened her eyes. It was as if a light had been turned off behind his dark penetrating gaze, and the fire between them had turned cold.

Confusion flickered over Raquel's features as she watched him, standing like a statue with a half-moon upon his shoulder. A soft glow of light ran between the tiny waves of hair upon his head as the moon's light played up his chiseled cheekbones, creating interesting shadows upon his handsome features. He was so alluring as he stood there. So strong. So masculine. So virile.

She saw his lips move, and somehow her mind, through the fog of desire, was able to comprehend the simple words he said.

"I will wait, *pataki*, until you unconditionally want me. I don't want a small part of you. I've got to have it all."

Then he turned his massive back toward her, and headed toward the shore.

Suddenly the breeze that blew upon her face was cold, and she found her nakedness embarrassing. Never before had she felt so rejected and empty. Hesitantly she looked toward the shore, and saw the Mayan girl, wet, in her tattered shift, kneeling on her haunches watching Nate's advance. The expression on her face glowed with womanly approval as he shamelessly stepped out of the water and retrieved his pants. Then the girl's dark eyes looked uncertainly at Raquel, for it was clear to her, this man was most certainly a prize.

It took all the nerve Raquel had to rise up off that stone and walk towards the shore. She tried to walk confidently with her head held high, but she found it was of little consequence whatever manner she chose.

Nate never looked in her direction as she made her way towards camp, and for some reason she felt even more humiliated because of it. Quickly, she donned the shift and combed out her wet tresses with trembling fingers.

Without another word, Nate made himself a spot to bed down for the night. The two women followed suit, Raquel sharing one of the old blankets with the Mayan girl. He never mentioned his trip to the village, nor could Raquel find the courage to question him about it. She was so confused. A kidnapper who was caring enough to find clothes for the hapless Mayan girl, and desired her, yet wanted her mind to want him as well as her body.

As she lay there beneath the beautiful Belizean sky, she became angry with the strange man who lay only several feet away. Angry because she did not understand him. But also she was angry at herself for beginning to have a certain amount of grudging respect for him.

There were other feelings inside that were beginning to stir, but she dared not explore them. Somehow she knew if ever released, they would change her neatly

packaged system of the rights and wrongs in human re-
lationships. A system that had formed her foundation
ever since she began studying psychology; its logic and
borders safe, and not the least bit frightening.

Raquel balled up in a fetal position upon the thickly
covered ground; the musty smell of the blanket wrapped
tightly about her, not because she was cold, but because
it provided a since of security that she longed for.

Yes, no doubt she was afraid. She was afraid if she
looked deep enough inside herself, she would find out
how much she wanted Nate not only because he could
protect her, but because his virility aroused her in a way
that she had never known before.

Behind her tightly shut eyes, unwillingly, Raquel kept
picturing his hard, muscular, nude body poised to enter
her, and a searing spark began to throb between her
legs.

She did not doubt he knew a lot about women and
how to please them. He had purposefully led her to
those waters where he knew she'd find pleasure, and she
knew, he knew, she could have been his. But obviously,
to this Nate there were things more important in life.
She had to admit it surprised her to know, just to have
a woman sexually wasn't enough. He needed her completely in his corner, trusting him under the most un-
trustworthy circumstances.

Yes, Raquel was beginning to find out Nate lived by
a strange code of ethics, possibly different from any
she'd ever encountered before.

Like a fish out of water Raquel flipped abruptly onto
her opposite side where her eyes rested upon his outstretched body, still and lifeless, well on his way to slum-

ber. It was his prostrate figure that entered sleep with her, but it was a totally virile, unabandoned, Nate, who possessed her dreams.

Chapter Seven

The Mayan girl's black eyes shone brightly as she emerged from behind the cover of bushes, wearing the colorful wrap skirt and white embroidered blouse Nate had presented to her earlier that morning. With her face clean and her hair brushed through with the aid of a bristly, but strong plant, an unusual kind of beauty had been awakened in the girl. There was a kind of regalness about her. Raquel knew, this was the real person behind the filth and tattered rags. The dignified tilt of her shiny black head, and a knowing calm behind her dark eyes reflected that. Nevertheless Raquel couldn't help but marvel at how remarkable the transformation had been.

Nate too, was pleased by the girl's metamorphosis, a slight nod of his head indicated his approval which was answered by a quick, beguiling, black-toothed smile. A resourceful twinkle in her eye, accompanied it, showing her memory of Nate's physical assets was still fresh in her mind.

A tiny tightening in Raquel's chest at their exchange surprised her. Why would she be jealous if Nate found the Mayan girl attractive?

Quickly she averted her gaze, just in case her heightened feelings could be read upon her face. For some reason, just the thought of Nate turning to the Mayan girl to find pleasure, deeply disturbed her.

Judging the girl's existence at the inn, she had to be profoundly aware of the things that really pleased a man. Could it be she was afraid once Nate had the Mayan girl he would no longer find her desirable?

As if by intuition, the girl approached Raquel with the second set of clothing, offering to show her the proper way to wear the multicolored wraparound skirt. Her black eyes searched deeply into Raquel's sable ones. It was an offer of friendship and trust.

After checking a shirt that he'd laid across a bush to dry, Nate swaggered down toward the opposite end of the concealed springs.

He watched the silent exchange between the two women, and he wished he'd been able to see the message the woman called Jackie had relayed in her eyes. Had the Mayan instinctively picked up a message of jealousy or disdain before she offered her visual bond of friendship? He didn't know for sure. But one thing he did know, the few days he had spent with this woman, her ways and actions contradicted the things he thought he knew about her. There was an inner strength and resolve he had not expected from a woman of her caliber.

Nate knew he was a good judge of character, and a damn good judge of women. Why hadn't she crawled up beside him last night to quench her own desire? It had been so apparent in her face, even her body poised and ready to receive him.

Back in the States he thought it was obvious she had been with many men, showing little concern about when or where. A woman as loose as that had needs and desires of her own that would eventually have to be fulfilled.

At first he'd thought the anger and frustration resulting from being kidnapped was the reason she had not given in to her promiscuous sexual nature. So he'd responded accordingly, playing the little game that many women liked to play. And hell, he didn't blame any woman for not wanting the likes of Jay or Al. But to be brought to the brink of pleasure that she'd reached last night, and not reach out to fulfill it . . . there had to be other reasons. This woman was either totally different from what he had expected, or she was a damn good con artist. His instincts told him it was not the latter, and that bothered him.

Yet, he couldn't be concerned with that right now. They had to reach Dangriga. Once there, the whole thing would come to an end, and maybe by then he would have the answers he needed. Until that time came, he would protect her any way he could.

It took only moments for Raquel to don the simple Mayan outfit. The knotting of the tangerine, red and mustard-colored wraparound skirt, riding low on her curvaceous hip, had been accomplished easily enough. Afterwards the Mayan girl helped her comb out her tangled locks, which had dried into a voluminous head of wild, somewhat cottony, black curls.

Speaking in her own language, the girl gesticulated and exclaimed over the texture of Raquel's thick mane, then demonstrated how it would be a magnet for bugs and other bits of nature if it remained loose.

Resourcefully the young girl produced a flowered vine. Starting at the crown of Raquel's head, she ornately, but delicately, twisted the strong plant through the locks until she came to the base of her neck, where the remainder of Raquel's hair was gathered in a large ball surrounded by several vermilion blossoms. The heady aroma of the flowers was heavenly, and Raquel closed her eyes as she sampled the scent.

As she opened them, she could see the look of admiration and approval on the Mayan's face, but unlike her she did not seek a look of approval from Nate.

Beneath profuse lashes, she watched him stride slowly back in their direction, then stop directly in front of her giving her a thorough and possessive going over.

"It looks good. Now you should really blend in, should the need ever arise."

For a moment his words of approval seem to lighten the emotional turmoil Raquel was feeling, but that moment of respite was quickly doused when she understood he was only concerned about her not being discovered, therefore keeping himself out of jeopardy.

Contempt filled her dark gaze before she turned away from him.

"Well, I guess this means we are ready, ladies," he signalled for the young girl to proceed before them, "lead the way."

They reached the outskirts of the Mayan girl's village in a short time. Raquel hadn't realized how close Nim Li Punti had actually been the night before, but as they circumvented the large Mayan ruin, she found herself gazing with astonishment at the sheer size of it.

There were numerous, intricately carved stelae towering eerily, their etched stone faces and figures telling a tale of long-gone Mayan triumph and tragedy. The smell was a strange mixture of stagnant air, weathered rock and plant life.

From what she could see, the majority of the ruin had not been reclaimed from the possessive forest whose vine-draped trees and shrouded bushes covered several buildings, creating large, uniquely shaped, foliage-molded mountains. Only a small section had been partially cleared. Raquel assumed this had been done by the archaeologist Nate mentioned the day before. It was around this section that they used the most care.

She understood Nate's cautious reaction, but not the one exhibited by the Mayan girl. There was a feel of fear and reverence about her as she skirted it. Her slightly slanted eyes were full of curiosity as she passed. She stole only covert glances whenever she dared to look at the ruins.

Raquel was surprised to see the gathering of thatch-roofed buildings hidden within the forest not far from Nim Li Punti. For some reason she had pictured the village sitting neatly on a plot of land totally cleared of foliage. This village, like Nim Li Punti, had an untamed feeling about it, as if it and nature were one.

The Mayan stopped several yards away from the unnaturally quiet gathering of thatched, single-room buildings. There was no speech or laughter to be heard, a strange feature for a well-kept village where people obviously lived.

Silently they advanced closer to the nearest cluster of edifices until an extremely large congregation of the occupants came into view.

A meeting of the entire village had been called. They had gathered upon the grass and moss, in what Raquel now recognized as the center of what appeared to be separate living communes.

A lone man was approaching the group. As he came closer Nate recognized him. It was Ponti, the man he had been introduced to the night before in the Kekchi village. His keen eyes narrowed as he surveyed the scene. Could the Mayan girl be from the Forbidden Village?

All eyes were turned in Ponti's direction as he crossed perpendicular to Nate, Raquel and the girl. Several of the men rose from their leadership seats upon the ground. They were followed by countless others, women as well as youngsters.

The women were dressed in the same manner as Raquel and the Mayan girl who stood silently beside her. The majority of the men were shirtless, wearing loose-fitting, white, calf-length cotton pants.

The entire scenario reminded Raquel of an old Western, the scene: A Mexican village, except the adobe buildings and dusty roads had been replaced by thatched buildings and an immense rain forest. The people bore an resemblance to Mexicans, albeit their straight black hair was of a finer texture.

Nate guessed Ponti had received the message he'd been waiting for: he'd gotten permission to see his family.

The three of them watched as he approached the crowd several yards away, and a burst of what the two observers assumed were shouts of welcome were heard. Suddenly, to Raquel and Nate's shock and amazement, Ponti was swallowed up in the swell of exuberant, trotting Mayans chanting and wailing, loudly. But their forward movement did not stop as they engulfed him, instead it increased in velocity pushing forward in their direction, only to halt when they enveloped the Mayan girl.

Inevitably, all four of them were caught up in the triumphant frenzy, but it was the Mayan girl who became surrounded by a small inner ring of elderly women, assessingly touching her face, skin and hair.

As the space between them widened, the young girl's eyes once again sought out Raquel's. The look within them alarmed something deep inside her. It was a look of resolve laced with fear.

In the midst of the excited Mayans, Raquel found herself beside the stranger who'd first attempted to approach the group. He looked out of place with his American-style haircut, jeans and T-shirt.

"Well Ponti, we meet again," Nate's rich voice boomed above the throng's noise. "Strangely enough, it seems like we've been given quite a joyous welcome."

Raquel's eyebrows lifted with surprise to hear Nate address the man by name.

"Yes, in some ways this is a happy occasion, at least many of the villagers feel that way. I don't know about Mircea, the girl who returned with you. I think she probably feels quite differently."

"Mircea ..." Raquel reflected upon her friend's name. "Why wouldn't she be happy to return to her own village?"

Ponti looked at the petite woman edged so closely against him because of the crushing crowd. He could see true concern for the girl's welfare written all over her attractive features. For a moment he hesitated, remembering the warnings of his parents and ancestors, "Never allow an outsider even a glimpse into our sacred rituals." But the beseeching look on this beautiful woman's face assured him, hers was not an exploiting concern, but a human one.

"She ran away to escape the fate that everyone here believes she was born to. A fate of blood and sacrifice."

Ponti realized he could not tolerate the look of shock and horror that spread across the woman's features as his words sank in. It was because of his feelings opposing these kinds of rites that he left his family long ago. Yet the rites were tradition—they would always support the elders, who never strayed from the laws of the tablets.

Rumors of these bloodletting sacrificial rites ran rampant amongst the nearby villagers. It was because of them that Balam had been given the name "Forbidden Village." Their Mayan brothers and sisters in nearby settlements had long ago let go of these ancient rituals.

"Sacrifice" the hushed word rolled numbly from Raquel's lips.

Nate remained quiet as he listened to the exchange, and his dark eyes surveyed the raucous crowd of Balamians. No doubt he felt for the Mayan girl's plight, but uppermost in his mind was what this could mean for himself, and Jackie Dawson.

As the Mayans' fervor heightened, they found themselves being carried along inside a huge crowd of Balamians as they proceeded back to the center of the village. The shrill note of handmade flutes shrieked loudly, and the older villagers began to stomp their naked feet upon the grassy plaza. Even the tiniest ones followed suit, their ignorance of purpose apparent in their darting eyes and fun-filled faces.

Raquel could see Mircea standing a slight distance in front of her on top of what must have been a stone slab, her eyes focused straight ahead of her, bizarrely glazed. Several feet away, a withered man with a leathery sack hanging heavily about his neck, commenced a ritualistic strut through the inner circle of women surrounding the tiny platform. He was minute in stature and weight, yet despite his deeply wrinkled face, his hair shone as darkly as a jaguar's black coat.

Once having danced his way to the altar, he removed the well-worn pouch from his neck, dug nimbly inside with knurled fingers, then finally extracted a curious shiny, black object.

As Raquel watched with intense curiosity, she saw Mircea accept a shallow pottery bowl filled with what appeared to be a string of narrow white rope. She held it with steady fingers just below her face, then she extended her tongue to its fullest length above it.

"What are they about to do?" Raquel asked as the aged man approached the girl. Nate responded by pulling her back against him, placing his strong hands protectively about her upper arms.

As quick as a wink the shaman took what looked like a spike of black glass, and forced it through the thickness of Mircea's tongue. There was no reaction of pain from her friend as he did so. To Raquel's abhorrence, this was followed by a threading of the white, bark cloth from the bowl through the open wound, and as the red of Mircea's blood crept down the thin stretch of paper, turning its paleness to crimson, the pitch of elation amongst the villagers was almost unbearable.

Stunned, Raquel turned her horror-stricken face into the safety of Nate's broad chest as her insides began to churn.

The excited group found joy in the Mayan girl's eyes

glassing over from the pain. For it was the pain, the Balamians believed, that would allow her to communicate with the gods. This was her heritage. This was Mircea's legacy.

Time seemed to stand still for Raquel as she clutched Nate's shirt and tried to make sense of the willful suffering she'd just witnessed, but her clouded mind could not make sense of what she'd just seen. *Mircea, dear Mircea,* she thought.

After a sufficient amount of her blood had been shed, the young girl's limp body was hustled off to one of the living units by a tiny group of Mayans whom Raquel assumed to be her family. As she disappeared inside the wooden door of the building, the jubilant sounds ceased, only to be replaced by a deadly silence as a sea of dark eyes rested on the intruders.

Shocked beyond belief, Raquel feared they would be chosen next for this grotesque show of pain.

It was Ponti's voice that broke the unnatural stillness. His tone was strong, yet it held a note of definite respect as he directed his words toward three of the Mayan men. Two of them waited as the shortest of the group responded. His words were rapid, his stance, stoic, yet his eyes held a tenderness no one could ignore. There was no doubt this man was Ponti's father.

Slowly the young man crossed the space between them, and was received by a tight embrace with arms so deeply bronzed they reminded Raquel of copper. This open display of love and tenderness contrasted peculiarly with the ritual that had just passed moments before. Raquel's diminutive frame trembled as she continued to lean against Nate for support.

Verbal exchanges continued amongst the group, yet

Nate's perceptive ears and eyes could tell when the conversation no longer centered on Ponti, but on himself and the woman he held tightly before him.

Strong head and hand gestures passed between the elders, and Raquel could tell something was afoot as the trio delivered cold calculating looks in their direction.

Barely moving her lips, she spoke so only Nate could hear.

"What do you think they plan to do with us?"

"It does not matter, *pataki*. I have plans of my own, and they do not include the Mayans."

Raquel gained strength from the conviction of his words, and even now in the height of her fear, she was painfully aware of his physical strength and virility. It was a heady feeling to know he would protect her no matter what, a potent aphrodisiac, for a moment she regretted not making love to him the night before. Looking at the intense faces surrounding them now, there was a chance neither one of them would ever make love again.

Raquel watched as Ponti leaned over and spoke into his father's ear. Contemplatively the older man nodded his head in agreement, his dark, perceptive eyes resting on their faces. Then he silenced Ponti with a final movement of his hand, and began to speak to his peers. At first they answered with silence, then reluctantly they agreed with his decision.

It was a stone-faced Ponti who approached the two outsiders.

"There's no easy way to tell you this," he solemnly informed them. "It's unfortunate that you were allowed to witness Mircea's initial bloodletting. If it wasn't for that, I'm pretty sure I could have convinced my father to talk the others into letting you go. So for right now, all I could do was buy you a little more time. You are to be the . . . guests of my extended family until the main ritual takes place tonight, during which you will be presented as part of the ceremony, the sacrifice," his dark eyes looked heavy with the burden of his words. "If I hadn't spoken up for you, it would have been over quickly, on the same small altar that Mircea's bloodletting took place."

One of the men loudly addressed Ponti, irritation apparent in his voice. In submission he nodded toward the Mayan and began to move in his direction. He spoke to Raquel and Nate over his shoulder. "It is the best that I can do," his eyes pleaded for understanding. "Now, you need to follow me."

On legs that felt like stilts Raquel walked behind Ponti. Nate's head towered above the crowd as they passed through it. By nature, the Mayans were a short people, and from the looks on many of their faces they found Nate's huge stature to be intimidating.

The two of them followed Ponti into a cluster of buildings not far from the one Mircea had entered. It was a single-room structure of medium size. A door on the opposite wall had been left ajar, allowing a view into a quadrangular-shaped patio. It was closed in by several other closely built buildings, just like the one in which they stood.

Some of Ponti's extended family had entered behind them, their voices blending together as they offered their opinions, but it was the females who ended up with the last say, directing Ponti to take Nate into another building on the opposite side of the patio, while Raquel remained behind.

She proved to be quite a curiosity for the Balamians, especially for the children, but after a few sharp words from an elderly female, they ignored her.

She leaned back against the wooden walls of the room and watched the family as they went on with their daily chores and made special preparations for the night to come.

Wood was brought in and piled in the middle of the room. It was stacked beside the place where the cooking was always done. Three large blackened stones were the base of the fire; deep grooves had been dug in the ground to make them a permanent fixture. Other articles, like herbs, vegetables, cooking and cleaning utensils were hung about, and Raquel got the feeling this room served only as the kitchen and eating area.

She could see other Balamians traversing back and forth between the buildings. There was a unity displayed in their actions that bespoke of more than family—but rather gave a sense of an interdependent existence. Raquel admired this sense of camaraderie.

Raquel thought about the people and the neighborhood in which she worked back in the States. She knew if this kind of thinking could be nurtured and carried out back there, many of them would not feel so alone when they fought the daily battle of survival. She determined, when she returned, she would initiate an extended-family program as part of her counseling.

A burning sensation commenced behind her dark eyes as water welled up inside, causing them to glisten. The clinic was no longer open where she could implement such a program, and right now, her chances were very slim of returning home at all.

She tried to feel anger towards Nate for putting her in

such a predicament, but now it all seemed like such a waste of energy. Whatever had driven him to be a part of the kidnapping ring that abducted her, had to have meaning in his life, for she knew now, he was not a criminal at heart, but a man of strong convictions.

The fire burned brightly, its smoke adding to the already soot-covered rafters above. Soon the smell of chili, sweet potatoes and tortillas wafted throughout, and Raquel's hunger mounted. Throughout the afternoon, groups of family members came in and partook of the delicious fare, but none was offered to Raquel.

Finally Ponti returned, his bronze features clouded with thoughts of the night to come. In a casual manner he walked near Raquel, secretly dropping a folded piece of beaten bark in her lap. With nervous fingers the girl clasped the paper, tucking it into the folds of the wraparound skirt. Her heart drummed inside her chest as she tried to imagine what had been written, and how she could read it without being discovered. For Raquel knew, even though it seemed no one watched her, the oldest female had taken it upon herself to keep a close eye on her.

After a few minutes of deciding what to do, she began to nod her head like a person fighting sleep. Several times she went through the jerky motions until she finally decided to stretch out on the dirt floor, eventually turning her back to the room as she deceitfully found a more comfortable position. It was there on her side, that she was able to read the note addressed to *Pataki.*

Make move at right time. Get close together.
Watch me. Don't be afraid.

Once again Raquel's heart thumped wildly. How could they ever escape from all of these Balamians? Already she could feel her adrenaline building, readying for fight or flight. If need be, it would be both, but she had no intention of dying here.

She thought of the fire that must have burned deep in Nate's eyes as he penned the scratchy note upon the rough paper. She could tell he was a man of deep passions and one day, she determined, she'd find out just how deep.

Lying on her side for as long as she could without slapping the troublesome fleas that nipped and bit at her ankles and arms, Raquel called upon the inner strength she knew she'd need in order to win. Like an invisible source, it had always been there whenever she needed it, and she knew the supply was infinite as long as she believed it was.

The young woman sat up, adjusting her skirt about her legs and feet, then patted the dust and dirt from her still neatly twisted hair. To the Balamians it looked like an accident when she broke one of the large, now withered, vermilion blossoms from the shriveled vine that encased it. But Ponti knew otherwise, when she sought his eyes with hers, then gazed longingly at the wrinkled petals. The flower would serve as her answer to Nate's message.

Gathering up left-over tidbits of tortilla, Ponti tossed the thick dough in Raquel's direction. Quickly the dogs pounced upon it slobbering, smacking and growling as they jostled for the offering. While retrieving several pieces that had fallen too close to the girl, he picked up the blossom and carried it out quickly in his hand.

The old saying, "funny how time flies when you're having fun" hammered in Raquel's mind as night descended quicker than she'd ever known it to do before.

She surmised that whoever coined that line had never been faced with a time when they were scheduled to die. Now the young woman knew, time also flies when death is approaching your door.

An uncanny quiet descended within the complex. Most of the women and children had long gone, leaving several of the men to watch over her. A group of candles had been lit inside, casting powerful shadows upon the walls, making the atmosphere that much more macabre as she thought of the fate the Balamians had planned for them.

Raquel sat ghostly still as she tried not to think about how these people steeped in ancient tradition planned to carry out the sacrifice. After what had happened to Mircea, she knew her imagination probably could not conjure up the likes of what they would do to two outsiders if they had the chance. Her breath started to come in short snatches at the thought of it.

Yet Nate had promised her their plans would fail, and despite all that had passed between them, she trusted his word.

Unknown to Raquel, Nate could see her as she sat drumming up the mental courage and fortitude she'd need to face the Balamians. The room in which he sat was dark. No candle had been left for him, only the moon's light outside provided some illumination in the simple surroundings.

He could tell from her posture that she was afraid, but he could also tell she would do whatever it took to save herself, and that was all he could ask of her. It was his fault that she faced such a horrible end, and it was his responsibility to make sure she never had to endure it. But how could he have known things would get this far out of hand?

It was an understatement to say that Nate was glad the Balamians did not think it necessary he be searched. That was one aspect of their cultural thinking that would work to his and the woman's advantage. As the day wore on he had paid close attention to their ways, and had concluded the Balamians would feel guns and modern weapons were the tools of cowards. Well, if need be he would be marked a coward, but he had no intention of being sacrificed.

As a child he'd heard stories about relatives of the Kekchi Indians who lived isolated in a village amongst the ruins. They were bloody, gruesome tales of pain and visions. That's why he'd known when Mircea extended her tongue what she was offering to do. Had she been a man, the piercing would have taken place through the male organ.

The veins and muscles bulged in his tan arms as he made rock-hard fists when a group of Balamians appeared and motioned for the woman to follow them. The depth of the need to protect her sprung up from deep within. Although it shocked him, he did not question its origin, he only knew he would protect this woman with his life, if the need arose.

Moments later he too was commanded to follow several escorts. Nate complied willingly, anticipating the right moment when they could make their move.

Raquel had expected to exit the building to a waiting crowd of anxious Balamians. Instead a stark, empty village awaited her through which she was quickly directed. Soon she realized she was headed for the ruins of Nim Li Punti. The instinct to flee was rising fast, and she turned to see if Nate was anywhere near her as they led her toward the sacrificial ground. As soon as she turned around to look, a massively built Balamian prodded her forcefully in the back, insisting that she keep her eyes straight ahead.

As they progressed, shouts and shrieks pierced the night. This was accompanied by drums and the jingling and clanging of metal. A fire which the Balamians built in the center of what appeared to be a large plaza, blazed wildly, illuminating the lichen-painted walls of Nim Li Punti.

No one noticed Raquel and her escorts when they arrived. All eyes were riveted upon the mass of swirling, animated bodies not far from the flames. At first Raquel thought they were fighting amongst themselves. Half of the Balamians caught in the quick of action wore brightly colored headgear decorated with red feathers, while the opposers wore bright feathers of yellow. Swords rose and fell methodically between them, while others tussled on the ground, brandishing wicked-looking knives and daggers, as their kindred spirits on the sidelines chanted and keened.

For a second Raquel was disoriented. Her nerves were as tight as a bowstring. Did they also plan to kill their own kind to appease these gods that they favored? But then it became clear to her, she was witnessing a mock battle.

Picturesque stelae loomed around them. Some of them depicted warfare, lovemaking and bloodletting. Others sported strange hieroglyphics Raquel had no way of understanding. The largest one lay like a sleeping giant wearing a huge hat.

Not far away Raquel could see Mircea seated

trancelike upon another altar. Hordes of vine-shrouded bushes and trees, sprinkled with bromeliads, orchids and other blossoms provided a magnificent backdrop for the eerie scene.

Mircea now wore a piece of colorful cloth that barely hid her tiny breasts. Her head was crowned with a headdress decorated in both the red and yellow feathers of the mock warriors.

Raquel was pushed in the direction of the platform on which Mircea sat, though she ended up only several feet away, her friend never acknowledged her presence. She was like a shell of herself, her tiny body motionless as it stood before the mass of clangorous Balamians.

Then the old shaman appeared out of the shadow of several tumbled rocks, gingerly carrying a sheathed dagger—the hilt of it, a masterfully carved jaguar. He lay the menacing object upon a special stand not far from Mircea. Like her, the shaman wore a headdress of mixed feathers. Several bowls of the ropelike beaten bark were also placed near the stand.

Raquel looked out into the excited faces of the Balamians, many of them waving spiked objects high above their heads as the momentum of the ritual heightened. Some of their wrists were entwined with strands of the beaten bark, waiting for the moment when they could give of their blood to the gods, their offering for the continuation of life as they knew it.

Raquel's dark anxious gaze fell upon Nate as he was being brought up the opposite side of the sacrificial altar. His tough visage found her and rested there. A slight snarl raised one corner of his ample lips, assuring her they would not be sacrificed without a fight, even though two strongly built Balamians held both wrists behind his back.

Ponti's tormented features were taut as he watched the scene upon the platform. The sight of Mircea offering herself as a sacrifice tugged at his tender heartstrings. His eyes rested upon her tiny face, then her slender hands. They were so delicate and beautiful, something to be treasured not destroyed. Yet, like the other Balamians, he too held a bloodletting instrument, made from a stingray's spine, within his grip, and the telltale sign of the ceremonial paper was also wrapped about his wrists.

It was not a coincidence the elders allowed him to return the day before the Vision Serpent ritual. His father had warned him, "the only way we will believe that you, Ponti, have truly returned to your people, will be that you too give of yourself during the Vision Serpent rites, so the cycle of life can continue here in Balam."

Ponti was very much interested in life, for at this very moment his highest concern was for not a single life to be lost.

Demonstrating his power, the shaman raised his aged hands, and the crowd as well as the warriors brought their revelry to a climax, but the low steady beat of a drumlike instrument continued its motion. It was time for the ritual to begin, and with squat, animal-like movements the shaman commenced his portion of the ceremony.

It was obvious to Raquel that he was telling a story as he swirled, dipped and swayed, motioning to the various stelae; the light from the huge fire made his shadow a live thing amongst the carvings. He danced until he worked up a steady stream of sweat that careened down the deep groves in his withered face. It was amazing a man of his age was so limber, displaying the stamina of a man much younger than himself.

A recitation of rites followed his performance. They were long and tedious, read from a book that Raquel thought resembled an accordion. She could not tell how old the book was, but it was terribly worn, and fashioned from the beaten bark the Balamians used for so many things.

Although Raquel was aware of the powerful movements of the shaman, the fire and passion that burned in Nate's eyes as he looked at her, brought an unexpected twist to the scene. Here she was, on the brink of death, and she could not draw her frightened gaze away from the message deep in his eyes.

He told her with his eyes how much he wanted her, to make her his and his alone. Even at this desperate hour, it was his deepest desire.

Raquel was overwhelmed, and his visual announcement to possess her was fervently met by one of complete surrender. She promised him with her gaze that she would be his if only they could survive.

Moments later, through apprehensive eyes, Raquel watched the sweating shaman approach her, an obsidian spike held calmly along his side. At first she was petrified, but as the elderly man drew closer, Raquel's instinct to fight back gushed forward.

She would not die this way. No! She shouted to herself. "No!" she shouted to the shaman. With a strength Raquel never knew she possessed, she freed herself from her two guards, and struck the shaman who was poised for the bloodletting.

Her defensive attack shocked everyone, and Nate

took advantage of the moment. Through pure brawn, he tore away from the men beside him. He executed a deadly blow to one of their windpipes with a steely elbow, then struck the other in the groin with a forceful knee. Both men clutched their bodies in pain, falling to the ground. In a matter of seconds Nate was at Raquel's side, wielding the 9mm pistol, hidden in his pants.

The Balamians nearest to the altar recovered quickly from their initial shock and several men launched a menacing attack. Adhering to the promise that he'd made to Ponti, to kill no one unless he was forced to, Nate shot one Balamian in the thigh, the other in his shoulder, causing another attacker to rethink his move.

"Let's go! Now!" he shouted to Raquel, tugging at her arm, directing her to the vine-draped bushes behind them.

Without thinking, Raquel made a swift move for the ceremonial dagger that lay on the pulpit—at least Mircea would be safe. It would have been the last move she made had it not been for Ponti, who blocked the blow of a livid Balamian wielding an ax.

The sound of the sharp weapon crashing down on the cracked pulpit nearly split her ears it was so close.

"You little fool!" Nate shouted, then grabbed her arm before leaping into the dark foliage.

Chapter Eight

Jay watched the *buyei* carefully light a long-stemmed, hand-carved pipe. Strands of blackish monkey hair hung uniformly from its bottom, shaking as the old high priest's unsteady fingers gripped the wooden object. His bulbous eyes stared, as the older man slowly inhaled the pungent herbs, then blew out a steady stream of greenish smoke.

Jay's gangly body swayed impatiently from side to side as he waited for the *buyei* to answer the question put before him. He did not care what the other Puntaborok villagers thought. He wanted to be done with this situation as quickly as possible, and that meant finding the girl and getting rid of her.

He rolled his yellow-stained eyes in the high priest's direction. It was obvious the priest was getting too old to run things. Even now, he didn't really know all the things that went on amongst the Shango, Jay thought with a smile. It was time for someone younger and stronger to take over.

"I think someone else should accompany you to bring the girl back. Al must wait here until a healing can be performed. Until then he can not be trusted or controlled," the Shangoain dialect poured slowly from his lips.

"But, mighty *buyei*, he is my brother. We have always worked together. He would not go against my word, plus I will need his strength in case the girl resists."

Another green stream of smoke floated above the *buyei*'s head. Pupils that used to be dark, but had succumbed to the grey tint of time, focused on Jay as he squatted before him.

"Jay, *Dada*, I feel there are other reasons you want Al to accompany you to bring back this girl." After a controlled pause he continued. "She is not to be harmed."

The *buyei* picked up a root carved into the shape of a woman from the divination basket, and tossed it between them.

"The fork of change is near." His tough finger poked the dried, blackened object. "We cannot change what was meant to be, *Dada*."

Jay lowered anger-filled eyes away from the knowing stare of the high priest. A familiar quiver surfaced in his stomach, reminding him that he knew the powers the *buyei* possessed, and it would not be wise to force his desires too strongly upon him. He glanced at his brother as he sat cross-legged beside him, playing with a large, unhappy centipede. Finally he nodded his head in compliance with the high priest's order.

"Take three of the other men with you. They will more than make up for the physical strength of your brother. The four of you will leave day after tomorrow."

Keeping his head bowed as he rose to his feet, Jay began to take leave of the high priest. It took several strong taps on Al's shoulder before he followed suit, mumbling to himself that Jay was interrupting his play-time.

There was no warm reception as the man and his brother entered their home, a stilt-topped building not far away. Acting more like a servant than a wife, Jay's spouse, Eva, lowered her head and shoulders as he came in, then muttered an offering of food. He gave the thin figure little attention as he crossed the room to a collection of containers, withdrew a crumpled envelope out of one of them, then stuffed the paper into his pants pocket.

"I am goin' out."

His wife's lowered eyes opened in surprise at this offering of congeniality. Their communication over the last three years had deteriorated to nothing, after it had become evident that she couldn't bear a child. Now she was a servant in her own home. It was only because of the *buyei* that they remained together.

As her dull eyes sought her husband's face, Eva realized he was not addressing her but his brother. Quickly she lowered her head again, and returned to the furthest corner of the one-room house, not wanting to draw too much attention to herself. She'd learned she was better off that way. Yet, she was very curious as to why Jay would leave Al behind; usually they did everything together. They were virtually inseparable. Maybe the *obeah* woman they had brought back from America had caused the change.

Eva's brown eyes shifted back and forth anxiously as she pondered the situation. Just the thought of any female having control over her husband pleased her. During their short marriage she had come to know just how much Jay disrespected women. To him they were simply objects to be used at his whim. With anticipation she concluded, the power of the *obeah* woman must be very strong to bring about a change in the relationship between her husband and his brother.

Large leaves lashed against her face, and Raquel stumbled over vines and fallen branches as Nate pulled her behind him at an exhausting pace. The shouts of their pursuers grew closer as she began to tire, still her mind urged her body to continue.

"Where are we going?" Gasps of air laced her words.

"I don't know where. Are you thinking about going back or something?" he replied, as they continued to run.

The sounds of the jungle seemed to come alive as night descended over the thick foliage, "No. I'm not."

"If you think about it, maybe they wouldn't be so hot on our trail if you hadn't stopped to take that damn dagger!"

"I couldn't just leave thinking they were going to carve out Mircea's tongue with it. So I took it!"

"Not her tongue, sweetheart. It was going to be her heart. So you better hope they don't catch us 'cause it'll be ours instead," he chastised her. "Because of your heroism, you may have made it easier for them to get two for the price of one."

The thought of letting go of the large hand that clasped hers as he dragged her along, flickered through Raquel's mind. Here he was blaming her for their predicament, and if it hadn't been for him, they wouldn't be in Belize in the first place.

"Don't blame this mess on me!" She tried to dig her fingernails into his firm skin for revenge. "If it hadn't—"

"Save your breath for running," was Nate's curt reply.

Minutes later, starving for air, Raquel's breaths turned into gasps as her intakes became more and more labored. She wanted to beg Nate to stop, but she was so out of breath she couldn't speak.

Nate listened to the strained breathing of the woman behind him, and he knew they would have to stop if only for a brief respite. Hastily he pulled her down with him behind a large hyacinth bush as he listened intently for the group of Balamians not far behind.

He was grateful for the cover of darkness, but he also knew the sounds they made crashing through the rain forest kept the Balamians on their trail. Nate looked at the woman hunched over with her hands on her knees, desperately trying to catch her breath.

"Are you ready?"

She answered weakly, and they were off again.

Suddenly, Nate released a sound of intense pain although he continued to run. Raquel assumed he had scraped his leg, or slightly twisted an ankle, because the sound was accompanied by a slight break in his stride. It wasn't until he spasmodically released her hand, collapsed, then nearly rolled into a partial clearing, that she knew it was much more than that. His body began to shake as if he were experiencing a chill.

"What's wrong?" she fell to her knees beside him.

He attempted to sit up, "I think it's a s-snakebite." Nate tried to look at his leg, but was overtaken by another, progressively stronger quiver.

"Oh God, not now!" she heard herself say as she peered down at the limb he was holding.

A small circle resembling a bruise could be seen above his ankle, it was too dark to see the punctures.

Frantically the young woman tried to think of something she could do as she heard the Balamians closing in on them. Maybe she could lance it like in the movies, and suck out the poison before it got into his bloodstream, but that would take time, and time was something they didn't have. She examined the ominous-looking bite once again.

A tightness gripped Raquel's chest when she raised his pants leg and saw a dark line forming, progressing up towards his heart. She thought *Somehow I've got to stop the poison from traveling upward! At least try to slow it down.*

Swiftly she grabbed a stick that lay near them on the ground. With trembling, but strong fingers, she tore a length of material from the rim of the shift she wore. Putting the cloth around Nate's leg about two inches above the menacing dark line, she tightened it with the stick in an attempt to stop the flow of blood between his heart and the venom.

Then unexpectantly, a crumpled vermilion blossom fell out of the denim material onto the moss-covered floor of the forest. Raquel clasped its withered softness in her shaking hand, "Oh, Nate."

She thought of the longing that filled her in the Balamian village when she sent the meaningful flower to him, and how passionately, with their eyes they had taken that silent vow. Somehow it was wrong for such a tiny thing as a snakebite to bring him down. His strength and passion for life was much more than that. He did not deserve to die like this.

Raquel knew she had promised herself she would never cry again, but now she saw, rather than felt the large bits of moisture dropping onto the tawny colored material of his shirt, forming dark circles as they landed.

Instinctively her hands went to his head and she gently lifted it, placing it upon her lap. She stared at his blank features as she rubbed his forehead, his face, his hair.

With resignation, Raquel waited for the Balamians to overtake them. Somehow her will to live had become connected with the man's life whose head she held upon her lap. A man who had kidnapped her, yet had protected her every step of the way. If he was to die, this would be the only embrace she could give him.

Raquel gazed affectionately at his strong face. Strange how in her mind the now-continuous quivering did not jar the handsomeness of his features. She marveled at how his thick lashes had formed a dark half-moon upon his high cheeks. Softly, as in a daze, she traced the shape of his broad, tall nose down to his lips, that even at first sight she knew, could have shaken the very foundation of her. Purposefully she placed a soft, lingering kiss upon them.

Out of the darkness, a figure appeared in the clearing. Raquel looked up with tired eyes expecting to see a Balamian with sword or dagger drawn, and a thick wrapping of beaten bark about his wrists. Instead a female approached.

Being overcome by exhaustion and mental strain and slightly relieved, Raquel calmly returned her remote, troubled stare to Nate's visage. Placing her face close to his, she began to hum a gentle melody as she continued her gentle administrations. If they were to die by the hands of this stranger, they would die together.

In silence, the odd figure exposed a large machete.

Raquel did not flinch as she raised it high above her head, then brought it down with remarkable force for a person her size. A splintering sound ensued as the woman hacked off a long strip of a large thorny plant nearby. She brought it over and dropped it upon Nate's legs.

At that moment two Balamians burst into the clearing, then halted abruptly as they surveyed the scene in front of them. Their gaze darted between Raquel, who appeared to be unaware of her surroundings as she embraced the barely conscious Nate, and the bush doctor, who pinned them with an unwavering stare.

It was she who spoke first, rapidly and authoritatively, raising her arms, then grabbing and shaking a talisman that she wore about her neck. By that time, several more Balamians had gathered, and disbelief and fear plastered their faces as they gawked at the shamaness. Suddenly they began to back away when the commanding figure took a powerful step in their direction. One last menacing word from her caused them to totally run in fear.

Squatting beside the man and the woman, she stretched out one of Nate's arms, and began to measure the strip of cockspur against its length. Carefully she cut the severed plant's dimensions to match his, then with wrinkled fingers, she forced the plant into his mouth, clamping it shut.

Through a mental haze Raquel heard the woman's rough accented voice.

"You make yo'r man chew this. He must chew it good an' swallow the juice, but he must not swallow the plant. The juices will fight the poison that has entered 'is body," Strong, heavily lidded eyes focused on Raquel as the woman spoke.

Following the stranger's instructions, the young woman began to massage Nate's jaws as she spoke to him.

"You hear that, Nate? She says you've got to chew this. It's going to help you. Do you hear me? Please, just try," her hand mechanically open and shut his mouth as part of the plant lay inside. Slowly he began to respond, unconsciously chewing on his own as she stuffed the remainder of the cockspur strip past his lips.

Satisfied with what she saw, the shamaness returned to the same plant. This time she used the machete to dig around and expose its root. She began to slice pieces off of the hard bottom.

"Remove the chewed plant from 'is mouth an' place it on the snakebite," she instructed over her shoulder.

With thumb and forefinger Raquel obeyed her command, patting the wet, sticky lump on the spot above Nate's ankle. He jerked as it made contact with his swollen skin.

"Now, one more time," the woman's raspy voice announced, as she stuffed the piece of cockspur root in his mouth. "'Tis won't cure him, but will delay the effects of the venom until we can get him to my hut."

Moments later the two women were balancing Nate's heavy frame between them, his arms draped about their shoulders. Dark, badly crinkled fingers, extracted the chewed root fiber from Nate's loose lips, then threw it on the ground. Satisfied, they began to make their way further into the rain forrest.

Chapter Nine

After Jay turned up the controls, the old air conditioner blew smooth gusts of cool air directly upon him as he lay on top of the knitted bedspread. He watched the sides of his mud-caked shoes slap together, while he waited in the comfortable surroundings of the Punta Gorda hotel.

This was the life he was meant to live. Not locked away in a village of elevated huts where the most modern of conveniences was a wood-burning stove, and the women smelled like dying fish. No, that was not the life for him. He was born to have money and power and he meant to have both.

Jay walked over and drew back the floral printed drapery, peering at the bright lights of the disco not far down the street. He had a little more than an hour before he was to meet Ricky Flint and his friends, and he planned to make good use of the time.

He withdrew the crumpled joint from his pocket, then lit it with an engraved sterling silver lighter that Ricky had given him almost a year ago during their first meeting. Running his thumb over the smooth-textured surface, he anticipated the time when items like this would be a dime a dozen amongst his possessions.

Jay chuckled to himself as he thought about his future. He would be in charge, never to bow to any man again. Soon, he would have the power he knew he was meant to receive. Soon, he would have everything.

Jay blew out the small flame that was swiftly progressing up the rolled cigarette. As he held the end near his wide nostrils, he inhaled deeply, enjoying the thick pungent smoke that drifted away from it.

Confidently, he walked over to the hotel door making sure it was unlocked, then climbed back upon the now-rumpled spread. Several deep pulls on the marijuana cigarette caused a forgotten seed inside to sputter and pop, the man smiled to himself at the familiar sound as a heady feeling descended upon him.

Jay was feeling the heat on his fingers from the almost consumed cigarette, when he heard a light tapping on the door. He extinguished the tiny tip in a glass ash tray on the nightstand beside the bed.

"Yeah?"

"It's Lindy," a soft female voice called from outside.

"Come on in and lock the door."

A rather petite woman wearing a lilac-colored spandex minidress and heels entered the room. Shutting and locking the door behind her, she leaned enticingly against it.

"Hello. I understand you're looking for some company for about an hour," Her manner of speaking was intelligent and her carriage just a slight bit haughty.

Jay had seen her several times before when he was in town. She worked out of the same house as Candy, his regular. But for some reason he'd never requested to see her even though he'd had the hots for her, and now he knew why. He had always felt he didn't deserve her, and that she felt she was better than he, no matter what her occupation.

Lindy's heavily lined eyes sized up the man on the bed. A precisely manicured hand smoothed the sides of her French rolled hair away from her rich brown skin. She could smell the lingering scent of marijuana in the room, and knew that accounted for the glassy look in his eyes. She could also feel something else she couldn't quite put her hands on.

"Yeah, t'at's about right, but I want more than your freakin' company. So why don't you come on ovah here and get to work," Jay commanded, wanting her to know her position.

A light of understanding clicked behind her dark eyes, and she slowly sauntered over to the dresser and placed her purse on its top. Silently, she pulled the elastic material of the dress over her shoulders, wiggling temptingly. She eased it over her rounded breasts and hips, until it was a purple pile at her spike-heeled feet. Keeping her eyes on the man on the bed, she kicked it away from her, then stood with her legs spread apart and her hands on her black-gartered hips.

Despite the calm Jay had determined to display, he licked his lips in anticipation as he assessed her almost-nude frame, had it not been for the garter, silk stockings and purple heels.

A look of triumph curled the corners of her pouty lips as she saw his reaction, and noted the growing bulge in the front of his pants. She'd seen his kind before. Straight from the forest, wanting to be big city. It was according to their frame of mind as to how they would react, so she'd have to be careful, for they could be un-usually cruel, or as obedient as a trained seal.

The woman's change in expression coupled with the effect of the marijuana, conjured up another image in Jay's mind and he touched the pale scar on the side of his face. He could see the woman, Jackie, standing be-fore him naked and ready to give of herself, letting go of the pretense that she did not want him. He remembered how his desire for her had nearly driven him mad. Her and her high-handed manners. He'd bet a hundred dol-lars she'd buck and scream like any other whore if he ever got inside her. He would still get his chance, he chuckled to himself.

"First, my money," Lindy held an outstretched hand in front of him, interrupting his drifting thoughts.

Harshly he slapped a fifty-dollar bill in her palm then rose to take off his clothes. No matter what women said, there was always a price for their stuff.

In the beginning he had believed otherwise, especially during the early months of marriage. Eva had been a virgin, and he remembered how proud he felt to have a woman that no other man had ever touched. Still the price for her virginity had been high.

She was young and inexperienced, and just the thought of that used to get a rise out of him. But he was patient, telling himself it would take time. Eventually he became her servant. She had him at her beck and call doing his work and hers. For certain she'd acted like she was the pot of gold at the end of the rainbow, and she had him believing it, because she was young and tender, and she knew he wanted a child.

The shaman had said if she was fertile a baby would be conceived within the first six months, but if she was slow to conceive, it would be at least a year. So he had waited. Settling for her lying there beneath him like a dead woman, giving little or no response only to find out she was no woman at all, and unable to bear him a child.

Jay's face relaxed into a satisfied smirk.

Well, after that, she got what was coming to her. If he was going to have to take care of a woman who couldn't satisfy him in any way, she'd work hard for that support. He wouldn't have a female that he was pumping into night after night remaining silent beneath him, openly denying his manhood. He had developed ways that would issue a response, be it pain or pleasure.

Before Lindy knew what he was about to do, Jay grabbed a hold of the mass of curls sitting on the top of her head, then bent her down over the full-size bed. Roughly, he kicked her ankles further apart with his still mud-caked shoes.

"If I'm going to have to pay you, bitch, you're going to work for your money," A snapping swat resounded off her rounded buttocks.

An appropriate whimper gushed from her lavishly painted lips, "Whatever you say, baby." She braced herself with strong arms as she bent forward.

Taken over by a lust-filled stupor, at first Jay didn't hear the knocking on the door until it turned into forceful pounding. The loud noise caught him off guard causing him to spill forth prematurely and a disappointed moan oozed from his puffy lips.

"Are you in there, Jay?" a deep voice demanded.

"Yeah. Yeah. I'm here."

"Ricky's waiting for you at the disco."

"Ain't you a little early?" Limply Jay pulled back, giv-

ing the prostitute room enough to saunter to the bathroom.

A pause ensued. "Do you want me to tell Ricky, *you*
want *him* to wait?" The question was richly laced with
insinuations.

"Na-aw." Panic struck him. He swallowed deeply before he continued. "Tell him I'll be right over."

He dressed hastily, leaving Lindy in the hotel room as
he closed the door behind him. It didn't take him long
to walk to the disco down the street.

"What is wrong with you, mon?" a woman snapped
after Jay rudely pushed her chair forward while making
his way across the crowded club.

He heard her irritated voice but didn't bother to respond. His gaze remained focused on Ricky, sitting at
the table with two other men. One he recognized; the
other, a large hunk of a man, was unfamiliar.

Rising out of his chair, Ricky extended an outstretched hand. "Jay, good to see you again, man. You
remember Rock, don't you?" he motioned to the familiar guy.

Jay nodded in agreement as Rock sat chewing enthu-
siastically on a stick of gum.

"And this is Mane-Mane."

He looked in the new guy's direction. His large,
braided head remained lowered as he meticulously lined
up several cigarettes on the plexiglass table.

Jay wondered which one of the Americans had
threatened him with telling Ricky he wanted him to
wait, as he gave them a none too friendly going-over.
Both of their receptions were cold, and he decided he
didn't care for either one of them. After all, they were
nothing but Ricky Flint's flunkies, jumping whenever he

said jump, and asking how high. Dudes like them would eagerly do his dirty work because they didn't have brains enough to do anything else.

During his first meeting with Rock, Jay found out how he believed the Belizean drug supply was an open playground for the States. So he had attached himself to Ricky Flint. He guessed Mane-Mane had done the same.

The sound of Jay's chair scraping the club's floor was drowned out by the loud reggae music. He looked across the table at Ricky's sparkling eyes, and wide, easy smile. His wavy, dark brown hair was pulled back to form a ponytail at the base of his neck.

He knew this man considered him as just a pawn in the game, and that's all he was when it came to Ricky's side of the board. But here in Punta Gorda, he could be the big man, the *oba*.

"Care for a drink?"

"Sure."

Ricky had barely raised his hand before a tall, chocolate brown waitress in a fuchsia cat suit appeared. Her wide smile was genuine as she glanced around the table.

"What d'ya having?"

Ricky motioned for Jay to place his order first.

Jay leaned back in the wooden chair, eyeing the woman's ample tush. "I'll have a Beliken & Crown."

"Make that four," Ricky added, patting the waitress's backside. "That's one thing I can say about you island-ers, you have plenty of everything," He watched the woman's rounded bottom rumble as she walked away, then grinned. "Everything that counts, that is." He

winked at Jay. "And of course that's why we're all here."
A fluff of lint on his designer shirt drew his attention,
and he aptly flicked it away. "Once you're able to tap
into a supply like this one, the need keeps growing and
growing. Some might think that's bad, but we know it's
only bad for those who really don't count. For folks like
us, Jay, it's a virtual gold mine."

Ricky waited for the waitress, who had hurried and
filled the order, to pour his beer into a heavy mug. Lifting the glass with a manicured hand, crowned by a tiny
gold pinkie ring, he boasted of things to come.

"This is to the future. After tonight there will be a
helluva future to look forward to."

Jay clinked his mug with the man's across the table.
By now he was full of anticipation, and the color of the
man's eyes had become an omen. They were a deep
green, the color of money.

Chapter Ten

Large rivulets of sweat ran down Nate's face onto the woven pad beneath him. Raquel sat nearby, drinking a mixture of herbs forced upon her by the shamaness. The strain of the Balamian incident had taken its toll, but she would not give in to rest until she witnessed the strange woman use her knowledge of herbs and roots to help Nate. She watched silently as the shamaness performed her task. Finally she was satisfied when the woman promised he would not die after all.

She sipped the relaxing mixture that tasted of chamomile, cinnamon and another flavor she did not recognize, and watched the older woman revive the fire inside the small, dirt-floor hut. It startled Raquel that she was not more panicked, that she felt so relaxed. She looked at the cup of tea in her hand and wondered if it were the herbs. She wondered if it were her trust in the shamaness. She wondered if she would feel this calm all the time if she simply knew Nate were nearby.

Skins and dried parts of various animals hung along the walls, mixed with different sized roots, carved figures and dried plants. The smell was a strange mixture of tangy sweetness and a gamy scent. Raquel was vaguely aware of how the hot liquid she drank helped to quell her desire to gag.

Eyes that appeared to be ancient would rest on her from time to time, while the elderly woman went about her tasks. She was distantly aware of the curious glances, but they did not move her either way. Nor did the figure's hunchbacked, skeleton-thin frame, crowned by a disarray of thick and thin dreadlocks, cause her the least bit of alarm. This person had brought them to a safe haven—one where the Balamians had not attempted to follow and were obviously afraid to trespass upon.

Outside, another pair of yellowish eyes watched the scene from the pitch blackness beyond the open flap of the hut's door. Raquel's hand paused in midair as she watched them come closer, until the slender, grayish body of jaguarundi walked menacingly through the opening. A low growl rumbled in his throat as his almond-shaped gaze seem to take in everything, paying special interest to the man who lay prostrate on the reed pallet. Slowly the shamaness turned toward the wildcat, and for a moment their eyes made contact. Now, the animal, like Raquel, seemed to freeze in midmotion, all except for his long swaying tail. Afterwards, as if receiving a message Raquel did not hear, the jaguarundi made a wide circle, only to retrace his steps and settle comfortably right outside the hut's door.

All this time she had witnessed the scene in the room through a kind of fog, and it was at this point the objects in the room began to swim about her. Moments passed, and before she knew it, the animal skins sans their hosts, began to come down off the walls and parley about the fire. Several ceremonial masks that hung in the corners provided peculiar sounds and chanting for the skins' bizarre dance.

Raquel never remembered at what point she lay down beside her very ill captor, placing her arm about his feverish torso. Nor did she know when reality turned into dreams, as she slept fitfully, surrounded by visions of warriors and jaguarundis.

It was early in the morning, and the young woman felt a deep urge to join her scream with the resounding noise of the howler monkeys perched in the rain forest trees. Their loud calls were free and uninhibited, making Raquel aware of her restricted existence.

She imagined it didn't matter if they were happy or melancholic, their voices would still ring out, and if they were lonely and feeling desperate as she felt, their loud cry would always be an outlet.

A day and a half had passed and Nate remained delirious, feverish. After the first night the shamaness decided he should be moved to a smaller hut beside her personal dwelling.

More than one of the forest animals had made their home in the vacant hut, and to her dismay, had to be chased out and shooed away. It was obvious the animals felt very comfortable with the old woman's company, and she with theirs; therefore, they didn't quite understand why this human creature did not find their company as appealing.

Raquel recalled staring down at the continuously bubbling broth, boiling in a large earthen container above the small fire. She didn't dare ask about the contents of the brew she'd been instructed to give Nate throughout the day. Its aroma reminded her of souring broccoli, the color being an appropriate vibrant green. Yet it was obvious to Raquel that the woman possessed a vast knowledge of the use of herbs and roots, unquestionably paling her limited wisdom, and for that she was grateful.

Raquel believed she could have stomached her outlandish surroundings much more easily if there had been any meaningful communication between her and her hostess, but there was none, not a mumbling word. Even carrying Nate to the other hut, and the shamaness's instructions to feed him, had been a series of head and arm movements, coupled with numerous glances from the woman's liquidy eyes.

It would have been different if she thought the woman could not speak, but she could, and that disturbed Raquel even more. It also made her wonder why the woman had intervened in the first place, when the Balamians were on the verge of killing them.

Had she not been standing in the midst of the rain forest, it would be easy to convince herself that being kidnapped, shanghaied and nearly sacrificed by a group of modern-day Mayans with ancient beliefs, was nothing but a bizarre dream. Now to be stuck with this person, was almost more than her overloaded psyche could endure.

Suddenly, along with the mounting squeal of several howler monkeys, the young woman let go a releasing yell, but because her sound was foreign, it caused the familiar forest clamor to come to an abrupt halt.

Raquel didn't feel the least bit embarrassed when the old woman stepped to the door of her hut and looked at her with blatant curiosity. As a matter of fact she felt somewhat satisfied that her crude therapy had drawn a reaction from her distant caretaker.

Minutes later, with nothing to do, she went back inside the hut to tend to Nate. She sponged down his hot face and neck with a dampened rag, dipped in a bowl of water made available for that purpose. His uncomfortable features tended to seek out the cool cloth, turning in the direction from which it came as he felt it make contact with his hot body.

His sensuous lips had become cracked, puffy masses because of the fever. Ever so tenderly, Raquel placed the damp cloth against them, hoping to ease their soreness.

She wondered what events in life had made this man of strong convictions take a path of crime. Somewhere deep inside her she felt it was all such a waste. Considering his demeanor and leadership abilities, he could have been anything he aspired to, but yet he had chosen a life that could eventually lead to prison.

Raquel lifted one of Nate's limp, warm hands into hers and began to study his strong fingers topped by amazingly well-kept, wide nails. She couldn't imagine his strength being contained behind iron bars, but more than that, it dawned on her, she couldn't imagine being the reason behind his incarceration.

Suddenly a strong urge to protect him surfaced inside her. The strength of it shocked Raquel as she looked down into his unconscious features. Small wrinkles creased his forehead as he turned uncomfortably. She reached out a gentle hand to smooth them away.

My God what was happening to her? Why should she care if he were imprisoned? It was crazy to worry about a man who had kidnapped her and placed her in such danger. Her whole life had been turned upside down because of him. If she made it back to the States, which was definitely uncertain at this time, she would have no home, and no job. And if she never made it back ...

Suddenly she realized how unwise her near-reclusive lifestyle had been, and how her adult life of separating herself from others mirrored her loner childhood. The only two people who had been close to her were her mother and Clinton Bradshaw. There was no one else who would really miss her.

Nate began to make small, silent motions with his parched lips, and Raquel wondered if he mouthed the name of a lover he'd left behind. Against her will the thought of it bothered her, and she had to admit she longed to know more about him, his childhood, his loves and dislikes.

Confused, her troubled gaze stared out into the kaleidoscopic rain forest, trying to discover her own feelings.

And what if he *didn't* survive. What would she do then? She'd be forced to find her way out of the forest, alone. But how would she do that with no knowledge of this country? Maybe she would eventually run into someone who would help her, or maybe Jay and Al would find her before she could ...

No. He would not die. I will make sure of that. I will personally make sure of it.

They had gone through so much together. Was that a sign they could possibly have a future despite their dire beginnings? Was there anything he could say or do that would make her accept him after all of this? Would he want to?

The onslaught of thoughts and emotions was nearly unbearable, so Raquel grabbed on to a more logical, clinical approach. Maybe the deep feelings she thought she was developing were simply a temporary reaction to the recent traumatic events. After all, for her, it was easier to sink into the comfort of loving feelings than confront the uncertain future she now faced. For there was one thing she did know—under extreme stress it was hard to calculate how a human being would react.

In the end it felt safest to look at their situation from a professional point of view. As a psychologist she had never come across a person as complex as this man, and naturally that would spark her interest to know more about him.

Raquel found a temporary comfort in her final conclusion, and she ignored the nagging gut feeling that told her it was not totally the truth.

The young woman reached for the wooden ladle lying on top of a large, pointed, clover-shaped leaf. She dipped it carefully into the broth. Patiently, she blew on its contents before administering it to the man before her. Droplets of green became caught in his mustache as she gently forced him to take in the liquid, afterwards wiping his mouth and chin as if he were an infant.

She readjusted the thin roll of cloth beneath his head and walked back outside. There she saw two porcupines eating contentedly in front of the shamaness's hut.

The image of a short-legged wildcat floated into her consciousness, and a nonverbal communication between him and her hostess ensued. She wondered if she'd dreamed it, but somehow the porcupines' presence insured her she had not. Plagued with loneliness, boredom and curiosity, Raquel walked past the undisturbed creatures and entered the doctor's home.

The even swishing of a jaguarundi's tail as he lay in a corner, proved to Raquel, that the encounter between the doctor and the animal had not been a dream. At first, she allowed the animal's piercing gaze to prevent her from entering, as did the somewhat cynical glance of the shamaness. Raquel's discomfort was obvious to her, yet she did not speak a word of welcome or motion for her to come inside.

A deluge of emotions ran through the young woman. Infantile feelings of wanting to shout at the crouching figure surfaced first. Would it be so awful to invite me in? This is ridiculous! Why did you bring us here anyway, if you really didn't want us here? Raquel could feel the muscles tightening in her face as her eyes narrowed in confrontation.

But it was the low growl of the wildcat that convinced her this would not be the route to take. The carnivorous sound made the hair stand up on the back of her neck and she thought, if this woman can communicate with the animals of the rain forest, what would she be able to do to me as well as Nate, who was virtually dependent upon her care?

So with a thrusting back of her shoulders, reliable logic won over emotion, and the young woman stepped further into the hut. Once again the overwhelming smell of animal remains mixed with various scents assaulted her, but this time she was determined to control her body's reaction.

A shallow woven basket filled with dried, crushed blossoms, caught Raquel's eye, so she sat cross-legged beside it, hoping their sweet fragrance dominated the space around them.

The jaguarundi released something akin to a purr, while a steady, smooth, grinding noise was being produced by the bush doctor as she ground a tiny pile of crushed green leaves into powder. She watched as the woman performed this task using a well-worn flat stone as the mortar, and another elongated rock served as a pestle.

As the young woman looked around, she began to wonder why this woman, who obviously lacked human companionship, had stored and prepared an untold number of liquids, powders and roots. Had the loneliness of the Belizean rain forest driven her to the brink of madness, as she felt she was being driven?

A nervous unbearable energy surged within Raquel as she realized, even though she had forced her presence upon her, her hostess had no intention of initiating communication between them. There was the possibility they could be there for countless days on end, and this woman would not have a need to act other than she was acting now. She was accustomed to not hearing the sound of a human voice, but Raquel was not, and to save her own sanity, she decided to do something about it.

"So . . . what are you preparing over there?"

A grayish yellow brow rose interrogatingly as the shamaness looked at the intent young woman, then returned silently to her work.

"Okay, so that's the way it's going to be," an unthwarted Raquel continued. "Well it really doesn't matter. You don't have to talk back. Just hearing the sound of my own voice feels like therapy enough. As a matter of fact it feels pretty good, and I'll just continue, if you don't mind?"

She spoke of her past job, her clients back in the States, and her practice of shaitsu and use of herbs. She spoke of her mother and her illness and her disappointment with Clinton Bradshaw. As time passed, it didn't matter that the old woman didn't participate in the conversation. Ironically, she thought of it as a visit to a psychologist like herself, but this time she was the patient, and the expressing of her thoughts and feelings began to have a cleansing effect.

She was careful not to speak of how she had come to Belize. Although, she really didn't know why. Not that she felt it would make a difference if this woman knew the man she was taking care of was part of a kidnapping ring. Living in the wild as the shamaness did, the laws and rules of society probably held little or no value in her eyes.

Time passed effortlessly, with the younger woman's continuous chatter. If her talking bothered the shamaness, she never expressed it, for in the midst of Raquel's talking, she had converted several small piles of herbs into medicinal powders, and stored them in dried, hollow guards.

Finally, feeling drained, Raquel decided to take her leave.

"Well, I guess that will be about all you can stand for one day. I can't promise this won't continue, at least until Nate is able to talk to me. How long do you think that will be?" she rambled on without expecting an answer. "Not that we've done that much talking in the past. But hopefully, soon he'll be well enough, and we can be on our way."

Raquel rose and dusted off the bottom of her wraparound skirt. She was surprised to glance down and see a papaya lying at her feet. It was rather strange. She didn't remember seeing the fruit when she initially took a seat on the ground.

"A papaya! Do you mind if I eat it?" Her wide, bright eyes searched out the elderly woman, but found only her back, cascaded with numerous dreadlocks. Then ancient eyes turned in her direction, examined her for a moment, and smoothly released her. Suddenly the thought appeared in her mind the shamaness had given her the succulent fruit. Astonished, she stared at the odd figure.

"Aw-aw . . . is this a gift for me?" she asked her reluctant hostess. But the shamaness simply turned away. Uniquely satisfied with the outcome of her visit Raquel left the hut to minister to Nate.

The following day mirrored the previous one with Raquel taking care of her recovering captor. Nate's fever had broken, but for some reason he slept continuously. It dawned on her, the brew she fed him probably contained a powerful, natural sedative.

Raquel gave a start as she saw the willowy figure of the bush doctor stooping near the fire—her entrances and exits were amazingly quiet, almost magical. She wondered about the woman's age, and how long she'd been living here, alone, in the middle of a Belizean rain forest.

She watched as the shamaness scraped what appeared to be a combination of finely chopped vegetables into the constantly boiling mixture, then she rose up and walked over to the young woman and man.

With nimble fingers she removed an old poultice that had been applied to Nate's leg the night before. She replaced it with several boiled leaves, still intact, that Raquel thought resembled wild burdock. Carefully she wrapped the pliable plants around the wound, then with her task completed, the bush doctor returned to her own hut.

Earlier that morning after finishing a breakfast of pineapple, banana and breadfruit, Raquel decided to visit with the distant shamaness, but to her dismay she found the hut empty. She was glad when the woman returned and she joined her in the space next door. This time she didn't take a seat on the dirt floor, but began a closer study of some of the objects, herbs and roots hanging profusely about. She was relieved to find the strong smell of the hut had little effect on her, and she marveled at how quickly the human body adjusted to its environment.

Her perusal was tentative at first, allowing the bush doctor to voice opposition if she chose, but as the moments passed and there was none, Raquel became more animated, calling out the name of herbs as she recognized them, though these were few and far in between. She imagined the number of herbs growing in Belize was astronomical, and that there must be many which even the most knowledgeable herbalists in the States had probably never heard of before.

For despite the emotional strain and circumstances under which she'd been forced to visit the country, its wild untapped beauty had not been lost upon her. It felt good to know the groping hands of civilization had not exploited, controlled or choked out the very essence of this country, as it had done to many others.

"And what in the world is this?" Raquel bent to touch a piece of bark that resembled the badly matted coat of a burnt red, shaggy dog.

"Don' touch that," the shamaness abruptly called out.

Raquel snatched her hand back as if she had been bitten.

"It ez gumbo-limbo. Your hand will burn an' blister if you touch it," the rough, accented voice of the bush doctor alerted her.

"Thanks for warning me," Raquel endeavored to keep a rousing satisfaction out of her voice.

"I see you have knowledge of the healin' plants," the raspy voice continued.

"Yes, I've worked with herbs. Still there are so many here I've never seen before. It's amazing. It must have taken you forever to gather all of them."

"Time for me ez of little importance, as it ez for you who live on the outside. Yet it was of the greates' importance for your man. Had he tended to the snakebite with the proper herbs when it first happened, the poison would not have had a chance to grab a strong hold on his body. But he did not and now he ez sufferin' 'cause of it," her liquidy eyes watched her. "But still, he ez young and strong, and it will not be long before you two mate again. I am aware of your anxiousness."

"Well, I—I," Raquel sputtered at the woman's directness. To say the least, it caught her off guard to go from having no communication at all with the woman to discussing such personal matters.

"Actually he is not—*my* man, so to speak."

Knowing dark eyes rose to the young woman's face. "Um-m," was her sole reply.

Now that the door of communication had been opened, Raquel refused to let it close again. "Do you think you could teach me about the herbs you have here and their uses?"

"Why?"

Startled again by her tactlessness, Raquel spoke the true answer. "Because I'd like to know more."

"There are many thin's that ordinary souls desire to delve in that are not the path for them to take."

"So are you saying I am ordinary or that you are extraordinary?" Raquel matched her insolence.

"Neither." The shamaness's thin frame lifted to its full height, but was still lacking because of her hunched back. "One must determine to be extraordinary if they choose to venture down the path."

"I didn't think that wanting to know more about herbs and their uses made me a wanderer down a particular path."

"It ez all a part of the whole. The healin' abilities of the plants cannot be separated from the spirit energy that created them. You must know the spirit in order to fully understand the healin'."

Once again, Raquel was impressed with the shamaness's wisdom, and her thoughts automatically centered on her own predicament.

"Tell me, what kind of people believe in the *gubida?*"

She tried to ask the question nonchalantly, attempting to draw attention away from her words by stepping up close to a mask of wood and fiber, examining it with great pretense.

"I do not mess in the affairs of others. That ez why I live as I do, so that my life can not be controlled by any group of people, or beliefs," the woman's voice was strong, resentful. With even steps she strode to the entrance of the hut, picked up a machete that lay nearby, then left without another word.

Raquel watched as the shamaness was swallowed up by the foliage of the rain forest. She reprimanded herself for being so impatient. Why couldn't she have waited awhile before she started asking questions about the customs and beliefs of the people in the woman's country? From her reaction there was no doubt she had hit a sore spot. It should have been obvious to her, there was a reason the shamaness had chosen to live alone. Now, at the moment when she had begun to open up and talk to her, she had pushed her too far. Raquel sincerely regretted her prying words, but she was only trying to seek help for herself.

"Get your lazy, stinkin' tail ovah t'ere and fix me some breakfas', but make sure you wash your hands before you do it," Jay roughly shoved his wife in the direction of the stove. "An' I don't want no more of those damn Johnny cakes. I want some fried feesh an' creole bread. Hurry up, too. I need to leave here by midday."

Eva shuffled toward the front door.

"Where you t'ink you goin'?" Jay demanded.

"I need to get some fresh feesh an' a few other thin's to cook wit'," she muttered.

"No, t'at's alright. I bought everything you need wit' me when I come in t'is mornin'." He looked at her suspiciously. "And the way you been lookin' at me, I don't trust you noway. You might try to put somet'in' in the food t'at'll make me sick," he stood menacingly close as he spoke. "So I'ma tell you right now, if anyting happens to me, today or next year, I'ma blame you. So rememba', if I don't die quick, you will go before me. You watch what I say," he clutched her pointed chin between his thumb and bent index finger, then pushed it back forcefully.

She caught her breath, inhaling the distinct smell of sweat, perfume and sex that still hung about him.

Minutes later, unchecked tears rolled down her dark face as she mixed bits of seafood and batter together to make the creole bread. Mucous ran from her wide nose, the result of her tears. Eva reached for a nearby cloth to wipe her face, then changed her mind. Using her open palm instead, she cleansed it, then immediately fashioned the chunky balls that would make the dough.

Jay gulped down the remainder of thick coffee and sat back after his meal, satisfied. He was glad Al had obviously drunk heavily the night before, for he had not budged from the pallet on which he slept. It would be easier this way, he and the men could leave without a scene.

He could hear Eva breathing as she sat on the edge of the bed with her back to him, and he wondered why she didn't eat the remainder of the creole bread as she usually did.

For a moment he slipped into the past when everything about Eva had once been smooth and round. Her cheeks, breasts, buttocks and calves, absolutely stimulating to see and touch. But all of that femininity had gone to waste because she wasn't able to bear him a child.

Ah! he thought. Why should he care if she ate at all? As long as she had the strength to cook his food, take care of his clothes and this house, it didn't matter if she ate.

A familiar feeling of resentment set in, and Eva's distorted unattractive features cast the older images aside. He deserved a better woman than Eva anyway. And when everything started rolling smoothly, he would have one.

* * *

The sun beamed high above when Jay joined the three other men inside the *buyei's* house. He was pleased with the selection of traveling partners the shaman had chosen.

"I plan to start the *dugu,* for Al in four days," the shaman's worn voice barely carried throughout the room. "The healing would be good if the woman could attend at its peak, her powers would be of great benefit. Either way, all of this must be settled before we go to Dangriga." His huge, tired eyes looked at each of the men as he continued. "The woman's presence with us will make the Shango that much more acceptable and powerful. When she is here, we will have time enough to convince her of our sincerity in wanting to reunite with the Garifuna, and she will understand why we have brought her to Punta Gorda." He sat quietly for a moment, then continued. "Already the scale is tilted in their direction, because the only *dabuyaba*—is housed on their land. Having her with us, will give us stature in their eyes." He drew a long breath. "Yes, scores must be settled, debts paid, but I am old now." His thin shoulders seem to droop with the admission. "The Shango must not be left without a *buyei.* We are the ones who must present ourselves humbly. Still it can not hurt to have the link already united with us. It would be a powerful sign."

Jay and the others nodded their agreement.

"Now go, my sons," he raised bent arms in release, "and let the spirit of the mighty *orisha,* Shango, be with you."

* * *

Consumed by thoughts of the shamaness, Raquel returned to the hut where she and Nate slept, and to a basket she was attempting to weave. She had given the man a mindful glance before turning to the container of slender reeds soaking in a dish of water. His eyes were closed, and there appeared to be no change in his condition.

The young woman scrutinized the irregularly shaped bottom that was to be the foundation of the basket. Slowly she began to shake her head. No one could ever have convinced her, that those basket-weaving classes during summer camp would come in handy one day. Yet here she sat, seeking solace in the task.

Hesitantly Raquel inserted the damp reed into what she hoped was the proper opening to begin her work again. Her smooth brows knitted together as her fingers tussled with the wrapping motions. A thick, black plait, she had twined at the crown of her head unraveled and landed on her bare shoulder as she worked, contrasting attractively with her copper skin, and the blood red color of the wrap she wore.

Earlier that day, it surprised her to find the roll of vibrant material beside her clothes when she emerged from bathing in a small nearby pool. Through experimentation and luck, she fashioned a combination African-like sarong from the folds. The soft linen felt good against her skin, and she wondered where the shamaness had bought it, for there was no evidence of a loom, and the material appeared to be quite new. She nearly laughed when she tried to picture the elderly woman sorting through piles of cloth choosing different patterns and colors for herself, when it was obvious from the nondescript robe she wore, and the way she had allowed her thick hair to naturally form into dreadlocks, such worldly things were not her concern.

Raquel looked down at the bright material, and she knew if she'd had her choice, red would not have been her preference. As a youth, her mother had always associated the color with sex, the devil and loose women. The latter term had included their next-door neighbor, Paulette, who loved red, and would allow Raquel to paint her nails in a variety of crimson shades, which sent her mother into a hissy fit every time. She recalled, there had been no love lost between the two women. Even on the day Paulette moved away from the neighborhood, the last words between them were ugly—her mother telling Paulette she was bound for hell. Paulette in turn dooming her mother to a life of pain and misery because of her "restrictin' nature."

Her mother's feelings about the color red had stuck with her, as had so many of her opinions and fears. You would not find anything red in Raquel's closet back in the States. It would be full of the proper clothing for a "professional" woman. Anything else would mean she was teetering too close to the edge, at least that's what she had always believed.

A pang of fear, anger, then regret, coursed through her. The chances of her having an apartment, let alone a closet of orderly clothes and shoes back in Miami was slim. They probably had been tossed out on the curb as she'd seen done before when a tenant was evicted for being delinquent.

A distraught, contempt-filled glance traveled in the direction of where her captor lay, and she was more than surprised when it was met by an unwavering stare, a fully cognizant gaze.

"Well, hello there." She placed the unfinished basket onto the dirt floor, then crossed the room to kneel beside Nate. Her depressing thoughts were quickly supplanted by relief to see him conscious for the first time since their arrival.

"Hello." The word was raspy, as his veiled eyes turned from the woman and looked around the hut.

"Where are we?"

It was difficult for him to speak, his voice was softer, strained, like a person finding out they could speak after a bout with laryngitis.

"You tell me," she offered him a sincere smile, then pivoted to dip a cup in a pail of cool water. "I've been here weaving baskets and studying herbs, while you decided to cop out and take a long, long nap."

Dark, inquisitive eyes searched her face. He was about to speak again, but she pressed the moist cup, with a hollow reed in its midst, in his direction. Automatically he attempted to rise to his elbows, but was overtaken by a dizzy spell. His chin slumped to his chest.

"Be careful," Raquel placed her slender arms about his shoulders, "You've been out of it for about two days. You have to be rather weak."

She didn't know why she wanted to comfort him, to make his awareness of his weakened condition more palatable, but somehow she felt it would not sit well with him to realize how bad off he had been.

Nate shook his head defiantly. He was unaccustomed to being pampered and catered to in this way, and he found his dependent state most annoying. With trembling lips he sought out the makeshift straw she offered him, quenching his dry throat, and stealing a moment to gather his strength. Feeling uncomfortable under her velvety compassionate gaze, he spoke roughly to her.

"And I guess I'm supposed to believe you hung around the entire time just to take care of me?" Cynicism edged the ungrateful question.

Nate knew he was being unfair, but it was shame that made him act this way. Contending with his weak physical condition was one thing, but to think, this woman whom he had kidnapped and forced to come to Belize, had stayed by his side, caring for him throughout the ordeal—that struck a sound blow.

Guilt and remorse churned inside him—they were feelings he had not experienced since childhood. It was all so foreign to him now, totally unsettling. It was as if a knife had cut into his armor and he felt weak and vulnerable as a result of it. Weakness was something he could not tolerate, and if this woman could bring out that side of him, he wanted nothing to do with her.

Raquel sat back on her haunches. "What if I say I did?"

"I'd say you were a fool, or worse."

Her eyes narrowed in anger. "Well I'll just be damned! And I'd say you were right!" She struggled to rise to her feet, but the cumbersome wrap prohibited a quick ascent.

Hastily Nate placed a solid but weak grip about her wrist.

"No, I'm sorry, *pataki*. Please, don't go," the words tumbled out before he could stop them.

Their eyes met for a moment before he closed his, then lay back inhaling deeply. His words were almost a whisper when he spoke. "I want to thank you." The message in his dark gaze as he looked at her again, was clear.

Raquel's shoulders slumped in resignation. She was tired of being on the defensive, tired of swimming against the current that had totally disrupted her life. Theirs was a most curious relationship. It would be almost comical if it weren't so intense.

She kept her eyes lowered as her mind filtered through her confusing thoughts, her small but able hands lay within each other in her lap. Maybe she could have left him with the shamaness and tried to find her way to civilization and freedom. But something wouldn't allow her to forget how he had never deserted her, and no matter how they had come together, she could not have left him at his weakest.

"Pataki." His long fingers, thinner than before, reached up to caress the side of her face, "Why couldn't things have been different?"

His simple words melted away the small amount of restraint she had managed to hold onto, and her smooth, petite hand reached up to cradle his. Moistness appeared in both sets of eyes, but Raquel's spilt over, dampening his hand as it remained there.

"I don't know why, Nate. I don't know why."

She mouthed the statement over and over again, crying out her anguish at the unfairness of life in presenting her with a man she knew she could love, but who was ultimately her enemy. The young woman turned her tear-stained face and lips further into his receptive palm.

Gradually, Nate allowed his hand to slide around to the back of her neck where he gently drew her down toward him, until he cradled her in his arms, mouthing terms of assurance and support—tender things that his mother had said to him when he was a child.

He turned and placed a kiss in the cluster of cottony, black curls that had formed around her hairline, then drew her in closer to his body, until he could feel her damp cheeks and nose pressed against his neck. She felt so small and soft against him, and he worried that she'd lost weight since the day she'd sat so defiantly on board the sailboat, the wind pressing against her face. All of that seemed so long ago.

Raquel found it was hard to breathe with her face buried so close against him, but it was oh, so comforting. Here within her captor's embrace she felt safe, even cared for. Here she didn't want or need to analyze her feelings, her thoughts, only to give in to them, for never had she experienced such an intensity of emotions.

Somehow they both knew they were crossing over into uncharted waters as they lay within each other's arms. Neither of them was willing or ready to tell the other the truth about themselves, but both were unable to ignore feelings that had developed between them. At the moment those things did not matter; for right now this was enough.

Chapter Eleven

It was barely dawn when the cry of a young animal woke Raquel. Heavy-lidded eyes forced themselves open because of the nagging noise. Outside, the sun was painting breathtaking strokes of gold, orange and rose across the sky. Carefully she slipped out of Nate's sleeping embrace, and ventured into the cool morning air. As she stretched outside the hut, feeling more alive and happy than she could ever remember, the long whining sound began again, and Raquel realized it was coming from inside the shamaness's hut.

With her features clouded over with concern, Raquel quickly entered the space, fearing it was the old woman, in pain or worse, dying. To Raquel's surprise she discovered the shamaness was not alone. Another woman, kneeling against a tree stump that served as a table, was with her, and she in turn held on to the object which was the source of the noise. It was a baby.

No sooner had the crying stopped, than it started again, as the shamaness took a large gathering of fresh herbs and swept them just above the young child's body in cleansing motions.

If the two women were aware of Raquel's presence, they gave no indication of it. The mother's eyes remained riveted upon her squalling child as the shamaness executed several more thrusting motions with the plants, accompanied by words Raquel did not understand.

Had Raquel been thinking clearly, she would have left once she came across this obviously private affair, but the entire scene caught her off guard. It was like watching the enactment of a story Paulette once told her involving an illness and a powerful cleansing. More than once she spoke of almost unbelievable spells and cures she attributed to the *orishas* or gods of a religion called *Santeria*. Raquel had been warned never to repeat these stories to anyone, and she hadn't.

Now that the ritual was complete, two sets of eyes turned in Raquel's direction. The mother holding the now-cooing baby, examined her with avid curiosity, while the shamaness's stare was almost piercing.

"Oh. I'm—I'm sorry. I didn't mean to interrupt anything. I just heard the baby crying and I didn't know . . . I'll just go back—" she nervously turned to leave.

The shamaness's voice halted her. "No. Wait."

Startled, Raquel stopped dead in her tracks.

Hearing the woman's command for Raquel to stay, the grateful mother spoke rapidly, bowing her thanks for the shamaness's help. Agilely she bent down and picked up a small basket covered with a white cloth. She offered the package to the older woman as she revealed its contents, a selection of colorful bird feathers.

Never once offering a smile, the doctor stoically accepted the basket from the beaming mother; and yet her distant attitude did not seem to bother the woman. Instead, shyly but with apparent admiration and a touch of awe, she looked into her stony features as if she wouldn't dare expect more from such a powerful person. Then, her eyes bright with joy and relief, she briskly walked from the hut and joined two other women Raquel hadn't noticed sitting in the rain forest at the edge of the clearing. Chattering like eager birds, they pointed excited fingers in the direction of the hut.

"You are ready to learn more about the 'erbs?" the shamaness addressed her. It was more of a statement than a question.

"Yes. I am if you are ready to teach me."

"What wisdom would there be in discussin' it if I were not ready?" she retorted, as she bundled up the ritual herbs that she intended to discard.

The woman's change of heart toward teaching Raquel was unexpected. She didn't know if she should be grateful or apprehensive.

"None, I guess," she remained rooted to the spot near the hut's entrance.

"Do you expect me to teach you from there?" her dreadlocked head tilted to the side, as she placed bony fingers on hips totally hidden underneath her clothes.

"No of course not. It's just that I need time to get ready."

A perturbed, mostly grey eyebrow rose to show the bush doctor's impatience with her would-be student, forcing the young woman to explain.

"Nate . . . the man I came here with, became conscious for a while yesterday evening, and I'd like to check on him this morning before we get started."

Without addressing her further, the shamaness

crossed the room and exited the hut. Raquel didn't
know if she had offended her again, so she sought to appease her. "I mean, I will do it that way if its all right
with you." She followed her, surprised she was headed
for the second hut.

"You should have told me when he awakened," she
rebuked her. "His broth mus' change now so that he
can quickly regain his strength."

"Well everything happened so fast I didn't have time
to think about it." Somehow the woman made her feel
like a careless child.

The shamaness swept into the hut with her pendulous
dreads reaching out about her, like antennas tuned to
receive the vast messages of the universe. She was not
pretty to behold. Actually she was a forceful sight, and
this caused a wide-awake Nate to question his lucidity.
He had no memory of the aid the woman had given
them, and was more than a little relieved to see Raquel
in her wake. Her presence assured him that he had not
crossed over to the other side while he slept, that he still
resided in the land of the living.

"You have been your own wors' enemy, man. Not
takin' care of that snakebite when it first happened. The
forces mus' be with you, a weaker person would have
died. Of course, I did not tell your woman that." She
jerked her head in Raquel's direction.

Raquel was forced to hide an amused smile behind
her hand at the absurd, confused look that appeared on
Nate's face. He looked in her direction as if asking for
reassurance, all she could give him was a comical
hunching of her small shoulders.

"A combination of beans and my special 'erbs should
get you started." The shamaness raised his pants leg and

checked the punctures, then shook her head with satisfaction. "That ez after you've drank plenty of the juices I will give to you."

Raquel just stood there looking rather dimwitted. She didn't know what to think of this talkative creature who had replaced the silent bush doctor of the last few days.

With uncharacteristic strength for her age, the shamaness removed the hot pot from the makeshift rack above the fire.

"Give it a few moments to cool, then throw the broth out into the forest, afterwards take it to the pond an' rinse it thoroughly, by then I will be ready to start the beans. Then you," looking directly at Raquel, "will be ready for your lessons."

A shroud of roped hair framed her angular face as she turned back to Nate, "Two days with my medicines an' you will be strong enough to travel, that ez if you don't use up too much of your strength on other things," she announced insinuatingly as she rose to depart, leaving Nate and Raquel stunned and amused by her last remark.

"After seeing her, I'm sure I have missed quite a bit over the last few days," he shook his head with disbelief, a half-baked smile on his face. "So you've got to fill me in whenever you get a chance, that is, between the chores you've been assigned and your other duties that have been heaped on you by your great and powerful master," he broke into uncontrollable laughter.

A picture of the dreaded, hump-backed shamaness pointing a bony finger and ordering the docile and obedient young woman around, replayed in his head. This was the same woman who had almost fought him every step of the way since he met her, even though he had to admit, she had reasons for wanting to go against him.

At first Raquel assumed it was the stress and strain, and powerful herbs he'd been forced to take, that had finally taken their toll on him. She had never seen this man truly smile before, let alone laugh, and somehow she didn't feel comfortable thinking that she was the prime target of his glee.

"What's so funny?" She attempted to keep a straight face, but it was all in vain, for his laughter was contagious. Before she knew it, she had joined in with the raucous noise, flopping down on the hut's dirt floor and laughing until tears ran down her cheeks.

Neither one of them really knew what was so funny. If they laughed at themselves for being in such an extraordinary situation, or at the outlandish statement the bush doctor made before she left.

Their unabandoned outbreak seemed to excite the animals in the rain forest as well, and their chatter and cooing swelled with the continuous laughter inside the hut.

Doubled over with hysterics, Nate stretched a frolicsome arm out and caught hold of Raquel's ankle. His touch sent tingles up her leg, and she playfully kicked at his hand so he would release her. They continued to laugh, both of them lost in a moment of complete camaraderie. It was marvelous to behold the twinkle of joy in the other's eyes, the sound of the other's laughter unknowingly becoming a treasured jewel.

Even in his semiweakened condition, Nate proved to be the stronger as he lay on his stomach supported by his elbows, holding tightly to both Raquel's feet. Still she resisted him, her knees pumping mechanically, while she attempted to pull down her wrap which was inching up because of her thrashing movements.

Suddenly two pairs of glistening, velvety dark eyes met and they stopped their childlike play, panting and catching their breath in the aftermath. In an instant an atmosphere of lighthearted laughter had turned into a communication of electrically charged passion, and a barrage of emotions surfaced in their eyes as they watched one another closely.

Nate's light grip on her ankles was doing strange things to her breathing, and Raquel could feel her heart begin to flutter.

"Pataki—"

Afraid of what he was about to say, as well as of her own response, Raquel cut him off. "I think the broth may have cooled a little by now," she looked for an inconsequential plug for the awkward moment. Gently she extracted her legs from his hold, he, in turn, did not resist her.

Although the pot still steamed, she found two large cloths to shield her hands and aid her in the removal of the metal container. She had to do something. Anything. The feelings that had arisen inside her as she looked in his eyes were powerful, more powerful than her ability to refuse him, more powerful than her ability to refuse herself.

Silently, Nate watched her movements with veiled eyes as she carefully walked to the entrance with her load.

"Pataki," the name was thick with passion.

"Yes," she barely recognized her own voice. It trembled with a tingling fear, a heightened anticipation. Feathery lashes raised to view the man who sat behind her on the dirt floor. Cordlike tendons within his firm arms stretched to their limits as he balanced himself, his fists, large balls in the dust, his knees spread evenly apart.

"You must give in to me willingly, . . . or not at all."

She nodded her head before walking through the opening.

Nate eased himself down onto his side. He could tell he was far from being his normal self, but from what he could remember, he felt much better than the day before.

Nate thought about the amount of time they'd lost, nearly four days. If his calculations were right, it would be about three days before they held the main ceremony in Dangriga. Initially he had planned to get there well ahead of the festivities, but it was far too late for that now. He would have to work within the time frame they had, hopefully nothing else would hamper their progress. Involuntarily his thoughts switched to Jay and Al.

It was obvious by now, Jay had a hidden agenda outside of wanting to have the woman present for the spiritual ceremony. Nate only wished he knew what it was. Yet there was one thing he did know. If he was right about Jay, it wouldn't be long before he would come looking for her, and he wouldn't come alone.

Nate's pulse quickened as his mind digressed to the feel of Raquel's slender ankles within his grip. They were tiny and feminine, like her smooth feet beneath them. He wanted this woman in a way he had never wanted anyone else. If he could make her come to him willingly, he knew that he could truly possess her, and it was so very important to him that he did.

It had taken him years to feel as if he really controlled his life, his environment. That's why it angered him so that he could not have foreseen all the things that had taken place since they reached Belize.

For years his family ties had made it hard for him to be in control of his own life, and now that he possessed control, he would never relinquish that power to anyone.

Nate remembered an awful time when he had felt totally helpless. Life's tragedies had poured their fury upon him, leaving him stunned and confused. Death is never an easy pill to swallow. It is doubly hard when it takes people you love, like Cecilia . . . and his mother.

Ever since he was a little boy, she had always taught him to have faith in the powers, allow them to mold his life, they would not guide him wrong. In the end, both Cecilia and his mother had died, a result of his people's faith. Their deaths did not destroy his belief, but they forced him to understand he must always have control of his own life, that way, the choices and their consequences would be of his own making.

That is why his feelings for this woman vexed him so. They had surfaced unexpectedly, an overpowering need to love her, protect her.

Nate knew he was an excellent judge of character, but if he went by what he'd gleaned since she'd been forced into his life, he would consider her a good woman. A strong one. The kind that he seldom came across in the circles he chose to travel in, and when he did he shied away from them. With his lifestyle, he'd found they were a hindrance and managed to complicate things. No. He preferred women with whom he knew where he stood. And all that was important to them was compensation in one way or another. That way there were never any strings attached, for he had learned the hard way, if you could love, you could also be hurt.

He wasn't so sure about this woman. But in the beginning he thought he knew what kind of woman she was. That she lived life in the fast lane, and that meant she carried all the baggage that came with it. Men. Alcohol. Drugs. Maybe the telltale signs had been stripped away here in the wilderness, but they would probably surface overnight when she was back in environment, he cautioned himself. Yes. She was doing what she had to do to survive, like a chameleon, adapting to her environment. Still, he had to admit, she was doing a damn good job of it. But he convinced himself, staying by his side and taking care of him was all a part of her game, a masterful con. That way, when he came to, he'd be beholding to her.

Nate rubbed the new growth on his face as he gathered his thoughts. The reality was, she could not have found her way out of the rain forest without help. Even if she had tried, her chance of finding someone who would really help her was very slim. Strange things had been known to happen in Central America. Women being sold into slavery was simply one of them. No, she'd played it safe, and he'd played right into her manipulative hands. Sure he was weak for her, and any man near death could have a change of heart. He would just have to remember who she was.

Purposefully he pushed away the nagging uncertainties about the woman. But one thing would still hold true—he would still have her on his terms. Then when they reached Dangriga their unholy alliance would come to an end.

He gathered himself together to try and stand. He had to start exercising, regaining his strength so they could leave tomorrow.

Slowly he rose to his full height, clasping his hand over his eyes as a lightheadedness overtook him. His left leg, adorned with the remnants of the bite and a dark poisonous streak was weakest, but he forced it to hold its own. He hobbled around the interior of the hut, grasping hold of convenient supports along the way. A pile of vibrant floral material caught his eye—it was the wrap skirt he'd acquired for the woman in the Mayan village. Immediately strong stirrings erupted inside him.

"Dammit! I'll have her tonight. Then this *obedah* will be out of my system. That's what I need to do," he tried to convince himself. "After that I'll be just fine," but a small voice inside of him wasn't so sure.

Raquel's hamstrings felt tight from all the squatting, as she tried to concentrate on the flowering plant the shamaness now insisted that she focus upon. Hours had passed since they'd entered the forest and the old woman began pouring out her knowledge of plants and herbs, their hazards and their positive qualities. Raquel could not figure out how the woman expected she would remember even one fourth of the things she'd been told. Even if she'd had a photographic memory, it would have been impossible.

Yellow pollen covered the tips of the shamaness's forefinger and thumb as she plucked the daisylike, tiny, white blossom with yellow interior from its downy stem. It was pleasantly aromatic with yellowish-green leaves.

"This plant's name tells of its main purpose, feverfew. It can break a fever." Her liquidy, heavily hooded eyes locked with Raquel's. "It was one of the 'erbs I mixed into your tea the first night, it ez also good to help calm a person, help them focus."

Raquel shook her weary head in understanding.

Briskly the shamaness stood up and made her way further along into the rain forest. Stooping again, she called to the young woman. "Here ez a very powerful 'erb," a gravelly chuckle rose in her throat. Raquel stood above her gazing down at the profuse, dotted leaf plants.

Impatiently the shamaness motioned for her to come closer.

"Smell."

Obeying her instruction, Raquel bent over stiffly, and inhaled the scent of the small leaves. She nearly choked from the unpleasant odor.

"It ez St. Juan's wort," the elderly woman informed her, satisfied that she would not forget its potent aroma. "It flowers yellow in the summer, and both its flowers and leaves can be made to give a red oil. It ez good for many thin's from stomach pains to asthma. But it can also bring on wonderful feelin's, if taken in larger amounts."

Raquel continued to hold the back of her hand against her nose, then allowed it to travele up to her eyes, where she gratefully closed them.

"I'm really thankful for all the things you've been telling me, but I'm so tired. Do you think we could do the remainder of this tomorrow?"

"I do not think you can afford to be tired."

With furrowed brows Raquel looked at her, confused.
"What do you mean?"

"You will need much knowledge to fool the Garifuna
an' the Shango, or the *gubida* will not come through
you."

Raquel stood stunned at the woman's words. Why
would the *gubida* come through *her?* What was she in
Belize for? What was going to happen to her? Questions
raced through her mind, as her knees buckled and she
almost sat down in the midst of the St. John's wort.

"What do you mean?"

"You are not Garifuna or Shango," the shamaness
barked at her. "If you are to be in the ceremony, there
is much you must know."

Raquel felt the hairs stand up on her arms as she took
in the eerie vision of the shamaness who remained on
her haunches beside her.

It was late afternoon, and the setting sun's dying rays
emanated brightly behind her powerful countenance.
Several thick dreads that grew from the top of her head,
appeared to be alive with energy, as dazzling hues of
gold, orange and red sparkled about them.

How could this woman have known why she was
here in Belize? Did her powers go beyond her knowledge of herbs and roots, into realms that Raquel had
been reluctant to even acknowledge? She had mentioned the *gubida* only once, and that conversation had
ended in vain. Never had she spoken of the Garifuna
and the Shango, yet the shamaness knew her very safety
depended on her assumed connection with these groups.

"I—I never said I was," Raquel stammered, feeling it
was useless to deny the truth.

"You know many believe you are," she squinted her

ancient eyes perceptively, "if they did not, you would not be here, or . . . you would be dead."

The grave truth of her statement made Raquel acknowledge a fear that she'd lived with since the beginning of this nightmare. If it were ever found out that she was not Jackie Dawson, her life would not be worth a penny.

Immense anxiety began to rise inside her as she thought of Jay and Al, a more poignant shudder shook her as she thought of Nate.

"But how did you know about this?"

"I may live alone here in the forest, but there ez little I don't know. Villagers like the women you saw this morning come to me for 'elp when they feel there ez no one else they can turn to. It ez at those times I am told many thin's," she licked her leathery lips. "She told me of a woman, a descendant of the Garifuna an' the Shango, a connection with the *gubida*, ez expected to attend the settlement ceremony in Dangriga. It ez a very important time. It will mean the bringing together of the Garifuna an' the Shango. A rift tore the groups apart many years ago.

"The diviners of both sides say the signs show this woman can speak to the dead ancestors of both the Garifuna an' the Shango. There must be communication between the ancestors, before there can be communication between the livin'. This ez what they believe."

The shamaness plucked two tender leaves from a group of St. Juan's wort, carefully she placed one upon her thick tongue, the other she offered to Raquel. Stunned, the young woman accepted the piece of plant, then mimicked the woman's actions.

"These are secret rituals. It ez taboo for outsiders to

know about them. Never are they involved. It would be dangerous for them to do so." Intently her old eyes watched as Raquel's frightened ones expanded as she listened. A strange smirk appeared amongst her wrinkles, as if she were drawing pleasure from the young woman's fear.

"Not because the Garifuna or the Shango would 'arm them, even though there may be some with powers who would place what ez called as *bilongos*, black magic spell, on the outsider. The real danger may come from the *orishas* for dabbling in their affairs. But if an outsider were to pretend to be one of the Garifuna or Shango, there would no doubt be those among the groups who would want to 'arm them."

Raquel swallowed visibly after the threat. The bitter taste of the herb was strong but seemed to have a rejuvenating effect upon the shattered woman.

Angry thoughts stormed through her mind as she thought about her unsavory position. She had not asked for any of this. There was nothing for her to gain. But here she sat in the middle of a Central American rain forest, staring into the face of a woman who spoke poignantly about her pending death. Defensively, Raquel struck back at her.

"So why are you telling me all this? You know I am not this person that they think I am, so why didn't you just tell them and get it over with?"

A spark of amusement appeared in the greying eyes.

"Because it would please me to play a part in foolin' those who did not want to acknowledge my power, simply because I am a woman."

Several brown nubs where teeth used to be appeared

as she skinned her lips back in what was supposed to be a smile, then her gaze took on a distant look.

"Yes, they all knew I had the abilities an' the knowledge, but they refused to accept me as a shaman, because I was female," she continued.

"I grew up in a small settlement between Dangriga an' Punta Gorda. Most of the people who lived there were Shango, although there was a Mayan village not very far away, so there was much mingling between them. That is why I am a mixture of Shango an' Mayan," she proudly stated. "I was a curious child, an' had been allowed to attend a small school for all of the children in the area. Because of my seekin' nature, the teacher, an Englishwoman, who had settled here with her husband, an archeologist, would send for special books for me to read. I became very knowledgeable about many thin's, but I also burned to know more about my people an' their beliefs, so I sought this knowledge any way I could. For years it did not matter, but as time went by and I matured, my Mayan father felt the time had come for me to wed one of the villagers. He felt I was becomin' too independent in my thinkin', and I was. I did not want to marry the villager he had chosen or any other man," she defiantly declared.

"The wisdom I had gained through the years surpassed any of the males in the village, even the *buyei*, an' I told them so. I told them none of the men were worthy of me, an' that I should be *buyei* of the village. Had I been of Garifunian descent this may not have been a problem, even though my arrogance must have roused them deeply. But being of Mayan and Shango ancestry, it was unthinkable. It ez important to the Shango that the *buyei* be male because they are named for the powerful and violent *orisha*, Shango, who ez the perfect symbol of the male sex.

"After that they tried to force my hand, but I ran away an' retreated far into the rain forest, to the place where I live now.

"Through the years my wisdom an' therefor' my power has grown. With time, there were incidents that spawned rumors of my abilities, frightening stories," her eyes gleamed wickedly. "Since then no one has dared to cross me, only those seekin' my help venture near to my home."

"So that is why the Balamians were afraid to attack you?"

"That ez why," she nodded gravely, then a compulsive glimmer entered her gaze. "But through you I can seek my revenge. The ultimate shame would be for an outsider to take part in their secret rituals, and by powers acquired through me, deceive them."

"So that's it," Raquel rose on to her knees. "You want to use me." Her anger and frustration mounted as she glared at her. "Just two weeks ago, if I hadn't agreed to being used by someone else, I wouldn't even be in the mess I'm in now. Once is enough. Thank you. After all of this, if I survive, maybe I will have learned my lesson."

"Ump . . . maybe. But there ez no other way for you to get through this without being discovered. I want to use you, but you need me in order to survive." The shamaness rose to her feet. "You are a very open spirit. What I want to do would be impossible if you were not," she eyed her appreciatively. "Word ez, a group of Shango men are headed this way, lookin' for a man and a woman. The woman ez the link to the *gubida*," the shamaness announced. "It will take them another day or so before they reach this area. You would do well to use this time wisely," she warned, then continued. "Let me pour the needed knowledge into your mind an' spirit. I swear it will not 'arm you. In the end, it will only aid you in the spiritual evolution that all human beings must go through."

Raquel looked at the strange woman who stood before her. She had called her an open spirit. The words struck a deep cord within her. Even as a child she had sought refuge in quiet moments alone. In her desire to escape her restricted environment her ability to open herself to her imagination had become acute.

Raquel couldn't help but think of how throughout her life, she had been plagued by the consequences of her mother's past. The lines and perimeters had been drawn early. Without a male in their house, and because of her mother's fervent religious beliefs, she had grown up under stringent rules. There had been rules and times for everything, and the system of rules could never be broken without dire consequences. Every good and evil deed one committed was being recorded, but her mother eagerly informed her, it would take many good acts to lessen the effect of just one sinister deed, and to her mother the simplest of mistakes was considered signs of wickedness.

Lucille Mason could see wickedness everywhere. She saw wickedness in the outside world and insisted Raquel remain within the walls of their home where it was safe. She changed her name from Mercenez, a constant reminder of Raquel's father's wickedness. Raquel would never forget how Lucy saw wickedness in a fatherly hug Raquel received from a fellow church member and loudly banished Mr. Harrison from their household.

In order to understand her mother's obsessiveness, Raquel decided to become a counselor and so that one day she would be able to help other people understand themselves.

She watched as her mother became more withdrawn and judgmental through the years, obviously fearing her daughter's march toward adulthood, and her inevitable leaving. Constantly, she cast taboos and roadblocks into her young fertile mind about many things, but especially when it came to the opposite sex, not knowing the long-term effects they would eventually have.

She knew it was bizarre to think, but somehow, at first she felt her mother was almost relieved to hear she had developed multiple sclerosis. It was something else to permanently bind her daughter to her side.

"You won't be able to leave me now," she had pleaded, eyes brimming with tears, but not a trace of sorrow in their depths. "It was because of my love and concern for you that I remained here, instead of following your father to the Dominican, where I could have been happy." Then she pointedly asked, "You won't leave me, will you, Raquel?"

Of course, every time her answer was no.

Now she believed it was her strong unyielding stance, demanding her mother be allowed to live with her and Clinton when they got married, that had put a strain on the relationship. Yet, there was another disturbing reason. She realized, her mother, spoon-feeding her negativity towards men throughout the years had been very fruitful.

It had taken years before Clinton had been able to coax her into making love, but then, the few times they had, it had been extremely unfulfilling for her, and undoubtedly for him. During their last words on the telephone, he had called her "cold and ungiving." It had hurt badly, but deep inside, Raquel felt his painful words were not true.

She knew there were times when consuming waves of emotions would rake through her. Like at the sight of a couple in a heated, mounting embrace in a movie, or while reading a romance novel, and now, at the touch or even a glance from Nate.

A sudden panic enveloped her. What if Clinton were right? What if her mother's teachings had helped to mold her into a woman who was simply unable to really give of herself? That she was able to feel at a distance, but when the moment of truth arrived she would completely shut down. A woman like that could never satisfy and hold Nate. He would only desire someone whose passion was as fiery as his own.

Now, once again, she faced being a pawn to someone else's past. But this was different, she thought, as she stared into the foreign, weathered face that watched her closely. The bush doctor's revenge on her past could be Raquel's ticket to life.

"What must I do in order to receive this knowledge?"

"I must make your mind an' spirit willin' to accept it. As you know, we don't have much time, but through your open spirit and the use of 'erbs, mainly the blue passion flower, I can mold them to what we both need."

The young woman's face was a concentrated mask

when she gave her answer. "Then let's do it quickly, before I change my mind."

Dusk was fast approaching when Nate looked out the hut's entrance for the umpteenth time. He couldn't understand what the woman and the shamaness could be doing in the forest for so long. It worried him a bit, but he felt if anyone knew these parts the shamaness did. So he would just have to wait patiently until their return.

The bean soup she'd prepared for him had become ready much earlier during the day, and he'd eaten most of the tasty concoction. Some of the seasonings were familiar, bringing up memories of when his family resided in Dangriga. But other tastes were odd—still it all comprised a unique blend.

As the day wore on, and he felt his strength returning, he became anxious for something to do. As he looked around, one of several pieces of wood he discovered during a walk around the clearing caught his eye. Picking it up, he turned it over in his hands, exploring the grainy surface. It was a beautiful chunk of dead cypress, and Nate thought it was large enough for him to carve a simple drumlike box, but he would need some kind of tool to do it. Because he had explored the hut thoroughly, he knew there was nothing here that could serve his purpose, so he decided to look in the shamaness's shanty.

It was Nate's first conscious visit inside the hut, and the variety and number of objects he saw amazed him. Slowly, his dark eyes began a perusal of the room. He was inside the cluttered space only a few moments, when his curious examination was cut short by the menacing growl of a lounging jaguarundi. Caught off guard by the animal's presence, he grabbed a nearly rusted knife. He quickly backed out with his carving tool in hand.

It took some time before the dull knife was sharp enough for carving. Being a perfectionist at heart, he attempted to remove all the rust on its surface against a flat stone. He had carved a lot as a boy, and he knew the edge had to be just so before the blade would render its best work. Finally he was ready to begin, and after removing the bark, he placed all his creative concentration on the light-colored wood. Time passed effortlessly as he worked, and before long the instrument was almost complete.

With proficient eyes, Nate checked to make sure the sides and the bottom of the hollow box fitted together smoothly before he began to place a carved top into place. He had cut different designs into the flat piece of wood, most of them long and slender, some with bulbous ends, others with prongs that stretched outward like fingers. The wood that remained, when struck, would yield a range of deep melodious plucking sounds, characteristic of a highly tuned bongo.

Satisfied the box was snug, he snapped the instrument's lid into place, then ran practiced fingers across its surface and sides. Using a rod he fashioned specifically for this purpose, he struck several of the prongs, and they yielded a lavish range of sounds. Yes, he thought, in such a short period of time he'd done well.

Settling with his back against the wall and the bongo box in his lap, he struck the prongs again, making himself familiar with each sound. It wasn't long before he began to beat out the rhythm of a familiar tune, while he waited for the women to return.

Chapter Twelve

Raquel stared at the beautiful flower sheltered underneath the thick cover of a healthy fern. Large yellowish petals, with a vibrant center of bluish-violet spikes, were crowned by pistils and stamens of equally complementary hues. Yet, what amazed her most, was the orangy fruit that had grown in the midst of its picturesque center.

"This ez what you shall eat," and the shamaness bent down and extracted the fruit from its home. "It ez very sweet an' delicious, an' will shield the bitter taste of the St. Juan's wort that you must also ingest." The elderly woman surveyed the area around them. "It ez good this passion flower has grown so close to the pond, for the water will aid me in what I must do."

Raquel looked out onto the tranquil water where the moon reflected luminously against its surface. Calmly she sat down beside its shore, and held the fruit that had been broken open by the bush doctor's withered hands. Determinedly she took a healthy bite from its center.

* * *

We've got your authors!

If you seek out the latest historical romances by today's bestselling authors, our new reader's service, KENSINGTON CHOICE, is the club for you.

KENSINGTON CHOICE is the only club where you can find authors like Janelle Taylor, Shannon Drake, Rosanne Bittner, Sylvie Sommerfield, Penelope Neri and Phoebe Conn all in one place...

...and the only service that will deliver their romances direct to your home as soon as they are published—even before they reach the bookstores.

KENSINGTON CHOICE is also the only service that will give you a substantial guaranteed discount off the publisher's prices on every one of those romances.

That's right: Every month, the Editors at Zebra and Pinnacle select four of the newest novels by our bestselling authors and rush them straight to you, even *before they reach the bookstores*. The publisher's prices for these romances range from $4.99 to $5.99—but they are always yours for the guaranteed low price of just *$3.95!*

That means you'll always save over $1.00...often as much as *$2.00*...off the publisher's prices on every new novel you get from KENSINGTON CHOICE!

All books are sent on a 10-day free examination basis, and there is no minimum number of books to buy. (A postage and handling charge of $1.50 is added to each shipment.)

As your introduction to the convenience and value of this new service, we invite you to accept

4 BOOKS FREE

The 4 books, worth up to $23.96, are our welcoming gift. You pay only $1 to help cover postage and handling.

To start your subscription to KENSINGTON CHOICE and receive your introductory package of 4 FREE romances, detach and mail the postpaid card at right *today*.

We have 4 FREE BOOKS for you as your introduction to KENSINGTON CHOICE

To get your FREE BOOKS, worth up to $23.96, mail card below.

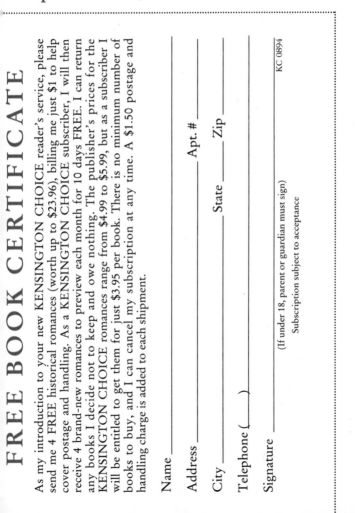

FREE BOOK CERTIFICATE

As my introduction to your new KENSINGTON CHOICE reader's service, please send me 4 FREE historical romances (worth up to $23.96), billing me just $1 to help cover postage and handling. As a KENSINGTON CHOICE subscriber, I will then receive 4 brand-new romances to preview each month for 10 days FREE. I can return any books I decide not to keep and owe nothing. The publisher's prices for the KENSINGTON CHOICE romances range from $4.99 to $5.99, but as a subscriber I will be entitled to get them for just $3.95 per book. There is no minimum number of books to buy, and I can cancel my subscription at any time. A $1.50 postage and handling charge is added to each shipment.

Name _____

Address _____ Apt. # _____

City _____ State _____ Zip _____

Telephone ( ) _____

Signature _____
(If under 18, parent or guardian must sign)
Subscription subject to acceptance

KC 0894

We have
4
FREE
Historical
Romances
for you!

Details inside!

There was no doubt in her mind what she was about to embark on would be considered an evil deed by many. Anything that acknowledged powers outside the church's belief in which she had grown up, would be considered a product of the devil, of Satan. But for her, that inner battle had been rectified long ago when she became interested in the Eastern way of healing. She realized there was so much she did not know or understand.

Her explorations had led her to shiatsu, a form of massage using acupressure. Now, as an adult, she believed anything that brought relief and joy could only come from the highest source, no matter what name a person chose to call it. She finally had begun to free her mind from the shackles of fear put inside her by her mother's misgivings. Yet Raquel knew that a part of her mind, the part that controlled her body, still remained in chains.

The shamaness was right. The blue passion flower's fruit was delicious, and she gratefully munched on its yellow pulp, avoiding the many seeds. Every once in a while she would place a leaf from St. Juan's wort into her mouth, until she had consumed more than she could remember of the tiny pieces.

As she neared the end of the second half of the fruit, she involuntarily began to focus on the moon's reflection in the pond. Like a giant luminous ball, it quivered ever so slightly in the water. It turned into a beckoning hand and seemed to draw her towards it.

Somewhere in the back of her mind she heard a plucking noise, and the reflection began to dance back and forth to its beat. Her transfixed eyes remained glued to the enticing surrealistic orb, as it bobbed to the rhythm of the pond's ripples.

Raquel thought she heard the shamaness chanting softly beside her, but she wasn't sure, nor did she care, as the most wonderful feeling began to embrace her. Willingly she gave in to the power of the moon's reflection and the vibratory hum of human sounds being whispered in her ear. Over and over again they would swell and fall in unison, until she anticipated the crescendos and valleys of the rhythmic noise. The young woman could not remember when she and the intonations became one, and time passed without notice. Her only recollection was of a wonderfully talented light, who could dance, sing and practically fly.

Some time later, Raquel's dark, flashing eyes began to focus on the weary ones before her. The shamaness looked exhausted, while she felt mildly energized but normal. There was no tingling in her fingers, she did not see a glow emanate from her body. Did the "magic", the power transference, work? Was her soul open enough to accept what the shamaness had to offer? Would she be able to fool everyone, including Nate?

"Are we done?" she asked nervously. "I mean, did it work?"

"Yes," the shamaness answered wearily. "The transfer ez complete." The old woman sighed as she recounted how there had been resistance in Raquel's mind before the channeling of her own mind's power and wisdom could be completed. With a satisfied smile, the shamaness watched her.

A deep sigh escaped the shamaness's pleated lips. "You won't see or feel a change, girl. The knowledge will only arise at the appointed time. That ez, when the *orishas* are called durin' the spiritual ceremony. Your life will remain the same," the elderly woman assured her. "The small leather pouch that I have placed on a cord around your neck, 'olds several very powerful female objects. A necklace of white and blue beads, seashells and stones found by the seashore. When the time ez right, you must place the beaded necklace about your neck, an' clasp the shells and stones tightly within your palms. You must think of the sea, an' the ocean, an' imitate its movements with your body, the rest will take place naturally," she balanced the tightly packed, small leather sack in the palm of her hand. "As for tonight, on an' off, you will continue to feel the euphoric, sometimes hypnotic effect of the 'erbs, but even that will be gone by mornin'."

Sensuously, Rachel began to rub her tiny hands across her head, but found her hair was no longer braided. Thick locks hung spiritedly about her shoulders, the moisture in the air adding to their volume, puffing them up into a black voluminous cloud.

"My hair—why is it loose?"

The shamaness managed a weak smile.

"Many do not understand the power of a person's hair. When allowed to grow freely an' in its natural state, it ez like a virtual tribute to the female energy in creation. Fertile understandin' an' yieldin' energy. It ez a tribute in its own right and should be worn proudly."

Raquel watched as the woman rose slowly to her feet. "Now, it ez time for us to go. I am finish."

As they approached the clearing in which the two huts stood, a soul-stirring rhythm of bongo beats could be heard. As if with the approaching steps of a powerful animal, they pranced in the dark, complementing the natural night sounds. The closer they came, the more compelling the music became to Raquel. By the time they reached the clearing, Raquel felt as if the beating had somehow entered inside of her. Sensually, with eyes closed, she moved her head from side to side, mimicking the sound with her continuous motions.

Despite her fatigue, the shamaness's eyes shone with anticipation. Secretly, she had known of the lustful effect the transference and wearing off of the herbs would have on the young woman, but she had chosen not to tell her. Her eager body would have no choice but to reflect the dose of spiritual power her mind had gained.

"It ez the life of the music you are feelin'," the grated voice whispered. "Some believe music ez a connection between the all powerful an' the mortal. So enjoy, young one. Bathe in the sensations that will arise in you, the emotions that will master you, for tonight will be a great night of blue passion."

With those parting words the shamaness entered her hut, leaving Raquel standing alone, just outside the place where Nate played the erotic sounds.

Slowly, but with excitement, the young woman approached the entrance, then stood with eyes aflame as she watched him play beside the fire.

Inside, searing tongues of orange and yellow appeared to leap to the beat, casting hypnotic shadows on the walls of the small hut. The entire scene was an aphrodisiac, fanning the flames of Raquel's potent desires.

Unaware of Raquel's presence, Nate's muscular shoulders were intensely hunched forward as he played the coercing cadence. A pumping bulge appeared and disappeared in his upper arm as he gripped the stick that ignited the carnal sound.

Thick lashes cast shadows upon his cheeks as he closed his eyes, oblivious to everything else. Suddenly, the soft pink tip of his tongue flicked onto the upper corner of his lip, as he leaned forward toward his instrument, feeling the beat he'd made.

Raquel's breaths began to come in deep rushes as his virility seemed to reach out and touch her. She grabbed hold of the sides of the entrance as a rousing tingle coursed through her, causing her to become weak in the knees and lightheaded. There was no doubt she could blame the surge of lustful feelings that were spilling over within her on the shamaness's herbs, but she could not deny the seed for them had been there all along. The herbs simply allowed them to break free.

It was at that moment Nate felt her presence. Purposeful dark eyes turned to embrace her, then became hooded at the unexpected carnal picture she made.

Raquel's head had dropped with the unexpected rush of desire. Now, as it subsided, she threw back her head, causing the jet, cottony billow surrounding her narrow face to quiver ever so slightly. It was then that their eyes locked, hers full of passion, his with a dawning curiosity.

Nate never stopped beating the box as his eager eyes traveled up from her trim ankles to the wide expanse of firm calf and thigh visible through the opening in her wrap. As a matter of fact, he began to beat the instrument even more intensely, beckoning her to join in with the rhythm, as he rotated his shoulders enticingly. He remembered how she had danced in the club before, and the thought of it caused his loins to tighten.

Nate had no idea what had occurred in the rain forest, but there was no doubt in his mind that the sensual creature standing before him would be his before the night was through. Somewhere, she had cast aside her reluctance to give herself willingly, and that suited his purposes all the more.

Abruptly, as if commanding her to begin, he struck a rapid succession of notes, then rose slowly to his feet. Taking catlike steps he began to cross the room in her direction. Each move, accompanied by the same five primitive sounds. By the time he had traveled halfway across the room, Raquel's body was replying to his unspoken challenge.

She began to anticipate each succession of beats, her frame swaying to its rhythm. Raquel would thrust her full breasts forward, leaning temptingly toward him long enough to entice him, only to withdraw as he stepped toward her. Her backward step rivaling his forward one.

It was only for a short period of time that Nate allowed the dance of prey and predator, for he couldn't help but be mesmerized as he watched her backing closer and closer to the flame, their shadowed forms reflecting the erotic scene on a gigantic scale.

Subconsciously, Raquel still played out her unwillingness to surrender to him through their mock chase. But because her dark gaze remained riveted upon his, she knew when he began to tire and wanted more. So like a sensual animal, she implored him to continue, promising him more if he would give it. It was the only way she could cope with the seething physical need that always existed, but had been made unbearable by the herbs. Her body yearned to be touched by him, but deep inside she was still afraid to surrender. So she siphoned off pleasure from the passion in his eyes, seeking its nourishment.

"Don't stop, Nate," she purred. "I will dance for you,

if you don't. I will do anything for you, Nate, if you don't stop." Teasing, heavily lashed eyes taunted him from beside the fire.

A deadly glint entered his dark eyes, and he caught a portion of his generous bottom lip within his teeth. He held it there.

"Oh-h. Do you promise?" was his husky response, and she nodded affirmatively, her pouting lips parting ever so slightly. "Um-m," the sound vibrated deep in his throat. "Well, I'm going to play for you, baby. Don't you worry about that." He picked up the pace of the sensual tune.

With lingering fingers, Raquel traced the rim of the wrap across the tops of her copper mounds, until they rested on the knotted material that held it all together, certain his gaze would follow her every move.

Unyielding, his eyes froze on her lithe hands as she prolonged the teasing motion, then laughed somewhat wickedly, before snatching it apart and thrusting the length of material to the other side of the hut.

Nate felt and heard his breath catch in his throat as she flaunted her nudity before him, the fire giving her reddish-brown skin a golden overtone. He knew he had seen her nude before, but this time, there was pure passion exhibited by every part of her. He allowed her a few more moments as the swaying, gyrating temptress, but he had come to his limit in visual fulfillment, and was ready for something much more tangible.

Displaying the agility of a panther, he lunged forward and grabbed her by her slender waist, drawing her into his bare chest, the leather pouch the only barrier between them as he held her possessively.

"I am through playing, *pataki,*" he stared down into

her smoky eyes. "Playing is for children and I am nobody's child."

The shock of his quick embrace helped to clear the lust-filled fog she had been under. A flicker of fear flashed in her velvety eyes, and her mouth parted slightly as if to murmur a sudden protest.

His perceptive gaze detected the ember of apprehension, and a deep growl emanated from inside his throat, "Ah-h, it is far too late for that, little one. There is no way I am going to let you change your mind."

A strong hand reached up to cup her chin, swiftly followed by his soft but firm lips upon hers. The height of desire Raquel had evoked in Nate was apparent through his searing kiss. With dauntless fervor his tongue sought out the moistness within, as his eager hands traveled down the length of her back to cup her exposed bottom. At first her mechanical response went unnoticed by him, until he sought to mold her more deeply into his hard frame, only to find what had been a lithe beckoning body, had now turned stiff and unyielding.

Abruptly he grabbed her shoulders, then shoved her far away from him in order to see the entire length of her. By now he was totally angered by her less-than-ardent response.

"Woman, I'll be damned if you will deny me tonight," he swore. "Who do you think you are playing with me like this?" he demanded, shaking her. "Or is this part of the cat and mouse game you play in Miami with all the men you go to bed with? Do you like to hear them beg for it?"

Once again he cupped her chin, but this time his hold was rough, demanding. "I will not beg."

Raquel stood speechless as she watched his fury

mount. She was confused by her own actions. She knew she wanted him, her body cried out for his touch, but her mind remained a captive of years of primness and order on which she prided herself. All her grand education helped her to analyze herself, but it couldn't free her. She felt so ashamed. How could she blatantly flaunt herself before him, then turn as cold as ice when he began to collect what she had offered.

"I'm not playing a game, Nate," she finally managed to say as his thumb and third finger pressed hard into her jaw bone.

There was pure anger in his eyes, but further inside their depths, there was a tinge of hurt. It was the latter that made Raquel continue.

"How can I make you understand when I don't quite understand myself," she pleaded. "I want you Nate . . . but I am just afraid. Afraid of you . . . of all of this . . . but also afraid of things from long ago that you had nothing to do with." Her slender hand came up to enfold the taut one that remained on her face. She shook her head passionately. "If we do this, what will it mean when this is all over? There are so many things you do not know about me, and I know so little about you." Her troubled eyes searched his for answers.

Nate did not know what kind of response he had expected from this woman, but he was sure it was not the sincere outpouring he had just heard. Overwhelmed by emotion he gently drew her head into his chest.

"Dammit, what kind of woman are you, *pataki?*" he swore at her softly, stroking her ebony cloud of hair. "I didn't come here equipped with a crystal ball so I can't say what is going to happen. But I promise one thing, as long as you are with me no harm will come to you. You have touched me in a way I've never been touched before."

Relief flooded her as she heard his reassuring words. Tenderly she looked up into his face. "And you have touched a place in me, Mr. Nate."

She rose on to her tiptoes and placed a lingering kiss upon his lips. "Two people couldn't go through this much together without consequences."

Nate's dark eyes clouded with emotion, then he sighed, deeply.

"*Pataki*, sometimes it's strange how life brings people together. And I know, it can't get much stranger than how we got here," he looked down at her intently. "But you've got to begin to trust me, and I got to begin to trust you. In the end our very lives could depend on it."

Raquel studied her captor's sincere features, and strong feelings began to stir inside.

"I may end up feeling like a fool, but for now, I know I must try."

Nate's gaze drifted from her ebony eyes to her promising lips as they formed the reassuring words. A sheen of moisture, caused their fullness to shine, beckoning him once again to touch them with his.

This time as his head descended toward her, he could feel her hands reach up to aid its progress, and his loins stirred with the promise of her touch.

A chilling weakness encased Raquel as his mouth covered hers. The utter softness of it began to unravel her and she whimpered.

Nate's deepest desire was to feel her give in to his touch, and from the moment their lips met, he knew she was all there for him.

With lingering motions he explored the inner sweetness of her mouth, feeling as if he could drown in its softness. Longingly he rubbed his temple against hers, then sought out her willing mouth again.

Feeling her flame of passion ignite, Raquel wanted Nate to know the depth of her desire, so she withdrew her mouth from his, tracing tiny, suckling kissing about his lips, as she murmured, "I want you, Nate. I want you." He enfolded her even more tightly inside his embrace. His caress was so intense she feared she might break from the strength of his arms.

In his fervor, he raised her inches off the hut's dirt floor, then kissed and plied the tender spot at the base of her throat as she wrapped her arms tightly about his sweltering shoulders.

Then like a man possessed, he snarled, "Now you shall have me, baby." He swept her up in his arms and carried her to his pallet.

With dark eyes smoldering, Raquel lay back with anticipation as she watched him unbutton and remove the cut-off jeans he had conveniently fashioned. She had no idea if the herbs had taken effect again, but she did know the hunger that churned within her was real and needed to be fed. Then as she watched the denim material slide to his muscular thighs, there was no doubt in her mind, Nate had the ability to fulfill her craving.

His eyes burned when he crouched above her, pinning her forearms to the natural material. Deliberately, he dragged his gaze from her face to her heaving breasts, causing their budded tips to constrict. He gave each darkened peak an encouraging lick to further their response; then cooed like a bird in the rain forest as they tightened even more.

"*Pataki*, you are so beautiful." He rose again to give

her a lingering kiss, only to withdraw before her lips were quenched.

Briefly his gaze returned to her swollen crests, only to travel further down her frame. Finally it rested on the profuse knoll of black curls, lying between the valley of her thighs. His eyes squinted intensely, as the involuntary pink tip of his tongue traced the shape of his own lip. He looked up into her eyes drunk with desire as he ground his teeth together, "Woman, I have waited for a long time. Now," he murmured, "you are mine."

Nate rubbed his face back and forth upon her curly mound, as if inhaling the female scent. Raquel's reaction mirrored his, as her head writhed from side to side anticipating whatever might be in store. There had never been this kind of intimacy between her and Clinton Bradshaw.

Nate enclosed the width of her waist within his hands before burrowing further into her center. His wetness sought out hers, and they mingled a honey sweetness, causing Raquel to cry out in sheer delight. He assaulted her over and over, until her hips began to rise and fall in a demanding motion.

"I can't take this," she moaned, "I feel as if I'm going to explode." And she grabbed his head, drawing it closer to her own.

Seething with his own desire, Nate released her, then readied himself in order to make them one. "Oh no, *pataki*. It is not nearly time for that. You must wait for me."

His possession was smooth. Hungrily Raquel arched her back as she received him, her moment was so close at hand, but Nate lay very still inside her, waiting for her passion to draw back from its crest. He wanted them to mount the peak of pleasure steadily, together. Raquel reluctantly followed his lead, too far gone to do anything else, hoping in the end to satisfy the exquisite ache he had initiated.

When he felt the time was right, he began to thrust inside her, causing ripples of pleasure to shoot through him. This taste of bliss naturally incited his motions, and his pace began to accelerate as he sought the sensations over and over again.

Never before had Raquel been pleasured so intensely, and she greedily wallowed in each stroke. He could feel her tighten selfishly about him, and he reached down further seeking to touch the very core of her.

Raquel and Nate clung to one another passionately as they rose, he whispering provoking words in her ears, assuring her of the pleasure she was giving him. His sensual words fueled their fire, and she met his thrusts, her voice turning raspy as she answered his erotic questions; the knowledge of her gratification fueling his own.

Suddenly the passion became unbearable and she cried out in her frenzy.

It was Nate's cue to join her as they clung to the peak of pleasure, then tumbled into a world of satisfaction.

Chapter Thirteen

The tricolored heron extended its neck ever so slightly. It resembled a stuffed bird, it stood so still. Its ruby-colored eyes remained fixed on the moving water below, watching and waiting for the right moment to surprise its morning meal.

Raquel sat quietly as the blue, maroon, and buff-colored bird stalked its prey, then with lightning movements, immersed its dark plumed head under water, afterwards emerging with the catch.

She'd come to the pond early that morning, memories and scents of the night before clinging close about her. She had intended to float in the forest's calm waters, but found it teeming with animal life. They, of course, were operating to nature's time clock.

At first, her disruption of the natural gathering caused some of the animals and birds to scatter, leaving behind a stubborn agouti on the opposite bank. His rabbit-sized body remained poised for flight as he assessed the unwelcome visitor.

* * *

Finally, he decided to continue his rapid lapping of the pond's water, concluding she was much too far away to do him any harm. After the agouti's bold stand, some of the other animals and birds began to return, but they were ready to retreat if she made even the slightest threatening move.

Raquel hugged her knees close to her newly awakened body. Parts of her still throbbed from the lovemaking the night before, and she knew it wouldn't take much to ignite the barely dormant stirrings within her.

Sooty lashes swept down on to high cheekbones, as she marveled at the ability human beings possessed to give such pleasure to one another. Still basking in the glow of her first true experience of being fulfilled, she wondered how her mother could ever have misled her to believe this natural thing between male and female could be wrong. It was all so powerful. And maybe that is where the problem rested. This kind of power used abusively could be devastating, but with love, it was the most wonderful thing on earth.

Raquel placed her flushed face against her updrawn knees. Love. How could she use the word in referring to a man who had participated in abducting her by force? Yet, amazingly, she had no doubt about the way she felt.

In deep thought, she dug her toes into the moss upon which she sat, and she knew her feelings for the man, Nate, had not just begun the night before, but days ahead of time.

Here was a man who didn't even know her real name, or who she truly was, and she claimed to be in love with him. Had she been back in Miami, counseling a young woman who spoke of being in love with a man in less then a month's time, a man who had committed a criminal act against her, she would have cautioned her to examine her feelings further. Might they be a strong case of infatuation? Or maybe even some kind of obsessive fantasy? She would kindly inform the misguided girl, that it takes true love a long time to grow and develop. She would say, "Most certainly it wouldn't be directed toward a man of this nature."

Raquel searched her logical mind for an answer to her own confused feelings. Maybe all of the things they had experienced together since coming aboard that sailboat, had sped up the natural ties and bonding that usually takes months and even years to develop. On the other hand, there is no way anyone would consider their "courtship" as natural.

The sound of nearly demented laughter echoed about her as she laughed at herself and the emotional predicament she found herself in, and the young woman covered her tangled hair with a settling fold of her arms.

Nate's search for Raquel had brought him within several feet of the water before he saw her. The strange laughter she expelled nearly sent chills up his spine, and his dark features clouded over with concern. It caused him considerable pain to see her in such mental agony.

At the moment there was nothing he could tell her that would ease her distress. He knew the words he might have chosen could even add to her heavy load. So he chose to remain silent, announcing his presence from the brush to warn her of his coming.

"So here you are," his tone was deceptively cheerful. "I wondered where you had gone so early this morning," he stooped and placed a playful kiss on the back of her neck.

Just the sound of his rich voice caused butterflies to

appear in her stomach, as his cool lips upon her back began creating an tremor. She dared not turn and look in his face, for she knew how she felt about him had to show in her eyes. So she attempted to match the non-chalant intonation of his greeting.

"Morning, Nate."

"Hey, this is a great idea," he said with a wide smile. She watched him stride purposefully toward the pond's edge. "I think I'll go for a swim."

Lithely he removed his cut-off jeans. Raquel couldn't help but stare with unabashed adoration at his athletic body. It was well defined, starting with his wide shoulders, his narrowing waistline, and firm buttocks. His legs and thighs were muscular like a runner's. Of all the animals she had seen at the pond that morning, Nate was undoubtedly the most beautiful.

Flashing her a pearly smile, he dove into the blue-green pond. Large spurts of water splashed her face from his body's weight, feeling cold in the early morning air. Nate emerged yards away, shaking water from his drenched face and head.

"What are you waiting for, *pataki?*" he called to her. "The water feels good, come on in."

She watched him float luxuriously on his back, as the soft rays of well-awakened dawn beamed down upon him. Raquel reminded herself that getting into the water was her sole reason for coming to the pond that morning, so she quickly unfastened her wrap, then tiptoed to the water's edge. She was on the brink of jumping into the chilly water before she remembered the leather pouch that hung about her neck. Protectively she removed it, hanging it on the sloping branch of a tree. She walked into the pond's refreshing embrace, closing her eyes as it rose higher about her body, until it reached her throat. Finally she struck out with a powerful kick, then turned on to her back, so the sun's rays could rest upon her face.

Nate watched her float alone, although he was very aware they could not waste much time this morning. Today was the day they would have to push ahead. Leaving this semi-private haven, to face the fate he had chosen for them. Had he known what he knew and felt now, he dared say he would not have involved her in this tangled web.

With powerful strokes Nate swam to a fringe of the pond where tall, slender reeds grew in abundance, and he broke off several handfuls of the plant. Straight away, he lit out to join Raquel.

Paddling on his back beside her, he told her to follow him in closer to the shore. Finally, they stopped, once her feet could firmly rest upon the ground beneath the water. Exposing her wet breasts to the morning air caused the tips to contract—the sensation deliciously reminded her of the night before.

"Here, let me show you."

Balling up the plants in his hand, he rubbed them vigorously between his palms until a soapy film began to form. Afterwards he circled behind Raquel, and began to gently rub the natural suds against her back. She moaned at his gentle, cleansing administrations. His hands felt strong as he lathered her back. To her pleasure, he did not miss the opportunity to explore the fullness of her buttocks, teasing her all the while.

"Oh, sorry about that," his lips touched her ear as he taunted her, "for a minute I forgot what I was supposed to be doing."

Raquel couldn't help but giggle at his mannish ways as he turned her to face him. "Oh boy, now look what you have done," he remarked, then smiled wickedly, but continued his mischievous bathing.

The reeds began to fall apart and lose their usefulness, but that did not stop the fond explorations of Nate's hands. Finally they could not resist the other, and they found a secluded spot to continue their lovemaking. The night before blurred in Raquel's memory—she was lost in the moment with Nate. Raquel wanted to remain in his arms, feeling his touch and his kiss, but there was a growing tenseness about him. She knew it was time for them to head back to the hut.

"I guess we need to be going back," she announced. "From what I understand we've got quite a way to go before we reach Dangriga."

The veiled look that appeared in Nate's eyes was not lost on the young woman, and she wondered what thoughts he hid behind it. Now that she had the shamaness's power within her, she hoped she no longer had to fear being exposed as a fraud during the ceremony. She was torn inside, because out of desperation part of her believed all the shamaness had told her, but another part of her still doubted if it were possible.

The shamaness had been the only person to tell her about the ritual. Nate had not, because he believed she was Jackie Dawson. How would he feel about her once he found out the truth? For him to have gone to the lengths he had to bring Jackie Dawson back to Belize, and to protect her to such extremes—how would he feel about Raquel Mason from Miami?

Raquel couldn't help but feel threatened by such tenacity. She knew from personal experience he was not an easy man to comprehend. Now her fear was twofold. Could she live up to what was expected of her once they reached Dangriga? And it frightened her to think of losing this man because of who she was not.

Neither spoke as they dressed, and they walked back to the clearing in silence.

"Nate!" an excited voice called as they stepped out into the open.

Both Nate and Raquel were surprised to see a somewhat hassled Ponti, safely standing several feet away from the shamaness and her mascot, the jaguarundi.

In his hands he carried a bundle of familiar objects, Raquel's belongings which she had left behind in Balam, and Nate's handgun, which he lost while fleeing from the Balamians.

If it hadn't been for Ponti, more than likely they would have been killed. In Raquel's exuberance, she gave the Mayan a friendly hug, causing him to flush with embarrassment. The damp material of her wrap still clung enticingly to her body.

Raquel noticed the flustered look on his face and stood back modestly, smoothing out some of the folds in the damp cloth. Still she couldn't contain her curiosity.

"How is Mircea?"

Ponti gave a boyish grin. "Fine . . . now that you have stolen the ceremonial blade. The elders are in an uproar. Most of them say there can be no more sacrifices until it is found. You see it has been in our village for thousands of years. Some believe it was used during the ancient bloodletting rituals," he rolled his eyes into his head playfully. "I don't know if it is that old, but there's no doubt it would be hard to trace its true origins back to the very beginning. So you see—" he stopped in midsentence realizing he did not know her name. "I'm sorry. You know your name," he confessed, abruptly.

"Ra—um-um." Raquel acted as if she needed to clear her throat as her real name nearly slipped off her tongue. "It is Jackie. Jackie Dawson," she weakly replied.

"So you see, Jackie, you have become a legend in our village. There are elders who are wondering if it is not a sign that the sacrifices and bloodletting should come to a halt. Maybe this will be the beginning of change for my people."

Raquel nodded with anxious appreciation.

Nervously, she felt for the leather pouch that usually hung about her neck. In a panic, she realized she had left it at the pond. Her wide eyes flew up to the shamaness's wrinkled face.

Turning hurriedly to Nate, she explained, "I forgot something back at the water. It won't take me but a few minutes, but I've got to run back and get it." Before he could answer she had dashed back into the forest.

Swiftly her feet crashed through the foliage. She was excited because of Ponti's presence, and to hear that Mircea's life might be permanently spared as a result of her efforts. She wondered if she could ever make such a difference back home.

She saw the pond in the distance. Oddly, there wasn't an animal or a bird in sight. Mildly curious, Raquel wondered if her rapid approach had frightened them all away.

Raquel could see the pouch hanging from the swinging branch as she approached it hurriedly. It took two hands to untangle the cord from the fingerlike limb. Specks of loose bark clung to it, and a few remnants flew into her eyes as she replaced the sack around her neck. Instinctively, her hands flew up to rub them.

Suddenly, a pair of rough hands covered her mouth and grabbed her about the waist. She kicked and squirmed wildly, although it had little effect on her abductor. He made no sound as he carried her rapidly away through the forest.

Raquel's eyes teared painfully as she tried to see who was responsible for the act, but the flecks in her eyes prevented her from opening them. In horror, she wiped at her face over and over again, feeling totally helpless.

Finally she was placed on the ground, and through blurry vision she whirled to face her assailant. But it simply made it easy for an accomplice to forcefully place a gag in her mouth, then tie another rag over her badly watering eyes. Frantically, she clawed to keep the wrap about her body, as her abductors dragged her through the rain forest.

They finally burst through on to what felt like a dirt road to Raquel. Somewhere near she could hear the laboring engine of a badly maintained vehicle. Suddenly, the motor revved up and the car's noise advanced towards them at a dangerous pace. Two strong arms reached down and pulled her into the car. Then just as swiftly as the car had pulled up beside them, it sped away down the bumpy road.

Nate offered Ponti the only seat there was in their small hut, as he told him of his snakebite, and the care and housing the shamaness had provided for them in their time of need. He was surprised to find out none of this was news to him.

"The villagers who chased after you came back and told of how "the powerful one" would not allow you to be harmed. After that, rumors abounded. They were saying, the woman who would be a shaman was housing the man and the woman responsible for the loss of the ceremonial blade. Although everyone believed this, no one from the village would dare to venture here to find out for themselves if it was really true."

"That is, besides you," Nate acknowledged.

Ponti nodded his head proudly. "I have always gone against the grain, but because I am smart, when I want to, I am able to hide the things I do that would upset my people most. When I left and went off to school, I did not care what they would think. Eventually I felt they would accept me again. And now that I have proven myself by trying to stop those who would steal the precious ceremonial blade," he said with a wink. "Now, I am very trusted in Balam. So much so, they charged me with getting rid of the belongings of the perpetrators. They do not want your negative energies in the village. So here I am getting rid of them." He placed Raquel's bundle on the floor and handed the handgun to Nate along with a roll of money.

Then a serious look blanketed Ponti's youthful features.

"I do not want to lead you to think that I do not love and respect my people. I just know that things must change," he sought Nate's understanding, "There are many things that the Balamians know that could be of exceptional good for the rest of the world, but I know as long as we continue to do bloodlettings and sacrifices, we will be looked at as nothing but senseless barbarians."

They shared a moment of companionable silence.

"I can't tell you how much I understand being connected to a group of people with ways that are not always understood by others," Nate said smoothly. "Things that as a young man I found hard to accept. And now as an adult, I fear, what I shall call . . . modern-day sacrifices. Either way, Ponti, the way of the Balamians or this more evolved way is wrong," he gazed off into the distance.

"Here in Belize, we are such a diverse people. Our heritages nearly span the globe. The tree is here, but it has been fed from as far away as Africa to China. In many ways, it is one of the most primitive places that lies in the midst of the civilized world. I think it will be quite some time before all our beliefs become tame . . . if ever."

"Yes, at times, we are far from tame," Ponti shook his head in agreement. "And that is the main reason I chose to bring these things to you this morning. I have news for you." He bent forward conspiratorially. "Late last night, the merchant that you met in the Kekchi village, was forced by a group of men to come and talk to us in Balam. They knew that an outsider would not be tolerated in the village. So they found the merchant, and they counted on his Mayan blood to allow them access. But before they came to Balam he says they had asked many questions, and evidently the merchant's answers led them to come to our village. He was very frightened, and more than a little pleased when he saw that I was one of the persons the head men chose to speak with them. From what I can understand, these men were very interested in your and your Jackie's whereabouts."

Nate's body became still as stone. His eyes took on a deadly glint, yet his voice was deceptively calm. "Were they Shango?"

"Yes." Ponti noticed a frightening change in his friend's persona. Slowly he eased back from leaning so close to him.

"They heard about the missing blade and the possibility that you may be staying with "the powerful one.""

"Were they still at Balam when you left this morning?"

"I cannot say. I had to come here in secret."

The thoughts in Nate's mind turned like a well-oiled wheel. He cursed under his breath for underestimating the speed in which Jay would come back to find the woman. It was evident they had not come by car, or they would have arrived in the area earlier. Nate did not think Jay would allow the shamaness's presence to keep him from coming for her, especially if he had back-up. Now he was sure the man's plans for the woman involved far more than he had confessed.

Suddenly Nate was keenly aware that Jackie had not returned from the pond. Without warning, he grabbed the firearm, checked it, strode forcefully toward the entrance of the hut, then broke into a solid run once he got outside. A startled Ponti was close behind.

Powerfully he shoved aside the large foliage that would block his way as he bolted for the water, his ears straining to hear the slightest indication that the woman was in trouble.

Yards away he crouched upon the ground, then began to crawl on all fours with the gun still held within his hand. He prayed Jay had not found her, but if he had, and there were more of them than he could handle, he would have a better chance by sneaking up on them; but most importantly, he did not want to unnecessarily jeopardize her life. Nate knew how badly Jay hated the woman, and that he would kill her without a second thought.

With cautious movements, he extended the length of his body outward, until he was on his belly, then made his way closer to the water by using his elbows. His muscular chest was still bare, and he knew that what he was doing was extremely dangerous—he had already had one encounter with a poisonous snake, now squirming along the rain forest's floor, his chances of being bitten a second time were very high. Abruptly he stopped, lying there for seconds at a time, listening. Then slowly he rose, peering at the water. His greatest fear took hold when he spotted the edge of the pond, and found she was not there. Instantly he rose above the foliage, forcing a school of startled reddish egrets to stop their morning hunt, and head for safety in the sky, in a red, blue-gray flurry.

Tense, he looked for signs of a struggle, but there were none. Yet he knew in his heart she had been taken, and taken by force.

He gripped and released the handle of the Glock pistol as a cold chill crept up inside him. Only once before in his life had he felt such uneasiness, but the memory of it lingered as if it were yesterday. Like a flash his mind went back to a time when he was a boy.

For Nate's mother, his father had been everything. Even after he was born, and Cecilia came to live with them, he remained the center of her life. Nothing had been too good for him in her eyes, she loved him so deeply. The fact he in turn loved her, couldn't have made her happier.

After Cecilia died, she began to change. The thought of a loved one dying frightened her terribly. The powers that be had failed her by not protecting the girl and in taking one so young. Since his mother was a person of deep beliefs, the impact of that event had a most profound effect. Even then as a child, Nate felt he could handle his cousin's death better than his mother, and he tried to comfort her the best he could. So did everyone else.

At that time, he was nearly twelve and had finally surpassed his mother in height. He had never noticed how small and delicate she was until then, and she became even more frail as time passed. Then slowly another problem surfaced. She became peculiarly paranoid about the dangers she said stalked her family.

The rift between the Garifuna and the Shango had caused a spiritual weakening of their villages. No longer was there a *dabuyaba*, religious temple, for the Garifuna to hold their important ceremonies. Now the only temple was located in the village of the Shango, and his mother viewed that as an extremely evil sign.

Nate's father tried to reassure her that things would be all right, but she clung to him even more. She always needed to hear that he would never leave her, even in death. And he would never love anyone else the way he loved her.

Then one day a young Shangoain woman appeared in Dangriga. All eyes were upon her as she walked through the small village. People appeared in the broken doorways of the clapboard houses, puzzling over what could have made this woman come to the Garifunian village, ignoring the awful split that had occurred nearly a half year before.

Nate remembered watching the woman progress up the dusty pathway between several of the buildings. He had been sitting outside his home finishing a drum his father had helped him fashion. The woman walked as if she were in a processional, carefully placing each foot in front of the other, until finally she reached the door of their house. His father was not home at the time, and it was his mother he called to speak to this unorthodox visitor.

Already fearful, she approached the door warily. Her apprehension grew when she realized the woman was Shangoain, her eyes widening with suppressed fear. Cautiously she spoke to her, then immediately asked what was her purpose for coming to the village, especially to their home.

Without an invitation the Shangoain stepped past his mother inside their front door. She never said a word as she started to unwrap the many folds of cloth that surrounded her thin frame. From the beginning, Nate had noticed how strange her dress had been, she was wrapped so completely. It was peculiar because it was a sweltering day, and he wondered how far she'd walked in the heavy, dark material.

His mother tried to discourage the woman's bizarre unveiling, but she ignored her as she continued to undress, keeping her steadfast gaze fastened to his mother's increasingly frightened features.

It had to have been obvious to the Shangoain that his mother was not well, for even at such a young age her fragile hands shook uncontrollably at her sides. She had to clasp them together in order to cease the embarrassing trait.

Eventually his mother saw her demands for the woman to stop her disrobing would continue to go unheeded, so she motioned for Nate to leave the doorway. Reluctantly he did so, yet he remained conveniently close to the house only a few feet away.

Moments passed, and suddenly he heard the swooning sound of a female voice. This was followed by the slamming of one of the doors inside. Shortly thereafter, the Shangoain woman appeared outside again, fully clothed. She turned a superior eye in Nate's direction.

"Boy, I want you to deliver a message for me."

Hesitantly he had nodded his head, all the time wondering why she had not passed the message on to his mother. It would have been far more appropriate for it to be delivered by another adult, because whatever her reason was for coming to Dangriga, it had to be of the utmost importance, and therefore a matter to be handled by the elders of the village.

His gaze fixed upon the woman's dark features which had the distinctive trait of the Shangoains, eyes that were extremely large. The shape of her face was round, and in its center was a nose so flat it was buttonlike, yet her lips were extremely thin. Large twists of hair rippled back from her face, gathering together in the crown of her head.

"Tell your father, he no longer has only one child. Soon there will be another. Tell him the mother is Vita, the Shangoain. He can find me in the town of Barooch, if he wants me." Stoically she turned and walked away.

It took Nate a few moments to recover from the

woman's stunning words, but when their meaning set in, he quickly entered the house looking for his mother.

An eerie feeling crept up his back as he stepped inside. The uncomfortable feeling confused him, for this was the house that he had grown up in, and had never known another. He called to his mother from the doorway, but she did not answer. Concerned he crossed to his parents' bedroom door, pressed his lips to the crack of it and called her name several times again. Still, she did not respond.

By now he was extremely afraid, he tried to open the door and found the knob turned easily. He called to her once more in vain. It was then that the most soul-shaking chill descended upon him as he walked into his parents' room.

At first he surveyed the entire area and did not see her, but as he turned to go back out of the door, he saw her small, slouched frame in the corner behind it. A thick flow of blood oozing from the deep cuts she had made in her wrists.

From the amount of blood she had shed, he knew he did not have time to run for help. So the boy did everything he could to stop the blood from flowing, but even while trying to save the last breaths of life in his mother's body, he knew that she was dead, perhaps had even died before he'd found her.

It was there on the floor that his father found them together. A disbelieving look of utter horror and shock took over his father's handsome features as he stared, but still, Nate had no merciful words to offer him.

"I don't know why you're standing there surprised." Nate's voice was inappropriately calm. "It is all your fault, you and that Shangoain woman, Vita, who says to tell you she is carrying your baby."

It was the first time in his life he had ever seen his father cry. It was an outpouring of deep, racking sobs that continued even while Nate was gone to bring back one of the village elders.

His father's depression went on for weeks, leaving him to fend for the both of them. Ironically, it was the act of a desperate man, one who didn't care about the future, that ended up changing their entire lives.

Ponti finally caught up with Nate, the latter's guerilla-like techniques had caused him to fall far behind. The lethal look on his companion's handsome features said everything, so the man waited to hear what plan of action he had decided to take.

"I'm going back to the hut for our belongings, and then I'm going after them. They haven't been gone long, so they couldn't have gotten far." He checked the handgun again to see if it was in good working order. "Hopefully she will try to slow down their progress, then I—"

"I don't know," Ponti cautiously interrupted. "By now they could have gone quite a ways if their vehicle was parked near Southern Highway."

"What vehicle?" he asked roughly.

"The men ... persuaded the merchant to let them use his jeep. He was in it, sitting outside his stall last night when they came up to him. They checked it over, found it was in good condition and had a tank full of gas. So they kept it."

Hearing this, Nate wasted no time in heading back

for the clearing. This changed everything. Now he would have to find a car, and fast.

"Does the guy who runs the store at Big Falls still have a couple of four-wheel-drives that he rents out?

"The last I heard, he does."

"Then I'll have to go there first before heading for Punta Gorda."

Nate knew there was no chance the owner wouldn't recognize him. Through the years he'd come through his place too many times. But now he had no other choice.

Hastily he threw on a shirt and a long pair of jeans as Ponti watched. The only belongings he had were his duffel bag and the things that belonged to Raquel, so he threw them all together. He was set to go when the shamaness entered the hut, like a watchdog, the jaguarundi was not far from her side.

There were signs of strain and fatigue edging her aged face, and for a moment Nate imagined her features had been altered in a kind of bizarre way. The change made her facial likeness more akin to the feline that was her constant companion.

Her voice was raspy when she spoke. "You are leavin'."

"Yes." His steely gaze rested on her. "Some men have taken the woman. These are men that will do her harm if I don't stop them, so I must go and find her."

"Oh-h yes," she shook her dreadlocked head in agreement. "But before you leave, I want to reassure you, that no one can stop the change. No one. She will remain safe," her commanding gaze locked with his.

Nate made a slight tilting of his head, a gesture of

thanks and recognition of her power. With this, the shamaness stepped aside and allowed them to pass.

Already Nate was several steps ahead of Ponti, determined not to lose even a minute's time. The youth was like a puppy, yapping at his heels.

"Maybe I should go with you. I could be of help."

Nate stopped momentarily at the edge of the rain forest. "I won't say I couldn't use it."

Ponti's brows knitted together as he thought it over. "First I will go back to Balam and tell my family I have some unfinished business I must settle before I completely return to the village. I'll tell them it will take me a few days to do it. His youthful eyes shone with excitement. After that, I will meet you at Big Falls."

"All right. It is up to you, but I want you to understand two things Ponti," his visage hardened as he turned to face the young man. "One. This is not a game and someone will probably get hurt. And two, if you are not there when I climb into that four-wheel-drive, I will leave without you." Without waiting for his response, Nate disappeared into the foliage.

Nate's thoughts were like a tornado, churning round and round, at its center was Jackie. Loving, passionate pictures of her that morning and the night before flashed through his mind, and hoped he would find her before it was too late. Just the thought of it caused beads of perspiration to break out on his forehead and above his lips.

He tried not to think of the horrible things Jay and Al would have done to her had he not been there, but there was no way to avoid it. Before he knew it he had called out in the wilderness, "I will kill them if they hurt her."

Exotic bird noises enveloped him as he progressed; the mocking sound of macaws and parrots were the most disturbing as they seemed to warn him in their humanlike voices, "rrah-rah, rrun, run, run . . ."

Chapter Fourteen

It was hard for Raquel to breathe folded up on the hard floor of the jeep. The humidity outside made the small stream of air where Raquel lay, stifling and thick with the musky smell of her new abductors. Two pairs of legs stretched out over her, concealing her from prying eyes and limiting her already restrained movements.

The young woman's hands remained tied behind her back making her arms ache despite the extra pad that had been placed on the jeep's floor for her supposed comfort.

Her eyes itched and burned something awful beneath the tight bandanna, and she could feel they were swollen. Maybe it was the kind of bark that had fallen into them, or the combination of that, along with the tightness of the scarf that had complicated their condition; but through a rising panic, she was sure, even if the bandanna were to be removed, her eyes had become so badly infected it would be impossible for her to see.

She strained to catch even the slightest indication of a human voice, but was only assaulted with the loud roar of the vehicle's engine. She couldn't imagine her captors sitting quietly for the period of time they'd been traveling. No, that wouldn't make sense at all. So she surmised, because of the open vehicle, the men's voices were being snatched away and carried outward by the wind, even making it difficult for them to hear one another.

Raquel's logical side urged her to be alert and listen, so she could be prepared for what they had in store for her, but another voice inside the horrified young woman warned her to remain in ignorance as long as she could. Deep inside she knew who was behind the kidnapping, and she knew the horrible things he was capable of doing.

Prolonged sounds of whimpering began to gurgle up in her throat as she shivered and wallowed in deep self-pity and fear. She buried her dirt-streaked face in the pad beneath her.

The nonchalant hand of one of her kidnappers reached down and shook her shoulder. She refused to respond.

"Heh, *obeah* woman, what is this?" His heavily accented voice sounded as if it were coming out of a vacuum. "You no can breathe with your face in there like t'at," and he turned her head to the side to insure she could. "We be there soon enough, and we can let you loose, okay?" he chuckled and patted her suggestively on the buttocks.

Raquel winced from his touch, and it was followed by an endearing pang. She allowed her mind to take her back to hours before when she had not shrank from the hands that touched and caressed her. Mentally she cuddled up to the thoughts of security that Nate's memory provided.

Moments later Raquel's comforting thoughts were interrupted as the jeep pulled off the road into the brush. Who would ever find her if they went off the path? Once again panic set in as her thoughts raced to try and anticipate what would happen next.

The squeaking noise of rusted hinges scraped her dark environment, then she felt a rush of fresh air upon her face and shoulders.

"Right here is as good a place as any," the voice said, and the swishing sound of feet parting grass followed.

Raquel lay as still as death, as if her immobility would help protect her.

"Well, I might as well join you," a second voice called, the same one that spoke of their impending arrival. She could hear the man grunt and groan as he removed his stiffened legs from about her, and joined the other outside the jeep.

Next, the distinct sound of a projected stream of liquid followed by another could be heard, all of this accompanied by one man's sigh of relief. Now Raquel knew they had not arrived at all, but that one of her captors had decided to make a pit stop, and a second had conveniently joined him.

"You t'ink we need to go off t'is highway before we get to t'at road t'at will take us straight in?" a third voice near her inquired.

The muffled response of a fourth person followed.

"Yeah, we've made good time haven't we *Dada?*" a now somewhat familiar satisfied voice called from outside the jeep. "It wasn't too hard findin' and catchin' her," his voice grew closer as he stepped back into the jeep and repositioned his legs. "And why didn't you tell me what a good-looking package the *gubida* had chosen to speak through." A fumbling hand reached down to find an easily accessed breast, squeezed it forcefully, then rolled the unwilling tip between its fingers. "Maybe aftah the ceremony is over, the *buyei* won't mind if we poke around a bit. I bet she has some other abilities we can appreciate besides speakin' with the ancestors." The man next to him laughed, while a third reentered the jeep, slamming the door behind him.

Their laughter was short-lived, as a frightfully familiar gruff voice barked, "Keep your willie to yourself, David. Plans have already been made for her."

The only sound that followed his brusque words was the gunning of the jeep's engine, and that loud noise was blocked out in Raquel's mind by the beating of her own heart. There was no doubt who that last voice belonged to. The knowledge of it caused her to lay frozen, stiff with fear in the bottom of the jeep. One of her greatest fears was happening. Jay had found her, and was taking her away, and only God knew what was in store for her next.

Nate waited impatiently while the store owner took care of two groups of eager tourists, one a family of five and the other, two women.

Although the father was ready to pay for the objects picked up by his brood, the two youngest children kept changing their minds as they came across new, more exciting souvenirs near the cash register. He looked grateful when the mother, who was straining with the hand of an unhappy two-year-old, put her foot down and told them to make up their minds or go without. Nate chuckled gently to himself before returning to the matter at hand.

Before coming inside he checked to see if there were any vehicles left to rent. To his relief, there were two parked out back.

Nate's anxious gaze drifted over to a taxi driver with his foot conveniently planted beneath the mandatory green license plate of his car. Even in this position he managed to rotate his slender hips to the blaring reggae music blasting from the car's crackling radio. Every once in a while, the driver would flash a wide smile in the direction of the two women whom he obviously had driven to Big Falls. One of them acknowledged him, while the other cast interested looks in Nate's direction. Nate raked over the woman once with an apathetic glance—who could compare to Jackie?

Out of his peripheral vision, he saw the tall, shapely blonde bend over and laughingly whisper words into her companion's ear. The other in turn looked to size him up, then reciprocated her friend's whisper. Seconds later the blonde walked over in his direction.

"Excuse me," she breathed, batting generously lashed blue eyes, then purposefully squeezing her tightly shorted hips between Nate and a nearby wall to look at the contents in a glass case behind him.

Wordlessly he shifted his position, leaning his hard frame a foot or so down from where he previously stood.

The blonde leaned over at an angle with rounded breasts thrust in his direction. The fashionable aqua-colored summer top revealed a substantial amount of cleavage, but her angle exposed even more to his conveniently positioned gaze. With slanted eyes he watched her with mild inquisitiveness.

A sheet of white-blonde hair draped over the side of her face as she stooped, covering her ploy. She daintily swept it to the side with a brightly polished hand, displaying two expensive diamond studs in one ear.

"May I help you?" the store owner called in his next customers, then for the first time he noticed the man leaning against the distant counter.

"Nate Bowman," he exclaimed, "How are you?"

Nate gave a quick nod of his head as an answer.

"I'll be with you in just a minute. I've got to take care of these two ladies. They were here first." He then turned his attention to the redhead who was walking over to his counter, followed by the blonde sauntering enticingly behind her.

"Yes," she replied, her American accent ringing in the air. "We'd like to rent one of your cars."

"Well I've got to tell you you're just in time. We've only got one more that's working. It's the black four-wheel Suzuki Samurai in the rear. Why don't you follow me outside, and I'll show it to you."

Nate's eyes narrowed with the man's pronouncement. "Do you mind if I come with you?" His voice was low, calm.

Before the store owner could answer, the smiling blonde extended her invitation. "Of course not, honey," she gave him a meaningful glance.

The four of them rounded the back of the building arriving at two mud-caked vehicles.

"I really hate that that other car isn't working. I don't like driving those things," the attractive blonde complained. She pushed her bottom lip out seductively, while eyeing Nate.

"I'm sorry," the store owner apologized, "but it's all I got."

"I tell you what," Nate quickly assessed the situation. "Since you two pretty ladies don't want to be bothered with it, I'll be willing to take it."

The redhead looked at him shrewdly, "I guess you would. There's nothing else here to drive. So you wouldn't be doing us any kind of favor if you took if off our hands, so to speak."

"Oh, but I would," he smiled slowly, showing even white teeth, a dangerous glint entering his darkly lashed eyes. "I'd be willing to talk the cabbie into taking you back where you'd be sure to get a nice air-conditioned automatic, and that way, you two lovely ladies could ride in comfort."

"Doesn't sound too bad to me," the eager blonde chimed in, but the redhead wasn't totally convinced.

"Ah come on, shu-gar," the blonde gave her companion a familiar hug, flashing her blue eyes in a way that was persuasive, then shimmying closer into the embrace. "Who knows, maybe we can convince this handsome fellow to come visit us while we're in Belize City," she turned insinuatingly to Nate. "We can pretty much guarantee you'd have more than your normal amount of fun," she smiled seductively.

Dark eyes gleamed knowingly. "Well I can believe that," he continued to smile. "Why don't you tell me where you're going to be staying, and I'll have to look you up when I get there."

The redhead's eyes lit up with anticipation. "Sounds pretty good to me. We'll be staying at the Chateau Car-

ibbean. Donna and I will look forward to seeing you,"
she blew a kiss to Nate.

Nate reciprocated with a snarl of a smile. "Well . . .
ladies, let me go and speak with the cabbie."

"Sure," the blonde acquiesced. "I saw a couple of
things I'd like to get before we leave anyway. Coming
with me, sugar?" she asked her girlfriend.

The two of them smiled and followed the store owner
back inside.

"How do you come off askin' me to take them to Big
Creek, now? Me and the redhead had some urgent
plans, and she never even mentioned drivin' there," the
irritated cab driver retorted.

"Well take your plans to Big Creek." Nate's voice was
deceptively calm. He'd used up all his diplomatic abilities on the women inside, and he had no intention of
furthering his skills in that area when it came to the cabbie. "I will pay you, for your trouble," a visible muscle
in the square of his jaw began to pulsate.

He was grateful the Balamians weren't even interested in receiving the negative energy off of his money,
and he peeled off two bills from the roll returned to him
by Ponti, pressing them forcefully into the driver's palm.

Grudgingly the man took it, and watched Nate walk
away with purposeful strides. On the way he passed the
two women with a similar amount of impatience. Once
inside the store, he placed what he knew was more than
a week's rental money on the counter.

"Keep the change, Pete. I won't be bringing the vehicle back here. I'll make sure someone delivers it to you
out of Dangriga in no more than a week."

Nate didn't wait for the store owner's response, he
simply headed for the Samurai.

With a powerful tug, he pulled back the stick to re-verse, and stomped down on the gas. Quickly, Ponti swung himself into the vehicle just before Nate made a screeching one-hundred-and-eight-degree turn. With the gas pedal to the floorboard, the Samurai almost leapt forward as they bounded past the front of the building, leaving the blonde, the redhead and the cabbie in a hail of mud.

Chapter Fifteen

Weak from fear and stress, Raquel placed her hands against her caked and swollen eyes as she kneeled on her knees. The stiffness in her arms made her discomfort that much more agonizing, but the feeling of utter helplessness because of her loss of sight preyed on her mind.

She tried to open her matted lashes, but it was to no avail. The tight bandanna had aided the infection. She had to accept that she was sightless and at the mercy of Jay and the Shango. The realization was stunning, and Raquel fell forward on her elbows with the heavy weight of it. Afraid, she listened to the voices around her.

"By the *orishas*, what happened to her eyes," an ancient male voice asked.

Jay looked at the unkempt figure that crouched in front of them. Her black hair was full of remnants from the rain forest, her wrap, crumpled and spotted with dirt and oil.

"It is not our fault," he said smugly, speaking English so Jackie was sure to understand them. He wanted her to know how little he cared about her welfare. "Her eyes were already becomin' infected when we foun' her. We had to keep them covered so she wouldn' see where we were bringin' her, *buyei.*"

"What is t'at?" the shaman asked abruptly. "Evenshally she would know anyway. T'is woman lives in the United States. At no time while bringin' her here was she a physical threat to you." He got up and crossed over to Raquel. "And look at her wrists, they are already raw the bonds so tight around t'em. *Dada,*" he turned an accusatory eye in Jay's direction, "t'is is the woman who will speak to our ancestors. She should not have been tied up like a animal for slaughter an' kept in the bottom of t'at car until you arrived here," his filmy eyes flashed. "It was not necessary and you know it. T'is is a shame before the *orishas!*" his lank arm trembled with anger.

Almost in a fog, Raquel listened to the defending words of the older man. Seeking any comfort she could, she reached out blindly in the direction of his voice, feeling the dust of the dirt floor beneath her hand until she came across the rough skin of the shaman's bare foot, she touched it imploringly.

"I have warned you, *Dada,* the *orishas* are not to be shamed in any way. T'is should not have happened."

"I was told to bring her here, an' I did," Jay could barely contain the anger in his voice. "Now I am to blame for her condition?" he spat back.

"Are you not *Dada,* named for the brother of the mighty *orisha, Shango?* It is to his brother t'at the real responsibility for the continuance of his good name is given. When I gave you t'is name, when you were only a young man, it was because of your love of *Shango* and your desire to protect what was *Shango,*" the high priest proclaimed. "Aftah the split with the Garifuna, your father let you come under my wing, an' for a long time I thought t'at you would be the next *buyei* for our village. But as you got older *Dada*, I could see in you a weakness for worldly t'ings t'at should never be present in a *buyei*. It is for t'at reason, and t'at reason alone t'at you have only been given the initiations of the seventh rank. I could not as *buyei* initiate you further. But because of my love for you, I have kept you close by my side. Do not make me t'ink now, *Dada*, that you were not even deservin' of it, because of your lack of understandin' and compassion."

The shaman pinned Jay with his fiery gaze.

Just for a second Jay felt the urge to challenge him, but it was a fleeting need. Quickly he dropped his subservient gaze to the hut's floor.

"Now you will be responsible for cleanin' her up, an' make amends to the *orishas*. Take her to your wife, Eva. Tell her what I have said. Afterwards, she is to stay in the house where Grace lived until we go to Dangriga. It is empty now, her burial was yesterday."

Surprised, Jay looked from Raquel to the shaman.

"What about the *dugu* for my brother. Is it not to be tonight?"

"There will be no *dugu*," the elderly man replied. "At least not here. More time was needed to prepare. It will be joined with the ceremony in Dangriga."

With shaky hands the elderly *buyei* reached down to aid Raquel in getting to her feet. "Here let me help you," both of them unsteady, he, from age, and she, from the trauma of the entire ordeal.

"Come here, *Dada*," he motioned for Jay to approach

them, "take her to your home an' have Eva look aftah her."

With determined control Jay took Raquel's arm, offered to him by the *buyei*.

"No! Don't touch me!" she screamed out, stumbling to the ground as she blindly tried to put space between them.

Jay clenched and unclenched his fists as he glared down at her.

"You see! She do not want any help. I do not feel anyt'in' for her," he touched the thickly scabbed scar Raquel was responsible for placing on his face. "From the very beginnin' of t'is she has been a negative source, so let her suffah. Just like Al is sufferin' now."

Wearily the shaman looked at the young man he had nurtured since he was a child, the dimness of sad acceptance blanketing his features, "You are wrong, *Dada*. She does not want *your* help. Now go an' get Eva. Bring her here an' let her take the woman to Grace's."

Angrily Jay stalked out to return minutes later with an ill-at-ease Eva. She tried to keep her face converted from the shaman's perceptive gaze. In an uncharacteristic fit of anger she'd threatened to go to the *buyei* about the treatment she was receiving from Jay and his brother. Jay warned if she did, he'd make sure Al had a new focus for his attention, her youngest sister.

Eva's calloused hand tugged lightly on Raquel's elbow, encouraging that she come with her. As the young woman obeyed and turned her badly infected features toward her, Eva looked uncertainly at the *buyei*.

"Take her down the street, child. Clean her up an' make sure she is well taken-care-of."

The woman nodded, obediently.

"An' Eva," the *buyei* called just as they were to pass through the door. "Aftah the ceremony in Dangriga we must talk, all of us." He turned an assessing gaze in Jay's direction.

Raquel allowed the thin woman to lead her silently down the path. She could hear several voices at a distance as they progressed, there was a hint of uneasiness in the low tones, and no one came up to them.

She guessed by now everyone had heard about her, and some of them like Jay, gave her no sympathy. But still, she could also feel their fear of an *obeah* woman, and what she might do should they cross her.

If Nate's initial feelings about Jackie Dawson shed any light on the situation, there was quite a bit of animosity toward her for abandoning her homeland and the responsibility she had in bridging the gap between the Shango and the Garifuna. Raquel surmised, maybe if Jackie Dawson had returned to Belize willingly, things would have been different.

The sun blazed hot on her face, causing the already-sensitive skin around her eyes to sting and burn. Even the protective touch of her own hands appeared to aggravate the condition. Unsure of herself, Raquel held on tightly to the arm of the woman beside her.

Finally the sound of broken clay erupted, startling the sightless young woman as they entered a house. Blindly, she had kicked an object just inside the doorway, causing the unexpected clatter.

Eva looked into Raquel's distorted face and could not help but feel sympathy for her. Word of how the young woman had arrived in the bottom of the jeep had spread quickly through the village. Eva assumed Jay was taking revenge against her for the magic she had worked on him and Al during their trip from the States.

Many of the villagers were afraid of the consequences such treatment of a *obeah* woman would have on the town. Others felt she was deserving of what had happened to her—she knew her responsibilities, but still had to be forced to do them.

As she looked at Raquel, Eva could not take sides. All she saw was a person in pain. She understood how it felt to have your face and body marred, to be used and to feel like a prisoner, having no control over your own life. Jay's wife decided to make her stay as comfortable as she could. It was something to take her mind off of her own troubles, and a reason to stay away from her home and Al.

"Don't worry," Eva spoke softly as if she were speaking to a child. "It is nothin' put a piece of the clay vessel from Grace's burial. It is a Shangoain tradition, but of course you should know t'at."

Raquel nodded her head.

"Now you sit here while I set up the tin tub for you to bathe. Grace did not have a bathtub, but she's got runnin' watah. I will heat some on the stove as well, 'cause here it is easy to use up the hot watah, even if you run it for jus' a short period of time. Not much electricity here in Puntaborok."

Eva talked to Raquel continuously as she prepared for her bathing. It was if she had not talked to anyone like this in a very long time, and the young woman found her steady voice comforting. She couldn't help but think how horrible her life must be, being married to a man like Jay.

She remembered the revengeful, sadistic way he began to look at her after she scratched his face and Al had been hurt, and she knew he was a man capable of deep cruelties. Raquel was very aware, with the condition she was in now, there was no way she could defend herself should Jay decide to take action against her.

"Eva? Your name is Eva, isn't it?"

"Yes."

"Is there anything here that I could use to put in my eyes?"

"Maybe, Grace used to grow all kinds of herbs in the back of her place. There may be somet'in' t'ere."

Raquel's spirits brightened a little when she heard this.

"Yes, there may be," she thought out loud and she began to search her mind for the names of herbs that would best serve her purposes. "Do you know anything about herbs, Eva?"

"No ma'am, I don't"

"Well maybe someone else in the village does."

"The *buyei* does, but his eyes are bad now an' it is hard for him to get around. He has not dealt in the herbs for many years." Eva looked over at Raquel's anxious face. "The only other person in the village who knows 'bout the herbs has already gone to Dangriga. A group of people who are helpin' to prepare for the ceremony, left a few days ago. I wouldn' trust anyone else here, ma'am, when it comes to somethin' like t'at."

Raquel's shoulders drooped with disappointment. If only she could see, she could choose the proper medicine herself. Her thoughts focused on the shamaness and the extensive lessons given to her in the rain forest. There were several herbs she had shown her with antibiotic qualities. How could she identify what she needed if she were blind?

It was at that moment Raquel made up her mind.

"Eva would you take me back to the garden? Maybe I can still choose the right herbs"

"I will if you like," was Eva's leery response.

"I will need something to place over my eyes while we are outside. The sun is awfully tough on them right now," she admitted.

After Eva provided a clean cloth that she gingerly tied on Raquel's face, they made their way to the garden.

"T'ere aren't very many of t'em, ma'am," Eva warned her as she looked around.

"Well maybe that is good, this way it won't take long." Remembering the shamaness stressing recognizing a plant by sight and smell, Raquel hoped she learned her lessons well. "Now if you would break off small shoots of the different herbs and bring them to me. Maybe I can discern through smelling them which one I need."

All of her life she'd been told when one of your senses is lacking the others become stronger to compensate for the inadequacy, and as she accepted the herbs from Eva's hands she prayed the saying was true.

Minutes later, several plants had passed beneath her nose with no luck, and frustration began to set in. Perspiration streamed down her face from the heat, and the salty solution burned as it touched her eyes beneath the cloth.

"T'ere are only two more," Eva said as she watched her.

"Okay, bring them, here."

Hesitantly, she inhaled the first of the last two plants.

An intensely thick scent wafted into her nostrils. It was sharp and leafy, and she could feel her heart quicken as she inhaled it. She thought she recognized the scent but she wasn't sure. Again she inhaled the small plant with shaking hands, this time, taking a deeper, surer breath.

"Eva, I believe this is an herb called Golden Seal," she announced excitedly. "If it isn't, it is something in the same family, and it must have the same qualities. Pick some more of these and we'll take them inside and boil them. I will need the liquid to bathe my eyes in. From the rest I'll make a poultice."

From the distance, the sound of several drums and a wind instrument reached them. The music was accompanied by a lone voice chanting a spirited tune. It was a vigorous sound, surrounded by the occasional howl of a nocturnal animal stirring for the first time as night began to descend.

Eva looked off in the direction of the sounds.

"They are beginnin' to prepare for the journey to Dangriga. Tonight there will be much singin' an' dancin' an' drinkin' of cashew fruit wine. In Dangriga they started weeks ago preparin' for Garifuna Settlement Day. It is a yearly holiday usually attended by tourists, but because of the uniting ritual, which you will be in, an' the *dugu* for my husband's brothah, many special things must be provided. The ritual and the *dugu* will take place first, an' it will be held in private. You see, our people must be in a receptive mood when they arrive in Dangriga, an' the celebratin' tonight should bring about the feelin's needed."

Raquel noticed a change in Eva's voice as she spoke of Al, and she wondered what kind of encounters she had had with him since his return from the States. From her own experience, she knew they could not be pleasant ones.

Eva poured several containers of hot water into the tin tub she had partially filled from the tap. The remaining water would be used to boil the Golden Seal. A generous handful of the dark green leaves was used to make the medicine, and she allowed them to steam and bubble just as Raquel instructed, until the water turned dark green. Eventually the plants were removed, and for a brief period the extract was allowed to cool.

Afterwards, she located a small swath of white linen cloth. A part of it was torn off and dipped into the soothing liquid. With it Raquel carefully cleaned her own eyes, allowing some of the pungent brew to seep inside. Once the cleansing was done, Eva placed two poultices made from the remainder of the cloth, and filled with golden seal and chamomile, on Raquel's swollen eyes. The young woman sat back gratefully and hoped it would work.

Minutes later, Raquel sank gingerly into the lukewarm water with Eva's steady arm around her. Because the tub was small, it was necessary for her to keep her knees close to her body as she lowered herself into the soapy water. At last, for the first time since her second abduction, Raquel was able to breathe a sigh of relief, and pray that Nate would soon come to find her.

It wasn't been easy to hide the Samurai in the densely treed forest, so they parked it quite a distance from the road that led into the village. Although Ponti was the younger man, his knees and back ached from remaining in the same position for such an extended period of time, and for the umpteenth time, he shifted his weight. He marveled at the control of the man beside him as he remained as still as death, watching the activities of several nearby musicians.

They had waited until almost dark before they ventured this close. He knew the man Nate's patience was wearing thin, and he contemplated how long it would be before he would take action.

"I wonder which house she's in," Ponti asked, feeling the need to talk. Nate had said very little since they left Big Falls. The feel around him was volatile, and Ponti thought it best not to breach the silence, until now.

"It's no telling. So we've got to wait for some kind of sign. Other than that, anything we do might put her in jeopardy, and I'm not taking a chance on that. Whatever move I make will be treated as the final one, because I'm going to do whatever I have to do to get her out of Jay's hands."

Ponti's stomach growled loudly as if it was responding to Nate's brusque words. The smell of roasting armadillo, and beans prepared with sweet potatoes was strong. He regretted not eating earlier. Their chances of eating anytime soon appeared very slim.

Several men and women had begun to gather in the area of the musicians and the food. One small boy, who looked to be no more than three, broke away from his mother to sway to the beat of the double-headed dundun drum, smiling all the while as a few people in the crowd edged him on. Systematically, other young males would break out into an energetic dance, with powerful movements and wide-spread steps.

"They're preparing to go to Dangriga," Nate informed a curious Ponti. "They believe everyone's spirits and energy must be at their highest to get through the ceremony that will go on for a few days. Right now, it would be good to be able to count on that belief but that just ain't the way it is. There are a couple of guys involved in this that I know you can't trust, and one of them has it out for her."

Several feet in front of them, a young man held up a goatskin fashioned into the shape of a hornlike pouch. Turning it up, he drank eagerly from its contents. Some of the liquid flowed from the corners of his mouth as he squirted the potent brew into the cavern, afterwards wiping his mouth with the corner of his free hand. With rhythmic weaving motions he made his way over in front of a young female. She in turn, kept her eyes focused on the ground as he danced animatedly before her. The small crowd roared with laughter when she made mockery of his movements once he turned his back and danced away.

At that moment a crashing noise erupted inside one of the clapboard houses. None of the villagers, neither Nate nor Ponti, could hear the sound, as the drums beat loudly, and the spirit of the evening's festivities were being launched to new heights.

"I never go wit' you no more," Al whined as he threw the large pottery bowl against the wall. His features showed his distress as he closed his eyes and roughly pulled the skin of his face downward. "You left me here fo' days. And now you want to go again wit'out me."

The childlike statement from the large man appeared out of place, and Jay sought a way to comfort his distraught brother. It was hard for him to see him like this, and his anger against Jackie Dawson was fueled.

"Aftah we go to Dangriga, Al, I will take you everywhere wit' me. It will be like it was befor'. You and me. Inseparable."

Al's thick lips turned down into a pronounced pout. "After Da-Da-Dangriga?" he repeated questioningly. "You told me tonight, Jay. Tonight I would go wit' you. You say there would be a party for me. Now you say another time. I no believe you, Jay. I no believe you."

He paced around the room in a circle, repeating the statement over and over again. Jay wished what he had promised Al was true, but the *buyei* had changed his mind and there was nothing he could do about it. Because of the condition Al was in, there was no way he could afford to take him with him tonight when he met with Ricky Flint and his men for the transaction.

His eyes were concerned as he looked at his brother. It was at times like this when he was lucid and thinking logical thoughts, he was sure he might be getting better. But it was the other times, when he was totally someone else, that worried him. Jay wondered if the healing ceremony would be of any use.

"Look, Al. I can't take you wit' me, mon. I just can't. But aftah tomorrow, I will stay here an' travel wit' you to Dangriga, an' I promise you t'ings will be fine from t'en on."

Startled, childlike, accusing eyes focused on Jay.

"I know why you won't take me. You are goin' to your secret place." A bizarre pride gleamed on Al's face as he spoke. "See I know, I know, about it. You did not want me to know, but I know, 'cuz I follow you there, the first night you left me."

"What are you talkin' about?" Jay's bulbous eyes narrowed with concern.

"You know. You know where, Jay."

Al sat down in a kitchen chair, and starting flapping his knees together, vigorously. A dim-witted grin crossed his face as he licked his lips with his wet tongue.

Jay stared at his brother. He wondered if what he said was true. In the beginning, he had planned to bring him in on everything once they got back to Punta Gorda, but the accident happened, changing all of his plans.

"No, I don't Al, tell me. Where is my secret place?"

Al replaced his leg movements with an aggravated rocking as he eyed his brother, then he abruptly stopped. His mood changed from excited to sulking almost in a split second's time, "I don't know, Jay. I don't know."

He laid his head within his arms which he folded over a badly nicked wooden table. He began to whine again like a baby.

Jay walked over and placed a comforting hand on his brother's shoulder. "It's gonna be all right, Al. T'ings will be jus' fine," he assured him. "Do you remembah that girl on the boat, Al? Do you? Well, she is here in Punta Gorda an' I have plans for you an' her."

Al peeped out at his brother from beneath his large forearm. Back and forth he wiped the mucus from his runny nose against it.

"You did like her didn't you?"

He shook his head, numbly.

"Well tonight when I come back, we're gonna pay her a visit."

"W-w-where she now?" Al blubbered.

"Eva is gettin' her ready for you, down in Miss Grace's old place. She's cleanin' her up to make her smell good all just for you, man. Now I want you to do one t'ing for me, and t'at's stay here until I come back to get you. Then we'll go and get t'at girl for you. All right?"

Grunting in between snorts of laughter Al answered him affirmatively.

It wasn't until Jay walked briskly out into the open path that Nate spotted him. The numerous trees hanging umbrella-like around his house, made it impossible to see the comings and goings there without being in the direct path of the moonlight.

A man on a mission, Nate watched as Jay paid no attention to the group of festival-goers. Hurriedly he strode pass them, then continued to walk towards the end of the village. As he passed one of the dwellings he was stopped by an elderly man. Nate assumed, by his dress, that he was the *buyei*. He could tell by Jay's stance that he was impatient and wanted their talk to end quickly. After another few minutes' delay, the two men parted company. The high priest headed for the celebrations and Jay continued on his chosen path. Nate and Ponti followed Jay under the cover of the surrounding rain forest.

Chapter Sixteen

Eva helped Raquel pull the plain shift over her head. It was necessary since her arms remained sore and hard to lift. Afterwards she busied herself carrying buckets of water out back as she emptied the tin tub. In the short amount of time they were together, the two women had developed a strange sort of camaraderie. The helping hand Raquel extended to Eva had served as a salve for her own dampened spirits. In turn, her comforting deeds and words could not have been offered to Raquel at a more needy time.

Once again the young woman touched her infected eyes. The itching and burning had ceased, and some of her sight had been restored. She was able to see through hazy slits, the results of the medicinal herbs.

As she combed through her wet hair, she thought of the shamaness, and felt gratitude toward the elderly woman who'd chosen an eccentric life of solitude, instead of a subservient one.

* * *

Suddenly, the clatter of an empty bucket being tossed to the floor startled her, and she turned in the direction from which it had been thrown.

Eva was standing just in the doorway, her eyes bulging with fear.

"What's the matter, Eva?" Raquel asked. Instantly her nerves became tight and on edge.

Before the woman could answer, Al pushed her inside, an unnatural look in his eyes as he salivated and grinned madly. Shocked, Raquel jumped to her feet, knocking over the wooden chair she was sitting on as she looked from Eva's horrified features to Al's deranged ones.

All was blurry because of her limited vision, but she could tell Eva was petrified with terror. Then she saw why. In Al's left hand an old-fashioned shaving blade, rusted with time, loomed threateningly at his side.

"What do you want?" Raquel murmured, as her mind wrestled with the scenario before her.

Al continued to grin stupidly. "I want you," he motioned with the blade. "Jay told me you were here wait'in for me an' later were we gone come get you togethah. But I—I didn't want to wait."

"Okay, I understand," she replied in an effort to reason with him. "But why do you need the razor?"

"So you won't run away. It wouldn't be nice fo' you to run away."

"I won't run, Al," Raquel lied as she tried to calculate how quickly she could get to the door without Al catching her. If only she could see clearly!

Taking a chance, Raquel made her move, heading for the door. Unluckily her foot caught on some object causing her to fall, but still she managed to grope for the knob. Just as she was opening it, Al's large frame slammed into her, knocking the breath from her body, and shutting the door once more. Raquel screamed over and over again hoping someone outside would hear her, but her cry for help was drowned out by the loud music of the preparatory celebration.

"You lied," he harshly whispered in her ear as he picked her up off the floor, and carried her with one arm around her waist. "I don't like people who lie. Jay lied. He told me he would take me wit' him tonight an' t'ere would be a party for me, but it was not true," his voice was wounded and childlike. "T'at's why I lied to him 'bout his secret place. I said I did not know where it was, but I do. It's the *dabuyaba* an' I'm gonna take you t'ere wit' me," he said decisively. "I'll show you what I do to liars. I don't break my promises."

Aimlessly Raquel kicked, squirmed and screamed as Al carried her out of the back door into the darkness. "Oh God, Eva-a-a, help me. For God's sake help me, Eva."

Inside, Eva remained petrified, tears flowing unchecked down her cheeks.

Minutes later Jay stepped up to the doorway of the last house in the village. At first, he acted as if he were about to knock and go inside, then suddenly he turned and backed into the shadows. Nervously, he looked to see if anyone saw him. Feeling comfortable that no one had, he ran across the path's end into the rain forest.

"Where do you think he's in such a hurry to get to?" Ponti enquired.

Nate didn't bother to answer. Wherever Jay was off to

he didn't believe it had anything to do with Raquel. Back at the celebration he'd overheard a conversation between two of the village women, talking about the *obeah* woman that had been taken to one of the villager's homes.

Stealthily, he made his way to the house Jay had stopped in front of, pausing at the door to hear if there was any noise coming from the inside, but there was none. He motioned for Ponti to hurry to his side.

"I don't know whose house this is, but it's as good a place as any to start looking for her. Now Ponti, all I want you to do is to stay back, because if I'm hurt we're going to need somebody to drive us out of here, and that somebody's going to have to be you."

Ponti nodded. "But what if you should get killed?" Fear of the unknown behind the wooden door weighed heavily on the younger man.

"That's a possibility, but not a probability," Nate calmly replied.

Vaguely satisfied, Ponti backed back into the shadows.

Adjusting his stance, Nate gripped the Glock in his right hand as he tried the door knob with his left. His heart beat heavily at the thought of being discovered but he was counting on the majority of the people being at the ceremony as the probability that weighed in his favor.

The knob turned easily in his hand, and he cracked the door, then waited for some kind of response from within, but only silence greeted him. Cautiously, he pushed it open with his right elbow, and the light from within the small house spilled out onto the path. As the opening widened, he could see there had been a struggle.

Nate was surprised when he saw the woman sitting passively on the back stoop with the door wide open. Her badly scarred back was exposed. Nate knew she had to have heard the door open, but she never turned to see who was entering the place.

Stepping inside, he inspected the room. Lying next to a tin tub he saw the bright red wrap Raquel had worn earlier that day.

Gently, he stooped down beside the woman whose salty tears had left white tracks on her dark skin.

"Where is she?" he asked then repeated the question. "Where is the *obeah* woman?"

Blankly, Eva looked into Nate's worried features, then with lips barely moving. "Al's taken her to the old temple. He say, he gone do to her, what he did to me."

As quick as a flash Nate was at the front entrance. "Ponti," he called. Instantly, the Mayan appeared out of the shadows.

"Go and get the Samurai, and meet me at the end of that road that forked off from the main one, coming in to the village. Do it! Now!"

Nate crashed through the foliage as he headed for the abandoned *dabuyaba*. He remembered its location well, for at one time, while he was still a boy, it was the only temple used by both the Shango and the Garifuna.

Branches and vines whipped at his face as he ran, the sight of the woman's scarred back spurring him on. He had to get there before the same gruesome thing happened to Raquel.

* * *

Al dragged Raquel into the thick darkness of the neglected building. The only illumination came from a small stream of moonlight that infiltrated through a crack in one of the dirt clogged windows. Holding on to her wrist tightly, he closed the door behind them, then he pulled her resisting body further inside. They passed between several rows of dusty benches before they reached the front of a large room.

Because of the darkness, Raquel's limited vision was practically useless, and an unfathomable panic began to rise inside of her.

"Let me go, Al," she pleaded. "You don't want to do this. It's bad! What you're thinking is bad, I tell you. And you're not a bad man, Al," she tried to reassure him through his demented mind.

Al was quiet as he looked around the dilapidated room. "We should go in t'ere." He dragged her behind him as he kicked open the door of a smaller room jutting off to the side of the large one. Bright moonlight streamed in as the door gave in to the weight of his thrust, and he slammed it behind them.

Satisfied, he let go of Raquel's wrist, and she peered helplessly into the semidarkness around her, frantically searching for an avenue of escape.

Strangely, this room was much cleaner than the first. Several large objects were lined up neatly against the wall. Remnants of broken benches had been piled in one of the corners, but the majority of the space was wide open.

"Yeah I like t'is room. It's much bettah than the first," Al rambled madly. "I can see bettah in here, and I want you to see what I do to you," he wiped the back of his hand across his nose.

He backed up to one of the containers against the wall, and placed the shaving razor upon it. Then keeping a watchful eye on Raquel, with jerky motions, he began to strip off his shirt and remove his pants. Finally he stood stark naked before her, grinning dementedly all the while. His thick, muscular body in contrast to the bizarre smile on his face.

A sickening bile began to rise in Raquel's throat as she watched him; the thought of what he planned to do to her, was utterly revolting.

"You gotta take off your clothes too," he stated, his tone absent of threat or anger. "I want to make pretty pictures for you" His eyes gleamed.

"I can't, Al. You've got to help me," she coaxed, her mind working quickly. Raquel began to back towards the stack of wooden remnants. "It will be better if you help to undress me." she asked in a quivering voice.

Al started across the room just as Raquel's back touched the wooden slats of the wall. Suddenly she turned and groped for one of the smaller pieces which lay near the edge. She grabbed it, sending a splinter deep into her hand. The pain was intense but Raquel did not care as she blindly swung the plank with all her might in Al's direction.

The wood landed with a sickening thud as it caught him across the face, breaking the skin with its force, its uneven edges cutting into the tender meat. Even so, the blow barely rocked him, and a cry like that of a mad, wounded animal rose from deep in his throat.

The unnatural noise horrified Raquel, and with a counter-swing she wielded the board again, this time catching him in his throat, causing him to grab it and double over with pain.

Seeing her chance, Raquel tried to skirt his massive body, but with one arm he reached out and caught her by the waist, as the other hand remained protectively about his own neck. She screamed again as he grabbed her, and in blind terror, she swung the slat wildly over her head, striking Al repeatedly. The powerful and mad Al shook her as if she were a rag doll, then released her as a piece of the splintering board pierced one of his eyes.

Like a cornered animal she dropped to the floor, scrambling to get behind him and to the door. With every ounce of strength she had she rose and lunged for the knob.

By now, Al's face was bleeding profusely. Seeing Raquel through a stream of blood, he caught her leg, forcing her to tumble sideways into the containers against the opposite wall. Raquel gasped as the board fell from her hand into the darkness of the room. With a triumphant laugh, Al climbed on top of her, placing his large hands about her throat. With eyes blazing wildly, he pressed her head back into a white dust that surrounded them, as he reached for the razor he'd placed on top of the containers.

She started to scream as his hand found the weapon and he raised it high above their heads. She closed her eyes to block out the horror of what was about to occur.

Suddenly, two loud bangs rang inside the room causing Raquel's eyes to fly open. For a second, Al's demented features seemed to freeze before he tumbled over to the side of her, dead from two bullets to the heart.

Raquel began to cry and shiver uncontrollably as Nate took her in his arms.

"It's all right *pataki*. It's all right. I am here now," he spoke to her comfortingly. "No harm will come to you, now, baby. No harm at all."

She clung to him, burying her face in his chest. "I thought I was dead, and I'd never see you again," she managed through racking sobs.

"No baby, it's all over with, just like a bad dream."

Gently he picked her up in his arms and carried her out of the temple. Moments later a set of headlights beamed in the distance, then pulled up beside them.

A silent Ponti looked on as Nate placed the young woman's limp body into the back seat of the car, then climbed up beside her, continuing to cradle her close in his arms. He rubbed her face and tangled hair, kissing her repeatedly, as he murmured reassurances.

As they drove down the moonlit back road, sprays of white powder floated inside the vehicle. Blotches of it were on Raquel's face, and a fine dusting was in her hair and on her shift.

"What the hell is this?" Nate muttered as he looked at it. Then he stuck a finger into a thick batch clinging to the side of Raquel's face and placed it in his mouth.

Smacking his lips experimentally, he exclaimed, "I'll be damned. It's cocaine."

Chapter Seventeen

"Shut off the lights!" Jay ordered, his voice hushed, excited.

Mane-Mane cut resentful eyes in Jay's direction. "What the hell for? Look man, you're getting on my freakin' nerves with all this bull—"

Reaching over Mane-Mane's muscular arm, Jay extinguished the lights as a nude couple full of cashew fruit wine stumbled drunkenly toward them. Their inebriated state was evidence of the orgiastic climax of the waning Shangoain celebration not very far away.

High-pitched squeals of pleasurable glee erupted from the female as the male's hands intentionally groped over her full frame. With anticipation, the couple fell to the ground continuing their sexual escapade. Quickly the woman's laughter was replaced with guttural moans of pleasure as they concluded the unabandoned foreplay exhibited only moments before.

Mane-Mane leaned over antagonistically towards Jay. "Don't you all have beds out here in the jungle to do that kind of thing? Or are you just so savage you all prefer making out on the ground like animals?"

"I wouldn't expect you to understan'," Jay retorted as he slid further into the car seat. Ricky's men acted as though they knew everything, that they were in control. But this was Jay's country, Jay's people. Soon he would control everything and these men would not talk to him with disrespect. He could almost taste all the power he would have if everything went according to plan. "It's the kind of t'ing only real men an' women know about," Jay continued to Mane-Mane. "Not punks who hide their true nature behin' big muscles, tryin' to make up for the tiny bulge in the front of their pants."

Mane-Mane's eyes lit up with anger, "You backwoods mother—"

"All right. All right. Cool it. Do you want them to hear us?" The other man, Rock, placed a calming hand on his partner's shoulder. "What the hell are they doing out here this time of morning anyway?" he asked Jay, irritated.

"T'ere was a celebration in the village. T'ey should be makin' t'eir way back towards the main street soon. Usually no one comes t'is far out. It must have been a very spirited ritual wit' lots of wine."

"Okay, we'll just wait them out."

Jay's prediction proved to be correct. Minutes later, the satiated pair made their way arm and arm back towards the distant music.

Still not wanting to take a chance, the trio started the car but kept the lights off; the moon provided enough illumination for them to navigate their way toward the abandoned *dabuyaba*.

"Mane-Mane, you and Jay go inside and take these sacks with you. Since this is our first haul we didn't stash that many bricks here, we're just starting to test the waters so to speak. "If everything goes smooth tonight, the next haul will be much bigger," he looked encouragingly in Jay's direction. "Now, only three of the containers actually have cane in them, the others are just dummies with debris and other crap inside."

"Yeah . . . yeah, I know. Remembah I was wit' you when the first drop was made," Jay was anxious to show he knew what was going on. Already he was outside the car with two of the large cotton sacks and a small spotlight in his hand.

Rock fastened a barely tolerable stare on his lean, suddenly impatient companion. "Just chill, man. I know that. I'm just doin' my job," he paused to let his point sink in. He needed to remind the newest member, whenever Ricky wasn't around, he was the man calling the shots. "While you two go inside, I'll stay out here, and make sure we don't have any unexpected guests. Mane-Mane, once you all check the place out, and find everything is okay, come back and let me know before you gather up the bricks."

Mane-Mane's braided head nodded with understanding. Then he grabbed the remaining sacks and flashlight, and joined Jay as he walked toward the building.

Carefully they opened the large wooden door, switching on their lights only after it had been closed behind them. Breathing heavily, Jay peered into the semi-darkness. He shined his minute spotlight around the dust-filled room making sure everything appeared to be the same.

Mane-Mane's eyes followed the path of Jay's light, from time to time blending his own luminous bubble with his partners.

A hoarse laugh gurgled up from his throat.

"Shit man, I'm disappointed. Ain't no leftover shrunken heads or human skulls laying around. Ain't that the kind of stuff y'all use to hoodoo each other with?"

"Screw you, man," Jay threw back at him while he advanced toward the side door aided by the flashlight.

Suddenly, the light focused on a large, muddy footprint planted firmly upon the door. Jay stiffened at the sight of it, then turned to Mane-Mane, placing a silencing finger across his thin lips.

Now, as alert as a bird dog, Mane-Mane pushed him aside. Cautiously he touched one of the thickest edges of the print's outline, and found it was still damp under the dry outer crust. A fatal look replaced the playful visage the huge bodyguard had worn moments before. He let the sacks fall silently to the dirt floor, and stealthily retrieved a .38 from the front of his pants. He motioned for Jay to continue shining his light in the direction of the door.

With amazing swiftness and one smooth action, Mane-Mane forced the door open, entered the room, and stood poised to confront anyone on the opposite side. He was counting on the element of surprise, coupled with the pitch darkness behind him and the glare of Jay's small spotlight to throw any would be opposers off guard. His heart beat loudly in his ears as his deepset eyes darted swiftly about the wrecked room.

"What the hell is this?" The words tumbled from his thick lips as his eyes landed on Al's nude, bloodied body against the tumbled containers, under a white coating of pure cocaine powder.

Pushing Mane-Mane aside, Jay forced his way in front of him. A painful pressure tightened inside his chest as he looked at his brother's lifeless body. Al's head lay cocked at an unnatural angle where the impact of the bullet had snapped his thick neck.

"Who's the dead freak laying in the middle of the stash, man?" Mane-Mane asked, not really expecting an answer. Before he could turn and look at his counterpart, Jay launched a mad attack on his back, a throaty scream of anguish echoing throughout the room.

"Don' call him a freak!" A thin but powerful arm locked about Mane-Mane's muscular throat, while Jay squeezed with all his might.

Gagging, the bodyguard tried to pry loose the viselike grip choking his neck. With fingers resembling talons, he desperately reached behind him, locking them into the side of Jay's thin throat. Squeezing his thick digits deep into his throat, Mane-Mane bent forward, and flipped him over onto his back. He followed Jay's fallen frame onto the ground, edging a forceful knee into his sternum, pressing his weight against his chest.

"What's the matter with you, man? Huh?" he managed between choking gasps, guardingly holding his throat.

Jay squeezed his eyes together, tightly, as he focused on the lingering pain beneath his jawbone. Tears edged their way from the corers of his eyes, and he fought against the pain and the mental picture of his brother's inert body.

"What's going on in here?" Rock spoke from behind them. His eyes were wide with foreboding and a few snorts of cocaine. A .38 similar to his partner's was visible in his hand.

"What the hell?" Rock reached down to pick up one of the hot spotlights, "All right, Mane-Mane, let him up," and he turned the lights glare on Al's stiff frame. "Damn, he sure is messed up. I wonder who he is," he shined the revealing white light lewdly upon Al's blank features, highlighting the thin covering of narcotics that blanketed the body and the area around it. "And look at all the cane that's on him. You got any idea who this is, man?" he turned to Jay, the situation and the drugs making his heart pump faster.

"He's my brothah," Jay stated as he weakly rose to his feet.

"Your brother." Rock's tone turned the innocent words into a crime. "What was he doing here?"

"I don't know," Jay held his shaking head in his hands. "As far as I know he nevah even came to t'is place. Nobody evah does."

"Well that's what you get for thinking village boy," Mane-Mane looked closely into Al's open eyes. "Rock ma-an, I warned Ricky against getting involved with folks like this boy. Now look-a-here. Part of the dope's messed up and we got a corpse on our hands. But see he don't want to listen to—"

"Shut up, man," Rock ordered. "He don't listen to you cuz you don't know when to be quiet. We need to find out how many bricks we still have left. We'll talk about everything else later."

Roughly Mane-Mane bent forward to move Al's inflexible body out of the way. Jay knocked his hand off of his brother's shoulder.

"I'll take care of my own brothah."

Rock and Mane-Mane rummaged for, then counted the remaining bricks of cocaine while Jay tried to cradle his dead brother's body in his arms, the natural effect of rigor mortis making his affectionate gestures nearly impossible.

"Nine, ten . . . Okay. That means we only lost two of them," the larger bodyguard concluded after placing the last pair of white rectangles in the sack.

"What do you mean, *only* two! Wait till Ricky hears about this. Those two bricks alone would be worth millions on the street," Rock's eyes flashed at his partner.

"Well hell, I didn't do it! Ain't no need to get pissed with me."

"Naw, you're right. But somebody's gonna have to pay for this."

Both sets of eyes focused on Jay and his brother.

"And I know jus' who," Jay said, almost to himself. "T'ey will pay for my brothah's death an' t'ey will not die quickly. I'm gonna make sure t'ey suffah," he spoke reassuringly to the corpse.

Rock and Mane-Mane looked at each other.

"That ain't the only thing around here that's gonna have to be paid for," Mane-Mane retorted. "Your damn brother getting killed is the least most important thing that needs to be considered."

A chill of fear ran down Mane-Mane's spine as Jay cast eyes shining with a bizarre light in his direction.

"I will put a curse on you . . . your mother, and every generation that comes after you, if you say anything else against him. I could be a *buyei*. Do not cross me. Do you understand?"

Mane-Mane knew about fighting with his hands and weapons, but being threatened with curses was unchartered territory, and almost frightened him more than a gun being pointed in his face. He threw up both his hands in a show of surrender.

"All right, man. All right. Yeah. Whoever monked up our stash . . . and did this to your brother, is gonna have to pay. They'll have to pay with their lives." He adeptly changed the subject. "I'll guarantee Ricky that."

"Yeah, you're right. We'll have to guarantee him something when we tell him about this," Rock sniffed and squeezed his nostrils out of habit. "But right now, we need to bury the stiff . . . I mean your brother, before this place is crawling with the law."

"No," Jay grabbed at Al's chest possessively. "He must be buried the Shangoain way. Not put in the ground like some worthless dog."

"Naw man, that's not what I'm sayin'," Rock explained, his patience growing thin, but like Mane-Mane he too was leery of curses. "Right now, it wouldn't do us, or your brother any good, if we get tracked down and put away before we can take care of the suckers who did all this. You see what I'm sayin'?"

Jay's bulbous eyes stared at him suspiciously.

"Since they offed your brother, I don't think they'll be running to the authorities right away. So we got a chance of finding them and paying them back. But if you take your brother back to your village like this, ma-an, ain't no way somebody dealing with the law ain't gonna here about it. Now you want to get the suckers who did this don't cha?"

Jay nodded affirmatively.

"Then just do what I say, all right?"

Rock watched as Jay and Mane-Mane carried Al into the main part of the temple to be temporarily placed under the platform. His drug habit compelled him to dab his finger into a small pile of cocaine, then inhaled it up his nostrils. The uncut narcotic caused his nose to bleed immediately. He patted it with a corner of one of the cotton sacks.

Eventually the three men returned to the vehicle, placing the remaining bricks of cocaine in the trunk of the car.

"Now, how do we find out if the people you think are responsible for all of this, are actually behind it?" Rock asked, gently rubbing his nose.

"It'll jus' take one stop," an unearthly calm laced Jay's words. "You all will have to stay in the car back off in the woods. If we drove up into the village, it would cause too big of a stir," he warned. "I'll tell you where to drop me off."

Jay entered the dark house silently. Once again, he waited to switch on the spotlight only after he'd closed the door behind him. His heart lurched as the light beamed directly onto Eva's emaciated, barely covered frame, hunching in a corner on top of a cot. Her eyes were wide open, but they did not blink from the glaring light. Any other time Jay would have spoken to her harshly, but her uncanny appearance made him think twice. Instead he cased the room with the unnatural light. Only after he was sure Jackie Dawson was not in the house did he address his wife.

"Where is the woman?"

Eva continued to stare directly ahead.

"D'ya hear what I said? Where is she? Did Al come here an' get her?" Jay demanded loudly, shining the light interrogatingly in her face, but to no avail. For a moment her features reflected fear as he mentioned his brother's name, but then that was replaced with the same blank stare.

Maybe he was tired from the entire ordeal, or even more unlikely he felt sorry for the pitiful picture his wife made, but for whatever reason, he didn't press her further. He switched off the light and closed the wooden door behind him. He didn't need Eva to tell him what had happened. The woman's absence told him everything he needed to know.

It was obvious Al had known about his secret place and had taken Jackie there. He had tried to have his way with her, she had fought him like the *echu* he knew her to be. Then Nate Bowman had come, probably during their struggle, killed Al and took her away.

Jay rounded the tiny house, only to stop on the side facing the rain forest. He needed a few moments alone before he joined the two men that waited for him. The intensity of the emotions rumbling inside him made it hard to think straight. It seemed like in a matter of minutes everything important in his life was being destroyed.

Al was dead, and his relationship with Ricky and the *buyei* would both be on shaky grounds after tonight. Even if he killed Nate and the woman, which he had to do to avenge his brother's death, it would not guarantee things in his life would be any better. Ricky could still decide he was too risky to deal with, and that would mean a loss of his future as he had dreamed of it; away from this village, living in Miami, having the best life had to offer. If that were taken away from him, as things would stand then, he would no longer have the high priest to support him. He would be ostracized, claimed dead to the Shangoains for killing the link to the *gubida*. The *buyei* would never forgive him.

Jay pulled hard on the reefer he'd automatically lit as his mind rambled through his current state of affairs. The one thing he was sure of, he had to make the people suffer who were responsible for his brother's death.

The man stared at the sky as he took several drags, then finished the hand-rolled cigarette, throwing the butt on the ground as he made up his mind.

He'd do everything he could to make Ricky give him another chance, that was the future he wanted, and that's what he still intended to have. After everything was over with, he would go back to the *dabuyaba* and give Al the best Shangoain burial that he could, but the truth about Al's death would have to remain a secret. He would convince the *buyei* Al had run off, and with his mind as scrambled as it was that would be easy for anyone to believe.

If Nate Bowman had killed him, which Jay believed he had, he figured Nate would not run and tell the authorities too quickly. So once he and the woman were dead, no one else would ever know what had happened. Most important, no matter how Nate and Jackie ended up dying, he'd have to convince Ricky and the others the Shango must never know he was involved in any kind of way. It would be the only way they'd be able to continue trafficking drugs in the area.

Automatically his mind went to Eva. She was the only person who knew enough of the truth to destroy the entire plan.

Jay's hand went to the switchblade he always carried with him. Already mentally drained, by now, he was almost acting entirely on instinct. He rounded the corner again and reentered the house, but this time when he turned on the spotlight, Eva was not there. His eyes went to the back door that was still ajar. She had managed to leave without him hearing her.

At first a feeling of unadulterated fear engulfed him, but that was replaced with a sense of relief when he thought of the threat he had made against her life if anything should ever happen to him. A satisfied smirk rested on his dark features. He knew his wife. The years had cowered her spirit. She would think long and hard before saying anything that could cause problems for him, and the state she appeared to be in, he didn't know if she was capable of thinking at all. Probably by the time she made her mind up to move against him, he would have found a more efficient way of taking care of her.

Jay let the calming thoughts wash over him, the effect of the marijuana aiding his endeavor. Feeling a sense of security, he shut off the spotlight and headed back to join Rock and Mane-Mane in the car.

Chapter Eighteen

"How much farther is Dangriga?"

Looking into the rear-view mirror, Ponti's voice reflected his weariness of body and spirit. The events of the previous day hung in his mind like a nagging movie. He didn't actually see what had happened in the temple, but he'd heard the unmistakable gunshots, and from the state the woman, Jackie Dawson, was in, there was no doubt in his mind Nate had killed the man responsible for it.

Over the last twenty-four hours he'd come to admire the man's steely strength, but he had to admit that admiration was tinged with fear. He believed there was very little Nate was afraid of, and a man without fear could be a dangerous man.

Ponti watched as Nate gently removed the wild strands of wind-blown hair from the woman's face as she slept comfortably against his shoulder, his ability to show such tenderness, starkly contrasted with the toughness he also possessed.

Thickly fringed eyes gazed out the window as he studied the very familiar territory. Because of Nate's knowledge they had been able to keep to the back roads.

"I'd say we've got ten miles to go, seven if we were able to cut through the forest," he responded to Ponti's question.

His deep voice caused movement underneath Raquel's closed eyelids, followed by the slight opening of her matted eyes. She could feel his arm draped snugly around her shoulder as thoughts of the morning's events drifted into her consciousness. She continued to remain very still, not wanting him to know she had awakened.

Raquel was afraid of what her reaction would be when she looked at him knowing he had killed a man, even if it were to protect her. Somehow her attempt to do the same thing in the heat of her struggle with Al did not lessen the weight of Nate's actions. She felt as if the arm about her shoulder was that of a complete stranger.

Truthfully, what did she really know about this man, Nate? That he had kidnapped her and forced her to come to Belize to be subjected to the horrors she had come to know? Yet in the midst of it all, had done all he could to protect her? That with the skill of a master sculptor he knew how to touch and caress her, bringing her to heights of passion she had only dreamed about? That he had killed a man, shooting him in the head at point-blank range without a second thought?

The look in Al's eyes when Nate shot him forced its way into her mind, and a shudder ran through her, causing Nate to look down and find she was awake. Their eyes met briefly allowing him to catch the glimmer of fear in hers before she quickly looked away. Nate's dark gaze looked emotionlessly ahead as she lifted her face from his shoulder, turning it in the direction of the opposite window.

"Here," he offered her a small container of bottled water and several crumpled napkins he'd found on the back seat of the car. "You can try and clean your eyes with this."

Raquel accepted his offering wordlessly.

The tepid water felt refreshing against her skin as she cleansed her face. She was relieved to find her eyes were almost back to normal, even though that discomfort had been replaced by another. Jarring pains shot up and down the length of her neck from even the slightest movement of her head, an achy reminder of her most recent brush with death.

Natural reflexes caused her to flinch from a particularly sharp pain, and Raquel's slender hand raised to cradle her bruised throat. Tears stung the back of her closed lids as she fought against the physical and mental discomfort.

Raquel felt a warm, caressing feeling on her thigh. She opened her eyes to see Nate's large comforting hand reaching out to console her.

Suddenly the sight of this comforting gesture infuriated her. Like a volcano that had been waiting to erupt, her raspy voice struck out, full of insurmountable fear and pain. "Don't you touch me. If it wasn't for you none of this would have happened to me." Dark, injured eyes overflowed with tears. "I can't stand anymore of this. I can't stand you."

Nate almost felt his heart stop at hearing the harsh words against him, nor could he stomach seeing her so distraught. Desperate, he enfolded her in his arms despite her loud protest, holding her tightly against him, willing the pain and hurt to go away.

Finally Raquel began to sob. It was a deep outpouring of the misery she felt as she gave in to the comforting embrace.

The fear Nate had seen in her perplexed eyes was more than he could bear. To accept that the woman you love, feared you and perceived you as a cruel and a heartless criminal, was hard to do. Yes, he had finally admitted to himself that he loved her. Seeing Al attempt to take her permanently away from him made his feelings clear: he desired her, he admired her and he loved her.

Yet Nate had mixed emotions about Raquel's reawakened fear of him. He knew in many ways they were still strangers. The moments of love they had shared were far less than the continuing nightmare she found herself in. He had no one to blame for that but himself.

As the moments passed, Raquel regained her self control, and she withdrew herself from his arms. Nate wanted to continue to hold her but he could tell from the stiffening of her body that she would not welcome him.

Raquel could feel his ebony gaze upon her willing her to look into his eyes. Curly, hesitant eyelashes fluttered during a moment of indecision before unveiling a tear bright, dusky stare. The unnerving chill of love, the warmest of emotions, trying to survive under these circumstances was felt by them both.

Although Nate's lips never uttered a word of apology, it was written clearly in the depths of his eyes. Raquel recognized the look but couldn't accept it.

Once again she was the first to break eye contact. He

had saved her life and she knew she still loved him, but she couldn't reach out to him any further, not after what happened with Al.

As she returned to looking out the window, bright splotches of color could be seen in the distance. The rain forest was very dense and traveling had been slow. She could tell that the road they had chosen was not well used, because in actuality it was little more than a path. The humidity had begun to build inside the vehicle as the morning progressed, and even though it was quite early and the massive cohune palms and guanacaste trees blocked out the majority of the sun's rays, its strong influence was beginning to be felt. All the jeep windows were now rolled down, it had become too sticky and hot inside.

"Hey, Nate. There are a bunch of women and children to the far right of us. They look like they're gathering something," Ponti exclaimed with curiosity.

"Yes, you're right. They're digging up cassava roots. There will be a lot of *ariba* bread made and eaten over the next few days, so they are making sure they'll have enough throughout the ceremonies."

"It is like the Mayan tortilla?"

"Somewhat."

Nate noticed Raquel's eyes brighten as she watched two Garifunian women accompanied by a little girl heading back for the village. On top of their heads they balanced baskets piled high with roots from the shrublike plant. He felt relieved to see even the slightest positive change in her. So he continued to talk, avoiding the heavy silence of moments before.

"It is a flat, dry bread, that is the very essence of the Garifunian culture, a legacy of our Carib Indian ancestry," Nate continued. "I say *our* because my father is Garifunian, but my mother was Creole. I basically know about the culture because of that, but the Garifunian are very secretive about a lot of their customs. There are things they never share with outsiders, not even their spouse."

A surprised look crossed Raquel's features as she listened to Nate talk about his family. For awhile now, she had longed to know more about him. It was a revelation to hear his parents were of mixed heritages, even though they were both Belizean. She envied what little knowledge he had of his father's people, since she had grown up completely ignorant of her own.

"As a matter of fact Garifuna means 'Cassava-eating people' taking their name from the Carib word *Karifuna,* of the Cassava clan."

Ponti nodded his head appreciatively, always anxious to learn whatever he could. Since he had grown up in Balam, he didn't know much about the other ethnic groups that populated Belize. The elders did not find it wise to share knowledge about other cultures. They felt the Balamian way was superior, and knowledge of others only helped to confuse their own villagers.

By now all of the women and children had become aware of the jeep. They stopped in the middle of their tasks, watching the vehicle's sluggish progress no more than a hundred yards away.

The dresses the women wore reminded Raquel of floral printed dusters favored by some of the elderly females who frequented the clinic, but these women also wore bright head wraps and scarfs.

While the women continued to watch their progress at a distance, two of the young boys began to run in the direction of the four-wheel drive. With agile grace their bare feet paddled against the forest floor. As they got closer they picked up pebbles and began to chuck them at the jeep. But their impromptu fun was cut short when they were abruptly stopped by a particularly vocal and nimble female.

As the vehicle passed the harvesters, and the distance between it and the women and children increased, Raquel could see all of them hoisting their loaded baskets on to their heads, and in a staggered line heading for Drangriga. Their easy movements with such an arduous task made her wonder what kind of people would greet them there.

For some reason it was hard for her to connect Nate with the women and children she saw toiling in the rain forest. From the very beginning, he had stood out from her other abductors. His naturally quiet, reserved ways—until provoked—seemed to separate him from Al and Jay. He was a man whose presence exuded power, unlike Art, with his youthful penchant to take instructions instead of give them.

Raquel choked back the urge to demand from Nate an answer for all that had happened to her. Why he had kidnapped her, then had chosen to protect her? Why was it so important to him that she participate in the Garifunian ceremony, that he would risk his own life to protect her?

Yet she knew she was afraid of what she might find out, and it made her feel that much more vulnerable. She was afraid the answer Nate might give would confirm the worst of her fears. That he was not a man with morals and principles who had simply been caught up in a mad scheme beyond his control. That he was in his

own way like Jay, all of his deeds a shield for his own
selfish needs.

Raquel felt a powerful urge to look in to the strong
features of the man whose face at times revealed bound-
less compassion. She sighed heavily. She hoped she was
right about Nate Bowman. She wanted to be reassured
that even if her logic had failed her, her inner guide, her
sense of good and evil and right and wrong, had not led
her astray. It was all so confusing. So much had passed
between her and Nate in such a short period of time,
she was having difficulty knowing what to believe.

Instead she looked down at her hands that were covered with dirt and her own blood. She was surprised to
see a large splinter lodged in the fleshy mound of her
palm beneath her thumb. As she picked at the splinter,
she realized her mind had been so overwhelmed with
the battery of recent events, and the engaging images
before her, she had managed to block out the pain of
the tender injury. Somehow seeing the violated flesh
made her feel its pain, causing once again an overall
feeling of defilement and uncertainty.

It had only been yesterday when she'd felt so sure
about her feelings for Nate, and her abilities to carry out
whatever was necessary during the ceremonies in
Dangriga, but now she wasn't sure of anything.

Unable to remove the splinter, she reached instead
for the small leather pouch that hung about her neck.
Her soiled fingers clung to its smoothness as she
searched for the power within herself to stay on the sane
side of her emotions. At that moment it would have
been so easy to cross the line, to let the current of
the mental gap between sanity and insanity sway to the
latter.

Oh God ... Spirit ... Will ... whatever I should call you. I need you to be with me now. Just let me be able to hold on. Her mental cry to the powers that be vibrated from within her, creating a strong shuddering, as she moved her lips to the words of the silent prayer, her richly lashed eyes closed tight in her seeking.

The intenseness that surrounded Raquel during this prayer-filled moment was felt by both Nate and Ponti. The younger man watched with true concern through the rear-view mirror, while Nate's dark gaze burned with a well-known torture.

The one woman whom he'd loved the most, his mother, had lived her last years of life balancing on the edge of sanity. Events not nearly as violent as the recent ones this woman beside him had suffered, had placed her on that precipice. He did not know if he could accept finally finding another kind of love, just as powerful, then losing her to a similar fate. Only this time there would be no one to blame but himself.

"It all will be over soon, *pataki.*" He sought to say the only words that he thought would comfort her.

A heavy silence prevailed inside the tiny vehicle as they progressed closer to the village. Raquel watched as the landscape changed from a dense rain forest to rising hills. Finally they took an ill-kept road called Hummingbird Highway that quickly changed names prior to approaching a shabby bus stand with a sign pointing toward Dangriga.

Time passed slowly as they entered the town's vicinity, a dilapidated fruit-laden truck creeping along contentedly in front of them helped to prolong the journey. As the minutes passed, Raquel realized the city of Dangriga was not another isolated village like Balam or

Eva's small settlement near Punta Gorda. Modern society had definitely made its mark here. From what she could see it was a neat, bustling town with restaurants, gift shops, a bar and a disco. Just like any city it had its more prosperous neighborhoods where the stilted houses were well kept, then, no further than a few blocks down, the housing climate changed, sometimes slightly, at others, drastically so. Just the sight and feel of the city gave her some reassurance that regular life still existed outside the bloodletting Balamians and vengeful Shangoains.

It was energizing to see a river flowing straight through Dangriga, populated with a variety of boats and people fishing. There seemed to be a festive attitude as they smiled, chatted and reeled in fish of all sizes and hues.

"Turn here," Nate instructed solemnly, pointing to the right. "It will take us down to the sea."

Ponti waited patiently as the traffic moved slowly through the streets.

Raquel could feel her spirits lifting as she watched the city's serene activities, but nothing was more healing than the inner calm inspired by the sight of the turquoise, clear Caribbean Sea. The spectable of its expansive waters lying before them assured her, there was definitely a master plan. One in which she and others like her, had in comparison, small but important roles to carry out. Raquel believed one either conjures up the faith to see oneself through or succumbs to the negative forces.

They turned down a road that ran along the meager beach. Like the river, it too had its share of people, but some of their activities were a little more puzzling to the young woman.

An older man placed a small colorful flag in the sand, carefully he began to smooth the surface of the tiny mound of sand around it. Raquel noticed the flag was one of several in varying colors, jutting out along the shore. The squeal of several frolicking adolescents drew her attention. There were several Creole boys chasing two girls of similar ages along the beach, the snapping pinchers of two large crabs helped to make the romp more exciting. The young females shrieked delightedly, as their dark, slightly waving hair, stretched out in the cool breeze. But their play was cut short by an older woman who beckoned the boys over in her direction. She and three other women were kneeling down beside—what Raquel assumed was a large hole in the ground. Curious, she continued to watch, as the reluctant young males turned from their pursuit of the fairer sex, and raced over toward the waiting older females.

One of the women was dropping what appeared to be several hot rocks, which she handled gingerly, with a piece of heavy cloth, into the opening. Soon after the boys arrived with their catch, those crabs along with others, were expertly bound in large banana leaves and what looked like sea weed, then placed in the gaping hole. Once the wrapped crabs were situated, the cavity was filled in with sand, and a small flag was placed above it to mark the spot.

With calculated timing, the two young females reappeared near the newly constructed oven, provoking the young males to go back to their previous chase.

The wheels of the Samurai crunched onto the pebbled lot of the Pelican Beach Resort. It was a good-looking hotel with a dock facing the sea. Several brown lounge chairs made with wooden slats had been conveniently placed facing the water, enabling guests to take advantage of the sun and the beautiful view.

It didn't take them long to check into the hotel where they secured two rooms. One for Ponti, the other for Nate and herself.

Rebellion wanted to raise its obstinate head when Nate directed her to their room and closed the door decidedly behind them. Had it not occurred to him that she might have wanted a room to herself? Even after all that had passed between them, did he still consider her his prisoner? She sighed, in actuality she still was. Not only because he had abducted her in Miami, but because in this short period of time he had managed to imprison her heart.

Never during her entire relationship with Clinton Bradshaw had she experienced such intense feelings ranging from fear to utter desire. It rattled Raquel to realize despite her cautious nature, what she did not know about Nate was less important to her than her growing feelings for him. She feared their intensity more than his cloaked past. Yes, she feared him, but she loved him more, and hoped her intuition was right: that he would never use that dark side against her.

The young woman inhaled deeply, her strong shoulders slumping with the weight of the past few weeks. There was so much to think about and do, now that they'd arrived in Dangriga.

A confused bird crashed into one of the windows of the hotel room, and Raquel's frightened eyes flew to the panes, expecting to see a vengeful Jay. She stood paralyzed until she heard Nate's voice.

"It is nothing to be frightened of *pataki*, only a bird," he crossed the room to place his arms about her. Nate felt her jump at his touch, then she began to shake uncontrollably.

He placed his bristly cheek against the cloud of black hair on top of her head, wrapping her even tighter in his strong embrace to still her trembling, and his fear of never being able to return to the blissful moments they had shared.

"You are my woman now, *pataki* and that means a hell of a lot to me. All I can ask is that you trust me to do the right thing by you. To take care of you. Can you do that?"

Raquel managed a few jerky affirmative nods of her head. But she was uncertain if she really meant it.

"Now, let's start with that splinter."

Nate had gotten everything he needed to remove the sliver from Raquel's hand when he checked into the hotel, and she and Ponti waited outside. The removal was painful, but necessary, and she couldn't help but be touched by the tenderness and concern Nate displayed as he carried out the tedious procedure.

"Now that wasn't so bad, was it?" he asked, dark, brown eyes looking deeply into hers as he held her hand, then placed a soft kiss in its palm.

"No" she managed, but was unable to respond further.

"Now let's run some hot bath-water. I believe I saw some bath crystals in here," he searched through the little set of bottles assembled in a decorative basket for the hotel guests.

"Here we go," he raised the small container with blue crystals for Raquel's inspection, then turned toward the bath tub. The rushing water thundered into the fiber-glass tub, its contents turning blue as Nate generously added the bath crystals.

She watched his accommodating actions with interest and a warm feeling of appreciation.

"Do you need me to help you undress . . . I know right now, your hand may make it a little difficult for you." He said with a deep whisper.

"No . . . I can manage. Thanks."

Raquel knew from the smoldering look in Nate's eyes that his thoughts weren't only occupied with her comfort.

"All right. I've got to go and take care of a few things. If all goes well, this will be over with sooner than you think," he held her gaze meaningfully. "I'll just be gone for a little while. Maybe you'd like to take a nap after your bath or order something to eat. If so, just put everything on the room. You will find your belongings inside the duffel, over there on the floor.

"All right."

"And *pataki*." She turned her head toward him, her hair softly falling around her shoulders. "As soon as possible, we will need to let the Garifunian priestess know that we have arrived. It's a matter of respect."

He gave her a comforting smile as he tried to mask his growing concern. Nate knew that by following this protocol he would ensure the good tidings of the nearby villagers and priestess. Every moment counted now, and he wanted to do everything he could to protect her.

Raquel could tell he was anxious. His gaze continuously strayed to the window and out onto the street below.

"Nate, I've got to know what's going to happen to

me." The statement loomed like an invisible wall between them.

"If everything goes right, *pataki*, you will be safe and on your way back to the States by tonight." Taking a deep, slow breath he looked down at the floor, then engulfed her with dark troubled eyes. "I never expected any of this would happen, but I will explain everything to you then."

"What do you mean?" Confusion and hope filled her weary eyes.

"Just trust me," his thickly lashed gaze implored her. "But I've got to go, *now.*"

At first she hesitated. She wanted to force him into telling her everything right then. But from the look in his eyes she knew that would be impossible to do. As they stared at one another Raquel remembered how, up to that moment, he had never lied to her. She knew she would have to believe that he was not lying now. Feeling totally exhausted she nodded her agreement.

"Good." Nate breathed a sigh of relief before reaching out to squeeze her hand, and closing the door behind him.

Raquel soaked in the tub until she almost fell asleep in its comforting waters. Stepping out, she wrapped the large, plain bath towel around her, then decided to wash her hair in the sink. It reminded her of the way her mother used to do it when she was younger.

She patted her hair as dry as she could before combing it out. She was surprised to discover the costume she'd worn to the party was also in the sack. The thousand dollars that had gotten her into all of this was still stealthily folded and sewn away.

Raquel parted her hair down the middle and formed

two French braids along the sides of her head, ending in
two ropelike plaits dangling against her shoulderblades.
She realized, as she inspected her features in the mirror,
the style made her look much younger. She also noticed
puffy sacks beneath her eyes, either remnants of the infection or visible signs of her weariness. Either way, the
braids, coupled with the swollen areas, had her looking
far from her best. But right now Raquel didn't care, she
would try to impress the priestess and the others when
she felt more up to it.

Raquel crossed the hotel room, patting the nape of
her neck and her edges with a hand towel, her eyes
straying to the window the bird had struck.

Several people paraded up and down the busy thoroughfare, going about their daily activities, oblivious to
the tumultuous events that had taken over her life. She
wished for the peace of mind they displayed with their
contented wanderings.

She noticed a woman wearing a colorful skirt and
watched her cross the street. Across the street, just inside
the doorway of a small shop was a man placing a phone
call. As she looked closer, she could see it was Nate. She
wondered what nature of business had forced him to
find a phone on the street instead of using the one in the
hotel room.

Raquel watched as he hung up and made two other
calls. His body and hand movements were intense as he
spoke, making sure his back was to the street. Finally
she saw him calm himself, then nervously turn to the
street as if he were afraid he had been overheard. After
forcefully hanging up the phone, Nate strode out onto
the sidewalk, then stood looking over at the hotel.

Quickly Raquel stepped back from the sheer paneled

window. Concealing herself against the wall, she hoped her rapid movement had not caught his astute gaze. It was an act that showed the lack of trust between them. His secretive calls outside the hotel, and her need for him not to know that she was aware of them.

Taking another covert glance, she watched as he made his way down the street, disappearing around the corner. Unnerved, she climbed between the warm covers of the bed, placing a dry towel on the linen-covered pillow to absorb the moisture from her hair.

It was about a half hour ago when he had asked her to trust him. Now, the uncertainty she felt as a result of his clandestine actions was that much stronger.

Raquel reached over to the nightstand and retrieved the leather pouch given to her by the shamaness. She placed the symbolic object about her neck. Normally she was not a superstitious person, but for some reason the small sack was the only thing that seemed to bring her comfort.

It was easy for her weary eyes to close as her mind brought up snatches of various thoughts between consciousness and sleep. Deep feelings of being trapped surfaced, telling her her choices were few. She could use the telephone to call the authorities, but she would be taking quite a chance. In a small city like this they were probably connected with the Garifunians. But even if they weren't, they probably wouldn't be willing to rub them the wrong way by dabbling in their religious affairs. As she drifted closer to sleep she came to the conclusion that trying to contact the States was out of the question. By the time help arrived all kinds of things could have happened. No, her best bet was to stick with Nate. She was afraid that anything she might try to do alone, Jay could be waiting for her. He would be ready, willing and able to snuff out her life in a moment's notice.

Feeling a kind of sickening fear wash over her, she submitted to the thought that Nate was her only hope. One that her heart irrationally placed complete trust in, but her mind failed to follow.

Chapter Nineteen

"Get that out of my face!" the usual smooth tones of Ricky Flint's heavy voice exploded, interrupting his telephone conversation.

The woman's thin but long eyelashes, swept down hastily, and her pretty features turned angry as she held her throbbing hand. A petite, silver, embossed tray lay face down on the sky blue carpet—its white contents almost invisible in its plushness.

Suddenly her anger dissolved into hurt, and the nostrils on her long nose slightly pumped in and out as her eyes glazed over with tears. One by one, crimson droplets spattered the carpet along with crushed pieces of glass; remains of the delicate crystal tube shattered by Ricky's blow.

Turning his back to the scene, the man pulled haughtily at the leather belt on his expensive pants.

"Just get over here," he yelled into the receiver. "Right now! You got that?" He slammed the custom-designed phone back into its cradle. Ricky turned his irritation back in the woman's direction.

"Why are you still standing there bleeding all over the fuckin' carpet?"

Not accustomed to this kind of treatment from her lover, the Creole woman struck back the only way she knew how.

"You *backra!*" Her dark eyes burned with harmful intent behind the racial categorization. "You can't talk to me like that."

Her timing was bad, and Ricky Flint delivered another blow. This time a backhand that sent her sprawling across the spacious sunroom floor. Classically designed billows of chiffon spread out delicately about her legs, and her heavy, dyed-auburn hair diffused in massive, curls lay above it. Stunned, she sobbed uncontrollably upon the expanse of blue carpet.

"This is not the time to cross me baby. Somebody's messin' up my business and I have no patience for that." He walked over and kneeled down beside her and began to artfully arrange the curls away from her already darkening cheek.

"Call Carl in here to clean up this mess, and here," he placed a few hundred-dollar bills beneath her nail-art-bedecked hands. "Go to one of those all-day spas and get pampered for daddy. By tomorrow you'll feel as good as new."

He rose to his feet and left the room, leaving her to weep alone.

About two hours later Jay's gaze strayed to the window, looking down at countless living walls of sculptured hedges, strategically grown to form an intricate maze. The collective pattern resembled two shattered sphere halves with a stone pathway down its center. Resplendent orchid blossoms pushed their tongued heads through the green blocks in intervals, giving the illusion of small fluctuating rainbows in their midst. Jay's eyes gleamed brightly as he took in the opulence from this high vantage point. From what he could tell, Ricky had carved himself out a wonderland that took up acres of his native soil.

Envy boiled up inside as he thought of the pitiful plot of land his entire settlement occupied. It wasn't fair that an outsider should possess such wealth, and he, a Belizean, should be so poor.

A resounding crack drew Jay's attention back to the room in which he stood, and a beautiful porcelain head of an almond-eyed female rolled, then wobbled toward his feet.

"Your freakin' brother is the reason I've lost over a million dollars of cane . . . and you got the nerve to stand in here while I'm talkin' and look out the window!"

Ricky's aggravated tones hung in the air just like his hand, holding a completed karate chop above the broken statue's birdlike body.

Jay eyed the expensive head of the siren lying in the thick bed of carpet, thinking only of how much of a waste it was to destroy the collectible piece. An Englishman he'd worked for as a child had owned quite a collection of invaluable things. As a result of working around such splendor and returning to his own impoverished surroundings, Jay promised himself, one day, he would have what the Englishman had, and more. Ricky's childlike outburst did nothing but increase his feelings of being more entitled to the good things in life than his extravagant boss. He would appreciate them more.

Slowly Jay's haunted, obsessed eyes traveled from the broken porcelain to Ricky's reddened face.

"Leave my brothah out of t'is." His hands formed strained fists at his side. "Already his soul is in danger of not makin' the trip to the othah side because I had to come here first before buryin' him properly. I will not let you or anyone else provoke him further, and have his troubled spirit remain on t'is side, nevah findin' peace."

"I don't give a good god . . ." Ricky's insult ended abruptly as Jay's thin lips began to move silently as in a chant, a piercing light emanating from his consumed stare.

During his years in Belize, Ricky had heard of many bizarre things that had happened to both natives and strangers alike who had crossed or wronged an emotional Shangoain. These things were spoke of fearfully and in whispered tones, as if just the mention of them in the wrong way would bring about an undesirable end.

There had also been Benjamin, a virile Creole whom he'd hired to help his gardener. The young man had angered his Shangoain cook by fooling around with her young granddaughter. Ricky had seen with his own eyes how he ended up incapable of pleasing any other woman as a result of their bizarre magic.

The drug boss looked into Jay's glazed eyes and rephrased his reprimand.

"All right. All right. Let's leave the dead alone. But I want compensation for the drugs that I'm missin', and if I can't have it in money, I want it in blood."

"I want their blood too," Jay stated flatly. "I want the pleasure of seein' them die by my hand, especially the woman. But I will have to kill Meester Nate first befor' that happens."

"I can understand how you feel," he continued to placate the emotional Shangoain as he felt around for the right words to say.

Ricky was glad Jay wanted to kill the people responsible for messing up his haul, even though that was not his motivation. In the end it would make it that much easier for him. This way he'd be able to gain total control of Jay. Committing a crime like murder was one of the best hole cards he could have on one of his men. As a matter of fact, on occasions, he had "requested" that some of his men do a job in order to bind them more securely to him.

He looked at the dark, slender man who stood before him, his body tense and rigid. Ricky could tell it wouldn't take much to make Jay snap, and that wouldn't be good for any of them. He had to play him like a well-tuned piano. Hitting the right keys would create such beautiful music, but the wrong ones would be disastrous. Ricky didn't want Jay's enthusiasm to mess things up. Murder had to be approached with a calm hand.

"Look, right now I want you to know you are not alone. You've got family. Rock, Mane-Mane and myself. We're all part of a large close-knit group. So I tell you what," congeniality permeating his gaze. "If you can take care of the guy, somebody else'll take care of the woman. Okay?"

"They will be at the Garifuna Settlement Day ceremonies, day after tomorrow. I will do it then," Jay announced, ignoring the question posed by his drug boss.

Uneasily Ricky looked at Jay, then at the two men who stood a small distance away from him. Rock continued to chew his gum as he watched his boss's face, waiting for even the slightest instruction. Mane-Mane rolled his index finger beside his temple, giving his un-solicited opinion of Jay's mental state.

"All right we'll do it day after tomorrow," he cun-ningly agreed, knowing Jay didn't care if he did or not. Under the circumstances Ricky knew he had to deal with him in a more subtle manner.

"Now that we've got business out of the way, why don't you and Mane-Mane step into the front sitting room and have Carl fix you some drinks. Rock, I've got a few things to go over with you, so you'll need to stick around for a few more minutes."

The two men watched as Jay and Mane-Mane filed through the double white doors, the latter closing the brass openers behind him.

"What d'ya think?" Ricky asked as he slumped down into the thick, maroon leather chair, placing his jeweled hands flat upon his desk.

"I think he's an uzi waiting to go off," Rock replied.

"Yeah, you're right," he began to drum his fingers. "But if we can point him in the right direction, he can do us a great service. The woman's got to be killed be-fore she can complete that ceremony."

"There are going to be a lot of tourists and things hangin' around for that ceremony. If any thing goes wrong, make sure it can be pinned on the man, Jay," Ricky continued. "He thinks he's not dispensable, but he is. There's another guy in that village just as greedy as he is, and would be more than willing to take his place as our contact. I really don't care about this guy Jay calls Nate. As far as I'm concerned he did us a favor by wastin' his crazy brother." Ricky smacked his hands together abruptly. "Messed up over a million dollars in pure cane just tryin' to get some snatch. It is his brother and that woman who need to pay for fuckin' up my co-caine. But he's gone, and now we got two reasons to waste the woman."

Chapter Twenty

Raquel was grateful to step inside the plain, but clean house. It allowed her some respite from the prying, inquisitive eyes of the Garifunians, who stopped their tasks to watch them advance down the road. Many had called out friendly greetings as they saw Nate, but none of the amicable words or looks had been thrown her way. But unlike the Shangoains who seemed hostile and afraid, the Garifunians appeared to be more curious, observing her as one would study a queer specimen under a microscope.

Once they reached the door of the small house, there was something in Nate's mannerism that made her hesitate. Somehow she felt he was uncertain about her accompanying him inside. But before he could explain, a wisp of a boy with a smile appearing too big for his face, opened it, giving Nate a warm welcome by embracing his waist. In turn, the man began to rub his closely shaven head.

"Brandon, what happened to your head, man? Marjorie must have gotten ahold of you this time," he teased. "You know I told you to watch out for those females. They like to get a fellow where it hurts whenever they can," he continued his fond needling.

The boy's eyes burned with amusement, yet despite his display of open affection, he never spoke a word.

"By the way, where is Marjorie?"

Raquel watched as the smile remained on Nate's handsome features, but a solemn look appeared in the depths of his eyes.

Silently, the young boy pointed in the direction of a lone door, his brown eyes clouding over with concern. "She's in there," he responded in whispered tones, then looked beyond the front door, "Where's Art?"

Nate kneeled down in front of the boy whom Art's mother had taken in, bringing his face parallel with his. "He couldn't come with us, Brandon," he spoke the foreboding words, his voice raspy. "But let's talk about that later, because right now I've got something for you."

With the ease of any six-year-old, Brandon brightened as Nate pulled a cheerfully packaged box from the shopping bag he was carrying and presented it to the boy. Small, eager fingers ripped off the colored paper, removed the lid of the box, and dug into the cloud of thin, white tissue. He stopped abruptly at the sight of his gift, a loud, "Gosh!" verbalizing his feelings.

"It's *The Rendezvous*," he exclaimed as he carefully reached down and retrieved a magnificently crafted sailboat. "Is it just like yours Mr. Nate?" bright eyes looking up at him admiringly.

"Just about."

"Wow, I've got to go show Chris," he ran for the door with his prize stretched out before him. Suddenly he made an abrupt turn. "Oops, first I gotta ask Big

Mama." He headed excitedly for the room but Nate caught him by the waist.

"That's all right, you go ahead. I'll tell her."

"Thanks." The word had barely been spoken before he disappeared through the door.

Nate watched him for a moment, then he turned to Raquel.

"I think it might be best if you stayed in here," his features solemn as he addressed her.

The words were put in the form of a suggestion, but Raquel knew they were a subtle command, as he motioned for her to take a seat in a hard-back chair at the table. She could feel all his attention had become focused on the room Brandon had pointed to only moments before.

Raquel watched as the door gave in to the even pressure from Nate's large hand. From her seat she could see inside the tiny room. It was barely large enough for the ornate, full-sized bed and dresser. There was a petite shaded lamp casting a soft glow throughout, and it was the only source of light, because the window shade had been drawn to completely block out the sun.

Nate approached the bed, somberly, even though it appeared to be empty from Raquel's vantage point. As he turned his profile in her direction, she could tell from his troubled features, someone of grave importance in his life was lying there. For moments on end, he stood in silence looking down at the still blankets. Finally, a slight arm rose up and reached toward him, and Raquel heard what she thought was a breathy version of his name.

Compassionately, Nate took the hand that reached

for him, knelt down beside the bed, and placed it against his cheek.

"How is my favorite girl," He gazed down fondly at the weak figure in the bed, concern making the deep hollow beneath his high cheekbones appear even more apparent.

"Mind what you say, Nate Bowman. It's been a long time since I was a girl . . . and your favorite? That will be the day when you call any woman your favorite."

Raquel could barely hear the soft words, but hear them she did, and it weakened her crumbling belief that she was someone special in his life.

"You never could take a compliment," he countered.

"No, I never could stand for B. S. and I still can't."

A look of resignation descended over Nate's dark features. "Marjorie . . ."

"You don't have to tell me. I know. Art is dead. It came to me in a dream the night he left."

Nate nodded.

She closed her eyes as she thought of him. "About two days after I had that dream I began to feel ill, and I tell you I get weaker with each day. But I know what's going on. The will of Art's spirit has attached itself to me." A weak smile crossed her wrinkled face. "He don't mean me any harm, he loves me, and he was a man of faith. That's why he wanted to help bring Jackie back to Dangriga. He wanted me and the *orishas* to be pleased with him. And that's the reason I think he's holding on to me. He wants to be present with me at the ceremony tomorrow," she stopped to catch her breath.

"I'm glad the ceremony is only a day away, then he will be free, and so will I," she finished.

Unintentionally, Nate glanced up looking in Raquel's

direction, causing Marjorie to do the same. Even this slight physical exertion resulted in her flopping back listlessly against the white sheets.

"Jackie . . . is that you, Jackie?"

Raquel's eyes opened wide at the mention of the name. Once again Nate looked at her, a veiled appearance fell upon his features.

Marjorie called out to her again.

"Ye-es," Raquel answered, hesitantly. "It's me."

A weak smile appeared on the woman's tired face.

She was the one who had shown him so much compassion at the time of his mother's death. Through the years he had done all he could to make her life as comfortable as possible. The presence of the modern furniture and fixtures reflected that, but even the generous contributions he made could not completely ward off the effects of the hard life Marjorie chose to live in Dangriga. She was stubborn about maintaining "the Garifunian way," and he respected that. Still, in his heart, he had vowed to do whatever he could to help her.

He thought about how hard he had taken Art's death, even though at the time he could not show it. He had drunk entirely too much that night when they first arrived in Belize, as he dwelled on how he would have to tell Marjorie her only son was dead.

"I knew she would come," she said almost to herself. "The *gubida* would never desert us. Tell her to come closer," she implored as her eyes opened slightly, then fluttered shut again.

Nate motioned for Raquel to join him at Marjorie's bedside. Her body shook with each step as she crossed the small space, the moment of her undoing becoming imminent. As she stood above the fragile figure, the tired eyes flickered open for a look at her, and showed a spark of confusion. Then, the woman exhaled loudly, fell back into a deep, almost coma-like sleep. A trembling breath of relief eased out of Raquel.

"I don't think she would have recognized you anyway," Nate commented. "You were a little girl when you left Belize."

Startled dark eyes looked up in his direction. Was there a hint of collusion in his voice?

When Nate returned to the hotel no more than an hour ago he appeared tense and preoccupied. Appearing somewhat relieved to see her dressed, they wasted no time in heading for the Garifunian settlement. He had said very little during the short time it took to get there.

Quickly she looked down at the figure who lay before them.

"I think we should leave and let her rest," Nate said as he took her arm. "The priestess is also expecting us."

There was little if any indication that this small settlement on the outskirts of Dangriga had ever been touched by modern society. Some of the doors to the simple clapboard houses were open for ventilation, allowing anyone who felt like it to watch whatever was happening inside. After taking several quick assessments of the interior of homes displayed in such a manner, Raquel concluded that Marjorie's house was probably one of the best furnished, if not the best, in the entire settlement. Somehow she knew Nate was the cause of her good fortune, and she wondered what compelled this strange man to do the things he did.

"Well, well . . . look what de win' done blew in," a

husky female voice called from the open structure they just passed. "If it isn't my mon, Nate, lookin' as good as evah."

An ebony-skinned female leaned against the inside frame of the weathered door, a set of perfect white teeth shining from her round face. Like the women in the cassava field she wore a dusterlike dress with floral print, but on her shapely frame, it was transformed into a provocative frock. The tiny buttons which traveled the length of its middle strained at their holes where her full breasts pressed against the light material, and groaned against the pressure her ample hips placed upon them. A wild arrangement of full hair framed her animated face, like a softly persuasive afro it reached out around her, touching her shoulders, giving way ever so slightly to the wind as she began to cross the space between them.

Raquel watched as Nate's eyes lit up with a familiar gleam that was quickly doused as a somewhat cynical, sideward smile forced its ways onto his features. The woman passed by Raquel, completely ignoring her. A natural scent mixed with a tangy floral smell drifted around her.

"Why did it take you so long to come back and see about your Belinda, eh?" She donned a pouty expression as she placed her hands upon her hips, her body almost touching his.

"How are you, Belinda?" He spoke, his richly lashed eyes intent on her face.

Slowly her full lips spread into a winsome smile. "I am good now that you are here." She placed her palm upon his chest, rubbing it ever so enticingly.

"You probably don't remember Jackie, do you?" He

turned in Raquel's direction. "You were both so young when she went to the States."

Her round eyes narrowed in speculation as they roamed over the silent young woman, stopping at her large, flashing eyes, "No, I don't."

There was no way for Raquel to deny the strong wave of jealousy that had washed over her as she watched the woman's exchange with Nate. It took all the control she could muster to keep from removing her clinging fingers from the material of his shirt.

"Strange that your sistah would be so jealous of you, Nate," Belinda's sultry voice took on a harsh edge. "But of course you have always been able to bring out the best and the worst in us females."

Nate's sister! But surely she was mistaken. Raquel opened her mouth to protest Belinda's words, but no sound emerged. Unsure of herself and shaken, she waited for Nate to straighten her out. Surely, she did not think Jackie Dawson was Nate's sister!

Just as Raquel expected, Nate addressed Belinda, but his words were far from what she expected.

"Maybe she wouldn't feel that way, if you weren't such a tantalizing creature," he continued to gaze in the woman's direction, the half smile fixed upon his lips.

With his words, Raquel felt as if she would faint—the switch from jealously to sheer shock was so strong. Through an emotional fog, she looked at the man she felt she had come to know and love, and she realized she really didn't know him at all.

There was a falseness to the smile he gave Belinda, though the woman seemed not to notice as she laid her voluptuous body against his in an invitational embrace. Obligingly Nate placed his arms around her as she leaned her head on his chest. He turned to look at Raquel above Belinda's mass of hair, the muscle in his strong jaw working convulsively. His dark eyes seem to burn into her.

"I will check back with you later," he assured the woman, but he continued to stare at Raquel while holding her in his arms. A flicker of remorse flashed in his gaze. "The priestess is waiting for us. Are you ready . . . Jackie?"

The name dropped on her like a heavy stone, and she realized Nate had never addressed her as Jackie before. She remembered how in the beginning he had called her Miss Dawson, in a distant way. But he never used the more familiar Jackie, because Jackie Dawson *was* his sister.

Before Belinda could remove her face from his chest, Nate reached out and clutched Raquel's arm. With his touch a feeling of total weakness seeped into her. All of a sudden she felt so tired. If only she had never accepted that envelope.

There was no logic behind what had happened to her over the last week. All of the time she had pretended to be Jackie Dawson, Nate had always known the truth. All the while she'd feared for her life and continued with the charade because of it, she had never been in any danger when it came to him. He had known all along she was an imposter.

From the flurry of emotions that flashed across her beautiful features, Nate could tell what Raquel was thinking. Belinda's timing couldn't have been worse. Any trust she had in him had been crushed, and right now, there was nothing he could do about it. But there was one thing she had to realize, this was not the time to reveal her true identity. She was in way too deep for that.

"Jackie," he shook her arm abruptly, causing the closest thing he'd ever seen to hate rise in her eyes.

"What is wit' her? She looks as if she was in a daze or sumt'in?" Belinda snapped.

"I'm surprised at you, Belinda, you of all people should understand. She's been sending herself through strong preparations in order to make a true connection with the *gubida* tomorrow, and it has not been easy for her after living such a pampered life in the States. But of course there's no need for me to remind you of this," he stroked her after speaking rather harshly in the beginning. "You have worked with the priestess, and have noticed the drain her spiritual travels can cause, something as plain as that would not get past a woman like you."

Belinda eyed Raquel with skepticism. "Yes, t'at is true. "But t'ere is a weakness about your sistah that leads me to t'ink she will not be able to stand up under the power of the spirits tomorrow evenin'."

Belinda held her head up haughtily. She looked down on Raquel for allowing the city life to spoil her, but at the same time, she felt envious because of it.

"She is stronger than she appears, I can assure you of that," Nate said with a nod. Secretly hoping that the time would never come to prove Belinda right or wrong.

"Well, I hope so fo' the people's sake and fo' hers. The entire village and remainder of the Shango will arrive early tomorrow mornin'. They will all be countin' on her. If she is able to call up the spirits of our ancestors but cannot carry them, horrible thin's could happen, ya know?"

"There is no need for you to worry, Belinda."

Nate slipped a protective arm about Raquel's shoulder as he urged her forward. She flinched at his touch, a repulsive feeling rising inside. She wanted to scream at him and remove it. Yet she dared not react as they started down the dirt road, many of the villagers' eyes upon them.

There was a bizarre feeling of dejàvu as she realized she was back where she started. She was all alone, and she could not depend on Nate.

Her nervous fingers sought out the leather pouch that hung about her neck, a tool of deception. Strange how this entire ordeal had started out with deceit. But to find out she, the deceiver, had also been deceived by a man she thought she had come to love, was the most bitter pill to swallow.

Chapter Twenty-one

"Nate, there is no need for you to remain here and be burdened with our spiritual talk." The delicate voice wafted toward them from the opposite side of the room. The tone was imploring but Raquel knew it was still a command.

The woman who sat before them was nothing like Raquel expected. After witnessing the Mayan shaman at work, and being trained by the shamaness in the rain forest, she had expected the priestess's countenance to be more, for lack of a better word, mystical.

The woman's soft, but even gaze, continued to rest on Nate as he rose from the chair and obediently passed through the door.

On leaving Belinda, they had time for only a few words before they were confronted by the priestess. She had taken it upon herself to meet them on the street while the majority of the village looked on. As she approached—she was a generous figure in African garb with a wide sun hat upon her head—Nate issued a warning to Raquel, "Whatever you do, don't let anyone know who you really are!" It was those words that echoed in her mind as he left her alone with the Garifunian priestess.

With hands much like those of a baby, she produced a pack of cigarettes and a lighter. Hospitably, she offered the pack to Raquel, who promptly refused.

"It is a shame you did not return to us of your own accord, Jackie. I know the *gubida* would be happier if you had." The priestess's smooth English oddly comforted Raquel, but not enough to dispel all of her questions and confusion.

There was a pregnant pause as she waited for Raquel to offer an excuse or apology for her action. She continued when none was given.

"Your brother has gone to great lengths to bring you here. We are grateful to him, and so should you be. It is the youth like you, who have weakened our society by disrespecting their roots, discarding the beliefs of their ancestors, and trying to become something they are not. That is why our people grow poorer with each year. It is a dreadful cycle. The youth see no promise for tomorrow, therefore they leave. And in their leaving, they take with them any promises they could have fulfilled in the future. There are only a few who look back and try to give of themselves once they are gone. Your brother has been one of them. Now, it is because of the prophecy, that has been spoken of for many years, that you are here. You are that foretold female descendant of the Garifuna and the Shango. Born out of a union performed during the night of the split. You were the only child conceived that night, and as a result have been endowed by the *gubida* to speak for them." Her ample figure rolled to the side, choosing a bunch of grapes to appease her eager appetite. With hands accustomed to traveling rapidly toward her cushiony lips, she popped a string of the deep purple fruits into her mouth. Suddenly, she paused with an aggressive gleam in her eye which she pointed in Raquel's direction.

"I have felt the energy of those who are filled with the power of the *gubida* before, and somehow yours is different," she squinted her already small eyes even more. "Powerful but different. By now, I know if the *gubida* are truly with you, they have instructed you on what to do to prepare for tomorrow. Tell me what they have said."

The priestess's obvious test for Raquel, caught the young woman off guard. Instantly fear shot up inside her. She dropped her eyes to the floor to hide the emotion from the woman's probing gaze. For moments that felt like an eternity her crowded mind searched for what would be the right answer, as the silence hung heavily between them. Involuntarily her hand sought out the pouch around her neck.

Foggy images began to appear behind her tightly closed eyelids, they grew in clarity as she gave in to them. As these pictures appeared to her mental eye, she relayed them to the Garifunian priestess in a surprisingly calm voice. She told of her eventual experience with the shamaness of the rain forest, of the water, the moon, her consumption of the blue passion flower and the St. Juan's wort. She spoke of gathering together the objects which she now wore about her neck inside the soft leathery pouch, gifts of the sea, and the earth, amidst the sparkle of bright beads. She told it as it unfolded in her mind, but she didn't realize until her tale was complete, and she was looking at the beaming features of the Garifunian priestess, there was one thing missing. As the occurrences of that night replayed in her mind, she was alone.

"Ah-h the most powerful preparations from *Yemoja*, goddess of the ocean." She smacked her lips appreciatively as she finished the last of the grapes. "It must have created a great yearning inside you," her sparkling eyes commented knowingly. "Did you find a suitable male to appease the fire and consummate the ritual?"

"Yes." The single-word response gave no indication of the shock Raquel felt at the woman's perceptive words. For a moment she reflected on the first night she and Nate made love. She had no idea the Garifunian priestess would consider the act a consummation of one of their rituals.

"Good. Now that I am certain you have been touched by our ancestors, and the ways of an initiate have been given to you, we can talk about the present." She adjusted her large frame on the well-worn, cushioned arm chair. "A place has been made ready for you, along with an attendant. There you will have the privacy you need for your vigil tonight. Once she tells me you are ready, a proper receiver of your female energy will be sent to you."

All of a sudden, she repeatedly smacked the backside of one hand against the palm of the other, and a hefty young woman entered the room carrying a large bundle under her arm. She kept her eyes riveted on the woman who had summoned her.

The priestess spoke to her in a dialect Raquel did not understand as the young woman, dressed in white, nodded her head reassuringly.

"Well now, everything is ready. She will show you

where you must go." Her dark gaze turned solemn, "And may the *orishas* be with you."

"I am proud, because I am the chosen one tonight," the sinewy young man boasted as he walked away from the fire. Several grunts and verbal acknowledgments of approval followed. The circle of males, young and old, agreed with him. They all considered being chosen as the receiver, an honor. Drawing their attention away from the fortunate villager, once again, a dried, decorated gourd, half full of cassava wine began to circulate.

With an air of insolence, the young man walked away from the group, a small burlap sack flapping against his hard hip. He had secured the hood beneath his belt after receiving it from the priestess. He wanted it to be handy whenever the time came for him to use it.

The feel of the cassava wine still burned in his chest, and he wished he could have stayed longer with his friends to help them finish the gourd. But he knew the time was drawing close, and just the thought of what was to come excited him. Through the trees he could see the lights from the houses, dotting the main area of the settlement, and even though he could not see it from where he walked, he knew, soon, he would be engulfed in the warmth of one of those lights, and in the arms of the one chosen by the *gubida*.

"Hey, what's your hurry?" a husky voice called out from the dark, causing the young man to turn abruptly.

"Who's askin'?" he replied, his rich, brown eyes searching the semidarkness.

Nate saw the telltale burlap sack hanging at the young man's waist, and his dark eyes narrowed perceptively. Night had arrived and there was no sign of the help he had expected. After the phone calls he had made earlier, he had been leery, but still hoped they would come back in time. Now he knew it would be sometime in the morning before they arrived. Nate had vowed to himself, and to the woman he had come to know as Jackie, that he would protect her, and protect he would.

He was glad he'd kept his word to Belinda, and had gone to see her no more than an hour ago. She had offered him a steaming plate of brocket deer and red beans and rice, prepared with coconut milk and spices. Belinda had always been a good cook, and he knew she would be insulted if he refused the offer. It was from her he knew a receptor would be chosen tonight.

"So, it is you who has been chosen tonight?" Nate added a bit of a slur to his speech, hoping the young man would not notice it wasn't there before.

Defined youthful features peered at Nate's face in the darkness. It was hard for him to see under the cover of trees and the influence of the wine. In the end, he concluded he did not recognize him, and he wondered how this stranger knew about such things. Secrecy in matters like this, when it came to outsiders, was second nature for Garifunians.

"What would you know about that?" his voice dripped with skepticism.

"Everything man. How old are you, nineteen?"

"Twenty."

"Oh yes, that explains it," Nate chuckled, turning up a near-empty bottle of cashew wine. "You were probably still a breast baby when I was taking care of business the way you'll be doing tonight." He made a show of draining the bottle. "I thought you looked pretty wet behind the ears. Are you sure you can handle it? Or are you going to need a little help?"

Nate made sure he remained in the shadow of the trees so it would be difficult for the young man to see his face, but he could clearly see the now-aggravated features of the fellow who stood before him.

"What you talkin' 'bout old man? I don't need no help from you or anybody else. My abilities around this village are well known. Maybe it's been such a long time for you, that you can't even imagine what I'm talkin' bout."

Tossing the now-empty bottle to the side and swaying a bit on his feet for emphasis, Nate made a show of attempting to open a second corked bottle with his teeth, loosening it just enough so it would come out easily with the slightest bit of pressure.

"I know more than you think I know, and ain't nothin' I can't take care of that you can," he baited.

"Yeah mon, I'm sure . . . just like that bottle cork."

Arrogantly the young man snatched the bottle from Nate's willing hands.

"Eh-h, wait a minute," he protested loudly. While inside he thought things were progressing even better than he planned.

With ease the young man removed the cork, and took a long swig from the bottle. Afterwards he wiped his mouth with the back of his hand.

"See there? I told you," he grinned as he held the bottle stretched out far from his side, then took another long, dramatic swill.

Yes, you sure did, Nate thought. But so did Belinda. He was glad Belinda's penchant for young men and good wine had put her in such a good, relaxed mood. She told him all about this particular young man and where he could be found. Now he just hoped there was enough hop in that bottle to put him out for the night.

Raquel's eyes focused on the exposed beams of the ceiling and the wooden planks that lay in between them. Over and over she counted them with the aid of the moonlight. She would try anything if it would keep her mind from straying to the burning ache searing inside her.

It had begun after she drank the tea. The feeling started in the pit of her stomach, fluttering like excited butterflies. Slowly it turned into a stimulating quiver, then finally an aching desire, blazing a demanding trail to the core of her womanhood.

She remembered feeling relieved when the young female attendant left her. The nagging desire had begun to take effect, overpowering her thoughts of escape. Embarrassed, she did not want the woman to know of her sensual predicament.

For a while she thought the girl would never leave. Her well-trained actions made it unnecessary for Raquel to initiate any of the preparatory rites. Instead she just followed the young woman's lead, taking whatever was offered to her, meditating at the times when she stopped in thoughtful prayer; then in the end, allowing her to place a soft, azure blue, caftan over her frame. It was then, as the cottony material slid over her nakedness, she first became aware of an awakening feeling within her chest accompanied by a somewhat heady sensation. As time passed these feelings increased, in a strange way establishing a feeling of empowerment. It was if she was at the height of awareness. An awareness of her femaleness and its creative powers.

Raquel didn't understand why she was feeling this way—was she actually the chosen one? She didn't understand why the ceremony's preparations seemed natural to her, normal, as if she were indeed fulfilling a legacy. As if she, Raquel Mason, not Jackie Dawson, was anointed.

Raquel's thoughts returned to the shamaness who shared her power with her. Perhaps the shamaness was right, perhaps Raquel did have an open soul, perhaps everything the shamaness had said and done was real. Perhaps, Raquel thought as she ran her hands gently along her thighs, everything will be all right.

A pleasurable wave ran through her. Raquel moaned with the sensation, feeling as if all her senses had been intensified. Eager fingers began to trace the shape of her own firm thigh beneath the smooth material, and her nostrils flared with the scent of the oils massaged on to her skin. A bittersweet, somewhat familiar taste still lingered in her mouth, a remnant of the aromatic tea she drank with her meal.

Unwillingly, images of the first night she made love to Nate surfaced in her mind, causing a staggered intake of breath. In a remote way the erotic pictures helped to quench the mounting fire within her, but in a deeper sense they only fanned the flames.

Hastily Raquel sat up on the bed, placing her bare feet on the furry skin that lay beside it. She forced herself to think of Miami, and her mother, and assured herself all of this would be over soon. In the end it would seem like a distant dream, or a more accurate description would be nightmare.

Like a restless cat, Raquel began to pace the floor, the feel of the smooth material moving against her skin arousing her even further.

Thoughts of the shamaness of the rain forrest flitted through her mind once again and she wondered why she had not been present in the images she relayed earlier to the Garifunian priestess. Something inside told her this was significant, but at the moment she didn't have the will to peruse the possibility, the aching in her loins seem to overpower all other trains of thought.

What sounded like footsteps and cracking branches outside the house made Raquel stop in the middle of the floor. Dark, intense almond-shaped eyes focused on the door to the one room building, and her bosom heaved heavily as she waited for it to open. Exaggerated moments went by, followed by nothing but silence. It wasn't until that moment that Raquel realized she had been intently waiting for something. But what?

A mixture of a laugh and a sob escaped her lips, for she finally realized what she was listening for. The priestess's words "Did you find a suitable male to receive your female energies?" . . . "Once you are ready, a proper receiver will be sent to you," echoed in her head. There was no doubt she was waiting for that "receiver." A suitable male. Any male!

Abruptly Raquel sat down on the bed, she drew her knees up to her chest and clasped them tightly together. What kind of ceremony is this, she wondered, as she laid her tormented face on her lap, causing her knees to be engulfed in a dark, cloud of hair. Her mind strayed to Nate. If he truly cared for her, how could he bring her

here knowing she would have to be intimate with another man-any man? And why did she still desire a man
to be with her now?

A warm burst of air and dim light, swept into the
room as the wooden door swung open, and a hooded
male stepped inside. Raquel stared up with wide, startled, damp eyes. Just the sight of him frightened and excited her, as he remained in the shadows near the door.
She sat paralyzed as she gazed upon his massive, muscular frame, which in the semidarkness resembled a
male statue. For a moment she thought there was something familiar about him. She cautioned her mind not to
play tricks on her. Nate was the only man in this settlement that she knew, and the priestess would not send
him, because she thought he was her brother.

Quickly she dashed away several tears that were making their way down her velvety cheeks. She tried to calm
herself so he would not see how nervous she was, then
she realized he could not see her, the hood was solid,
making it impossible.

Just this tiny realization of his helplessness sparked
boldness in Raquel. She knew her eager body had been
well-primed with herbs for this male who stood before
her, and the logical side of her nature was being silenced
by an earthy desire.

Slowly she rose from the bed as several hedonistic
tremors ran through her, like a spider with a victim in
her web, Raquel became the predator, and she eyed her
catch with anticipation.

The young woman took deep, trembling breaths as
she crossed the room and stood before the man. This
time, she allowed her gaze to linger on his taut frame as
she assessed him, starting with his broad, tan shoulders,

traveling downward. She could tell he was not nervous, his chest rose evenly, causing the sharply defined musculature encasing his abdomen to rise as well.

Raquel's dark lustful gaze stopped at the simple wrap he wore around his hips, a slight smile turned up the corners of her full lips as she thought of how easily it could be removed. This caused her sable eyes to become smoky with passion as she imagined what lay underneath it.

Possessively she reached out and touched one hardened pectoral, then ran her hand across his chest to the other. The feel of his rock-hard body caused her to moan again, and she closed her eyes as an exquisite sensation throbbed between her legs.

Almost with a will of its own her hand trailed down to the side of the wrap covering his maleness. With one swift motion she removed it, causing his shaft to spring forward. To Raquel's lustful eyes it appeared massive, and she longed to take it inside her.

Somewhere in the far recesses of her mind a small voice called out in protest to what she was about to do. But then another part of her, a strong inner-knowing, calmed her fears.

From that point on, not once did she question her thoughts or actions. She was being guided by a force, natural in its nature, but unnatural in intensity. It was as if she had become totally possessed by the spirit of desire, pushing her forward to assuage its needs.

Anxious, she led him to the bed and helped him lie down on the sheet. Her eyes never left his body as they burned with a dazed passion, soaking up his maleness which was in a state of semireadiness. She nearly tore the blue gown as she removed it from her body with such haste, and left it in an abandoned heap upon the floor.

With animal-like agility she straddled the man's strong body, as thoughts of impaling herself upon him engulfed her. Writhing because of the fire between her thighs, Raquel lowered herself upon his frame, needing to feel the closeness, but at the same time aware that he was not yet poised for entry. The feel of the rough hood against her skin, interrupted her sexual revelry, so with trembling fingers she grasped it, then hastily withdrew it from his head. Dazed with lust she did not focus on his features, at the moment they were not important. Nothing was important outside of the aphrodisiac's persuasive power, and ultimately quenching her own sexual need.

With hooded eyes Nate watched Raquel's passion-filled features as she threw back her head then arched her back. A mixture of emotions fought inside of him. The desire to fill her aching body almost overpowered him, but a nagging resentment echoed in his head as he realized she didn't care who fulfilled her need.

He had heard of how potent the possession could be. This, coupled with the proper herbs would be overwhelming. But to see the woman he loved eagerly mount a man she did not know only angered him.

"You want it so badly, do you?" his silky voice was laced with anger.

Raquel's dazed eyes tried to focus on the face of the man beneath her. His voice was familiar, but it sounded like a murmur against the waves of passion pounding in her head and through her body. Yet, somewhere deep inside she knew him.

Suddenly he grabbed her beneath her armpits, then easily turned and pinned her beneath him.

"The female spirit may be riding you, *pataki*, but I want you to know, that it's me, Nate, that you are giving yourself to. Do you hear me? You are mine, dammit, and no one else's!" He shouted as he clasped her chin in his hand.

He knew it was his fault she was in this predicament, but just the thought of her wantonly giving herself to a stranger had driven him to anger.

Nate's harsh words helped to clear Raquel's fuzzy head. Like a person functioning out of a mental tunnel, a vague realization of what was taking place began to unfold. Suddenly her almond-shaped eyes became lucid and full of loathing. Why hadn't he made her aware of who he was before now? No. He just let her go on humiliating herself in front of him! And now he was speaking to her like she was some common whore. It was his fault all of this—the kidnapping, the jungle, the ceremony—and she hated him for it.

"Who in the hell do you think you are, huh?" she insulted him. "I don't trust you one bit Meester Nate," she gave the best imitation of Jay's accent she could muster. "You drag me down here to this God-forsaken place and I end up going through hell and more because of you. Now you say I belong to you? I don't belong to you or anyone else." She raised her hand in an attempt to strike him.

Quickly he caught her hand, then forced both her arms above her head where he clasped her wrists together while his other hand descended over her mouth.

"What are you trying to do? Let your friend out there know we are having a disagreement." His eyes raked her features sarcastically. "Oh no, *pataki*, you must be quiet. This is not the time to let anyone know the truth about me or you. What would they say if they thought I had gone through all of this to be with my sister?" He placed warm lips against the hollow of her throat as he spoke, emitting a derisive snarl as she struggled against him.

"You keep moving like that, and it won't be long before you are raking my back in pleasure," he provoked her with a crooked smile. "I just wanted to make sure you knew who it was you were giving yourself to." He stared into angry eyes that were beginning to glaze over with passion. "We are not enemies, *pataki*, we just had a bad beginning. You'll see. And one day I will make it up to you."

Totally aroused now, his searing lips descended on hers as she lay pinned helplessly beneath him. At first she attempted to turn her head to avoid his assault, but he was relentless in his quest, in the end capturing them completely and forcing their surrender.

He kissed her long and hard, angry at himself and at how things had turned out. Never could he have imagined on that fateful day, when he first saw her, that things would get so out of hand.

The taste of her lips fueled his desire, and once again he sought out the hollow of her throat. It was as if he could not get enough of her. Drunkenly he blazed a trail of kisses from that tender spot to her taut caramel breasts below. He took each brown nipple between his lips, nibbling and sucking until they were hard and erect. Despite herself Raquel responded eagerly, thrusting the mounds in the direction of his hot lips, needing and wanting more of what he had to offer. As swiftly as her clearheadedness had descended it vanished, washed away by the passion he fueled and something else she did not quite understand, nor did she care.

The fire between her thighs flared, rising to a pitch that was unbearable. Like a wild woman, she bucked her hips against his torso seeking appeasement in any way she could. With strong hands Nate sought to restrain her, as he continued his downward descent. Firmly he covered her breasts with his large brown hands, molding the mounds into pliable flesh as she moaned her desire.

He entered his tongue into the heart of her blaze, and found it literally sweltering to the touch. Eagerly he sought to cool her while satisfying his own hunger.

The sounds of pleasure that rose from her were guttural and thick, she was beyond knowing who he was or even caring, but he knew it was he who was abating her flame, and for the moment that was enough.

From the time Nate entered her, he knew it would be like no other lovemaking he had ever known. She was an active volcano drawing him inward, clasping hold with an intensity that took his breath away. Even though he was astride, there wasn't much he could do but ride the wave of passion that spurred her on. He wrapped her tightly in his arms, murmuring words of endearment. It was all he could do to endure the journey, but when her time came he was ready to render his last most powerful strokes, sending them both over the precipice to the cliffs below.

Hoarsely he moaned into her ears, "I love you, *pataki*," as they plummeted into the valley of pleasure.

Chapter Twenty-two

The gathering of Garifunians parted naturally as the Shangoain *buyei*, accompanied by the remaining villagers entered the settlement. Eva's eyes darted nervously from side to side as she progressed with the group. Like the others, she held her back rod straight and her chin high as they moved along. She was glad one of the village women had given her a new shift to wear for it gave her the extra boost of confidence she needed. Still, she was glad to be walking deep in the midst of the crowd. It gave her a sense of protection.

A quiver of fear ran through her as she thought of what she had done, and what Jay would probably do once he found out. Then Eva calmed her own fear by thinking of what the *buyei* had promised. He assured her no one was put on earth to suffer, and if she left Jay she would be protected by the *orishas* and by the Shango.

Like the other Shangoains, Eva knew some of the Garifunians considered their coming to Dangriga an act of submission, and admission of wrongdoing on their part. Yet they, the Shangoains, considered it more an act of faith. The prophecy said the special ceremony

must take place in the *dabuyaba*, and Dangriga housed
the only active temple of their faith in Belize. Obviously,
those who could see the future had known this would be
the only way to bring the two factions together, and outside forces had worked against the *dabuyaba* in the
Shangoain village eventually closing it down.

Eva strained her neck to see the black and white
feathers of the *buyei's* headdress as he led the group several yards ahead of her. Despite all its elaborate splendor, it was still hard for her to see anything but the tips
of the piece, and the reason for this made her sad. Time
had humbled the *buyei's* proud, erect posture. Now his
shoulders displayed a pronounced droop, causing a need
for him to crane his neck and head like a bird whenever
he spoke to someone taller than himself. She pictured
his almost feeble progression as he led them, and she
knew it too pointed up their weakness in the Garifunians' eyes.

The gathering of Garifunians began to move in a parallel fashion along with the Shangoains, following them
into the interior of the village. Several tourists who'd
come early for the Settlement Day festivities focused
their attention on the advancing crowd. They gathered
together naturally in a curious bunch, in a place that allowed them clear view of the entire scene. Questioning
glances and words passed between them as they checked
their watches. It was only 11 A.M. and the ceremony
wasn't due to start until that afternoon. An elderly man
informed the others he'd been told they would have to
leave and return at the proper time when the Settlement
Day ceremony began. Several others chimed in they
had also been told the same thing, and looks of excite-

ment and apprehension settled on their faces as they wondered what was in store.

The tourists watched as the growing congregation made a large, thatched roof on stilts their final destination. The crowd began to speak in hushed tones, as they waited, and a feeling of anticipation surfaced. Suddenly all movement and sound halted as the Garifunian priestess stepped forward to meet and welcome the Shangoain *buyei*.

She looked quite different from the day before. Gone was her sun hat and scarcely matching African garb. Today's circumstances called for a more elaborate mode of dress. A well-twisted and coiled white wrap, sprinkled with gold threads, topped her generous features, and this of course, was accompanied by a matching outfit. Like a queen in all her glory, the Garifunians' religious leader calmly surveyed the group before her. If she had even the slightest feeling the Shangoains had finally succumbed to her people she did not show it as she tilted her voluminously enshrouded head, then extended a meaty arm inviting the *buyei* to join her under the cool thatched roof. It was amazing to see how elegantly the large woman maneuvered herself in the long fitted skirt and top; the sleeves so stiff it resembled a shield.

Looks of pride were exchanged among the Garifunians as they watched their opulent priestess accompany the waning Shangoain *buyei* back to their seats. A cool drink was offered to both leaders, and they sat in a companionable silence as they consumed it.

Without instruction, the Shangoains and Garifunians split up and joined their fellow villagers, who had already mapped out separate areas where cooking and other activities were taking place. Both groups knew after today's ritual, they would have to accept the other as their brother or sister in faith, yet, inside, they still housed a need to show that in some ways their own people were superior.

So with no open challenge spoken between them, they set out to out cook, and out perform what they considered the rival group. They knew their people were alike in many ways, but there were small things that drew a fine line of distinction, and their cooking was one of them.

In the Garifunians' camp, smoke rose from shallow troughs dug out and filled with wood to form an open fire, and large pots hung by their handles on branches stretched out well above the flames. Inside the kettles, a broth had just begun to form between the pieces of gibnut and armadillo. The meat would be allowed to stew until it was juicy and tender to the touch. Other dishes, seafood and vegetable alike, were prepared with coconut milk and spices indigenous to the area.

The Garifunian cooks carefully sampled all the condiments to insure their freshness and potency before adding them to the main fare. This was an important meal, and the women couldn't chance overlooking even the smallest detail.

On the other hand, the Shangoains' culinary talents had been largely influenced by the Spanish conquerors. In their camp, several females poked sticks into slabs of beef which popped and sizzled atop large piles of coal, as the meat cooked in the open. There were big iron pots nestled down in the red and white carbon, and inside, chunks of meat cooked slowly in a variety of tangy sauces. Looks and words of satisfaction or disapproval were passed between the concerned cooks as they tasted the spicy mixtures.

Not far away, huge tortillas were being stretched and made ready for the time when they would be filled with beef, eggs, or beans, either singularly or combined. One carefully rolled tortilla could provide a small meal for at least ten people after it was sliced and dished out. From the painstaking activity in the village, it was obvious both groups were intent on preparing their culinary best, which would be consumed by all.

While the women were busy with the food, the men continued to make last-minute repairs to the costumes that would be worn during the Garifunian Settlement Day ceremony. Over the years wear and tear had gotten the best of some of them, so with pride, they added new feathers or paint where they were needed.

Still groggy from the night before, the young man who had been chosen as Raquel's receiver, smoothed out the colorful feathers of the cape he would wear during the historical reenactment. Because of the power he received from the medium the night before, he would wear the most prestigious costume in the ceremony. He would be Chatoyer, the legendary leader of the Garifuna, who led their last historic battle against the British nearly two hundred years ago. Chatoyer's people had fought courageously, but still the confrontation ended with the surviving Garifunians being captured and deported to the island of Ruatan near Honduras. The ceremony is held each year so they would not forget their ancestors' bravery.

Suspiciously, he combed the crowd of men for the one he met on his way to the medium's house the previous night. His mind was foggy about what had actually taken place, and even now his head seemed to pound and swell as he tried to concentrate. All he remembered was waking up in one of the hammocks hanging amongst the trees throughout the village for convenience' sake. He had no actual memory of last night.

Bursts of laughter erupted from the group of men beside him as the ever-present bottle of cashew fruit wine made its rounds. Just the thought of drinking it caused his stomach to churn, and a slow feeling of nausea to rise.

A strong hand clasped the young man's shoulder, and he looked up into a half-smiling face above him. The glare of the sun behind the stranger blurred his facial features as he began to speak words of praise.

"Congratulations, I hear you're going to be Chatoyer during the ceremony."

"Yes, I am," the younger man grimaced as he answered. In the back of his mind he thought there was something familiar about the man's voice, but he couldn't place where he'd heard the voice before.

"You should be very proud," Nate said, his voice like silk. "I happened to be turning in as you were leaving the medium's place last night. You deserve the honor of being Chatoyer after receiving such power."

"Uh . . . you saw, I mean . . . thank you." He donned a self-assured look as he acknowledged the compliment.

"You are welcome," Nate replied, his steely gaze boring into the young man's confused features before he rose and walked away.

A perplexed look surfaced on his face before he put his doubts to rest, accepting the man's word. He could be proud because he had performed his duty as the medium's receiver, and today during the ceremony he would be given even greater honor.

Nate frowned as he rested his foot in the low fork of a tree, and scanned the active crowd. It was almost noon, and soon the *gubida* ceremony would begin. He had never intended for it to get this far, and he scolded himself for not being able to get the woman back to the States before now. He knew it was now too late for that. Obviously she'd been able to convince the priestess of her authenticity, but Nate knew talking was one thing, performing the mystical tasks involved in the ceremony would be another.

His dark eyes searched the outskirts of the settlement. He knew it was still early, and he hoped Ponti and the men would manage to come in time. He was deeply concerned about her performance in the ritual—a ritual he had never witnessed before. He only hoped it would all be over soon. Then he would be in a stronger position to protect the woman from anything Jay and his people might have planned. For there was no doubt in his mind, they would make their presence known in the settlement, and when they did, their main objective would be to silence him and the woman.

A group of men in the Garifunian camp began a lively beat on a set of drums. This was soon answered by a similar cadence from the Shangoains'. It didn't take long before bands had formed on both sides, each one striving to out play the other. Clusters of energetic children began to shuffle their feet and shake their hips and shoulders in a fashion they'd seen displayed many times by other adults. Nate watched as Belinda joined a group of them, showing them how a well-seasoned woman could spice up the moves. Her antics brought forth whoops and hollers from both the Garifunian men and the women.

Encouraged by their sounds of approval, Belinda danced toward the young man who would soon wear the costume of Chatoyer in the settlement day ceremony. A lopsided grin surfaced on his young features as he watched her, then with slightly glazed eyes he rose, and accepted to become her partner.

Feeling the music, his neck moved back and forth like a rooster as he danced toward her. Both sets of eyes were focused on the others, and they smiled the smile of lovers who knew the other could most certainly satisfy their needs. Once again this spawned a reaction from the crowd, but this time there were innuendos, sexual in nature.

As time passed, sporadic dancing and music broke out in both camps as the cashew wine flowed, and the people's spirits rose in anticipation of the events to come.

Chapter Twenty-three

Still drowsy, Raquel fought against the tangle of sheets binding the lower half of her body. At first she tried to block out the unwelcome sunlight that had awakened her, but eventually, her heavily lashed eyelids fluttered open to the demanding light. It took a few moments for her to orient herself, but when she did, her heart began to race within her as she thought of what the day would hold—coupled with flashes of the previous night.

Now, in the bright light of day, the night's events seemed almost impossible to believe, and she looked around the house to see if she could have imagined it. But the blue heap of material on the floor told the entire tale. It had not been a dream. What she had done . . . and how she had acted . . . it had all been real.

A slim, nervous hand reached up and pushed a mass of bushy hair away from her face. Afterwards she sat up, squinting in the direction of the window where the sun was forcing its way inside.

The sight of a large thatched roof on stilts caught her eye. Immediately she recognized the robust priestess, and she guessed the man who sat beside her was the Shangoain *buyei*. Without warning, an icy chill ran down her spine as she thought of the role she would soon play, and the danger she might meet should she fail.

Once again thoughts of running away entered her mind. Panic-stricken eyes searched the growing crowd outside, and her heart lurched as she saw a group of tourists standing idly by. To the north of them she could see several parked cars. If only she could get to them! Maybe she could get them to help her!

Without further thought Raquel threw on the light blue caftan and headed for the door. Maybe she could secretly hide out in one of their vehicles, and wait for the time when they would leave.

Excited by the thought of escape, she cracked the door to peer outside. After going over the area quickly, she thought there was a chance she could circumvent the center of the settlement, and approach the cars from behind. Shoving the door aside, she made her initial step to run for the cover of the nearby woods.

"Mornin'," a respectful, strong voice greeted her. "So you finally woke up, did you? I thought you would sleep the whole morning through. I was just about to check on you again. I been in there twice, trying to see if you wanted breakfas' or something."

Badly startled by the assistant's presence, Raquel answered a short, "No," then immediately closed the door.

Her nerves on edge, she tilted her head back against the wood, and with a trembling hand she squeezed the leather pouch hanging about her neck. Frustration filled her moist eyes as she looked down at the ill-shaped object. In so doing, she caught sight of a large, dark bruise on her forearm. The unsightly spot made her think of

Al, then drove a horrible fact home. If she failed during the ceremony, the Garifunians and Shangoains might do her harm, but there was no doubt if Jay caught up with her while she was trying to escape, he would kill her.

Perspiration broke out on her forehead. Raquel decided she would be better off taking her chances performing the ritual. She would do as the shamaness of the rain forest advised her. She had said she was an open spirit. So she would will herself to open to the voices of her intuition, and simply allow that part of her to flow. Raquel knew for her, that was easier said than done. But if all else failed, she determined, she would put on a performance that would win her an academy award, if need be.

Raquel was very skeptical about her abilities to yield to such spiritual beliefs. All of her life she had purposefully kept that kind of thinking at bay. As the years passed, she had convinced herself those quiet moments of childish imagination were only possible because she had been so young. To her, intuition meant uncertainty, and she had no room for that. Controlling logic had been her foundation, and now her very life depended on being able to let go of that.

An insistent knocking erupted behind the door, followed by the assistant's voice.

"I know you said you didn't want anything, but I got a basin of hot water for you to wash up in, and some fruit for you to eat. Madame Sofea would never forgive me if I didn't take care of you right. D'ya hear?"

Raquel eased up on the pressure she was applying against the door. "Come in," she invited her, half-heartedly.

Obedient, the young assistant picked up a large bowl filled with steaming water and stepped inside. Her stride was purposeful as she crossed the room and sat the container on a hand made wooden table. Beside it she placed two washcloths. Raquel watched as she went out again, returning with a package beneath her arm. There was also a bowl of oranges, grapefruits and tomatoes.

"Once you have eaten and washed yourself, here is the dress you will wear for the ceremony." She laid the brown paper packet on the bed. "I will not disturb you again until everythin' has been made ready, and the people have gathered for the ritual." The young woman started to cross the room to the door, she stopped and looked back, "Should you need me, I will be waiting outside."

Raquel sat down at the table. Despite what she told the assistant, she was hungry, and she began to peel one of the aromatic oranges as her eyes traveled to the brown package on the bed. Now, there was no turning back. She would go through with the ritual.

Automatically, Raquel began to rely on her ability to carve out a logical understanding of how she could perform what would be expected of her. Through her years of study, she had come to know of a part of the mind, which, when given the right atmosphere, even under the most bizarre situations, would react impulsively, answering the need, even when it was totally opposed to the person's personality or abilities.

Images of the night before surfaced, and she was ashamed to think how unabashedly she'd responded, letting go of all restraints without hesitation. She had been ready to do whatever was necessary to appease the potent desire burning in her veins. It just so happened

Nate had been the one to come to her. She was appalled to admit that, at that time, she would have given herself to anyone.

There was a part of her that was thankful it had been Nate. But now, knowing how he had lied to her, using her even after she thought things had changed from the time he'd forcefully brought her to Belize, she could find only a bittersweet comfort in it.

In some ways, it hurt even more to have given herself to him. It further cheapened her love, seeing how he had completely used and deceived her.

Raquel sat eating the orange in silence, and listening to the tangled sound of music outside the window. She thought of the men who approached her outside the Caribbean club that fateful night, and she wondered what connection they had with Nate, if any.

A sickening feeling churned in her stomach as she thought of how ruthless he must be to have deliberately put her in such a dangerous situation, just to satisfy his own means. She was stupid to trust him, and even nurse him back to health in his hour of need. How he must have secretly laughed at her kindness, and used what he considered to be her weakness to his advantage. Now that he was back on his home turf, he could afford to tell her the truth, because she had nearly served her purpose. Whatever that may be! Wouldn't it be most ironic if he and Jay were actually working together, putting on this outrageous farce for reasons they only knew.

Raquel's anger rose with a disappointed kind of fear as her mind conjured up all sorts of reasons for the last ten days of her life. She knew she could use the anger to give her the strength she would need to survive what was in store for her.

After finishing another piece of fruit, Raquel attempted to wash her body with a sliver of soap she found on a cabinet. Deep in thought, she dried off with the second cloth, then slipped back into the caftan.

Curiosity drew her to the brown package on the bed, with trembling fingers she unwrapped it. The objects inside were simple, a string of sparkling blue and white beads, a floor-length shift in a similar shade of blue, and a large-tooth comb missing several of its prongs. A cynical smile touched Raquel's full lips, such a simple outfit for a medium who was expected to perform such miraculous works.

With the comb she managed to style her hair. She thought it should reflect the simplicity of the dress and beads, so she decided to redo her braids. The two plaits began at her forehead, outlined the edge of her hair, and met in the back where she braided them together, making the final braid into a ball.

For some reason she felt an unnatural calm as she sat on the bed with her head against the wall, waiting for the time she would be summoned. Raquel closed her eyes, shutting out the world, and tried to focus on the center of peace she had come to know on rare occasions during her sporadic meditations. As she concentrated, she knew, no matter what methods she used to conduct the ritual, the answers would all have to come from inside her. She just hoped they were the right ones.

Chapter Twenty-four

"Hey, what is this?" the middle-aged, red-haired man protested. "I didn't come all the way down here in this god-forsaken mudhole to miss any of the action. I'm ready to par-r-tay. And I heard you've never been to a party till you've partied down here at one of y'all's festivals. And now you're telling me I'm not allowed," he raised his voice at the teenage Garifunians who had linked arms to block his way.

A group of tourists interested in the outburst lingered conveniently behind. Unlike the others who had contented themselves with shopping in the only gift shop, they wanted to see if there was even the slightest chance they would be allowed to see the forbidden ritual.

"This is not for outsiders," one of the louder, bolder teenagers replied, then clasped the wrists of his human chain counterparts even tighter, causing the others to do the same.

"Oh it's not? We'll see about that."

The large man attempted to shove his way through the teenagers' block, but he was abruptly stopped by two adult males approaching from the rear.

They didn't speak a word as they grabbed him beneath his armpits, and forcefully dragged him back to the middle of the settlement while he shouted obscenities and the other tourists shuffled off to do some shopping.

The red-haired man continued to grumble as he sat in the spot where he had been discarded by the two Shangoains, but he made no attempt to follow them as they entered the rain forest.

As the minutes passed Raquel knew it wouldn't be long before the assistant informed her the villagers were ready. Once again a light sheen of perspiration broke out on her forehead, and a little voice inside admonished her, calling her a fool for even attempting this. Maybe she was a fool. Maybe she had even become as confused as some of the patients she'd counseled over the years. But there was one thing she was sure of, that she was willing to do whatever it would take to bring this ordeal to an end.

Yet Raquel knew there was something else that compelled her, even though she would deny it if she could. It was a persistent, inner nagging, telling her there was more. Something on an almost imperceptible level coercing her to carry out this task, guiding her with forces she did not understand.

The young woman ran both of her hands over her eyes, and tried to rid her mind of that train of thought. It was futile at this point to try and reason why her life had led her here. It would only drain her, and she would need all the powers of concentration she could muster for the ritual.

A knock sounded at the door, and as Raquel rose to answer it Nate came into view far outside her window.

He was carrying Marjorie, her small body appearing frail in his arms. Brandon's smaller steps looked hurried beside Nate's long strides as they crossed the mud-caked road to enter the rain forest. There was a scowl upon his handsome features when he turned and gave the settlement one hard, searching look before disappearing into the thicket.

Impatient from no answer, the assistant cracked the door and spoke into the tiny space.

"It is time for the ceremony to begin."

Raquel took a deep breath and steadied herself, "I'm ready," then she walked over to the door and stepped outside.

The assistant acknowledged her with a slight smile, but without further adieu she turned and walked toward the rain forest.

The green darkness of the tree-canopy-covered forest was a stark contrast to the tropical sunshine beaming down on the rest of the settlement. The transition was almost mystical, for this was a totally different world, ruled by nature and its forces. The assistant's movements through the brush seemed to reflect Raquel's thoughts. She was no longer the pragmatic creature from the settlement, but one who showed even with the slightest touch, that she honored nature and its gifts. Almost with reverence she pushed aside the branches and vines appearing in their way as they progressed deeper into the forest, her feet moving soundlessly upon the ground.

It didn't take long for them to reach the circle of villagers, gathered around a partial clearing. Immediately, countless pairs of dark eyes engulfed Raquel as they entered the center area covered by moss and other growth favoring a close relationship with the earth.

The Garifunian priestess and the Shangoain *buyei* sat on the opposite side of the clearing. In their hands were small gourds, covered with netting, connected by cowrie shells. Both nodded as she entered the circle, shaking the minute instruments in a welcoming salute.

It was then Raquel noticed the other musicians. They were seated on the ground with their legs crossed, holding the same instrument, varying in size.

Obviously the welcoming rattle was their cue, so with controlled hand and arm movements, they began a low, rhythmic, slating sound. Over and over they played the same pattern until their bodies naturally joined in, their upper torsos and heads following the repetitive beat. With perfect timing, the light, hollow pulse of a bongo drum fused with it, giving the cadence a lulling, resonate sound. Some of the younger Garifunians and Shangoains began to imitate the body movement of the musicians until the entire gathering seemed to sway in unison, beguiled by the trance inducing music.

A moment of confusion nearly disrupted the beginning of the ritual, when both the priestess and *buyei* attempted to speak at the same time. An awkward silence followed as they both gestured, indicating the other should be allowed to go first. Finally, the *buyei* accepted the priestess's act of courtesy, and spoke briefly to the crowd.

"We have waited a long time for t'is, and out of respect for the *gubida* we should not delay it any longer," his trembling, but strong voice floated outward. "T'is ceremony will renew the bond between the Garifunian an' Shangoain people, makin' it stronger than evah. An' through this unity our faith will also be strengthened by us giving the proper honor an' praise to the gods an' goddesses of our ancestors."

The *buyei* finished his introduction by picking up a small cup of water that had been sitting between him and the priestess. He turned and offered it to her. Following his lead, she accepted the object from his knurled hands and began to sprinkle several drops of the water on the ground. Afterwards she shook her rattle, and spoke in a loud voice.

"We praise Olodumare and all honored ancestors who live at the feet of Olodumare in the world thus to follow. We praise our personal ancestors and salute the priests of our houses. We also salute Yemoja-Olokun and Shango and the many gods of our people."

Verbal agreement resounded throughout the crowd at the priestess's words. Finally, when the crowd became silent, the music began again, but this time it was louder, and all eyes turned to Raquel.

Her anxious features searched the faces of the villagers surrounding her, then reluctantly her gaze stopped on Nate's concerned face and Marjorie's thin countenance, leaning against his chest.

She could feel the crowd's expectation as they stared at her, it was almost a suffocating feeling. She tried to relax enough to think of the advice the shamaness of the rain forest had given her, but her mind drew a blank. The music seemed to become more insistent, the sound of it feeling as if it were literally trying to enter her head.

Suddenly Raquel felt overwhelmed. She became lightheaded as if she might faint, and she dropped to her knees. Weakly, she leaned forward and placed her face against the cool moss blanketing the forest floor. It was hard for her to breathe, and despite herself, she tried to call out to Nate for help, but no sound came from her lips. Finally, her fading gaze connected with his, just as it looked as if he had decided to come to her. Then everything around her went dark.

There was a part of her that was aware of everything, but somehow time had been suspended. She could see her body crouched in the forest, the people around her, and Nate on a perpetual verge of reaching out to her.

The part of Raquel that was conscious, turned its attention toward the rain forest, then merely by focusing her thoughts on its interior, she began to travel at an amazing speed. All the colors of the forest blended together as she whooshed by, and before she knew it, she was standing outside a cave. Two bright eyes glowed from within it, then upon seeing her they began to move in her direction. It was an animal. A jaguarundi. When he emerged from the cave he came and laid his body down at her feet, as docile as a kitten.

As Raquel knelt to rub his soft fur, his piercing eyes seemed to draw her gaze within them, and an image of the shamaness of the rain forest appeared in their yellowish depths.

She was lying alone in her hut upon a pallet. The rise and fall of her thin chest was almost indiscernible beneath the numerous layers of cloth, and her once-powerful dreadlocks lay limply about her. The vision clutched at Raquel's heart, and her feelings went out to her mentor that she should be alone in her hour of death.

Then suddenly, as if she could feel Raquel's emotions, a slight smile appeared on the shamaness's withered face. Slowly she began to speak, and somehow Raquel could hear her coarse voice purring in the wind.

"Do not feel sad for me. Soon I will be totally re-united with the source of all power. And that ez the key to all knowledge, girl. All that lives has a spark of that power within, as you do. Clasp hold of the pouch an' give praise to the ocean an' her life-giving forces. Ask for her compassion, an' she will help bridge the two worlds that you seek. My timely passing will open the way for you." Her last words were only a blur, then her dried lips were still and Raquel knew the shamaness of the rain forest was dead. Oddly, at that moment, she did not feel grief. If she trusted her mentor, she would have to believe all that she had said. Maybe now she would find the acceptance she could not find here on earth.

Abruptly her mind focused on the pouch. She needed it to call on the ocean's power, yet it still hung around her neck as she crouched in the forest. A profound yearning to hold it overcame her, and with that urgent desire, in a split second, her spirit and body were re-united. During that second, she was totally aware of be-ing in the clearing, the people, the music. But as soon as she called on the force of the ocean to show her com-passion, her consciousness totally deserted her.

Chapter Twenty-five

She could barely make out the face above her, but as the moments passed, and her fluttering lashes halted their erratic movement, she realized it was Nate's face. Her confused mind began to fill with all sorts of questions. But Raquel knew they would have to wait, because breathing deeply was all she was capable of doing. She felt exhausted, even her head felt heavy as she attempted to turn it on Nate's lap. Finally she realized her portion of the ritual was over.

Two villagers had taken her place as the center of attention, and they were in the throes of what she could only call some kind of trance. The man and the woman resembled marionettes being controlled by invisible strings, their body movements jerky and unpredictable.

The music had also changed from the repetitive cadence she remembered, to a more animated, invigorating, sound. This was matched by the movements of the chosen villagers.

The entire crowd had become energized, and by the satisfied looks on the priestess and *buyei's* faces, she knew she had been successful.

"What happened?" she asked weakly. She found her throat was parched as she attempted to speak.

One smooth eyebrow raised, perplexed, "You tell me," Nate's dark eyes glistened as he looked down into her face. "You looked like you knew exactly what you were doing a little while ago."

She closed her eyes, not understanding what he meant, and too tired to reply. When she opened them again, she saw the assistant kneeling down beside her, offering her a drink. Hastily she took the container, gulping down its contents without a second thought.

A thin hand reached out to take the empty cup from her, and Raquel's eyes opened wide with disbelief when she saw it was Marjorie. She was deathly thin, but deep within the depths of her eyes was the sparkle of life.

"I want to thank you for releasing my boy," her voice was barely more than a whisper as she spoke. "Now it is time for me to rejoin the livin'. Brandon needs me, and I know now, Art has safely crossed over to the other side."

Raquel could only nod her head lamely.

As Marjorie walked away, two village women approached them and gently removed Raquel from Nate's care. She was moved to a seat of honor near the priestess and the *buyei*. There she was given time to recuperate, and with amazement, she watched the remainder of the ritual.

Raquel could tell, despite his helping her, Nate was grateful when the women took her from him. It was obvious he was on edge, and even the compelling activity inside the clearing could not hold his attention. His watchful, steely gaze continuously searched the surrounding rain forest. His concern was somewhere out there, not within the circle of satisfied Garifunians and Shangoains.

The young woman watched as the villagers, whom the priestess said were being ridden by some unseen forces, unexpectantly dropped with exhaustion. Quickly several caring participants came to their aid, and moved them to places where they too could rest. The music continued to play for a while longer. It was as if the musicians had to come down from the peak where their music had taken them. Shortly afterwards, the sound of the bongos and the rattles came to a halt.

A meaty, dimpled hand was shown to the crowd as the priestess sought to gain their attention.

"I know there is only one question that both the Garifunian and our spiritual brothers, the Shangoain, would like to ask the ancestors. And that is, "Are you pleased with what we have done here today? Has the spiritual rift between our people been mended by these works?"

Words of encouragement and affirmation intermittently rose from the crowd, and Raquel could tell this question-and-answer period was also a part of the ceremony.

The question had been asked, and now a divination would decide if the answer was a positive one. If it was, blessings would be bestowed on both of the villages, or if the contrary were true, afflictions would rage among the people for not pleasing the *gubida*.

The Shangoain *buyei* produced the divination tools from a sack he carried at his side. They were four hollow coconut shells, and Raquel could tell they had received much use through the years. What used to be their hairy outer part had been worn down, until now the fibers resembled a sprouting beard.

Ceremoniously the *buyei* wet each one of the shells. Once done, he cast all four on the forest floor. The villagers watched the process in a hushed silence. Three times he threw them, and three times they landed face up. Raquel had no idea what the results of the casting meant, until the last throw was met by exuberant shouts from the pleased crowd.

This time the priestess did not try to calm the congregation, so above the excited raucous shouts she announced, "We have surely been blessed today! Now let the Settlement Day festivities begin."

Jay grabbed the first painted mask and shirt he found. Working fast, he removed his top and quickly replaced it with the costume. His anxious fingers found the small buttons on the old rayon top difficult to work with, and he cussed at the shirt under his breath.

"Look through there, and see if t'ere's anythin' t'at will fit both of you," he instructed Rock and Mane-Mane.

Rock resented the authoritative attitude Jay had taken since arriving in the village. He would have made it known, but he realized nabbing some of the costumes that were to be worn during the ceremony wasn't a bad idea. This way their faces would be covered, no one would be able to identify them, and they'd surely blend in with the crowd.

He signaled his okay for Mane-Mane to search through the small stacks of shirts and masks as he kept watch. He could see one of their backups perusing the gift shop, while the other joined in with the large crowd of tourists waiting for the festivities to begin.

"You ain't found nothin' yet?" he barked, as he rubbed his index finger back and forth beneath his nose.

"Hell no! These damn things are too little for either one of us. That goes to show you what I've been saying all along. These suckers, just like Jay, ain't nothing but—" he stopped and looked in the man's direction, to see if his remark would hit home.

But Jay's anxious eyes were focused on the spot where the villagers would reenter the settlement. He'd waited a long time to settle the score with Nate and the woman, and revenge was uppermost in his mind.

Unable to get a rise out of him, Mane-Mane continued.

"Maybe we should go back to our original plan and just wait for Jay to round up the woman. Once the guy sees she's missing, he's sure to follow, and we can take care of both of 'em at the same time."

Jay's eyes seemed to light up as he heard Mane-Mane mention Raquel. "Yes, leave the woman to me. I'll take care of her."

"What d'ya mean you'll take care of her?" Rock jumped in. "You're suppose to bring her to me, and I'll decide how it's handled from there." Hell, Rock wanted Jay to do the killing, but not out in the open where everyone could see. As obsessed as he had become, there's no telling what he might say and do that would ultimately connect him with their organization. He told Ricky this guy was going to be hard to handle. But all he could say was, "Just point him in the right direction, and let him do the dirty work."

Jay simply stared at Rock. It was a long hollow look, as if he could see right through him.

Rock hated to admit it, but ever since they found Jay's dead brother he'd begun to feel uneasy around the guy. There was something spooky about him, just like this stare he was throwing down on him now.

Jay insulted him in a voice as piercing as his stare. "I don't take no orders from nobody like you." Then he walked away, disappearing into the nearby brush.

The crowd at the clearing jumped to its feet no sooner than the priestess's words were spoken, and the musicians began to play again. This time the bongos and rattles were joined by other drums and an old guitar. The Garifunians and Shangoains joined their voices in song as they made their way back to the settlement. At first their revelry sounded like a low hum to the tourists, but it rose in pitch as they got nearer to the settlements border.

Raquel was well entangled in the joyous crowd. Despite her fatigue, she could almost feel the energy from their happiness. She knew, not even in a thousand years would she be able to explain what had happened back there, but explain it or not, something miraculous did occur, and she had played a major role. But her moment of triumph was cut short when Nate showed up beside her.

"We-ell, that was quite a show you put on back there, *pataki*, I didn't know you had it in you. Are you sure you haven't done this kind of thing before?"

There was a slight smile on his face, but his eyes were bright like an animal's whose senses were tuned for danger. Possessively, he placed his large hand around her forearm and held it tightly.

"If it isn't my dear . . . brother," she spat at him. "I'm glad my performance was greater than even you had expected. But that shouldn't surprise you. Being great performers and deceivers tends to run in the family," she retorted angrily, trying to remove her arm from his grasp with no avail.

"You can let go of my arm now," she hissed between her teeth. "Haven't I served my purpose? Or has that calculating brain of yours come up with some other way you can use me?"

"Yes, in a way you've served your purpose, and very well I should say," his voice was harsh. "And now I want to make sure you get to keep doing just that." His already-firm grip tightened at the anger and distrust in her voice.

Dark, almond eyes looked up at him with accusation, "Don't start that again." Wincing, she looked at his large hand on her arm. "And you are hurting me!"

Nate's voice softened, and so did his grip as he looked down at her.

"I'm sorry, *pataki*, but we didn't make it this far for me to lose you now. I know after all this you may find it difficult to believe, but I only want to protect you. You see—"

"Liar! You're nothing but a liar!" she screamed cutting him off, then managing to yank herself free. But no one could hear her, or paid her any attention as the excited crowd burst out into the settlement.

The strong forward thrust caught Raquel up in the throng. They were joined by the tourists who were moving in closer to get a better look at the Yankunu dancers jauntily advancing toward them. Their costumes depicted the dress of the villagers' ancestors, some much more elaborate than others.

Large hand-painted masks covered their faces as they waved sticks and other objects, representing the weapons they used to fight the British during that fateful battle.

Raquel caught a glimpse of Nate's contorted features as she was carried outside of his reach. For the first time since she'd known him, she saw fear and apprehension in his eyes, and she knew without a doubt, those feeling were not for himself but for her.

The appearance of the dancers further enlivened the group, and almost everyone had joined in the celebration. Food and wine was being passed about freely, as the villagers celebrated Garifuna Settlement Day, and the favorable results of the ritual.

Staggered, boisterous phrases of praise resounded all around as the young man dressed as Chatoyer entered the scene. His bright feathers seem to vibrate in the sunshine as he twirled and turned showing his prowess, energized by the crowd's approval. Several eager villagers hoisted Raquel up and maneuvered her nearer to the symbol of their legendary leader, putting her down in the front of the crowd, so he would surely see her.

Just as the excited crowd expected, the young man's eyes gleamed within the ferocious mask when he saw the woman he thought he had coupled with the night before, and he began to prance saucily before her, surrounded by the other Yankunu dancers, drawing an even more jubilant response.

Raquel stood tensely before him with the villagers

shouting words of encouragement at her back, not sure what they were encouraging her to do.

One of the dancers reached out and grabbed her by her wrist, and began to pull her into their circle as she was being pushed from behind. Energized, he began to cavort with her by his side. She could tell he expected her to duplicate his movements, but the picture of Nate's face only moments ago still loomed in her mind.

Suddenly a string of shots rang out from an automatic weapon. The eruption seem to come from the area where the tourists had parked their cars.

Raquel's heart lurched with fear at the sound of the loud blasts. It was Jay! He'd finally caught up with them. Suddenly all she could see was Nate lying in a pool of blood and Jay standing above him, a satisfied smile on his face after killing the man who'd fatally shot his brother.

"No—o!" The mad scream rose from the depths of her as she tried to break loose from the dancer who still held her arm. She had to find out . . . to go to him!

The sound of the gunshots caused panic to break out amongst the crowd, and people were shoving and pushing one another to find cover. In the pandemonium, the dancer who held her hand began to drag her in the opposite direction of where she wanted to go. Once again she tried to extract her hand from his, but he held it even tighter. It was then, she realized, she was being forcefully led by the masked man.

Jay began to lead her away from where he knew Rock and Mane-Mane were waiting. He would not allow them to tell him what he should do with the woman. He already knew what had to be done. She had to be made to suffer, just like Al suffered. And he would be the only one to do it.

"What are you doing?" Raquel screamed as her plight began to sink in. "You better let go of me!"

Furiously she fought against the iron-tight grip, trying to break free. The man was headed for the cover of the rain forest, and she knew she would be in even graver danger once they entered it.

Obsessed, Jay paid little attention to her pleas as he dragged her deeper into the forest. Sweat poured down his face beneath the mask because of the heat and the effort it took to control the woman. His breaths became ragged with exertion, and his heart pumped faster as he focused on the fear in her voice.

Finally reaching a point far enough within the brush, he stopped and removed the papier mâché cover.

A slow, unnatural smile spread across his thin lips. "So we meet again, *echu?*" A terrifying mixture of hate and lust burned in his eyes as he addressed her.

The shock of seeing Jay's face beneath the mask was nearly too much, and it took all the strength Raquel had to remain steady on her feet.

"You shouldn' be surprised to see me. Don' tell me you thought I wouldn' come aftah you." The sound of his large switchblade releasing sliced into his words.

"Yes. I knew from the very first you were bad luck," he spat on the ground beside her feet. "Yeah, I know of all 'e talk of you an' the *gubida*. But 'e stories are fairy tales, told to people who are afraid to take control of t'eir own lives." He meaningfully tested the point of the blade against his index finger, drawing a quick spurt of blood. Once again he looked up at Raquel. "You were bad for me an' my brothah, Al. But you were no good even before t'at. I tried to get rid of you, but somehow it didn' work. I would have taken care of you from the very beginnin' if it hadn' been for Meester Nate. He was *always* t'ere to protect you . . . but he isn't here now."

Jay's horrible eyes burned into hers as he grabbed her by the throat and drew her to him. "No, he isn' here now." Each word caused bursts of his coarse breath to blow into her face, and Raquel closed her eyes against him.

Grinning, he meticulously moved the blade from her throat downward with the needle-sharp tip of the knife. Putting pressure against the thin material of her shift. It pierced the papery fabric easily, drawing a pencil thin line of blood on her skin as he went. Savoring the moment, and his feeling of power over her, Jay stopped at the tender spot between her breasts.

"Yeah, the man who talked all t'at fancy talk 'bout protectin' you because of the ancestors, ain't nowhere aroun'," he snorted. "But now I know he jus' wanted to keep Al and me from you, cuz he wanted you himself," he applied more pressure against the knife. "I wonder where he is now, *echu*. I wouldn' be surprised if he isn' layin' not very far from here wit' his brains shot out by Rock or Mane-Mane."

"Guess again, Jay."

Raquel's eyes flew open to see Nate standing several feet behind the man, his gun drawn.

A flicker of surprise clouded Jay's bulbous eyes at the sound of Nate's silky voice, and he tightened his hold about Raquel's neck.

"If you have a gun Meester Nate, an' you decide to shoot me at such close range, the bullet will go right through me into t'e woman. Or by t'e time it enters my body, I will have plunged t'is knife deep into her chest. Either way she will be dead."

"That's true, Jay. You both will be dead. But I will be alive. And I'm the one who bent over and put my gun against your no-good, crazy brother's heart. Put him out of his misery just like a rabid dog. I killed him Jay. And once you're dead there'll be no one to avenge him," he paused to let his words sink in. "But if he were my brother, Jay, I'd want to kill the person who killed him."

Raquel could feel the knife quiver against her chest and she knew Nate's words had reached their mark. Jay's grip on her neck tightened and she winced in pain.

"You shut up 'bout my brothah, you no-good sonuvabitch! I will—"

"You will what?" Nate's voice was deadly smooth as he spoke. "Kill me, Jay? How you gonna do that as long as you're holding the woman? If you let her go, I promise you, I'll put down the gun and you can have me. I'm the one who actually killed your brother, not her. I'm the one you really want."

There was a moment of indecision before Jay spoke again.

"Well, you come 'round here where I can see you and t'en we'll talk."

"I'll come, but I don't want to talk. See there's a chance I can get near enough to you, and shoot you before you can stab the woman. And I'm willing to take that chance. So to keep it fair, I'm going to stop here and count to three. On the count of three, I will drop the gun, but while I'm counting, you better be pushing her away, and have released her when I'm done."

"One . . ." Nate's dark eyes narrowed as he watched

Jay's veins in the hand around Raquel's neck protrude. "Two . . ."

Her breath was cut short as Jay began to push her over to his side. She could feel his fingers constricting around her neck, and she knew he was trying to choke her. Her hands flew up to her throat in an effort to pry his maniacal fingers from around it.

"Three."

Suddenly he pushed her on the ground, and she heard the thud of Nate's gun when it hit the moss-covered floor. Like an animal, Nate sprung toward Jay, grabbing the arm which held the ominous switchblade. Both men struggled, pitting their strength against one another, as they rolled through the brush.

Focusing his strength, Nate forced Jay onto his back, and applied his weight against the arm holding the knife. Jay's teeth ground together as he tried to hold onto the weapon, but finally Nate prevailed, and the switchblade was knocked into the thickness of a nearby bush.

Pushed beyond the point of anger, Jay let loose an enraged yell and kneed Nate in the groin, causing him to double over in pain. Jay knew he had to take advantage of the moment, and he lunged toward the Glock Nate had thrown on the ground. Panting and feeling the hard, cold metal in his shaking hands, he aimed the gun in Nate's direction.

"Now, not only am I going to kill you, Meester Nate, but I also get to kill the no-good bitch. No-ow," he groaned, "it will end as it should end by my killin' the two of you."

A broad, demented smile beamed on Jay's face as he pulled the trigger, only for the bullet to go off into the ground a couple of feet in front of him. Like a wooden soldier being pushed face down, Jay's thin body pitched forward. The butt of the switchblade sticking out of his back as Eva stood above him. Motionless she stood watching as his body convulsed with his last painful breaths. Then almost, as if realizing what she had done, she abruptly looked up at Nate and Raquel, then turned and ran into the rain forest.

Chapter Twenty-six

A large, wet area was forming on the back of Mane-Mane's T-shirt, compliments of the sun. His muscles rippled underneath the soggy material as he adjusted his body, trying get more comfortable.

"Shit," he hollered loudly. "The hood of this damn car is burnin' my face," he complained as the top of his frame lay across the blue vehicle. His eyes rolled to the side as far as they could in an effort to see what kind of reaction his remark had drawn. To his dismay, it drew none. Sniffing, Rock lay beside him cussing beneath his breath. Both men were handcuffed. Their two accomplices were draped across the vehicle on the other side of the hood, bound in the same fashion.

Raquel tried to listen at a distance along with several villagers and tourists, to—as she guessed—law-enforcement officers haggling about what had taken place. It was hard to hear because of comments from curious onlookers.

A short man in uniform, pointed an accusing finger toward Nate and the five men standing near him. She knew Nate had to have heard the remarks, but saw that he continued to explain events calmly to the group around him.

Raquel could barely concentrate as her mind and senses continued to reel from the scene in the forest. Once they had reentered the village, things happened so fast she could barely keep up with them.

She remembered Ponti rushing to their side, and upon seeing the blood from the shallow cut on her chest, asking if she were okay. Weakly she had nodded, and with his support walked with him and Nate across the main thoroughfare of the village. Abruptly Nate stopped, instructed Ponti to take her to a shady spot, and handed him the pistol Jay had attempted to use only minutes before.

"I think the danger is over," Nate cautioned, "but if not, don't be afraid to use it."

Still shaky, but pleased to have Ponti by her side, Raquel watched as Nate walked toward the parked cars where several men were being held at gunpoint by apparent tourists. Moments later, Belizean law-enforcement officers arrived on the scene, and after a few words with Nate and the other men, placed handcuffs on the prisoners, who were now lying across the cars.

A short official, obviously the one in charge, showed growing signs of irritation as he spoke to several other officers. Distrustful glances were cast toward Nate and the men around him as they continued their conversation.

Suddenly, the officer shoved his way through the ring of men surrounding Nate, and confronted him. The back of his hand smacked against his palm repeatedly as he spoke. All of his gestures were wild and irritated during the exchange.

Raquel looked on as Nate stood quietly, his tall frame looking almost relaxed as he leaned into one hip. Beads of perspiration gleamed on all of the men's faces as the sun beat down on the scene.

Several minutes passed and Raquel was slightly amused that the official had not run out of steam, but it was apparent Nate had heard enough. Interrupting the man's speech, he turned to one of the men behind him, and immediately produced several folded papers and a small, leather billfold.

The official was plainly offended by Nate's actions and placed his hefty hands on his hips as he watched him warily.

"What the heck is going on over there, Ponti?" Raquel asked totally baffled.

"It's a long story," he hedged. "Maybe I should let Mr. Nate tell you about it."

Surprised, and a little irritated, Raquel looked at Ponti's cloaked features, then back at Nate and the men around him.

After a minute's perusal of the paperwork the official abruptly flung them back into Nate's outstretched palm.

"I should know about things like this before they take place," he protested over the murmur of the crowd.

Further confused, Raquel watched as Nate spoke to the man, then showed him the contents of the leather billfold. The official shook his head as if he'd been defeated, asked—Raquel perceived—more questions, then threw his hands up in submission and rejoined his men.

Barking instructions, he watched as his officers placed the handcuffed men in the back seats of two of the four-wheel drive vehicles, then secured them further by handcuffing them to the interior of the car. Satisfied they had performed their duties in an adequate manner, he made a slight nod in Nate's direction, got into another vehicle and drove away, followed by the cars filled with two new sets of prisoners.

For a moment their eyes met, and Raquel was more aware than ever that she knew nothing about this man with whom she'd spent the most dangerous, yet fulfilling week of her entire life.

Nate's attention was drawn back to his men and they exchanged a few more words. Afterwards they dispersed in several directions, while Nate advanced toward the priestess and the *buyei*, who were seated beneath the large thatched roof.

Once again Raquel could tell that several questions were asked and Nate supplied the answers. On this occasion, taking his time to explain what had occurred, thus showing them more respect than he had shown the law-enforcement officer. Sporadically, the priestess and *buyei* nodded their heads in understanding as he spoke, until finally each one laid their hands upon him, giving him their approval.

Raquel wondered if he'd told them the truth about who she was, and if so, why were they still pleased with him? And the officers—they'd nearly treated him as if he were their equal. It was all so confusing, if he knew he had their trust, why had they hidden like criminals the entire time they were in Belize? And why had he actually participated in kidnapping her, if he was such friends, so to speak, with the law?

By now totally perplexed, she watched as the two heads of the Garifunian and Shangoain communities bid him a fond farewell and began to cross the dusty road progressing in her direction.

There were so many questions she wanted to ask and things she needed to say, but once he reached her, she was speechless.

Nate understood the myriad of emotions playing across her still-beautiful, but somewhat-drawn features. She had lost weight, and the bruise on her face was at its peak. He wanted to take her in his arms and tell her everything would be okay, but coming from him, he knew those words would sound empty and meaningless.

"*Pataki*, we're ready to go home now." His expression was veiled as he looked into her face.

For some reason the phrase she had waited to hear for so long angered her. And the word which he had come to call her grated on her nerves. So after all this, he would simply tell her we're ready to go home! He didn't think he owed her any kind of explanation as to what had actually taken place! So ... she should be grateful to be alive and that was it!

"Just wait a minute!" her incredulous eyes cut into him. "So that's it, huh? This is crazy! You think you can just walk over here and offer to take me home like we just went to the movies or something?"

"No," his eyes continued to search hers. "I understand—"

"We're ready to leave any time you are, Mr. Bowman," one of the men interrupted him.

"All right," he answered him, but his eyes stayed fastened on Raquel's. "Look, I've got a lot to tell you, and this isn't the place to do it. It'll be better once we're on the plane."

Their dark eyes locked in a silent battle.

Wanting and feeling like she deserved more, Raquel thought of protesting further, but another one of the men approached Nate, insisting he had some pressing things to discuss with him, then he began to physically pull him aside. After a few choice words in his ear, the understanding countenance he'd shown her only moments before disappeared, and he became engulfed in the conversation at hand.

Wordlessly he cut the man off with a movement of his hand, "We need to talk about this on the plane." The man nodded his head in agreement.

With distressed features, Nate turned and addressed Ponti.

"I've got to go now, but you know what to do."

"Yes, I've got it all written down right here." He patted a leather binder Raquel had not noticed before.

"Good, because from now on you're going to be one of my main people working between the States and Belize. Let's consider this as your first assignment." He patted him on the shoulder.

Happily Ponti nodded his compliance, then turned a more solemn face toward Raquel. "Here." He passed her the bundle filled with the costume from that fateful night, and a few other belongings. "These are yours."

She held the objects in front of her, staring at them. They brought back so many memories, she could feel unwanted tears gathering behind her eyes, stinging them. To hide her emotion, she quickly hugged him around the neck, "Thank you, Ponti," she murmured, as she tried to gain control of herself. "If you ever see Mircea again you tell her I will never forget her."

"I will see her. And I will tell her," he promised.

"Well we've got to go now." Once again Nate took

control, as he helped Raquel into the back seat of the four wheel drive. One of his men, already behind the wheel, revved up the engine once Nate seated himself.

Almost with disbelief Raquel settled back and began to wave to the many curious, but accepting villagers who remained behind. The *buyei* and the priestess both acknowledged her as they passed, and it wasn't long before she could hear a bongo beat, inviting them to forget the sorrows of the day, and join in the celebration. Only a matter of minutes had passed and they had left the village behind.

"The plane is not far from here," the man driving the vehicle informed Nate. "John brought it down in a nearby bean field."

Nate showed little reaction to the man's words. She could tell his thoughts were already far away.

"A private plane?" Raquel questioned.

"Yes," Nate replied, but would provide no further information.

"Well may I ask whose plane I'll be flying in, or is that too much to ask," she exploded.

Not liking the tone of her voice, the driver attracted her gaze in the rear-view mirror, disdainfully answering, "Mr. Bowman's, of course."

"Yours?" Raquel demanded of Nate.

"No. My father's."

It was a white and blue Beechcraft that seated six people. The pilot and two of the other men were already aboard. The cars they had used were turned over to two of the men from the village, who drove away before the plane took off.

All the men addressed Nate as Mr. Bowman, except for the one who said they had important matters to discuss. He took the seat across from Nate's, and began to immediately shovel papers in his direction. A fourth man, in his twenties, took the seat opposite Raquel. He had a no-nonsense look about him, and Raquel felt he would not be open to her questions or idle conversation.

As the small craft lifted off the ground the young woman's adrenaline soared with it. Taking one last look out the window, she spotted a large jaguarundi, standing at the edge of the rain forest, watching the plane's ascent. Goodbye, she called out to him silently, acknowledging the living symbol of her mentor's spirit.

There was a mixture of uncertainty and elation as they climbed and she realized it was finally going to happen. She was finally going home!

The flight was a relatively short one, but during the entire time not once did Nate attempt to speak to her. It was true the man who sat beside her constantly fed him information, but Raquel still felt that was no excuse for ignoring her. As the flight progressed, she felt more and more alienated from the man with whom she'd shared the last week of her life.

Unfastening her seat belt, Raquel sat on the edge of the cushioned seat and placed a demanding hand on Nate's forearm.

"You've got to tell me what's going on here? What happened back there in the village, and who are these men?"

She tried to speak at a level that only Nate could hear, but no sooner had she said the demanding words than both of the men pinned her with an impatient stare. The one who seemed to have the closest tie with Nate handed him another envelope, emphasizing that he felt the business at hand was more important than Raquel's questions.

"*Pataki*, my sister, Jackie, has died." He paused a moment at Raquel's gasp. "And unfortunately, her death has set off a whole chain of events. I cannot tell you anymore right now. I promise we will talk once we reach Miami." His dark eyes were sad and sought understanding, but she could tell he was anxious to get back to his conversation with his aide.

It all felt very strange, for in a matter of minutes things had changed, drastically. In the primitive world of Belize they had depended almost solely on each other, but now as they flew back into the present, into their world, she felt as if they were becoming strangers once again.

The young man beside her leaned forward, "Is there anything I can get for you, Mr. Bowman?" his demeanor reflecting his willingness to serve.

Raquel never heard the response. She just watched as he returned to a restful position and looked out the window. His subservient attitude toward Nate only fed her uncertainty. The feeling was magnified by the respect all of these men showed him, men who obviously felt they owed him their allegiance. Who was Nate Bowman?

All of a sudden she felt out of place, and she glanced nervously about the plane with its immaculate interior, TV, VCR, and telephone.

Now, there were only two things she knew about the man, Nate Bowman. His family was far from poor, and from what she'd witnessed in Dangriga, they also had plenty of clout in Belize. Yet she knew there were all sorts of ways to make money and gain clout in a Central American country, and not all of them good.

Raquel looked at the young man who sat across from her, and almost by telepathy he turned his head returning her gaze. Quickly, she dropped her thick, lashes, but he continued to look, a long measuring stare. Self-consciously, she placed her hand over the bloodstain smearing the front of the slashed shift. Suddenly she realized what she must look like to this fastidious young man.

Embarrassed, and wanting to explain, she looked directly into his face, but she could see he had drawn his own conclusions. They were clearly written in his eyes. They were of two different worlds. She was not a woman who belonged in the world of private planes and the best life could offer . . . not this woman discovered in a dance club and given a fifteen hundred dollars to play a game.

This time it was Raquel who turned and looked out the window, perturbed by Nate's silent and pompous judgment, and fearful he was not the only one who shared those feelings.

When they landed a small crowd of people met them at the Opa-Locka airport, all of them wanting to talk to "Mr. Bowman." At first Raquel stood idly by, watching the interactions and waiting for Nate to look for her. But as the moments passed, and the men in their business suits, and a particularly well-kept female vied for his attention, she knew her chances of speaking to him would be slim to none.

A sick feeling of disillusionment began to rise inside her as the minutes, rolled by, and she questioned her logic for remaining there. Why was it so important that she speak to him anyway? No matter what, he still played a part in the kidnapping, bringing her close to death more times than she cared to remember.

Still she stood and watched, her mind fighting with her emotions, remembering how it felt to be in his arms, the things he had promised, the moments they shared, if only . . .

The woman reached up and laid an affectionate palm against Nate's square jaw, her china-doll hair swinging back from her meticulously made-up features as she looked up at him, welcoming him back. This woman's actions forced Raquel to face reality. There was no reason for her to wait. She didn't belong here. Not because she didn't deserve the things they had, but because she knew nothing about them, and they knew, and cared nothing about her.

It wasn't hard for Raquel to locate the women's bathroom. Once inside, she washed her face and changed her clothes. Resourcefully, she donned the shift she was given when she first arrived on the sailboat, completing her outfit with the skirt from the costume.

With steady fingers she ripped open the bralike top of the festive outfit, and to her relief found the one-thousand dollars still inside. With unshed tears in her eyes, Raquel looked in the mirror, took a deep breath and patted the thick French braids that circled her head, "Well this is it, girlfriend, I guess it's time to go home."

Chapter Twenty-seven

"Are you coming tonight, Sam?" Raquel called out as she headed for the door.

"I'm thinking about it." He frowned, then rubbed his hand through his hair. "You know how I hate politicking and all the brown-nosing that goes with it."

"Well look at it this way," Raquel advised, "It's a chance to get a free meal, and drink some good wine for a change."

She smiled at the man who had proven to be her right hand during the last five weeks.

She had been back only three days when she was contacted and told the clinic would be reopened, financed by a well-established foundation. They were also looking for a director to head it up.

Her aspirations had never included being director, and after Belize . . . she only wanted to practice her profession with a little more open-mindedness, and live her life as carefree as she could. So for her, taking on the director's position was out of the question, but she had someone in mind who would be perfect for the job. That person was Sam.

* * *

They had worked together before, and she knew he had plenty of expertise in business and social services, actually many more years than she had served as a professional psychologist.

So she called him up. Luckily his number was the same and he was between jobs, but she still had to convince him to take the position. With a couple of lunches and emotional support to persuade him, he finally accepted. Raquel knew Sam really loved his work, and just needed to get ahold of his midlife crisis long enough to join the world of productive human beings again.

"All right, you've said the magic words." Sam laid his grey head on top of the cubicle wall. "Where do I go and what time?"

"The announcement's on the bulletin board," she spoke as she headed for the door. "It's been there for a little over a week."

Even though Sam was the director, it was Raquel who had organized everything before the clinic opened. It had taken a couple of weeks, and both their efforts for the place to begin to run somewhat smoothly. It was at that point, she had warned him.

"Look, I wouldn't be doing this if we weren't friends, and if I had done any less than begged you to take this job. But now that the place is pretty much on the right track, this is it, the ball's in your court. You take on your responsibilities and I take care of mine."

Privately she was thankful for the onslaught of work, it kept her mind occupied, and her body tired.

Raquel felt truly blessed when it came to how things had worked out once she'd returned to the States.

Her fears of having been evicted were foremost in her mind as she rode along in the taxi. She expected to see remnants of her belongings littering the curb. But to her relief, nothing like that had occurred.

The landlord was the one who had been thrown out by the owners of the apartment building. She found a letter beneath her door, telling how he had "misappropriated and embezzled funds." It had stated they had no way of knowing who had actually been paying their rent and who had not. So under the new management, all tenants were considered current, and the upcoming rent would be due at its usual time.

Raquel couldn't have asked for a better arrangement. She had been given the break she needed, and with the ten thousand dollars she'd earned from her charade; she had enough money to catch up her important debts.

Yet it was the phone call from the Devon Foundation that truly seemed like a miracle; they wanted to reopen the clinic where she had worked. In contacting the previous director, they discovered he had already committed himself to other employment. But they informed Raquel he had spoken very highly of her, and of her dedication to the facility. With such a strong commendation, they wanted her involved in the reopening, if not as director, then as the resident psychologist performing the same duties she'd performed in the past. Strange, it was almost as if things were exactly the same. As if Belize was only a dream.

Raquel reached up in front of her and pulled down the sunvisor that sported a mirror on its backside. Immediately her dark eyes focused on the almost invisible line that traveled down from the pulse point at the base of her throat, then disappeared into the folds of her blouse. This faint scar, along with the objects she'd stored in a shoe box in her closet, were the only proof she had ever been to the Central American country. There were many things, however, she could not see that were also proof of her ordeal.

She had come to accept and believe the power of the human mind and spirit was far greater than she'd ever imagined, and she was determined to use her new-found knowledge in her work as a psychologist. In many ways she had been strengthened by the ordeal, gaining confidence in herself and her ability to perform and survive under the most demanding circumstances. Raquel was no longer afraid to trust her own instincts, to stray from the beaten path and go with the flow. Those were the positive things she had brought back with her.

But there were also the dreams that had haunted her since her return. Jumbled menageries filled with all sorts of things. Some of them frightening, some bizarre, most of them included Nate Bowman. She'd promised herself if they persisted, she would seek some kind of counseling. As a professional she knew it was the right thing to do. Yet she was hesitant to follow her own advice.

Raquel rolled down her windows as she got on the highway. The forceful movement of the muggy air helped to free her thoughts of Belize. Tomorrow she would take her mother the book she bought her.

She was relieved to find out she had worried very little about her, and had assumed she had taken that long-talked-about vacation. Everything was like before. Almost.

The young woman checked the address she'd written down on her pad. The even numbers were on the right hand side, so the Devon House would be located on the left side of the palm-lined street.

Raquel saw the lines of parked cars before she reached the address, so she decided it would be fruitless to try and find a convenient parking space; therefore she parked several houses away.

The neighborhood possessed a distinct character. The architecture of the old stucco buildings was unique, each house having its own special qualities, though they were no bigger than average in size. Most of the homes had been transformed into commercial properties, giving the businesses a personal touch.

Raquel's heels clicked on the flagstone walkway as she passed the ornately hung sign, and mounted the two steps to the entrance. The main door consisted of an oval-shaped glass trimmed in wood. Through it, she could see the people eating and drinking inside. She determined, she would mingle with the crowd no more than thirty minutes. That should be sufficient time to pay her respects to her employers, and then she would slip away and go home. Sam was the one who was obligated to spend a more "meaningful" amount of time at the affair. He was the director.

"And your name is?" An elderly gentleman in a dated suit extended his hand in Raquel's direction.

"Raquel Mason," she switched the glass of wine to her left hand. "I'm the resident psychologist at the newly reopened southwest clinic."

"Oh, yes, I know all about it. My name's Robert Kellner. I'm on the Devon Foundation board. For some time we had been considering backing an organization like yours, and when we were told the clinic had recently closed, we thought it was a prime opportunity to pursue our goals." He smiled at her. "Let me show you around the Devon House. I've been involved with the foundation for many years. And I think we've done some pretty good things."

Raquel followed Mr. Kellner about as he showed her several rooms in the house, furnished with antiques and memorabilia from the foundation's various projects. Hors d'oeuvres and wine were available in two of the rooms, and Mr. Kellner took it upon himself to introduce her to the different groups of people they encountered on their tour.

Finally, they reached the last room which served as the foundation's museum. It housed their most-prized possessions. Raquel could tell Mr. Kellner got pleasure out of telling her the stories behind the objects that were displayed, and she listened contentedly, enjoying his company and the knowledge he shared with her.

"Hey Bob," a plump, middle-aged woman called from the door, "there's somebody who just came in who's looking for you."

Mr. Kellner apologized for having to leave so abruptly, then he disappeared after the woman who'd summoned him.

Raquel drained the wine glass and looked around for a tray to discard it.

"There's one over there," a silky voice spoke from the doorway.

Raquel nearly dropped the glass when she heard the familiar voice. She turned around quickly to see Nate Bowman standing behind her. He was dressed in a well-tailored, black, double-breasted suit. His hair and mustache were groomed to perfection. The sheer shock of seeing him was overwhelming enough, but the business-like persona he carried compounded her reaction.

Still she held on to her composure as she crossed the room to the trash can he'd indicated, her heart pounding beyond belief as she spoke.

"Well, I see you're not wearing your kidnapping clothes today." Even to her own ears the statement sounded lame and somehow inappropriate.

"No, I'm not. That's because abduction isn't my usual occupation," his dark eyes were steady as he watched her. "Would you like to know what is?"

Her hands trembled as she turned to face him, "Should I?"

"I hope s—"

"Mr. Bowman," the deep voice cut into his words, "there's a guy downstairs who wants to speak with you."

Raquel recognized the young man who had been seated opposite her on the plane ride back from Dangriga.

"Not now," his tone was impatient. "I've had enough interruptions. This is important." He turned and looked at the young man, "This woman is important."

"Yes, Mr. Bowman," his eyebrows lifted in surprise. "I understand."

Nate took a step inside the room, then turned and locked the door.

"There's so much I've got to tell you, *pataki*, but I need to know that you are truly open to me, and willing to hear what I have to say."

He had crossed the room and was standing in front of her, a hint of cologne wafting around him. Involuntarily Raquel took a step back. Over the past five weeks she had tried to occupy her waking thoughts with anything and everything but this man and what he had awakened in her. She felt ashamed of her feelings for him. That she would fall in love with a person who had kidnapped and used her the way he had. There could be no doubt she had missed him. But somehow not seeing or hearing from him had made it easier. She could pretend it had never happened. It was all a dream.

Raquel looked into his face, and she didn't know if she wanted to slap or kiss him. Several locks of wild hair framed her features, expressing their independence from the ball she'd gathered at the crown of her head, as well as from a separate cascade of rich, black hair beneath it.

Her emotions were like an electrical current, each one touching off another until they flowed together in a powerful stream. Everything had been his fault, and now here he was again abruptly reentering her life, but this time he was offering an explanation for wreaking the havoc he had caused. Was she willing to listen? Could she? She had tried so hard to bury his memory. It had been the safest and most sane thing to do.

Nate reached out to touch her face.

"No . . . please don't,' Raquel turned away from him, then her dark eyes flashed back at him. "What makes you think you have the right to touch me? We are no longer in the wilds of Belize, and I'm no longer your prisoner."

"All right," his eyes clouded with pain, "I won't touch you. But I want you to sit in this chair, and give me a chance to tell you the truth. That is all I'm asking. After that you can make up your own mind."

He went and perched on a nearby windowsill and waited for Raquel's answer.

Nervously she tugged at the top of her navy blue suit.

She wished she could stop the blood that was racing through her veins as she looked at him, heard his voice. As he sat with the sunshine outlining his dark frame, she knew she had lied, for part of her was still his prisoner. She knew he still held her heart and always would.

Slowly Raquel descended into the chair he pulled up for her. She focused her eyes on her hands as she held them in her lap. "All right. I'm ready."

Relief flooded his rugged features as he watched her. Suddenly his neck settled down on his chest, like a man who had carried a heavy burden for a long time and now would be able to relieve it. "Where do I begin?" he said almost to himself as he turned and looked out the window. "I guess I should start at the beginning."

"You may not remember, but I was there the night Benjamin and Thomas offered you the money to impersonate my sister. We all sat together and watched you as you danced in the club, and I knew you were perfect for what I had planned. There was a strong resemblance between you and Jackie, your size, your complexion, and she wore her hair similar to yours." His eyes focused on her face as if he were seeing her for the first time, then he continued.

"It was strange because, even then, I found you very attractive. But I watched as you danced so enticing and intimate with the guy on the floor that night. You made my blood boil, and I thought I knew what kind of woman you were. I have known so many, *pataki*. They have been the kind of women I have allowed in my life. The kind who always look for new thrills and do not have any problems getting paid for them, if they can."

Raquel looked down at her hands as she thought of the dire circumstances she had faced that night and how desperate she was. Now, when she looked back, she knew she had acted rashly.

"I watched them make you the offer through the window of a limousine parked out front, and when you accepted the envelope, it I knew I had judged you correctly. It was after that when everything went haywire." He walked over to a nearby bookcase, and ran his fingers along the leather-bound backs. "You see my sister Jackie was very ill at the time." His eyes had a faraway look when he turned to her.

"From the time she came to live with my father and I, she'd been a very independent, high-spirited young girl. It was after my mother died and we were moving to the States. You see Jackie is my half-sister. Her mother was Shangoain. You know the story, the one conceived on the night of the rift."

Raquel nodded that she remembered.

"Well, when my mother found out about Jackie, her mother was still pregnant with her. It was because of my father's infidelity that my mother committed suicide. Afterwards my father nearly lost his mind. He didn't care about anything, me . . . the property . . . anything. He just wanted to let everything go. Not that we had much at the time, but we did have some land that had been owned by my mother's family. But as my mother became less and less competent mentally, my father had her sign ownership of the property over to him for safekeeping." He laughed dryly to himself. "That almost ended up being a mistake with the frame of mind he was in after her death." He paused as if to gather his thoughts.

"You see my mother was Creole, and the land was located near Belize City where a lot of development was going on. Eventually some developers felt our land was the best location for their project, and they offered us a small sum of money for it. My father was willing to let it go at that price, but I had heard stories about how a family could become rich off of the outsiders who were coming in, wanting Belizean land. I was a young teenager then, but I convinced my father to talk to one of the lawyers in Belize City before he signed the papers. The lawyer put together a real good deal, and invested part of the profits in some more land further inland. We still own that land today. It's covered with orange and grapefruit orchards, where the majority of my family's profits come from. We provide the citrus that grocery chain stores make their orange and grapefruit juices from, here in the States." He sat back down on the windowsill. "A very lucrative enterprise."

"A couple of years passed with good profits, we moved to the United States, and Jackie moved with us. Jackie's mother was ostracized by the Shango because her child was part Garifuna. Years passed before it was prophesied Jackie would repair the rift between the Shango and the Garifuna, and the year and the date when this would take place. Wanting the best for her child, Jackie's mother, who is now dead from cancer, gave her to my father. It was common knowledge amongst the Garifuna that she was my half-sister. Some, like Marjorie and Belinda knew her. But no one among the Shango knew.

"From the very beginning it was hard for my father to control Jackie, and as the money poured in, and Jackie became a teenager, it was almost impossible. I did the best I could while I was around, but at the same time I was trying to live my own life. I guess, because of the money, things came rather easy for us. And through the years I must admit I've done some things I'm not too proud of. It seems I've always been attracted to danger. Finally I learned how to channel that energy in a positive way. I began to spend a lot of time out of the country, in Belize in particular, and I started working with the National Drug Advisory Council. It's Belize's DEA. My father was having some problems with poachers trying to grow their drugs in our fields. Being a part of the NDAC gave me control over the situation, I thought.

"Unable to control Jackie, my father hired a man to keep his eye on her because she started hanging out with all sorts of unacceptable people. But before he realized it, she had gotten the bodyguard under her thumb with her charms, and he ended up taking her to these places to meet these friends of hers. One thing progressed to another, and before you knew it the cans of beer were joined by marijuana and so on and so forth, until she started using cocaine, eventually freebasing.

"Everything happened so fast, by the time I caught wind of it she was a heavy user. Because of our family's wealth and our Belizean contact, she was getting the majority of her stuff from the homeland. Three nights before we found you, Jackie had smoked some coke laced with cyanide. The guy who my father had hired to watch her said she suffered a bad seizure as a result of it and that sent her into a coma. I knew it was no mistake she'd gotten a bad package." He pressed his hands deep into his pants pockets. "Someone wanted her out of the way, and I had to know why." Deep in thought,

Nate turned and stared out the window, almost as if he had forgotten Raquel was there.

"At first I didn't tell my father. He's old and sick, and had never really recovered from losing my mother. I had to try and see if Jackie would pull through before letting him know what was going on.

"You know, in a way I felt personally responsible." His dark eyes searched hers. "Here I was a big NDAC agent, and couldn't even protect my own sister from the drugs they may have been growing on my own land. So I came up with the bright idea to have someone pretend to be Jackie at a big function. One that just about everybody we knew would know about. We'd make it invitation only, and that way we'd have a list of just about everybody there. So if any of the folks who attended the function had anything to do with Jackie receiving the bad package, I felt some kind of way they'd show their hand," Nate nodded his head in retrospect. "And they did. But it wasn't anything like I expected.

"Right before the party, I found out a group of Garifunians and Shangoains had banded together to take Jackie back to Belize. Evidently she'd been contacted several times by the priestess and the *buyei*, telling her about her spiritual obligations, and what it would mean to them if she would come voluntarily. But Jackie, being in the condition she was in, found the whole thing rather funny. I found some letters in a box she had under her bed. She had written on top of it with some red lipstick, marking it 'voodoo.'

"Well as you know, the spiritual heads of the Garifuna and the Shango didn't think it was a funny matter at all. They were dead serious about it, and so they decided if she wouldn't come on her own, they'd make her come. Once she'd performed her duties as the link to the *gubida,* they'd allow her to return to the States. But she was going to meet her obligations one way or another.

"Art was one of the men chosen by the Garifunians. Once he got on the mainland, he contacted me, telling me about the plan. *Pataki,* I felt responsible for bringing you into a situation that was about to get out of control, so I did the only thing I could think to do. I detained— with ample funds—the other Garifunian who was to be a part of the kidnapping ring, and I took his place. Art simply thought I wanted to watch out for my sister. So it was he and I who met up with Jay and Al at the appointed time and place. It was easy for me to hook it up, by saying we were independent dancers and musicians hired for the party. We showed up with the rest of them, in costume, part of the entertainment for the evening."

Raquel reflected on the first time she'd seen Nate, his muscles rippling in his arms as he played the drum for the feathered dancers. She remembered there had been an animal magnetism about him that had strongly touched her.

Nate watched her eyes cloud over with memories and he wanted so much to make her understand, all along he had just wanted to protect her, even before he realized he had come to love her.

"I never intended that you would spend one night in Belize, *pataki.*" His thickly lashed eyes pleaded that she understand. "I had made arrangements for my men to meet us in Dangriga when the sailboat arrived, but after the storm, we landed much further south than I expected, and it became a totally different ball game.

"Jay was part of a grapevine between here and Belize.

We intentionally put out that Jackie would be at the party that night, and that's why we hired you. Jay wanted to insure the job was done right the second time, so he made himself a part of the kidnapping gang.

"I knew things were going to be dangerous when Jay threw you in the car. I had to establish myself as the head of the group. I finagled using my boat and all to try and have as much control of the situation as I could.

"At first I just thought he was a bad apple, then I suspected more. I decided to take you through the ceremony because I knew there was a connection to Jackie's overdose and the reunification. It wasn't until you ended up in that abandoned temple where the cocaine was stored that I was sure about Jay. It was Jay who made sure my sister got ahold of the bad cocaine. In their ring, he was the only one who knew the Garifuna and the Shango wanted her to come back and perform the ritual bridging the rift between them. But Jay knew if she were allowed to do that, his little party would be over. If he got rid of Jackie before she ever came back to Belize, he could continue using the old temple as a storehouse for the cocaine until it was shipped to the States. The rift between the Garifuna and Shango would continue, and his life as part of the Belizean drug world would grow and prosper, and his pockets along with it.

"So you see *pataki*, I could not let you know that I knew who you were. I knew as long as you thought hiding your real identity was the only thing you had that was keeping you alive, you would play your role as Jackie Dawson to the hilt."

Raquel shook her head at the complex story Nate had laid out before her.

"So how did you find me? You didn't even know my real name."

"I had Benjamin inquire at the building where you'd left your car. He asked if they had towed a car fitting the description of yours. Of course they said yes, and they told us where it had been taken. They also said a pretty, young woman had been in earlier that day asking the same thing. You made quite an impression, *pataki*." We figured it was you, and we went from there."

"But that still doesn't explain what you're doing here."

"My father is on the board of the Devon Foundation. After I had you checked out, very thoroughly, I realized you used to work at the clinic that had closed down. I encouraged my father to suggest that the Devon Foundation take it on, and reopen it," he smiled at her cunningly. "I figured you would be attending this little get-together as part of your working duties."

"So after five weeks you finally got around to making time in your busy schedule for the charity case, huh?" Still, she could not help but distrust him. Unconsciously she sought a way to tell him so.

"Oh no, *pataki*." He walked over to the chair and bent down in front of her. "I had never planned to let you out of my sight once we got off that plane. But before we even left Belize, I was told Jackie had died, and my father was taking it very badly. My mind was in a whirlwind as all these papers were being put before me, getting things in line in case my father also passed away. If only you had waited for me, *pataki*. Once I was back in Miami, there was Jackie's funeral and so many other things that demanded my attention. It was impossible for me to break away. But there wasn't a day you weren't in my thoughts."

He covered her trembling hands with his.

"*Pataki,* I could never forget the woman I'd come to know in the rain forest of my homeland. The strength and the courage she showed, and her willingness to love me, no matter what. Did you think I could ever let you go after what we shared?" His voice almost sounded angry.

"Deep in that forest I promised myself, no one would ever have you but me. You were mine, and we would live to share our lives together. It was that hope, and that promise that kept me alive."

Raquel could feel her heart pound through her chest. "How can I believe all of this is true? How could I ever forget?" Her dark eyes searched his frantically. "*How* do you start over from something like this?"

"How?" he looked straight into her face streaked with tears. "Like this," and he wiped the tears away. "Hello, my name is Nate Bowman." His voice was low, silky, "What's yours?"

"Raquel," she answered uncertainly. "Raquel Mason."

"It is so wonderful to meet you, Raquel," His voice caressed her name. "Don't ask me how, but for some reason I just know, you're the woman I've been searching for all my life."

"I am?"

"Yes, you are."

Two pairs of dark eyes searched each other.

"Well, I want to warn you, the bad memories of what happened may be with me for a long time."

"And I'll be there for you, *pataki,* if you need me. Reminding you of how we discovered our love for one another, and if it hadn't been for those bad times, we may not ever have found each other." He touched her face tenderly.

"I'm afraid to try!" Her moist, dark eyes shone brightly, above her full quivering lips.

"Don't be," he reassured her. "Just call on the strength I know you have deep inside."

Their eyes held until their lips naturally gravitated together. Raquel and Nate kissed tenderly for a long time. Then, with his lips lightly touching hers she heard him say, "Now, *pataki*, now you are truly home."

Dear Readers,

I can't express how excited I am about my writing career. I look forward to sitting down and writing stories for you with the same kind of sizzling romance, action and adventure that I've created in *Beguiled*.

I hope we can establish a sharing relationship, one where you express your feelings about my books, and I promise to write back to you whenever you reach out to me.

You can write me at the following:

Eboni Snoe
P.O. Box 800028
Roswell, Georgia 30075–0001

I look forward to hearing from you soon.

FUN AND LOVE!

THE DUMBEST DUMB BLONDE JOKE BOOK   (889, $4.50)
by Joey West
They say that blondes have more fun . . . but we can all have a hoot
with THE DUMBEST DUMB BLONDE JOKE BOOK. Here's a
hilarious collection of hundreds of dumb blonde jokes — including
dumb blonde GUY jokes — that are certain to send you over the
edge!

THE I HATE MADONNA JOKE BOOK   (798, $4.50)
by Joey West
She's Hollywood's most controversial star. Her raunchy reputation's brought her fame and fortune. Now here is a sensational collection of hilarious material on America's most talked about
MATERIAL GIRL!

LOVE'S LITTLE INSTRUCTION BOOK   (774, $4.99)
by Annie Pigeon
Filled from cover to cover with romantic hints — one for every day
of the year — this delightful book will liven up your life and make
you and your lover smile. Discover these amusing tips for making
your lover happy . . . tips like — ask her mother to dance — have his
car washed — take turns being irrational . . . and many, many
more!

MOM'S LITTLE INSTRUCTION BOOK   (0009, $4.99)
by Annie Pigeon
Mom needs as much help as she can get, what with chaotic sched-
ules, wedding fiascos, Barneymania and all. Now, here comes the
best mother's helper yet. Filled with funny comforting advice for
moms of all ages. What better way to show mother how very much
you love her by giving her a gift guaranteed to make her smile
everyday of the year.

*Available wherever paperbacks are sold, or order direct from the
Publisher. Send cover price plus 50¢ per copy for mailing and handling to Penguin USA, P.O. Box 999, c/o Dept. 17109, Bergen-
field, NJ 07621. Residents of New York and Tennessee must
include sales tax. DO NOT SEND CASH.*